THE
OTHER SIDE
Book Two
Disembodied Living

Sea Elle Wolf

THE OTHER SIDE
DISEMBODIED LIVING
Sea Elle Wolf

Copyright © 2025 by Sea Elle Wolf
Library of Congress Control Number: 2025910546

Table of Contents

For Frances

Prologue

NIGHT OF THE WOLF MOON

One Year After the Wedding

It was a cold night in January. Inside the dimly lit tavern, people sipped pints and exchanged idle banter, with the occasional moments of rowdy laughter ringing out and bouncing across the room. A small bartender stood with his arms folded, staring at the television mounted on the wall with interest. The newscast was barely loud enough to be heard over the boisterous crowd.

"...it was here on this idyllic green pasture of misty farmland that a gruesome discovery marred what should have been a peaceful morning on the Doherty property," the reporter stated in journalistic fashion.

A stocky man wearing a brown denim jacket with a sheepskin collar sat at a nearby table. He craned his neck toward the set to listen more closely to the strange report that had captured his attention.

"So, I come out here with my son like we do every morning. We noticed about three or four them cows were missin'. So we wondered about looking for our cattle only to discover they were in the south pasture near the edge of the woods. They'd been ripped apart! Maybe a black bear or bobcat got to them, but frankly, I can't reckon what kind of animal coulda done that sorta damage. Maybe it was even something..." the farmer visibly grasped for the right word. "...unnatural or something."

"Unnatural? What do you mean? What are you thinking?" the reporter asked in a serious tone, then pointed the microphone back toward the farmer.

"Well, like, maybe it was a *werewolf*," the farmer on the TV suggested. "Or, I don't know, an alien or something!"

The stocky man in the brown denim jacket barked out raspy laughter. "Werewolves and aliens! Ha! Is *this* the 'trouble' you warned me about, Travis?" he teased his buddy sitting across from him.

"No, dude. It's not just some mangled cattle," Travis replied defensively. "In a small town like Nocturne, shit gets real *backwoods* real fuckin fast," he said with ominous authority. "Trust me, Ricky, out here, it's nothing like Boston where assholes like you come from."

"*Oh, okay!*" Ricky replied with exaggerated sarcasm, followed by more derisive laughter.

Today was Ricky Carlson's first visit to Nocturne. He made the three-plus hour drive from Boston to see his buddy, Travis, who had recently purchased a plot of land and moved to the area to tend it. The two friends arranged to meet at a tavern called Charlie's Bar and Grill on the edge of town. Travis had warned Ricky that strange occurrences had been on the rise lately, so he wanted to keep a low profile and avoid Main Street in downtown Nocturne. This warning did not deter Ricky; it was the prospect of trouble that finally motivated him to make the long trip. He loved any excuse to cause fights or get into mischief. However, once he arrived in town, Ricky was disappointed as he gazed up and down the sleepy streets and realized that Travis had played him for a fool. Nocturne was just another dull, rural Massachusetts town. In fact, it seemed downright boring—just as he had suspected from the beginning. He had not seen anything remarkable.

Ricky shook his head and was about to take another sip of beer when a sultry-looking brunette walked through the tavern door. He coughed and choked on the cold suds in his mouth.

"Holy shit, dude, look at that!" Of course, he and Travis immediately seized the chance to showcase their most charming attempts at seduction. They made lewd catcalls, inviting her to sit on their laps and whatnot, but their advances were unsuccessful for reasons that eluded them. The attractive brunette merely ignored them, walked to the other side of the horseshoe-shaped bar, and took a seat on an empty stool. The bartender trotted over and retrieved her order, and a martini appeared before her a few moments later. She calmly sipped her drink as she seemed to wait for company.

Ricky couldn't take his eyes off this woman. Even the girls back home in Boston weren't this attractive. The brunette slipped off an expensive-looking black coat, revealing a form-fitting black dress underneath. The faintest glimpse of a red bra strap peeked out from under the sleeve on her shoulder. Ricky's jaw dropped; he was utterly transfixed by her.

"Man, what a stone-cold fox. That chick was built for fuckin," Travis commented crassly as he wiped the foam from his mouth with the back of his sleeve.

"Step aside, bro. Watch a big-city boy give this honey the thrill of a lifetime. I bet the small-town clowns around here just gawk and don't have the stones to actually talk to her." Ricky rose with inflated confidence, strode across the bar, and approached the woman. She lifted an electric gaze toward him, a quizzical expression upon her face.

"S'cuse me, ma'am, but I was wonderin if I could buy you a drink?" Ricky asked coolly. An amused, almost vicious smile spread across the woman's viper-red lips.

"Oh, no, darling," she drawled, her Eastern European accent was subtle yet noticeable as she looked him up and down. "At least buy *yourself* dinner first."

"Appreciate it, darlin', but I already ate."

"Ah, such a gentleman! Now you're all set to go fuck yourself," she said as she took a sip of her martini.

Travis howled with laughter from across the bar. Ricky stared at the woman for a moment longer, then scoffed dismissively as he turned and walked back to the table to rejoin his friend. Nevertheless, his face did not convey defeat.

"It's no problem," he remarked with a darkly arrogant smile. "You can't say I didn't try the polite way first."

Over the next hour, Ricky laughed and drank too much with his friend while keeping one eye on the woman. Nobody joined her during the time it took for her to finish her first drink, and she ordered another. Once the second drink was delivered to the bar, the woman took a sip, stood, put her coat on, and headed toward the back hallway toward the restrooms. Ricky sat frozen as he watched her walk away. Just before disappearing around the corner, the woman shot him another electric gaze. *Bingo,* he thought. Ricky was always one to seize every opportunity.

"Alright, I'm goin' in," Ricky said.

"Man, your ass is gonna get arrested one day. Or worse..."

"Will you shut up! Drink your beer." With that, Ricky quickly stumbled out of his chair, walked to the other end of the tavern, and casually leaned across the bar top near the woman's glass. He pretended he was going to order something, but fortunately, the bartender had his back to him. Instead of getting his attention, Ricky quickly slipped a small tablet into the woman's mostly full glass and stuck his finger in to stir it. Then he quickly pushed off the bar, launching himself enthusiastically toward the back hallway where the restrooms were located to keep an eye on the woman's movements.

As soon as Ricky entered the dimly lit hallway, he caught a glimpse of the back door closing as a burst of cold air swept past him. He stared at the door in bewilderment, then glanced up at the neon sign above it—EXIT. Could it have been his mark who just left? He quickly peeked inside both restrooms and confirmed they were empty. *It must have been her who left. Damnit!* Ricky doubled back into the hallway and stumbled through the exit.

The back door of the tavern burst open, and Ricky stumbled belligerently into the alley. A single light attached to the building illuminated the thick, icy fog hanging in the air. Fresh snow blanketed the ground and rooftops beyond. The brilliant light from the Full Moon reflected off the white surfaces, making his surroundings substantially visible.

Ricky steadied himself and scanned both directions of the alley. To his dismay, he did not see the woman anywhere in sight. His gaze fell to the ground, eyeballing the dainty footprints in the freshly fallen snow. The tracks led away from the bar and disappeared into the shadowed woodland behind the tavern. A defiant laugh escaped his throat, leaving his breath lingering like smoke in the air. He briefly contemplated his options. It was cold that night, and visibility inside the woods would be low. However, those conditions could actually end up working in his favor. The scent of used cooking oil wafted over from a nearby grease trap as he headed into the daunting forest.

One deliberate step after another, Ricky made his way through the dark trees. He grew increasingly impatient as he ventured deeper into the forest, following the footprints in the snow. Scanning the dense vegetation, he briefly wondered if this was worth all the effort. He could save himself a lot of trouble and go back to his buddy, Travis, and the beer left sitting on the table at the tavern. But his half-erection urged him forward, compelling him to keep looking a little longer. As he searched for any sign of the woman beneath the cover of the shadowy trees, he paused and glanced back. Ricky could just barely make out a faint glimmer of light from the alleyway. Again, he contemplated going back.

The soft sound of feminine laughter floated from the darkness deep within the woods. Ricky spun around, frantically searching for the source. His startlement eased into delight, and a malicious smile spread across his face. He snickered quietly to himself, shook his head at his priorities, and then began jogging toward the seductive laughter.

The trees grew denser, yet he continued to hunt. Visibility was low, and he soon began to feel demotivated once more. Sure, she was attractive, and he wanted to get some action, but the inconvenience was starting to weigh on him. After a few minutes, he paused to catch his breath.

As he surveyed his surroundings, a vague disorientation began to surface, soon followed by another sensation—Ricky felt someone watching him. He spun around and caught a glimpse of a dark figure disappearing behind a nearby tree trunk. *Finally*, he thought to himself as he rounded the tree trunk. To his dismay, nobody was there.

"Okay, I give up. Where are you?" his frustrated voice boomed into the chilly silence. He had intended to sound threatening but was starting to feel frightened himself. Only the cold, dark stillness of night answered him. It was time to give up. Ricky turned and began to head back. A twig snapped somewhere behind him, causing him to spin around wildly. The dense tree trunks made him feel claustrophobic. The sound had been so close that the sight of nothing felt jarring. *Fuck this shit,* he thought, walking hurriedly back the way he came. *This is way more trouble than it's worth*, he thought with angry defeat and growing panic. He heard a faint rustling sound from somewhere to his right. Ricky swung around to see nothing but empty forest staring back at him.

"Who's there?" he called out sharply. His instincts tingled, warning him that something was wrong. Maybe that bitch had tricked him into coming out here, lured him to follow so that her boyfriend could jump out and rob him.

Ricky turned to walk back the way he had come, but he realized he couldn't see the light from the tavern or alleyway anywhere. He looked down to search for his footprints in the snow, only to discover multiple tracks leading in various directions; some appeared to be animal tracks. More alarming than that, they seemed to belong to a large predator.

"It's okay," he reassured himself as he fought the urge to panic. He felt vulnerable and disliked that feeling. He was fairly certain the alley was right behind him. Ricky frantically retraced his steps, searching for his footprints. He jogged around for several minutes, but no light from the alleyway appeared. Another noise behind him made him jump. Once more, he whirled around and desperately scanned the dark tree line. It felt as though he was being stalked.

At that moment, the clouds parted, revealing the magnificent Wolf Moon in the sky. Ricky felt grateful for the thin slivers of moonlight streaming through the barren tree branches above. Pockets of his surroundings became visible, including a ferocious-looking creature he glimpsed out of the corner of his eye. Sensing its presence, Ricky swung around to look directly at whatever was there but only found the large tree trunks mocking him. Ricky started to run. If he returned to the tavern, this would all be over, and he would be safe. He ran for what felt like an eternity but still couldn't find any light filtering through the trees. A stitch in his side forced him to stop and catch his breath. Hopefully he had lost whatever was following him. The sudden sound of a low growl behind him confirmed this was not the case, and Ricky began to move once more.

Ricky felt his legs grow weak and fatigued when streaks of faint orange light from the alleyway came into view through the dense tree line. He gulped icy air into his lungs, realizing he hadn't run this much since high school gym some twenty years earlier. No longer hearing anything pursuing him, Ricky finally stopped, turned, and confirmed that nothing was behind him. He'd made it, he realized with a deep sigh of relief. A dry laugh escaped his throat as he reminded himself that he needed to get his priorities in order. If something seemed too good to be true, it probably was. Who knows? He had likely just escaped getting robbed or something. That little bitch was just playing games with him. He laughed and shook his head as he headed back toward the bar. Hopefully, Travis was still there waiting for him.

Before he could take another step, Ricky's legs were swept out from underneath him. He fell forward onto his stomach, and his chin struck the ground hard, causing him to see stars. Ricky blinked and noticed the light from the alleyway receding as it grew more distant, then vanished completely. He was being dragged by his ankles at incredible speeds through the forest. He tried to call out for help, but the ground kept slamming into his face.

He struggled to break free, but it felt as if his ankles were locked inside a bear trap. Then, finally, it was over. Whatever it was had released him. Ricky lifted his disoriented, bloodied face from the ground. His shirt was torn to shreds and caked with mud and ice. Road rash covered his exposed skin—his palms, face, neck, and even his belly where the shirt had lifted from the force of being dragged.

The sound of heavy breathing suddenly registered in Ricky's awareness. He hesitantly turned to confront his assailant and found himself face-to-face with the snapping jaws of a large wolf. His scream echoed into the night but was soon silenced.

Chapter One

THE SEER

San Pedro, California

"Althea, it's not your fault," Mrs. Canere comforted, gently wiping the tears from her young daughter's face. Seven-year-old Althea looked up at her mom through a veil of fresh tears.

"Mom, I tried to tell them what I saw. I really tried," the little girl whispered and sobbed. "They didn't believe me! They said I was just making up stories." Her mother kept lovingly stroking her daughter's face while holding her close.

"I know it hurts, my darling. You did what you could. Those who lack the gift of sight often find the concept difficult to grasp. What happened to Brian isn't your fault."

"Mrs. Canere," the uniformed officer compassionately interrupted, "I believe we have everything we need from your daughter. Hopefully, the description she provided will help us catch the bad guy and bring Brian home safely."

Upon hearing this, Althea wept harder. She knew this was not true. While she was able to provide the detectives with a detailed physical description of a man she had never laid eyes on before, unfortunately, she wasn't able to share with them that her classmate, Brian, had already been killed. As if reading her mind, Althea's mom squeezed her hand, signaling her not to reveal this detail. If the authorities knew Althea had any knowledge of the little boy's death, it would only confuse and unnecessarily complicate the investigation. She understood the silent instruction and remained silent.

The pair drove home in heavy silence. After a few miles, Althea's mom turned to her daughter. "My darling, I know that having the ability to see certain details of a person's *past and future* may feel overwhelming. It felt that way for me too once. When I was your age, I struggled to accept myself and my abilities. I felt like an outsider. But I can assure you that learning to trust your *inner voice* will free you from the burden you are feeling. Remember, the greatest gift you can give yourself is to love and accept yourself for who you are. And don't worry; they *will* catch the man who did this to Brian."

Althea remembered how it felt to gaze out the car window on that tragic day. In that moment, life taught her the importance of listening to her inner voice. However, she came to understand that revealing her powers to those unfamiliar with clairvoyance was not always the most effective approach, as ordinary people often found it difficult to believe. Consequently, she adapted by learning to insert herself naturally into situations to influence outcomes. Later, during her high school years, Althea befriended a girl named Rebecca and successfully prevented her from being trafficked by a so-called family friend. From that moment on, she honed and refined her inner sight abilities into a focused and effective tool. She realized that her mother had been right all those years earlier, after the tragedy that had befallen her second-grade classmate, Brian. Her inner voice became one of her greatest gifts in life. In adulthood, Althea discovered a more organic method to share her visions.

Althea Canere was a *seer*; it was a gift passed down through her family for generations. At twenty-nine, she stood tall and slender, with a heart-shaped face and dark brown eyes. Although her natural hair color was brown, she often changed its hue and style; currently, she sported long crimson locks. Strong and athletically graceful, she was considered a classic beauty by many. She lived in the apartment above the metaphysical shop she owned and operated called Stellar Remnants. It was through the mystical atmosphere of Stellar Remnants that she could openly offer fortunetelling services to those who genuinely sought divination guidance and to others who merely desired entertainment.

Typically, Althea's psychic abilities manifested through premonitions. Whenever she was near someone—or even a group of people—her heightened intuition interacted with the auras of others, granting her a level of clairvoyant insight. The signals, strength, and clarity of her premonitions often varied based on an individual's consciousness and their connection to both their surroundings and other living beings, whether flora or fauna. When encountering a crowd of people, the premonitions arrived all at once, like the static of multiple radio stations playing simultaneously. Althea had trained herself to separate, extract, and focus on one prophetic vision over another as she deemed necessary.

Over the past few years, Althea had begun experiencing unusual dreams featuring a woman whom she had never met named Erika. Although Althea was unsure why fate was presenting these dreams to her, her instincts suggested that there was a destiny to fulfill with this person. A couple of months after one of these dreams about Erika, Althea noticed another stranger passing by her shop. This stranger was not Erika but a mousy woman who caught Althea's attention. In the brief moment when their eyes locked, Althea gazed into this woman's soul and sensed that she was somehow connected to the person she sought.

Just over a year later, when a bridal shower group entered Stellar Remnants, Althea was struck with a premonition so strong that it felt like a lightning bolt. The prophecy was so significant and linked to monumental events that she could almost sense it from a mile away. As Althea walked out of the back room and entered the store lobby, she saw the same mousy woman she had observed passing her shop so long ago. Back then, Althea had tried to catch up to her on the street but ultimately lost sight of her. Even in that fleeting moment, Althea sensed she would cross paths with this woman again. Now, through a twist of fate, the same mousy woman had finally wandered into Stellar Remnants on this very night. She was a gatekeeper, holding the key to the road Althea was destined to traverse. This would prove to be one of the most important karmic obligations she would fulfill in her lifetime.

North Hollywood

Just after 9 pm, the sidewalk outside the small metaphysical shop glowed with neon pink light spilling from the large palm-shaped sign mounted in the shop's window. Next to it, a sign featuring script lettering displayed the store's name—Stellar Remnants.

Inside the shop, the rich aroma of freshly burnt sage lingered in the air, while numerous candles rested on small dishes holding water, their wicks flickering as they burned. An orange tabby cat named Gingersnaps graciously hosted the group of intoxicated bridesmaids who had wandered into the store moments ago on a whim, seeking a psychic reading for the bride-to-be. However, it was a different member of their group that the shop's proprietor had singled out and asked to accompany her into the back room. Now, the women joked and laughed as they explored the shop, waiting for their friend.

"Where is Erika?" Althea asked the stranger standing before her. The pair stood in a small room filled with the scent of palo santo, and thin wisps of smoke wafted through the dim glow of several lamps scattered throughout the space. The walls were painted lavender, and the room was decorated with various purple and green accents. Despite the tarot card reading table in the center of the room, Althea had not invited the stranger to sit. This moment had been a long time coming, and she couldn't wait any longer. "Erika," Althea repeated. "Where is she?"

The visitor raised her eyebrows as if trying to decipher how to respond to the question. Relaxing her mind, Althea searched the wavelengths between them for more information.

"I'm sorry," the woman finally spoke up with an awkward giggle. "I'm sorry, but I actually don't really believe in this sorta thing," she said, gesturing toward the tarot cards and candles. "My friends and I just came here for our friend, Jessa. She's about to get married. We thought we'd have a laugh. Sorry! Not at you! Just..., ya know... have a bit of a joke. I mean fun! I was trying to say, 'have a joke' and—"

"That's okay," Althea responded dismissively, unintentionally interrupting the woman. "I'm just wondering if you can tell me where Erika is. Do you know anyone by that name?" she asked, again probing this woman's soul, but it quickly became clear that a mental blockage was present. This was confusing. It was almost like certain elements of this person's consciousness were absent, as if they had been deliberately erased. What kind of being would be capable of erasing someone's memory, she wondered.

"But come on! No offense to you or your business; I mean, everyone needs to make a living, but you can't tell me that fortune-telling is *real*," the stranger scoffed.

"Honestly, I really don't need you to believe it's real. It's not important right now. Can you *please* tell me how I can get in touch with someone *you know* named Erika? She's probably about my height and has ashy brown hair. I think she has green eyes. Does that ring a bell?"

"Hmmm? Oh... Erika Navarro? Wow, it feels like I haven't thought about that name in forever!" the mousy woman stammered, her eyes roved around the room as she seemed to search her thoughts.

"Navarro! Awesome! The more information you can provide, the better!" Althea encouraged.

"Um, let me think. The last time I saw Erika was at her family's house."

"Okay, where was that?"

"You know what? I really have no idea," the woman laughed nervously.

"That's fine. Let's begin broadly. Can you tell me which county or state she's in?"

"On the East Coast!" The woman's face lit up at the recollected detail, then immediately fell into concerned dismay once more. "Oh, my God! What's wrong with me? She's on the East Coast. It's northern. Not New York. It's Boston, but not Boston. Massachusetts!" She looked relieved once she finally wrestled the word out.

"Massachusetts! You're doing great. This is wonderful. Thank you. Where in Massachusetts? You said it's not Boston?"

"Okay, I got this," the woman said with determination. "It's their family name. It's a town that sounds like a melody. It's beautiful, with forests and mountains. It's Chopin. It's nighttime and song."

"Nocturne?" Althea inquired, making an educated guess.

"Nocturne! That's it! Nocturne!"

Althea quickly retrieved her cell phone and entered the location name into the maps application. Sure enough, the town she had never heard of appeared—it was 2,964 miles away.

"Amazing! Okay, when did you see her last?" Althea persisted.

"Huh, you know what? It's the funniest thing, but I'm actually not really sure. That's really strange, right?"

"Think!" Althea urged. "The last time you mentioned seeing her was at her family's home, which we confirmed is in Nocturne. When did you travel there?"

"Geez, that was, I think, like two summers ago," the woman speculated. At this remark, Althea realized that she was being sincere. Something must have happened to cause her confusion.

"That's okay. I'll help you try to remember," Althea patiently coaxed. "You probably had to take some time away from your life to go visit. Maybe inform your job or someone close to you? You likely had to purchase an airline ticket."

"Oh yeah! It's starting to come back to me now! It was for Erika's birthday, which I know is in August! It couldn't have been her last birthday, but I'm pretty sure it was the year before that!" Once more, the woman appeared briefly relieved as she recalled the additional details, but then she shifted sharply into worry as she exclaimed, "Oh no!"

"What is it?"

"I think I might have left her in a *bad* situation, but I can't remember why I feel that way. Has that ever happened to you? It feels almost like it's at the tip of my brain. I mean, at the tip of my tongue! But it's just not coming to me for some reason! I have this strong feeling that it was a bad situation, and now I feel awful for leaving her behind."

The two were interrupted as the beads hanging down from the door frame parted, making delicate sounds as they clicked against each other.

"Um, Nikki?" It was the ringleader of the bachelorette party festivities. "Jessa is out here waiting for her turn. It's *her* special night, you know," the Maid of Honor chastised.

"No, I'm sorry," Althea interjected. "I can't provide any services tonight. Please express my apologies to the bride-to-be for the inconvenience. If you bring her back another time, I will make it up to her with a complimentary reading. Again, please accept my apologies, but something important has come up."

The haughty woman scoffed, "Seriously?"

"Seriously," Althea confirmed with conviction. The woman's jaw tightened as she rolled her eyes at Nikki.

"Mia, I'm sorry!" Nikki exclaimed. "Something has happened to Erika; I think she's in trouble! I think she needs my help."

"Oh well, if it's for Erika!" Mia replied in a high-pitched, mocking tone, offering one more eye roll before turning to leave the room. Althea dismissed the situation much quicker than Nikki, rolling right back into her line of questioning to keep Nikki focused.

"Okay, Nikki, is it?"

"Nicole."

"Nicole, please stay focused and don't worry about Mia for now. I sense that she and Jessa won't be friends for long anyway, because Mia is sleeping with the groom-to-be. So! It sounds like your gut is telling you that you left Erika in a *bad situation*. Do you know how to find her family's house? You mentioned it was their last name. Is the family's last name Navarro or Nocturne, like the town? Do you happen to have an address?"

"Oh! Let's see," Nicole said, perking up again at the chance to be helpful. "I'm not sure!" she responded enthusiastically but then seemed to process the words that had just escaped her lips. "That's strange. I *should* know, right?"

"That's okay. Perhaps you have the address noted down somewhere? You probably had to book a ticket?"

"Yes, that's a great point! I should have all the info on my phone," Nicole said as she searched her cellphone.

While Nicole searched for details, Althea's cat Gingersnaps appeared in the doorway, signaling that the rest of the party had departed as the purring feline sought more attention. Upon seeing her cat, Althea realized she needed to start making plans for her imminent trip. She had numerous responsibilities in her life, home, and business to think about, and she had no idea how long she would be away on this destiny journey.

"Okay, here it is," Nicole finally confirmed. "I flew into Boston, Massachusetts, and it seems I rented a car. And look! Here's the address right there—Dragos Manor," Nicole said as visible chills overcame her body.

"Thank you. Listen, I need to go to Nocturne to check on Erika. I'll have to think of a good reason to be there, but I'll come up with something."

"You can always say that you know Nicole Ramirez! That I told you about that place."

"Hmmm, maybe," Althea mused. "No offense, but I might need something with a bit more impact; otherwise, they might not let me stay long enough to figure out what's happening. Is there anything you think I should know before I go there? Anything at all that you remember about the family or the area?"

"Nothing I can think of! It's a pretty normal place!" Nicole stated with lighthearted authority.

"Are you sure?" Althea pressed. "You mentioned that you thought you left her in a bad situation."

"You're right! I did say that. Oh wait, it's ghosts! There are ghosts! Her family's home is haunted," Nicole said casually, sweeping her hand dismissively through the air.

"Ghosts?" Althea asked with surprise, then lifted her phone again and typed in *'Dragos Manor, Nocturne, MA.'* A handful of articles and several paranormal websites listed Dragos Manor as a historic, haunted hotel in Nocturne, Massachusetts. From what Althea could see from a quick search, the establishment did not appear to have a formal website of its own.

She randomly selected a more recent article, though it was still several years old, and began skimming through the text. It provided a historical overview of the infamous estate. Toward the bottom of the home screen was an image of an old newspaper advertisement from 1939. The ad was positioned between a large *General Electric* television promotion and a caricature of Charlie Chaplin with an announcement beneath. The Dragos Manor ad was modest, featuring a black and white photo of a magnificent four-story gothic mansion and a bold headline that read—*Dragos Manor, Nocturne, Massachusetts.* The body of the text simply stated: *Richly improved experience offering convenient bookings throughout the year. A long-famed, phenomenal adventure that will leave guests filled with mystic wonder.* Althea's eyes scrolled to the bottom of the page, where she saw a cheesy tagline that read, *"Book your next stay at Dragos Manor. We're dying to have you!"*

"Oh wait," Nicole's face was quizzical for a moment. "I guess that is strange, isn't it?" she admitted sheepishly, as she must have finally realized that ghosts were not commonplace.

Okay, so it was some sort of haunted house that Althea would be dealing with. She realized that this detail could possibly explain some aspects of her strange dreams.

"Ghosts, huh..." she mused. "I should reach out to my programmer friend, Kit. At one point, she mentioned a software prototype for a paranormal investigation tool she was working on. So, I guess I'm a ghost hunter now," Althea reflected for a moment before turning back to Nicole. "I can't thank you enough for coming here tonight. You have been extremely helpful."

"Of course! I'm happy to help! I *want* to help."

"Nicole, is there *anything else I need to know* about Erika, her family, or anything at all before I go out there?"

"Nope! Nothing else comes to mind! That is definitely everything!"

"Thank you. I have a lot of plans to make."

"Is there anything I can do to assist?" Nicole asked hopefully.

Althea felt apprehensive. "It would probably be better if I went out there alone. I don't want to let on that I know anything about the situation. I can assess the circumstances passively to avoid drawing suspicion."

"Please let me help somehow! Erika is my best friend, and I feel so guilty that I almost forgot about her." It was Nicole's turn to press. Just then, Gingersnaps rubbed against Nicole's ankles. She bent down and scooped the cat up. "I could watch your cat and the shop if you'd like. I'm actually looking for a job right now anyway! You can train me! I'm sorry for what I said earlier about not believing in this stuff."

Althea looked at Nicole skeptically at first, but soon recognized that a viable solution was presenting itself to her and that it was likely part of the karmic journey she was about to begin. After weighing the various factors, she ultimately decided against introducing resistance into the equation.

"Thank you. I will gratefully and humbly accept your help. Staying in close contact will likely be useful in case I need to consult with you as I embark on this journey."

Chapter Two

NEW MOON, OLD PATTERNS

Darkness enveloped Dragos Manor and its surrounding landscape. The grand, century-old Gothic Revival estate, with large, rust-colored stone walls and pointed dark gray rooftops, loomed menacingly against the moonless January sky. The vast woodlands circling the property resembled turbulent ocean waves in the night, with the treetops swaying rhythmically in the howling, moaning winds.

"Mom? Mom, I know you're in there," Erika Farkas—formerly Erika Navarro—whispered into the darkness. Her voice was hesitant as she spoke through a hole slightly smaller than her face. The hole had been crudely chiseled into the brick wall separating her from the mysterious room beyond. While the space on the other side had once been unknown to her, it had since become very significant after Erika learned that her mother had not died a tragic death in a fabricated car accident, as her family had told her for nearly her entire life. Just over a year ago, Erika was finally told the truth—her mother had taken her own life in the room beyond this wall.

"I know you're in there," Erika repeated. "At least, I hope you are," she added, conflicted about what she truly wanted to hear in response.

Despite the circumstances, Erika had accepted long ago that her mother had indeed died and was buried at Nocturne Hills Cemetery nearly a decade earlier. Yet, something deep inside her told her that there was even more to the story than her family was telling her. This was because, in the two years since returning to Dragos Manor—the haunted mansion-hotel owned and operated by the Dragos family—Erika had uncovered so many secrets that she realized she had never truly known her family at all.

Growing up, Erika led a very normal and ordinary life, despite experiencing more than her fair share of loss. She lost her father at a young age and her grandmother during her teenage years. Most notably, the sudden death of her mother when Erika was seventeen compelled her to leave her hometown of Nocturne, Massachusetts, in haste. Seeking comfort in a new environment, she moved to California, where she eventually met her fiancé, Ryan Wilson, after college. Erika and Ryan shared a happy enough relationship for a few years until Ryan was brutally murdered in a horrific manner. This tragedy led the then twenty-five-year-old Erika to leave the West Coast and return to the East Coast, to live with her maternal side of the family at the long-rumored haunted estate in Nocturne. Once back at Dragos Manor, Erika quickly learned that her family was far from normal. In fact, they turned out to be quite paranormal.

"Mom, please! If any part of you is in there, give me a sign. I promise I can handle it. When I found out that the rumors about this place were true—that it *really is* haunted, sure... I freaked out, but I've learned to live with it! I found out that I have werewolves in my family! I know *you* were a werewolf! I know I'm... I mean, I guess I'm some kind of werewolf, but I don't change or whatever. Sounds so fucking absurd saying all this out loud, but I want you to know that I can handle it! I've seen the ghost of my dead grandmother! I married a damn werewolf, for God's sake! I've swallowed so much supernatural bullshit since I got here; seeing the ghost of my dead mother would be the least weird thing that's happened to me! I know you're in there!" Erika's voice broke. She was unsure how to push the negotiation further since she had been coming up to the 4th floor for months and seemingly pleading into a void of nothingness.

"Grandaunt Ana told me you're up here! She told me that you literally killed yourself trying to lock that *thing* away—*the Mother*. If she's in there, keeping you from me, you can tell her I'm not afraid of her! You can tell her to march over here and kiss me on the—"

A faint tapping echoed from the cavity beyond the bricks, causing Erika to stumble over her words. She quickly pulled her cell phone from her pocket, turned on the flashlight, and aimed it through the hole in the wall. The area beyond seemed unremarkable, but it was more than just a storage space. The room was large, filled with numerous beds, cupboards, and pantries, yet it was pretty evident that it was unoccupied. Dust covered much of the floor and furniture, indicating that nothing had moved inside for a long time. She switched off the flashlight, feeling frustrated and angry, but also terrified that her life was destined for endless heartache and struggle.

"Fine, if you won't see me face to face, I'll do it my way!" she called out. Erika turned, exhaled her disheartenment, and sank down along the bricks, settling onto the dark hallway floor. Her long, ash-brown hair cascaded over her shoulders, and her usually vibrant green eyes appeared dull in the shadows. Her long legs stretched out before her, crossing gracefully at the ankles. Lifting the pewter hand mirror with its paisley backing that she had brought with her, Erika gazed longingly at its reflection.

She first discovered this antique mirror hidden away inside a vanity drawer in her late mother's abandoned suite. The first time she looked into it, Erika saw what one would expect to see—a reflection of herself staring back. However, something about her appearance seemed more hollow than usual, almost as if something was missing. She had not been able to pinpoint it in the moment, but, after many sleepless nights ruminating on the incident, Erika realized that she looked like a broken, empty vessel. The next time she gazed into the mirror was on her wedding day. That time, Erika did not see her face—nor anyone else's face, for that matter. Instead, she saw an image of the brick wall on the 4th floor, concealing the area where her mother had taken her own life. Once Erika slowly began removing bricks from the wall, the mirror started to behave in a very strange way. Whenever she wasn't on the 4th floor, it would show the black hole in the bricks, almost beckoning her to visit. Even more unsettling was that when Erika brought the mirror up to the 4th floor and gazed into it, her mother's image stared back at her. This was a significant reason that compelled Erika to find out what exactly happened on the other side of the wall.

After overcoming the initial shock of seeing her mom in the mirror's reflection, Erika quickly found comfort in the image, even though she wasn't sure if it was truly her mother. One reason for her uncertainty was that the reflection in the mirror mimicked all of Erika's movements—if Erika blinked, her mother blinked; when she smiled, her mother smiled back; and when she mouthed the words *"I love you,"* her mother silently expressed the same sentiment. Even if some kind of magic was at play, making this portrayal possible, seeing her mother after so many years of absence brought solace to Erika's heart.

Erika forcibly averted her eyes from the mirror. She refocused her thoughts on the mysterious space behind the brick wall, undoubtedly the most intriguing thing about the 4th floor. Frankly, it baffled her. She wondered why her mother had chosen this place to end her life. Why had this room been bricked off for so long? Where was that thing Ana had warned her about? *The Mother*. Erika had never seen it. From what she could tell, all that sealed-off room held was dusty, old, forgotten furniture. Still, Erika had been cautioned never to go inside. However, after a series of events left her feeling disillusioned and crushed, Erika decided to ignore that warning. By now, she had removed about half a dozen bricks since she first broke through that barrier just over a year ago, on the night of her wedding.

Erika stood up again and pressed her face against the hole in the bricks.

"Mom, I need... I need you. I'm fighting like hell to regain control over my life. After losing you, everything has gone to shit! I have this insatiable desire to prove to myself that I can handle anything, but I'm not sure that I can! Ana retired and left me in charge of this place and our family. I'm running this haunted hotel, but it feels more like it's running me. I married *Blake Farkas*. Everyone expects me to have his babies. And not just any babies... they're saying I'm some rare non-transforming werewolf. How come there are no other werewolves in the world like Marius? You can't tell me my offspring will turn out as a *hybrid* werewolf like him simply because I'm half human! That doesn't make any sense! This is all too much! You kept all of this from me my whole life, and now I have to deal with it! I know you're in there! I saw you! I saw you that day I found this hand mirror in your old room. I saw you down in the cellar when Blake rescued me from the Mischief poltergeist. I saw you on the evening of my wedding. What other shadow woman would be following me around?

A sudden sound from deep within the cavity captured Erika's attention and snapped her out of her frantic rambling. The faint rustling on the other side of the bricks made her blood run cold as she desperately searched for her cell phone. After checking her empty pockets, Erika scoured the floor until she spotted a dark rectangular silhouette. She picked up her phone and thrust it through the hole. Once again, the room appeared uninhabited, with only dust and cobwebs as the remaining residents. She sighed and decided to give up for tonight. As she had come to expect, the real answers most likely lay hidden within the pages of a family story that kept its secrets well buried.

The Venetian silk drapes were drawn in the cavernous suite on the 3rd floor. Chimney glass oil lamps flickered, casting shallow glimmers of golden light throughout the otherwise austere suite. The Edwardian décor was neatly arranged yet modestly displayed throughout the room. Anastacia Dragos—Ana for short—sat upright in the center of a plush bed, surrounded by numerous decorative silk pillows trimmed with Nottingham lace frills.

Despite being in her nineties, the now-retired Head of Household of Dragos Manor maintained a relatively youthful appearance and exuded an air of commanding dignity, even while resting in bed. Although she had spent the last year secluded in her bedroom suite, Ana still took great pride in her appearance. Tonight, she wore a black velvet dressing gown adorned with pearl-colored beads and sequins. Her salt-and-pepper hair was meticulously styled in victory rolls, and she applied a tasteful amount of makeup in case any unexpected visitors dropped by, such as the one she suspected had come to visit her that evening. Ana's sharp facial features were twisted into an unsettling smile as she spoke into the empty room before her.

"Sophia? Sophia, I know you're in here," she whispered into the vastness of her suite. No response came. Nothing moved, except for the shadows dancing and swaying in the flickering lamplight. Although Ana understood it was possible for Sophia's spirit to be present on the 3rd floor, she recognized it was highly unlikely. While the brick wall on the 4th floor was intended to keep the living out, more importantly, there were many more nonphysical partitions in place to keep the dead in. Still, Ana swore she had heard her late grandmother-in-law's unmistakable, silvery voice just moments ago.

"Come now, Sophia. I know you're there. Show yourself," she challenged, her voice laced with hesitation, conflicted about what she truly wished to hear in response. Maybe she had imagined it. Or perhaps her mind was playing tricks on her, and the isolation was affecting her, just as her son Marius had recently expressed concern about.

Several factors contributed to Ana's desire for solitude. It was not solely linked to her retirement as the Head of Household of the Dragos family; rather, Ana felt she no longer had a place in the world, let alone in her family's magnificent home. The truth was that Ana believed she had ultimately failed to live up to the legacies of past Dragos matriarchs. She had failed to protect the resident spirits of Dragos Manor when all three hundred had mysteriously vanished on the night of Erika and Blake's wedding. A pang of sorrow resonated in her heart as Ana thought of her late sister-in-law, Daniela. That night, Daniela's ghost had even speculated that *the Mother* had returned just before she and the others disappeared. Ana silently berated herself. Despite the irony, Ana knew Sophia Dragos would have never allowed any of this to happen.

"Sophia, please! If any part of you is here, give me a sign. After everything you've done for me, I would never turn you away. Even with all that has happened, I still believe that you have the ability to separate from *her*," Ana paused, briefly unsure how to proceed in the negotiation.

Even with the troubling circumstances surrounding the latter part of Sophia's life, Ana had always admired the late founder of Dragos Manor. After all, Sophia had taken Ana in when she was shunned by werewolf society in Romania. Being a werewolf who could not transform was deemed unacceptable at that time. Ana endured discrimination, frequent slurs, exclusion, and, worst of all, ostracism from her own family.

When she came to live at Dragos Manor in the early 1940s through an arranged marriage to Sophia's grandson, Elek, Ana finally felt accepted for the first time in her life. Upon meeting Sophia Dragos, Ana discovered the type of matriarch she aspired to be. She learned everything from Sophia, a powerful *Leader of the Pack*, as that title used to be called.

Both ardent and graceful, Sophia forged a remarkable path in life. While many regarded her as a true beauty, it was her determination and resilience that primarily defined her. As was customary in werewolf culture, Sophia passed the role of *Leader of the Pack* to her next living female relatives. In this case, her grandsons' wives, Daniela and Anastacia Dragos, inherited the family home and business. Decades later, after Erika's grandmother Daniela passed away, Ana became the sole *Leader of the Pack*, or *Head of Household*, as the title evolved into by the turn of the twenty-first century to better align with human society.

"You came here to ask about Erika because she now carries the proverbial torch. I know what you're thinking—why is *she* the Leader of the Pack while I'm still around? Well, I'll have you know that it wasn't because I gave up. Circumstances became quite complicated. I did everything you taught me; I ran a tight ship, always honoring the pride and traditions of our homeland. Sure, Dragos Manor experienced its financial ups and downs, but you, more than anyone, should understand that! Then suddenly, I looked up one day and realized that the whole world had changed. It wasn't me! It was them. I simply could not bear it when I discovered that Cristian, my only grandson, is—"

A faint tapping echoed throughout the vast space around her, causing Ana to stumble over her words. She swiftly craned her neck around, searching the room for the source of the sound. The room before her appeared unchanged and empty, leaving Ana feeling discouraged.

"Fine, if you won't talk with me face-to-face, I'm done wasting my time conversing with the phantoms of my imagination!"

Ana sank deeper into bed, exhaling her disappointment. She tried to fall asleep; however, agitation coursed through her as she struggled to quiet her mind. Suddenly, she sat up again and spoke boldly into the room.

"Sophia, I know you found a way past those bricks. Even if you aren't in this room right now, I feel you *in my bones*. Please don't be angry with me. Marius forced me to place those spells on the bricks after what happened to—" Ana faltered, fearing she might be touching on a sensitive subject. She decided to delicately shift the conversation to avoid offending her deceased mentor.

"I'm not sure if you realize this, but Erika married the Farkas wolf. Never in all my life did I think a Dragos would marry a Farkas, not after a century of the Romanian and Hungarian Lycan feud. To this day, I still cannot believe those Hungarians are living in our beautiful Romanian home. And get this, Sophia, the 'peace offering' that was made to the Farkas family is that Erika will give Blake Farkas *hybrid offspring*. No one has ever stopped to wonder why the history of Lycanthropy, only my two sons, Marius and

Anton, possess the unique abilities of hybrid werewolves," Ana snickered. "Oh, Sophia, you must forgive me for going along with that fairytale, but it had to happen to save our family home. Also, since we're on the subject, it's strange, but recently, I swear I've been seeing my father outside, standing near the trees on the eastern lawn. Do you think it's possible there's another—"

A sudden sound from deep within the recesses of the room captured Ana's attention, snapping her out of her frantic rambling. There was a faint rustling coming from the shadows in the corner of the suite. Her blood ran cold as she desperately searched for the source. After a moment of craning and straining, a coy smile crept across her lips, sharpening her already pointed features.

"I see you," Ana whispered with delight.

Chapter Three

DRAGOS MANOR'S HEARTBEAT

Several Weeks Later

The bright Worm Moon pierced the dark sky like the shimmering eye of a creature stalking the night. Winter was over, and March had brought vibrant green vegetation and various blossoms to the sprawling grounds of Dragos Manor. Yet, despite the renewed atmosphere, a hollow silence lingered in the cool nighttime air.

It was nearly midnight. Inside the late 1800s estate, the expansiveness of the ground floor lobby felt like the murky void within the belly of a massive whale. A few wall sconces made a feeble attempt to illuminate the antique Edwardian décor peppered throughout the home. The gigantic house vibrated with a faint rhythmic hum, almost as if the very structure possessed a heartbeat.

A tall Australian woman in her mid-twenties, with long blond hair and high cheekbones, crept up the staircase toward the 2nd story where the guest rooms were located. This woman was Kathryn, and she clutched her cell phone like a crucifix, the flashlight switched on and guiding her up one emerald-carpeted step at a time. When she reached about halfway up the stairs, the grandfather clock on the ground level bellowed a loud chime that rang out eleven more times, signaling that it was midnight. The sudden sound nearly made Kathryn's soul catapult right out of her body, leaving her corpse poised to topple over and die right there on the steps.

This is what I get for letting my friends convince me to go on a holiday at a haunted hotel; she silently berated herself. *I wonder where those wankers are, anyway,* she thought as she took a breath to steady herself and then continued up the staircase.

Kathryn hesitated at the top of the landing and shone the flashlight down the long hallway stretching out before her. It had a daunting and foreboding quality. *Classic,* she thought. For some inexplicable reason, there were no light switches in sight. *Great way to sell that scare factor,* she mused. It was working; Kathryn was scared. *It's not real; it's just pretend,* she reminded herself as she started down the hallway.

Like everything else in this place, even the doors seemed spooky; they were antiques made of solid oak stained dark brown, featuring extruded linings and decorative Valma brass handles. Each entryway had a mounted brass number plate. The odd room numbers were on the left, while the even numbers were on the right.

Kathryn sighed and started down the dark hallway. As she passed each door, she tilted the flashlight to illuminate the number plate, helping her orient herself and gauge how much farther she had to go before reaching her room, number 216. Upon reaching room 205, she heard the soft creak of a floorboard behind her and got the distinct impression that someone's eyes were on her. Assuming her friends had followed her, Kathryn turned with some relief to see who had joined her on the floor, but to her horror, the hallway behind her was empty. Chills ran down her spine. Her fight-or-flight response kicked into high alert as she frantically scanned the hallway. She had distinctly heard a sound, yet by all appearances, she was alone.

"Hello?" she called, trying to suppress the tremor in her voice. "Is someone there?" When no response came, she quickly directed her flashlight toward the nearest doorway on her right—room 206. *Alright, I need to get a grip and just get to my room,* she thought as a nervous giggle escaped her lips. Still, she moved with more urgency as she continued.

She only made it a short distance before another sound broke the silence. Kathryn froze, listening intently, trying to discern what the new noise was and where it was coming from. A faint scratching, reminiscent of a rodent gnawing inside the walls, seemed to come from behind a nearby doorway. Kathryn directed the flashlight beam toward the number plate—room 208. She was about to dismiss it and continue on, but the scratching sound quickly grew louder until it resembled human nails clawing at the door.

26

Someone was desperately trying to escape that room. The scratching soon gave way to muffled sounds of movement. Whatever it was, it sounded far too large to be a rodent. Moving closer, Kathryn carefully pressed her ear against the oak door and listened. As soon as she did, she heard the crashing of furniture, then an awful thud of body weight hitting the ground, followed by faint gasping. *Someone was in trouble*, she realized, as panic flooded her eyes.

The door across the hall abruptly burst open, and a tall, gangly man appeared in the doorway. Kathryn jumped, startled by his abrupt presence. The man stepped into the hallway, shutting the door behind him. He was an attractive Latino man, wearing a crisp black button-up shirt with white flowers, and his hair was clean and slicked back from a recent shower.

"Oh my God, Ignacio! You scared the proverbial shit outta me, mate!" Kathryn exclaimed in her Australian accent while holding a hand to her chest and then placing two fingers on her wrist. This man was her friend, Ignacio—Nacho for short.

"Yeah, I can see that from your sweat mustache," Nacho teased. "Also, thank you for specifying 'proverbial.' I'd be alarmed if this were a *'literal'* situation. Whatcha doin', hun? Did I just catch you creepin'?" Kathryn glanced back at the door she had just listened through. It was quiet now.

"I heard some strange sounds," she explained defensively. "But now I realize I probably just heard you being inappropriate with some little twink you have trapped in your room. If you could take even just five minutes from your incessant Eiffel Towering—" she began to tease, but was interrupted when the door to Nacho's room burst open again, revealing two slender young men in their early twenties, both with wet hair. They clearly didn't expect to encounter anyone in the hallway, as they froze in Kathryn's flashlight beam, appearing like startled deer caught in headlights. "You are so predictable," she muttered with amusement as the femme boys hurried down the hallway toward the staircase.

"Hey, you can just stow your judgment, little Miss Bogan. Where are you off to anyway?" Nacho asked nonchalantly.

"If you must know, I was on my way to my room to grab some *party favors* for Stanley and me, but I got sidetracked when I heard you all making those strange sounds."

"What sounds?"

"I don't know. It sounded bloody animalistic. Like you had them tied up in your bed, and they were struggling to escape or gasping for air or something."

"First of all, they couldn't get enough of what they were gasping for," Nacho said with a sly smile.

"Oh my God, gross!" Kathryn exclaimed, her face twisted in disgust at the crass comment.

"And second, you weren't hearin' us bangin' in no bed. We *Eiffel Towered* in the shower like civilized adults," Nacho confirmed with an air of sophistication.

"Well, you sound downright *terrifying* when you're having sex, mate."

"Come on! We couldn't have sounded *that* scary," Nacho scoffed. "What exactly did you hear, anyway?" Then, as if answering his question, the strange sounds started once again, but this time they came from the room across the hallway—number 210. Strange scratching from behind the doorway gave way to heavy objects crashing around the room, followed by a hollow gasp like a death rattle. Nacho and Kathryn exchanged a knowing glance. "I mean, people do be bangin', ya know," Nacho offered with a coy smile as he shrugged it off.

"Oh my God! What losers! Who comes to a haunted hotel as *epic* as this just to play smash-ups? That sounds bloody boring! No offense," Kathryn feebly offered. Nacho stared back at her with a deadpan expression. "What I meant was that I wouldn't want to miss a single second of the festivities here! We're staying *three weeks* in this little, hidden haunted gem! Literally, it's a chance of a lifetime!" she exclaimed. "Speaking of which, I want to hurry up and get back to the party. Would you mind escorting me to my room, darling? It's scary as buggery up here. I mean, haven't they ever heard of lights in this place? We paid good money. We paid for some bloody lights!"

"Fiiine, I'll go with you on one condition. You gotta share your coca," Nacho negotiated.

"No duh, queen! Right this way, Madam," Kathryn directed.

"Mademoiselle!" Nacho corrected in his best Patsy Stone impression.

The pair continued down the dark hallway on the 2nd floor of Dragos Manor. As they passed the next door marked 211, they heard sounds of a struggle once more. Oddly, it was the same noise they had heard in 210, coming from behind a different door. Nacho and Kathryn exchanged glances.

"Lotsa horny gals up in here tonight," Nacho playfully suggested as the pair continued onward. However, as they passed the next door and heard the same sounds again, Nacho quickly ran out of quips and could only manage a feeble, "*Daayumn.*"

After the pair passed room 213, hearing the same strange noises again, Nacho remained silent. Nor did he have anything to say as they passed rooms 214 and 215, all the while hearing the same eerie sounds coming from within each room. What was even creepier was that the ferocity and brutality seemed to intensify with each passing door. Once they arrived at Kathryn's room, number 216, everything finally fell silent.

"Phew," she whispered with relief. Kathryn was certain they were thinking the same thing—what if those sounds were coming from inside her room as well?

She rummaged through her pocket and pulled out the room key, clutching it in her small hand. After inserting it into the keyhole, she turned the lock and slowly twisted the black oval knob. The door creaked open to reveal a dark, shadowy room.

"That's odd," Kathryn remarked. "I could have sworn I left the light on." As she lifted the flashlight into the room, the beam briefly illuminated an unnaturally tall, spindly figure, but the flashlight flickered and went out. Their surroundings plunged into complete darkness. Suddenly, the sounds of a full-blown physical altercation erupted from within the room before them. It sounded as if someone was struggling for their very life, and a deep, rattling gasp of terror and panic filled the space.

She and Nacho screamed in unison. She reached over and blindly searched for a wall switch. When she finally found it, she flipped it on, but no light appeared as expected. Kathryn and Nacho continued to scream together.

"Where is the goddamn light?" Nacho demanded.

"There's a lamp over there by the bed!" Kathryn replied urgently, as the terrible sounds escalated. Nacho bravely rushed into the room and frantically reached for the nightstand. At last, the light clicked on, and everything fell quiet. The room appeared as Kathryn had left it, with her suitcase open on the floor, slightly rummaged through. The pair looked around wordlessly, fear still etched on their faces.

"That was insane," Nacho murmured. "What was making that sound?"

"Maybe it was coming from next door after all?" Kathryn commented, feeling doubt about her own speculation.

"Am I crazy, or did you see someone in this room when we first—"

"Whatever, I'm over it. This is starting to piss me off. It's probably the hotel staff playing pranks to make their little *haunted house* seem more authentic. There's clearly no one here now. Look under the bed," Kathryn directed, and Nacho complied as he glanced underneath the bed.

"Nothing," he confirmed. "Let's grab this coke of yours and get back to the party. Maybe we can do a bump or two first to calm our nerves," he suggested.

"That is the *best* fucking idea I've heard all night, mate." Kathryn shook off her nerves and walked over to her luggage. She retrieved a clear plastic bag containing the desired white substance, and all residual fear melted away into anticipation of the upcoming high. Nacho pulled a small gold coke spoon from a chain around his neck and handed it to his friend. Kathryn plopped down on the edge of the bed and took the first spoonful, quickly snorting it through one nostril, then handed the baggy and spoon over to Nacho, who did the same and took a second sniff through his other nostril.

As they were enjoying themselves, a quiet scratching sound resumed once more. The friends exchanged bewildered glances. However, after the controlled substance entered their bloodstream, they seemed less frightened as the rodent-like clawing noises persisted.

"This place is such a trip. I can't believe how haunted it is," Nacho remarked as Kathryn took another sniff of the snowy substance.

"I know! My flat in Melbourne used to be *haunted as*," Kathryn laughed. Nacho looked confused.

"Haunted as what?" he asked.

"Oh, that's just some Aussie slang, mate. It would be like Americans saying *haunted AF*," she continued to laugh until her chuckling gave way to a contemplative look. "Does that sound like it's coming from under the bed?"

"Ugh, I'm feeling way too good for you to try and scare me, bitch," Nacho said, raising another tiny spoonful of white powder to his nose. Suddenly, his arms flew into the air as his body lurched forward, and he was forcefully pulled to the floor. A white powdery cloud hung in the air while adrenaline snapped Kathryn into action. She lunged for her friend as Nacho was being violently dragged under the bed by an unseen force.

"Help! Kathryn! Help me!" he screamed. She grabbed her friend by the forearms and tried to stop him from disappearing into the recesses under the bed.

"I've got you! Just hold onto me!"

"Please don't let go! Please don't let me go! Something's got my ankles!" he pleaded with a frightened, sweaty face. Kathryn engaged in a tug-of-war with her friend acting as the rope. She winced and strained, then opened her eyes and glanced underneath the bed to see what had him. Red glowing eyes viciously narrowed in her direction.

"Holy shit, what the hell is that?" she yelled. Upon hearing this, Nacho's screams grew louder and more frantic. Then, the pair suddenly flew backward, with Nacho landing on top of Kathryn. The friends stared at each other; terror filled their faces. They both spun around to look underneath the bed. It was dark. There were no red eyes staring back at them any longer. Kathryn grabbed her cell phone and turned on the flashlight. The beam of light confirmed that there was nothing underneath the bed.

Both friends let out a long sigh as their fear receded, replaced once again by the boldness of the narcotics high. They turned to look at each other just as the dull, rhythmic vibration of EDM bass echoed from downstairs. Nacho and Kathryn held each other as they processed the situation they had just experienced. A smile slowly spread across their faces.

"That was *fuckin insane*! I wish we had captured that on video for our socials!" Nacho squealed.

"I can't *believe* that just happened! Oh my Gawd, wait until I tell Stanley!" Kathryn exclaimed as she stood, brushing herself off. Nacho picked up the baggie of coke and his tiny gold spoon, and the pair exited the room, laughing hysterically as the door slammed shut behind them with a loud *bang*.

Chapter Four

QUEEN OF THE CASTLE

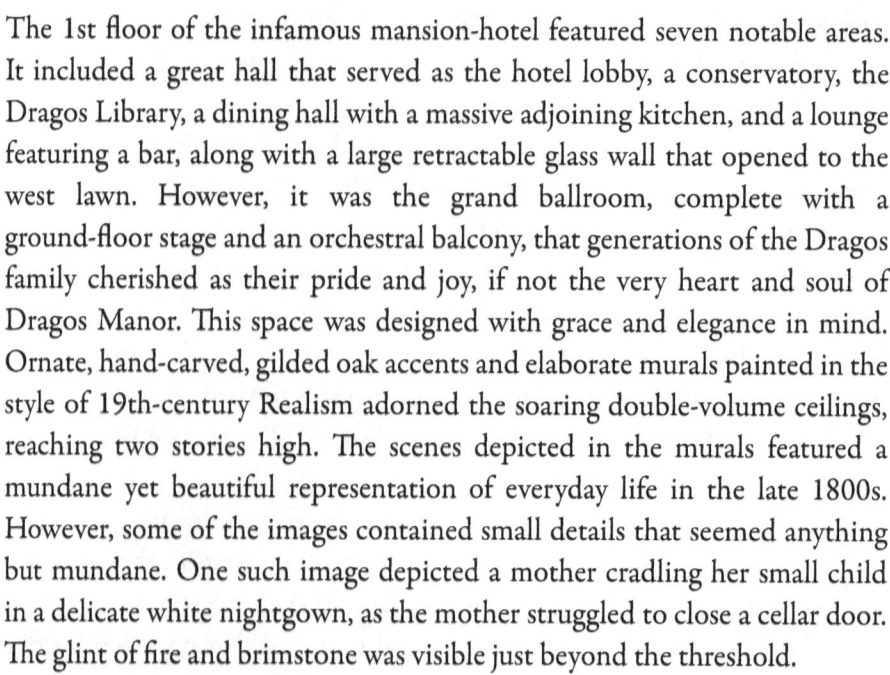

The 1st floor of the infamous mansion-hotel featured seven notable areas. It included a great hall that served as the hotel lobby, a conservatory, the Dragos Library, a dining hall with a massive adjoining kitchen, and a lounge featuring a bar, along with a large retractable glass wall that opened to the west lawn. However, it was the grand ballroom, complete with a ground-floor stage and an orchestral balcony, that generations of the Dragos family cherished as their pride and joy, if not the very heart and soul of Dragos Manor. This space was designed with grace and elegance in mind. Ornate, hand-carved, gilded oak accents and elaborate murals painted in the style of 19th-century Realism adorned the soaring double-volume ceilings, reaching two stories high. The scenes depicted in the murals featured a mundane yet beautiful representation of everyday life in the late 1800s. However, some of the images contained small details that seemed anything but mundane. One such image depicted a mother cradling her small child in a delicate white nightgown, as the mother struggled to close a cellar door. The glint of fire and brimstone was visible just beyond the threshold.

Red and pink lights flashed across the anxious faces of the mother and the frightened child she held in her arms as the song "Freaks" by Timmy Trumpet & Savage blared from numerous speakers. The vast space was dark and humid, with hundreds of bodies jumping feverishly to the music, their forms highlighted by strobing beams of light. The red lights snapped off, replaced by tiny pinpoints of white orbs that swarmed around the ballroom like fireflies. Then, the entire room went dark before solid blue beams of light illuminated cages raised just above the crowd. Inside, Go-Go dancers gyrated vibrantly to the Melbourne bounce music pulsing throughout the room.

There were many types of individuals in attendance at this rager—erotic humiliation was happening in one corner while voyeurism and BDSM were occurring in another.

A jovial group of people dressed in werewolf costumes, decorated with various pieces of glowing jewelry, skipped through the crowd. The dance floor resembled a feeding frenzy filled with creatures driven by an insatiable hunger for lust, stimulants, and raw, visceral interaction. Rows of tables were arranged in a horseshoe shape around the perimeter of the dance floor. Servers delivered expensive bottles of champagne, liquor, and wine to guests who had paid a premium to sit at these VIP tables.

At the center of it all sat Cristian Dragos. His hair was thick, dark, and neat, featuring a prominent widow's peak. His eyebrows resembled large caterpillars, and although he was clean-shaven, a hint of a dark five o'clock shadow lingered beneath his fair skin. As Cristian took a long drag from his cigarette, a glint of light caught the large gold wolf head ring on his middle finger.

Surrounding him was his entourage—a group of younger local werewolves from Nocturne who called themselves the Killers. This group included the Aristide brothers, Beo and Malcolm Jr., two charismatic individuals endowed with all the southern gothic charm passed down from their Haitian French Creole father, Malcolm Sr. There was Loki Lupu, who was quiet with short, dark, wavy hair and a patchy beard, while River Landis had a mischievous air about him, sporting wild, greasy, light brown hair loosely slicked back on his head.

The friends sat in a spacious owner's lounge on the stage near the giant windows of the ballroom's eastern wall. The heavy curtains were drawn shut to block out the Full Moon in the sky that evening. Security guards loitered in front of velvet ropes, ensuring no one dared approach the thick, occluding drapes. Cristian, Beo, Malcom Jr., River Landis, and Loki Lupu casually sipped their drinks while watching the boisterous crowd like a turbulent riptide undulating on the dance floor. Bottles of Grey Goose and Dom

Pérignon were scattered across the cocktail table before them.

"Can you believe we've only been open one week? It blows my mind how quickly this thing took off!" Cristian shouted jubilantly as he beamed at the crowd, thrilled that his plans were coming to fruition.

"Didn't I tell you it was a good idea to promote this thing through our connects from the rave and music festival circuits?" Beo chimed in with a satisfied grin.

"It's after midnight, we're out in the middle of bumfuck nowhere, and newcomers are *still* rollin' through! You see! This is what I've been talking about for years! All the wasted potential in this place!" Cristian marveled, continuing to ride the wave of his success. "*This* is our crowd. *This* is what I know how to do best."

At that moment, Kessler Vulpe staggered out from the swarm on the dance floor and stumbled up the steps of the stage. A couple of women laughed and giggled flirtatiously beneath his arms, one resting on each of their shoulders. Cristian could tell by their scent that these women were human.

"Cristian! I fucking love this place! You are the *queen* of Nocturne nightlife! We have needed something like this for far too long! It's about time!" Kessler stammered through an exhilarated smile that spread across his entire face.

"Yeah, it's cool, guys," Loki remarked in a soft, unenthusiastic tone that was barely audible over the loud music.

"Ugh! What is it? What's wrong?" Cristian asked, noticing Loki's sullen demeanor.

"He's got *blue moons,* dude," River eagerly chimed in. "That's the werewolf equivalent of 'blue balls' from a lack of transforming. I've got them too! Don't you guys feel a bit *backed up* in your solar plexus from missing out on the Full Moon tonight? What are we doing sitting inside?"

"River, Loki, feel free to take off," Cristian responded dismissively over the sound of the crowd. "In fact, all of you are welcome to leave! No one is forcing you dicks to be here night after night, eating *for free,* drinking *for free,* partying *for free!*"

"You could use this as an opportunity to be *blue moons* deep in honeys!" Kessler added, somewhat tactlessly, while pulling the fawning women into a tighter embrace, causing them to giggle once more.

"Look at yourselves! Are you guys even werewolves?" River chastised with repugnance.

"River, don't you get it?" Cristian fired back. "Look around! This is *huge* for us! Yes, it's a big deal for my family, but it's also important for Lycans as a whole! Nothing like this has ever existed in New England! Hell, maybe even in the entire country! Look out there," Cristian gestured towards the dancefloor. The Killers all turned and surveyed the crowd. The dancefloor was packed with partygoers. People dressed in werewolf costumes continued to dance through the festive throng. "Sure, *most* of those individuals are human, but I'm sure you can sense that some of those beings out there... are werewolves."

"Why does it have to be one thing or the other? Why can't we have something groundbreaking for Lycan society and take the curtain down?" River challenged.

"Because you idiot! Not all of them *are* werewolves. I don't mind that this is a *rumored* werewolf club, but I'm not ready to break a considerable number of laws and blatantly have a pack of werewolves running around in front of a bunch of random-ass humans! It's one night. Please, go outside if you want to," Cristian invited. "No one's stopping you!"

"What is he talking about?" one of the women under Kessler's arm asked.

"Don't worry about it, Shoshanna," Kessler downplayed. "He's high as a kite."

After being told to leave, a flustered River stood up with a glare, and Loki reluctantly followed. The disgruntled friends walked out of the ballroom, through the lobby, and towards the front door. Before they exited, River pulled off his shirt, revealing his smooth, muscular chest. Loki followed suit, exposing his more slender frame. His skin was pale, contrasting with dark hair that covered much of his chest. At that moment, two non-binary newcomers wearing goth attire walked through the front doors into Dragos Manor.

"Looks like someone's getting lucky tonight," one of the goths quipped with a mischievous grin as they walked by the shirtless pair.

"I'm jealous," the other agreed, casting a knowing look at their friend.

The two new arrivals continued toward the rhythmic music emanating from the ballroom as River and Loki stepped out into the night. Both immediately began transforming into their werewolf selves, shedding the remnants of their clothing. Once the transformation was complete, the two large wolves paused to admire the magnificence of the bright Full Moon. Then, together, they threw back their heads and let out a celebratory howl as they bounded off toward the woods.

Inside the ballroom, Malcolm Jr. joined Kessler and his companions on the dance floor, leaving Cristian and Beo alone in the owner's lounge. Beo leaned over and affectionately grasped Cristian's chin. The gesture of affection gradually lifted Cristian out of his dismal mood from the argument with River and Loki. Beo leaned in and gave him a long, tender kiss, causing all residual frustration to melt away. When Beo leaned back and gazed lovingly into his eyes, Cristian exhaled a sigh of relief. At least his boyfriend was on his side.

"Babe, I know this club is your baby, and I understand why you don't want to leave it, but River's right," he started, to which Cristian leaned back, groaned, and rolled his eyes. "I'm feeling the blue moons myself... in my solar plexus. *Mr. Bitey* feels all cooped up inside."

"Well, like I said—River, Loki, and Mr. Bitey are all free to go outside whenever you want to. I, on the other hand, want to stay *right* here. Please just let me enjoy my moment. I mean, never in my wildest dreams would I have thought that all my wishes would come true! But look... here I am... Cristian Dragos, Head of Household of Dragos Manor—the most renowned, albeit rumored, werewolf nightclub and haunted hotel on the East Coast!" Cristian exclaimed, feeling high on the sentiment.

"Yeah, for now," Beo added under his breath. Cristian's elation dropped as he glanced over at his boyfriend.

"Ex-squeeze me?" he asked incredulously.

"C'mon, babe! You know that I am so, *so* proud of you. Look how much you have accomplished in such a short period of time! It's just that... I worry that if you get your hopes up too high, it will hurt once Erika snaps out of it and picks up the reins again."

"Ha! I don't see *that* happening anytime soon! I mean, have you seen her lately?" Cristian asked. Beo winced.

"That bad, huh?"

"Let's just say—she's incapable of driving this thing. She'd get a DUI! This business is running like a well-oiled dogsled being pulled by poltergeists and hellhounds. She'd crash and burn so fast."

"Are you done?" Beo asked with infinite patience.

"Never! Maybe! Fine, yes! What?" Cristian relinquished, finally taking a breath.

"Look, honey, I believe in you. I always have. But I also worry about you too. I don't want to see you get hurt. If you build your castle on a strong foundation, you will have a solid kingdom for years to come."

"Okay, you're starting to sound like Marius. Also, you lost me with your construction analogy. I'm making a fuck-ton of money, so I can buy as many 'foundations' as I need," Cristian countered with a flirtatious smile. Beo stared back at him with subtle defeat in his eyes. Cristian knew not to dismiss his partner too much if he wanted a chance at romance later that night. He relented. "I understand what you're saying. I know this thing took off quickly, and it drives you crazy that I'm a *shoot-from-the-hip* kinda guy, but you've gotta trust me. I make shit happen. This *is* the foundation of my kingdom. Erika has made it crystal clear that she does not want to rule. She only seems interested in getting lost... just like her mom, *and* her dad, for that matter. And while that's really sad, you have to let individuals own their karma. This is my fate. It's my destiny. I can *feel it*. Plus, like I said, we are raking in a boatload of cash! Not only do I never have to worry about money again, but at this rate, I can finally buy all that happiness I keep hearing about," Cristian joked.

"Just be careful. There's a French saying, 'Plaie d'argent n'est pas mortelle.' It means, 'A financial wound is not mortal.' For you, it should mean—money isn't everything."

"Okay, honey. Let's talk about something else! Or better yet, let's not talk at all!" Cristian said and leaned in again for a kiss, but when Beo didn't budge, Cristian realized his mistake. Beo raised a sharp eyebrow, letting his boyfriend know he was not pleased with this remark.

"So, should I just add this to the list of off-limits topics?" Beo asked pointedly.

"What off-limits topics? What are you talking about?" Cristian fired back.

"Well, let's see. In addition to this most recent *Godfather*-Esque inclusion of '*Don't ask me about my business,*' there is the subject of your Bunica, which, granted, I understand is difficult for you to talk about. But I'm your boyfriend, and I wish you felt that you could open up to me."

"Beo, I don't know what you want me to say! I'm sorry I had to keep my distance for a while after my Bunica found us kissing in the kitchen last year. I know how I acted back then still hurts you, and I'm sorry," Cristian exclaimed defensively. Beo ignored this and continued on.

"There is also the subject of what happened to Curt. It seems very strange to me that Adrian somehow ends up dead around the same time Curt is never seen or heard from again." While Cristian had been ready to engage in the relationship sparring exercise, his shoulders slumped as he slowly closed his mouth after arriving at this line of questioning. "Yeah, that's what I thought," Beo muttered. "Ya know, I think the two things might be related, and I think *you* know something about it! And I'm not the only one, Cristian! Everyone in town thinks you know something about it! If something happened, again, I wish you felt like you could confide in me."

Cristian's heart thundered inside his chest. This subject had come up numerous times over the past sixteen months since Cristian had pushed Curt, Nocturne's resident werewolf hunter, from the rooftop courtyard of Dragos Manor, causing him to plummet four stories to his death. And while it was Curt who had killed Adrian on the rooftop that night, unfortunately, Cristian could never be honest with Beo about any of it. Not if he wanted to protect his boyfriend from the other werewolf hunters who arrived in town the night of Erika and Blake's wedding. The group had remained in Nocturne ever since, investigating what happened to their missing comrade, incessantly questioning everyone in town, and putting together a timeline of events leading up to Curt's disappearance.

Letting Kessler in on the homicidal secret had been one thing. Cristian and Vittoria needed help covering up the crime, and Kessler, due to his quasi-bloodlust, gladly agreed to take part. However, Beo was another story. Cristian just couldn't allow his boyfriend to get caught up in his mess, which could end up having dire consequences since it was strictly forbidden for werewolves to harm hunters. So, Cristian sighed and repeated the same narrative that everyone had settled on that fateful night.

The story was that Marius and Erika were at Dragos Manor the evening Curt disappeared. Cristian, Vittoria, Blake, and Kessler had all spent the evening hanging out on the ridge, overlooking the gorge, and howling at the Moon. However, poor Adrian had been out roaming the forest that night and accidentally wandered onto a farmer's property. The farmer's rifle must have been loaded with a silver bullet, which led to Adrian's untimely death.

"I told you," Cristian explained weakly. "The farmer must have fabricated a silver bullet."

"Yeah, I've heard your story—the mysterious farmer with his convenient silver bullet. And Adrian just a sitting duck on his property. Where did you say that farm was again?" Cristian only shook his head at this question. "Ya know, I saw Adrian at Erika and Blake's wedding before he and your other house ghosts disappeared that night, and I could've sworn there was a blade wound on his neck. That seems more hunter MO to me."

"Beo, I..." Cristian stammered but quickly found himself at a loss for what else to say, so he feebly finished the false narrative. "I promise you, I don't know what happened to Curt."

Chapter Five

THE CONSUMER

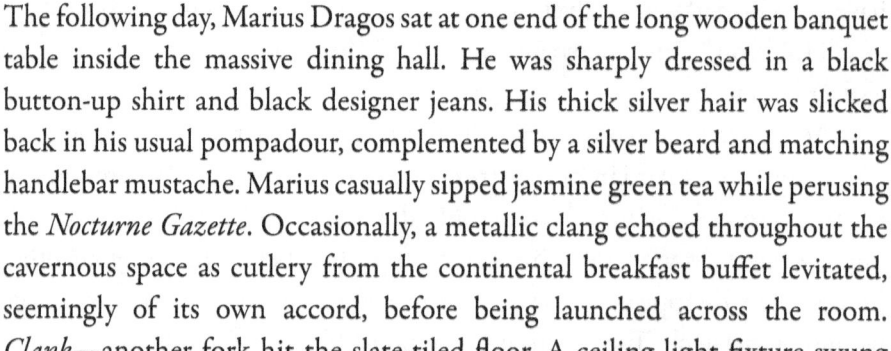

The following day, Marius Dragos sat at one end of the long wooden banquet table inside the massive dining hall. He was sharply dressed in a black button-up shirt and black designer jeans. His thick silver hair was slicked back in his usual pompadour, complemented by a silver beard and matching handlebar mustache. Marius casually sipped jasmine green tea while perusing the *Nocturne Gazette*. Occasionally, a metallic clang echoed throughout the cavernous space as cutlery from the continental breakfast buffet levitated, seemingly of its own accord, before being launched across the room. *Clank*—another fork hit the slate-tiled floor. A ceiling light fixture swung slowly from side to side as the bulbs buzzed and burned overbright.

At the far end of the table opposite Marius, a couple of haggard-looking hipsters nursed cups of steaming coffee. They wore sunglasses, no doubt to subdue the hangovers that surely pulsed behind their eyes. They nervously eyed the stainless-steel cutlery scattered across the floor, along with the chandelier swinging and buzzing with electricity overhead. Despite their hushed voices, there were nervous undertones about the prominent poltergeist activity.

Cristian rounded the corner, looking as fresh as a daisy. He casually swung by the remnants of the buffet, poured himself a cup of coffee, and added a small amount of non-dairy creamer. He plucked one of the levitating spoons suspended in the air and began stirring his coffee. When he finished with the spoon, he attempted to hand it back to the invisible entity that had been levitating it, only for the spoon to fall to the ground with another *clang*.

Cristian spun around, walked over to the banquet table, and plopped down into a seat near his uncle, letting out a big sigh as he did so.

"Ahhh, good morning, Marius," he greeted cheerfully as he took his first sip of coffee.

"Good afternoon, Cristian," Marius corrected, his tone light yet wry.

"Okay, I know what you're gonna say," Cristian began defensively.

"Oh, really?" Marius asked with manufactured amusement as he folded his newspaper. "..and what is it that I'm going to say?" The question seemed to catch Cristian off guard as he scrunched his eyes and shook his head in bewilderment.

"That was meant to be, like, rhetorical or something. I don't *actually* know what you're gonna say! I mean, it's just a figure of speech. Something you say when you know that your uncle disapproves of your really impressive nightclub, even though it is *single-handedly* saving our family home," Cristian rattled off neurotically, then scoffed.

"Come on, Cristian. You can do better than that. Dig deep. Try to imagine what I would really say," Marius challenged.

"Excuse me, but can you both please keep your voices down? Y'all are talking really loudly, and we have gnarly headaches over here," one of the hipsters arrogantly requested. "Also, I'm not sure how y'all are doing these little 'parlor tricks' of yours with the silverware and lights, but it's a little *over-the-top campy*." Cristian turned and gave this person a long, hard stare until he averted his eyes in beta-male fashion.

"*You* are the one who paid to stay in a haunted hotel; then you question what you can't explain when it's happening right in front of your face! And don't tell me to keep my voice down in my own dining hall!" Cristian fired back. The hipster stood up and tapped his friend on the shoulder. The pair left as Cristian turned back toward Marius again and let out a long sigh that came out as more of a groan.

"I don't know, Marius, you would probably say that 'A fish in a river does the backstroke upstream during the storm only when he stares at a smiling crocodile in the mouth' or some shit like that," Cristian guessed sardonically.

"That is not at all anything I would ever say, dear nephew," Marius smirked. "For one thing, that statement was nonsensical, and for another, there was no thought or care behind the sentiment."

"Okay, fine! Spit it out! What is it then?" Cristian asked. Marius leaned forward, meeting his nephew's irritated gaze.

"I see a lawless nature that is abundant in your nightclub. Greed, sex, drugs, depravity. The atmosphere is the epitome of the term 'consumer.' To eat greedily and unconsciously, appetites will only grow into insatiable hungry monsters. And I must say, you yourself have been seeming more desensitized and disconnected from your family lately."

"Marius, look... I appreciate that you want everyone to live more conscious lives, but this is the real fuckin' world. Okay? It's just how it goes! The business is thriving for the first time in literal decades! Not only were we able to give the Farkas family a return on their investment in only a week, but also, at this rate, we'll never have to worry about money again!" Cristian stated with pride. "No disrespect to my Bunica, but this place has been squandering its potential for *way* too long. It's about time that a HOH came into the picture and took up the reins like this.

"And I suppose that Head of Household you're referring to is yourself?"

"I mean, it sure as hell isn't Erika! Look around. When was the last time you saw her? And the last time you saw her, was she anywhere near sober?" Cristian challenged.

"Please understand, Cristian. It is not my intention to make you feel judged or that I am diminishing your accomplishments, but as a smart business owner, you need to allow room for feedback. And, more importantly, as a family member, you need to allow room for loving concern," Marius commented in earnest. "Part of this concern comes from me, your uncle, who cares about you and your mental and physical well-being. But another part comes on behalf of the other Lycan families. They have been watching what you're doing here and complaining that you are being reckless."

"I'm well aware of what the *MESS* has to say about me."

"Excuse me?" Marius asked.

"Mihaela Lupu, Elena Vulpe, Shanice Aristide, and Serafine Landis. Take the first letter of all their names—*MESS*," Cristian clarified. "But trust me... if it were Erika running this business, no one would question it for a moment! It's just because it's me; I'm not a female werewolf, and males aren't allowed to be Head of Household. But what did you expect me to do? With

Erika's *extreme passiveness* in her role, someone needed to step in and do something. Erika said that she didn't mind if we tried out my ideas, and now look at us! We can't be afraid of a little success, and I'm being careful!"

"Are you being careful, though? Success is one thing, but given our situation, I would expect you to operate a little more inconspicuously. Those werewolf hunters have been pressing everyone in town, and rumor has it that they know we were the last ones to see Curt alive. It turns out that he had told a few people in town about the relationship he was having with Erika," Marius said in a hushed voice. Cristian blew a defiant raspberry at this.

"Oh please... those hunters have nothing," he said, unfazed by the remark. "No trail. Nada, zero, zip, zilch. They're just grasping at straws. Plus, you just said it yourself. That bullshit about Curt sneaking around with Erika... That hunter was such an arrogant prick; I bet he had enemies all over the East Coast," Cristian huffed, leaning back and taking another sip of coffee. Marius eyed his nephew suspiciously; his heart ached for Cristian to be honest with him, but sadly, Marius had a strong suspicion that he wasn't. Considering the information Marius had, he worried that his nephew might be in over his head.

Almost two years ago, Marius and Malcolm Aristide Senior stumbled upon a witness through the Gather at the Goat circuit who possibly implicated Cristian as the main conspirator in a murder-for-hire plot. Curt turned out to be the hired henchman, his accomplice was a werewolf named Adrian, and the victim was Erika's fiancé, Ryan. This left the unknown conspirator who had planned the entire scheme. Later, Cristian, Adrian, and Vittoria instigated a fight with the werewolf hunter, which resulted in Curt killing Adrian and Cristian pushing Curt off the rooftop of Dragos Manor. At the time, Cristian said his actions were done to protect Erika. However, Marius knew that if there was any legitimacy to his suspicions that Cristian hired Curt to commit the heinous crime of murdering his cousin's fiancé, it provided a strong motive for Cristian to want to silence the werewolf hunter.

Regardless of the reason, Cristian killing Curt put the entire Dragos family in danger, since the Werewolf-Hunter Pact strictly prohibited a werewolf from harming any hunter. So, against Marius' higher instincts, they collectively decided to cover up the crime. To make matters worse, Marius feared disastrous consequences for his family if Erika ever found out there was even a slight chance that Cristian was involved in her fiancé's brutal murder. Their family would be torn asunder. And Marius knew the truth always seemed to have a way of coming to light. These were the reasons he was concerned for his nephew, who, despite his horrible mistakes, was someone who felt more like a son to Marius.

"Cristian, I must admit, I still don't understand why you thought you had to push Curt," Marius began somberly. "We were all up there. We could have subdued and restrained him, then reported him to the hunters. His murder has added an extra layer of complexity to our entire situation and is forcing us to *lie* not only to the werewolf hunter organization but to our friends and neighbors as well."

"Are you kidding? We couldn't have turned him in! The hunters are just a bunch of crooked outlaws. He would've gotten away with it and then framed me for Erika's fiancé's death. He threatened me as much."

"But why would he have specifically framed you? Why not frame me? Why not frame the Farkas family? It could have been any of us," Marius argued, then paused as he found himself in the same place he had encountered repeatedly since the nightmarish incident. He sighed and took a deep breath. "Cristian, I know we've gone through this several times..."

"Oh, Jiminy Christ," Cristian huffed.

"But I need to know the truth," Marius pressed. "Was there another reason behind your actions? Do you know more than you're letting on about what happened to Erika's fiancé? Because if you're in trouble, Cristian, I can help you figure it out. *We* can figure it out together."

At this remark, Cristian fixed his gaze on his uncle and let out a long, tense sigh through his nostrils. He blinked and rolled his eyes toward the ceiling, taking a moment to either regain control of his emotions or formulate a response. After a short while, he turned his attention back to Marius.

"No," he said firmly. Marius remained steady. He had decided long ago that if Cristian was in over his head, he would help his nephew navigate the difficult road, should there be any truth to his somewhat founded speculation. Cristian began filling the silence with further explanation. "As far as I know, Curt acted alone—well, besides hiring Adrian. I sense that you mean well, Uncle Marius, but the fact is that you have been questioning me about this for over a year now. It's reached the point where you need to decide whether you believe me or not. Because I can't keep saying the same thing on repeat."

Marius pondered his nephew's words before responding.

"You're right," he finally said.

Cristian inhaled deeply, seemingly ready for a counterargument, but then released an exaggerated exhale as he exclaimed, "Wait, what?"

"You're right," Marius reiterated, "I can't keep asking you the same questions over and over and expect a different answer. You understand the position we're in regarding the hunters' investigation. You stand by your actions and explanations, and I must accept that. But you also need to recognize this—the reality is that we're *all* at risk now because of your actions—the *whole* family. Committing such a heinous crime and then concealing it from the hunters and our community calls for you to pump the brakes on your business for the safety of us all. We don't need to draw any more unwelcome attention to ourselves. Historically, the Head of Household successor has always adhered to the precedent set by previous ones. That said, if you intend to remain a proxy in this role, I sincerely implore you to work through the issues with your grandmother." For a moment, Marius thought his words might have made an impact. Cristian's face seemed to bear the weight of contemplation as he mulled over these words.

"I hear your advice, Uncle. I will do what I can to keep a low profile, but I don't think visiting Bunica will help at all. She doesn't accept me because I'm gay, and I can't change that. Believe me, if I could wake up tomorrow and be... different, I would do it."

Marius sighed. "It breaks my heart to hear you say that, my dear nephew," he said with heartfelt sincerity. "There's nothing wrong with you. You never need to change yourself; not for your grandma, not for me, not for anyone. You are wonderful; I think you shimmer and shine when you allow yourself to. Again, you should stay connected to our family, the Lycan community, and, most importantly, to *yourself*. Within your awareness and conscience, you will find peace and acceptance."

At that moment, Vittoria and Kessler walked through the dining hall doorway, smiling at each other. Vittoria looked up, saw Marius and Cristian, and suddenly stopped.

"I just remembered; I forgot something... somewhere... else. I'll be right back!" she stammered and rushed off. Kessler watched her leave with mild confusion but continued toward the buffet. He poured himself a black coffee and joined Cristian and Marius at the table.

"Think about what I've said, Cristian," Marius advised, then stood up to allow the two friends to enjoy their afternoon coffee.

As Cristian watched his uncle leave, his mind raced through all the events that had led him to this pivotal moment. Once Marius was out of earshot, he turned around to vent his frustrations to Kessler.

"First, Beo starts accusing me of having some level of involvement in Curt's disappearance!"

"Ahhh, you do..." Kessler remarked.

"Then my uncle starts accusing me of being involved in the death of Erika's loser human fiancé!"

"You were..." Kessler commented.

"All freakin' year, it's been the same thing with those two!"

"With whom?" Vittoria asked as she slinked in to rejoin her friends.

Kessler quickly rattled off the details, getting Vittoria up to speed. "Beo thinks Cristian killed Curt—he did. And Marius thinks Cristian was involved in killing Erika's boyfriend—he was." Cristian ignored this.

"At least now, I think I *finally* got through to Marius. I basically told him to stop asking me the same thing over and over! Nobody cares! Let's move on, for Christ's sake!" Cristian finished his tirade. Kessler nodded mechanically, his wide-eyed expression suggesting that his mind was elsewhere.

Cristian shook off his irritation and was about to take his final sip of coffee when something caught his attention. He lowered his mug, sniffed the air, and then his eyes darted over to Vittoria.

"Again?" he demanded.

"Darling, I'm sorry. These creeps make it so easy for me," Vittoria drawled with little emotion as she stood and walked over to the buffet. She poured herself a black coffee, then brought the pot over to Cristian and filled his mug before returning to her seat.

"Yeah, I know killing lowlifes and losers has been your *kink* lately," Cristian snidely remarked.

"Don't judge me, darling. They are the ones who deserve it the most."

"So, that's why you didn't come in here a moment ago—you were avoiding Marius because you *reek* of death!" Cristian ridiculed, waving his hand through the air to disperse the odor.

"Hey, I just have to say I'm impressed," Kessler interjected, defending Vittoria. "At least you both have the guts to actually kill someone! I've always wondered what that's like. Cristian, I know you've only killed one person, but you, Vittoria, seem to be really good at it! Maybe you could take me out with you sometime? Show me the ropes..."

"Well, I hate to break it to you, but you're both going to have to pause your gruesome killing spree for a bit or move your operation outside of Nocturne because my uncle and the other HoH-es are on my case about 'keeping a low profile.' They think Club Dragos is getting too much negative press, so to speak."

"Whhaaat? That is ridiculous! Don't they see all the benefits your club has brought to this town?" Kessler responded in disbelief. "Increased revenue for the township and whatnot. I tell ya, you might be ruffling some dusty old feathers in this measly one-horse town, but it's for the greater good!"

"Ugh, God, I know. But if Marius were here, he'd say, 'I happen to know that horse, and he has always spoken very highly of us,'" Cristian joked. Vittoria sneered at her friend's feeble attempt at humor.

"My point *is*—sure, you might be breaking the status quo, but that doesn't have to be a bad thing! You're shaking things up! I think what you're doing for werewolf culture is groundbreaking." Cristian's demeanor began to take on an air of self-importance in response to Kessler's words.

"Darling, I'll be the first to admit that the Hungarian perspective on interacting with humans has its flaws," Vittoria continued. "It's misguided from a biological standpoint, especially with the introduction of hybrid werewolves into our species, and it's also been wrong from a socioeconomic perspective. Let's face it—inherited Lycan wealth is diminishing among the old families. Your nightclub brings our culture out of the shadows. And why not leverage those little beasts to our benefit? Let humans support our lifestyle instead of us tiptoeing around them, trying not to disturb their fragile ecosystems while they only cling to fallacies that their feeble little minds can tolerate. They can't even reconcile their own differences. Can you imagine how they'd respond to other beings? Ha! Their delicate illusion of social constructs would crumble completely."

"Thank you, guys! I'm glad at least someone sees how important my club is. Honestly, I can handle the hunters; I can handle all the nonsense from the Heads of Household, but I need Marius to drop the murder accusations, and I need Beo to stop questioning me about Curt! We got into it again last night. Why are those closest to me constantly so suspicious of me?"

"All you need to do is hold firm with all of it," Vittoria said. "The old ways are dying, darling. Dragos Manor is yours. And as far as those crimes, nobody can touch you. There is simply a lack of evidence. It's a small annoyance that will fade away with time."

Chapter Six

SEEING SOMEONE

The chime signaling the elevator's arrival echoed across the 3rd floor of Dragos Manor, where the family's living quarters were located. Moments later, the doors opened, and Marius stepped into the dimly lit corridor. Despite the open drapes on the east and west-facing windows, the 3rd floor always felt muted and subdued. The walls were covered in navy-blue wallpaper decorated with small silver paisley patterns, while brass wall sconces lit the way along the hallway to the various doorways. A brisk pace carried Marius swiftly to his mother's bedroom suite.

Shortly after Erika and Blake's wedding the previous year, Ana officially announced her retirement and then abruptly confined herself to her bedroom. Although Marius was unsure of the exact reasons for her isolation, he suspected that the main cause stemmed from a conflict between his mother and nephew over Cristian's sexual orientation. Despite not agreeing with his mother's stance on the subject and frequently voicing his opinion on the matter, Marius made it a point to visit her daily to try to maintain some semblance of family togetherness. Additionally, he began noticing several concerning observations following his mother's withdrawal and wanted to keep a close eye on the situation.

The first thing he noticed was that Ana Dragos appeared to have experienced a sharp decline in her mental and physical health. Most days, the former Head of Household seemed unintelligible. She often spent hours talking to herself or with individuals not seemingly present in the room. Every now and then, it appeared as if she might even be conversing with the very house itself.

The second thing Marius discovered was that paranormal activity had significantly increased in recent months. It seemed that the resident poltergeist, nicknamed *the Mischief*, had escaped from the cellar—where it had been previously confined—and gradually made its way to the upper floors of the house. This led to an increase in paranormal activity, including objects moving of their own accord, unusual electrical phenomena, and countless other frightening occurrences. While it was possible that the absence of the other house spirits might have given the Mischief free rein, Marius suspected that it was more likely happening because Ana had taken a step back from her duties as Head of Household. He knew that some of those duties included maintaining spells to contain the house spirits.

The last thing he noticed troubled him more than anything. Marius discovered that a few bricks had been removed from the wall on the 4th floor. This partition had remained sturdy and intact ever since Marius himself laid the bricks nearly ten years earlier. What puzzled him most was that he couldn't determine whether the breach came from the inside or outside. While all the occupants of Dragos Manor denied removing the bricks, Marius feared Erika might have had something to do with it. The question that kept him up at night was—what if all three of his concerns were somehow connected?

Marius sighed as he gently rapped on Ana's chamber door. After a brief wait, an elderly man in brown slacks, a white button-up shirt with suspenders, and a tweed flat cap answered the door. Tom, the old groundskeeper who had worked for the Dragos family for nearly four decades, stood in the doorway.

"Marius! Great to see you, lad! I'm pleased to say you've come on a good day! She's just finishing her tea now, and we've even briefly chatted about a few modern topics, such as the spring blossoms in the gardens. Ms. Ana also mentioned what she's craving for supper tonight! Shepherd's Pie, can you believe that? I never thought she liked British foods, but your mother always surprises me; she really does!" Old Tom was genuinely a cheerful person. This warmed Marius' heart, knowing his mother had such a devoted and caring companion. Over the years, the friendship between Tom and Ana seemed to have evolved into something more meaningful, but both were very private about their affairs, so Marius was careful never to pry.

"I appreciate your being here for my mother, Tom. She is truly fortunate to have a dear friend like you by her side," Marius said to the elderly groundskeeper, then turned toward his mother. Ana was sitting up in her bed. A tea tray rested on her nightstand, holding empty cups and a small plate with a few crumbs. Ana gazed out the window on the far wall, which overlooked the front lawns and vast woodlands. She mumbled softly to herself as Marius approached.

"Sophia, Martisor is nearly upon us. We must remember to get the white and red string for the girls," Ana muttered.

"Oh, dear," Tom said, moving closer to Marius' side. "It seems she might have already retreated into the past. Ms. Ana appears to find comfort in old memories and conversations with long-gone friends and family members," Tom explained.

"Hello, Mother," Marius said with a smile. His words seemed to capture her attention. She fell silent and turned her face toward him, but her gaze remained fixed on the window. Her eyes appeared hazy and unfocused.

"I'm quite worried about how dreadful the sky looks. I'm not sure Tuesday will be a good choice for Baba," she continued, discussing the Romanian tradition of Martisor. Marius had noticed this behavior developing in his mother and had become somewhat accustomed to the challenge of engaging her in conversation. He was not discouraged.

"You're looking very well today, Mother." Ana said nothing. "I wanted to come by and update you on how things are going around here. Our hotel business is doing quite well! The good news is that we no longer have anything to worry about regarding the banks. Dragos Manor is completely safe! I know how much anxiety our previous debts caused you. I wish you had told me about the problem sooner. Regardless, we are doing fine now—more than fine, in fact! And it's all thanks to Cristian. He has really stepped up and demonstrated his natural aptitude for business. Isn't that wonderful?" Ana did not take her eyes off the window across the room. Marius persisted. "Mother, it would be good if you and Cristian spoke. I can tell how much he misses his Bunica. Surely, you must miss him too? You were the one who raised him, after all! He's doing well, but I can see that he needs you. He seems to be a little lost, and I think it would be good for everyone if you two reconnected. He's the same person he's always been—nothing's changed. Deep down, I know how much you love him." Marius searched his mother's face for any glimmer of presence. Then, after a moment, she seemed to arrive.

"And where is Erika during all this?" Ana finally emerged in the moment.

"Erika! She's... well... she just needs a little time. I'm happy to say that Blake is a wonderful husband to her! He's patient, and it's clear how much he cares for her, but... she seems to be struggling to find herself." At this, Ana scoffed, snorting laughter through her nose.

"In my day, marriages were arranged, and individuals were thrust into unions. There was no period of adjustment, no tears, no whining or complaining. You held your head high and were grateful to serve your purpose."

"Honestly, that sounds quite traumatic, Mother," Marius remarked matter-of-factly.

"I *beg* your pardon! Marrying your father was not *traumatic*!" Ana retorted, clearly insulted. "The only 'trauma' I ever experienced, so to speak, came from my children! Not from you, of course, dear Marius, but from my grandson Cristian," she inhaled sharply through her nostrils, "...and that no good brother of yours! They are cruel, selfish creatures who only ever think of themselves! Honestly, I shouldn't be surprised that Cristian abandoned our family the same way his egotistical father did!"

"Mother, no one is perfect. Loving and accepting yourself for who you are, living your truth... that's the closest we can get to it. Imperfections come together to create perfection. As long as no one is being harmed, adults loving other consenting adults is truly no one's business but their own."

"I know, Sophia, I agree. He's always been a dreamer, that one," Ana replied, but it was clear her response was not intended for Marius.

"Mother, did you hear what I said?"

"We really should do something about that male caller who stands outside. I do worry about him. It gets so cold and dark outside at night. But he insists on being out there day after day," Ana continued, craning her neck around Marius to gaze out the window.

"Mother, you should be proud of Cristian. He is dedicated and loyal to this family, which is why he's working so hard to ensure our business succeeds. But he needs to know that you still love him. I'm concerned that this rift in your relationship might cause him to disconnect even further. Both of those kids need your support and guidance; otherwise, I'm worried everything will come crashing down around us. This house is too much for us to manage alone. You need to teach Erika the knowledge and spells to maintain it."

"He just stands there," Ana replied.

"Did you hear what I said, Mother? The magic at Dragos Manor is off balance! It has been since those bricks were taken from that wall. The house spirits are gone, and the Mischief has reached the 2nd floor! You told me that if it reunites with its other half, it would be a catastrophe! You cannot just check out! We need you to work with Erika to restore balance."

"He just stands there, watching us."

Marius abruptly stopped talking and absorbed his mother's words. Her gaze stayed fixed on the window.

"Wait. Who's there, mother?" he asked, then turned to Tom. "Who's she talking about?"

"To be honest, I'm not sure. She keeps mentioning a man standing on the edge of the forest. I tease her and ask if she's been *seeing someone*—a secret admirer, perhaps," Tom chuckled. "She's been talking about him for quite a while. I figured he must be someone from her past. Plus, she's been 'spending a lot of time' with Ms. Sophia lately, so I gather she might not be fully present in this decade, if you catch my drift, lad."

"Yeah, maybe," Marius murmured thoughtfully. He then turned to Ana. "Mother, where are you seeing the man? Is he here now?"

"Oh, I'm sure he's out there, always on the edge of the forest." Her words sent a chill down Marius' spine. His mind raced with thoughts of the hunters who had been prowling around since Curt's disappearance. He stood up, quickly approached the window, and looked out at the beautiful sunny afternoon over the grounds of Dragos Manor. He scanned the perimeter of the forest, but he saw no sign of anyone. Marius turned back to face his mother, worry etched on his face. Despite Ana's objections, he might need to call in a doctor even though she had firmly insisted that she didn't want any fuss.

After kissing his mother on the forehead, Marius said goodbye, and he and Tom left Ana's room—Marius to continue his day and Tom to clear the used dishes from the suite. Once in the elevator, Tom tried to comfort Marius.

"I understand that you're worried about her, but I believe she's doing well overall! She's getting good rest and eating properly. Aside from the occasional conversations with those not present, she seems quite happy to me. Trust me, I know your mother well and am keeping a close eye on her. If I notice any signs of concern, I'll be sure to let you know right away."

"Well, I really appreciate it, Tom. I truly do. However, I also think it might be wise to get a doctor's opinion just to be safe."

The bedclothes rustled as Ana pushed the comforter aside. The elderly Dragos matriarch stood and stretched, then started shuffling to the far window on the east-facing wall.

"I'm well aware of that, Sophia. I told you, I'm not sure where she's been. She certainly hasn't visited me in a long time. When I see her, you'll be the first to know." Once Ana reached the window, she gazed out toward the eastern edge of the woods surrounding Dragos Manor. As she had come to expect, she saw the figure of a man watching the house. He looked familiar, yet she couldn't distinguish who he was from that distance. He stood beneath the shadow of the pine trees, just out of the sunlight. When he noticed her looking down at him, he raised his arm and waved. Ana hesitantly lifted her wrinkled hand and slowly waved back.

"You see, just like I said, always right there on the edge of Noctambulist Forest," Ana said, seemingly to no one.

Chapter Seven

HOUSE OF CARDS IN THE AIR

Calmness enveloped the woods surrounding Dragos Manor. A gentle, sweet-smelling breeze danced through the piebald patches of shade beneath the dense trees. A variety of woodland creatures went about their business in the branches of the canopies. Below, a figure moved silently among the trunks, careful not to make a sound to avoid drawing attention to himself. The last thing he wanted was to scare away the squirrels and birds, all of whom were enjoying the peaceful atmosphere of the sunny spring afternoon.

A tall, muscular guy with shaggy dark brown hair and amber eyes emerged from the edge of the woodland tree line. Blake Farkas felt relaxed yet pensive after spending the previous evening in nature. However, serenity was fleeting as the tall, imposing structure of Dragos Manor came into view. Technically, this was his home. It had been since his marriage, yet it somehow failed to bring his heart solace the way a home should. For a brief moment, his will betrayed him as Blake glanced back longingly toward the forest where he had just come. The thick tangle of trees, ground vegetation, and small wildlife seemed to call him back. For Blake, this was where peace resided, roaming the evenings during a Full Moon in his werewolf state. Nowadays, these were about the only moments in his life that felt restorative and uncomplicated. Life was simple, instinctual, and authentic as a werewolf wandering the forest at night. Turning back to face the gothic, haunted mansion, he sighed again as the inevitable realization washed over him. Sooner or later, he would have to go inside.

Home—Blake contemplated the word for a moment, turning it over in his mind. *What a strange concept 'home' is. Truthfully, it's what I've desired most throughout my life. And yet, I did not have a home in Hungary. I did not have a home with my parents. They were always too distracted by the wrong things happening in the world—things that did not truly matter in life. There was no genuine interest in family, friends, community, or nature. My heart has longed to find my home—the place where I belong with the love that's meant for me.*

Blake sighed at the thought of love. *However, things do not always turn out as you dreamed in your youth. I have heard the American saying, 'Home is where the heart is.'* Blake pondered this phrase while gazing up at the imposing Gothic structure before him. He squinted, as if it caused his eyes discomfort. *If this saying is true, then my heart is made of stone and is haunted. But I should not complain; it all comes from my choices and decisions. I thought I could build my house of cards in the sky. And that is what hits so close to home. Something is missing. It's as if I don't know the words, but I can hum the tune by heart. My broken heart.*

Once more, Blake sighed and let his melancholic thoughts about home and heart wash away like pebbles rinsed from shore by the tide. He understood what *home* meant—or at least had a sense of what he wanted it to be, how he wanted it to feel. He found himself struggling to uncover it within the hardened walls that loomed before him. He also struggled to find it within his marriage. Yet, he had learned to expertly temper his disappointment. He recognized that the circumstances of his marriage were as fragile as glass, and because of this, he knew never to cast too many stones.

Blake vowed long ago, no matter what, that he would stay. This commitment formed the foundation for all his actions. Despite the dread of living within those cold walls and how starved his heart was for even the damaged love he and Erika had established but seldom nurtured, the reason he chose to stay was simple—he loved her. Whether his wife could not or would not provide him with a home and family, he was determined to offer those things to her. He exhaled a deep sigh to release the turmoil bottled up inside him. "*Eat your heart out,*" he thought sarcastically as he stepped toward Dragos Manor to find his beloved wife.

It had been about fifteen months since the wedding, and each day afterward was challenging for both him and Erika. Despite their strong bond and undeniable connection, Blake was keenly aware that his wife was not in love with him—not in the way he had hoped to be loved by his partner. While this realization repeatedly broke his heart, he had made vows and a commitment to her; those meant something to him. Honor was important to him. Blake saw himself as the source of strength that Erika needed and the stability she had lacked.

He worried about his wife's safety inside that house. Most nights, she would disappear into the deep recesses of the upper floors and not emerge again until the next day. She had shared very little information about her mother. What she had revealed to him was enough for Blake to understand that the circumstances surrounding her death felt familiar. When he asked, Erika never wanted to discuss it. Because of his culture, Blake held privacy in high regard; while he did not pressure her to open up, he knew he needed to find out more. More about the history, the magic, and the skeletons buried in the closets. All of it. That would be the only way he'd have a chance to try and save his wife.

The large front doors of Dragos Manor swung open, and Blake stepped inside, dressed in black jeans and a t-shirt, both slightly damp from being discarded outside the previous night ahead of transformation. As he had hoped, the coast was clear, so he made his way across the lobby, attempting a stealthy return to his bedroom suite. Once he reached the far end of the lobby, a *ding* echoed from the elevator. The doors of the cart opened, and out stepped Marius. For a brief moment, Blake considered changing course, not because he disliked Marius, but because he knew the older Dragos was perceptive. Blake wasn't in the mood to answer any probing questions. It was too late.

"Good afternoon, Blake. Are you just getting in? You must be tired."

"Yes, well, sort of. I napped earlier in the forest, then I woke up and decided to take a walk to enjoy the morning," he replied, making a strong effort to conceal the hurt feelings in his heart. After nearly two years in America, Blake's English had improved significantly. Gone were the days of getting lost in translation, though he still occasionally struggled to turn a phrase and often used unintentional malaphors. "I was putting pennies into my thoughts," he added with a weary smile.

"I see," Marius said, studying Blake's expression. "Is something bothering you?"

Damnit, how does he do that? Blake wondered. "No, no. I'm fine. Everything is fine," he quickly lied, trying to perk up his demeanor. "I was just on my way to find Erika."

"Alright, then. I suspected as much. To be honest, I haven't seen her in a while. I've been all over the house... even on the 4th." Marius and Blake exchanged a look of unspoken understanding at this comment. Marius, too, must have noticed that Erika had been spending many evenings up there. "You can check your room, but truthfully, I sense she isn't here," Marius said gently. Blake nodded solemnly and switched gears.

"No, I meant to say that I would look for her in town. I mean, catch up with her there," Blake stammered. "I was just on my way into town to pick her up. She probably wanted to have a night out since I wasn't home last night."

"Here," Marius said, reaching into his pocket to pull out a small ring of keys and tossing them to Blake. "Take the pickup. I don't think your car is here either." Blake caught the keys with a jingle as they landed in his palm. He nodded in thanks to Marius. "Well, see ya later, alligator," Marius said with a friendly smile.

"Goodbye, crocodile," Blake replied before making his way back through the lobby and stepping out the front door into the afternoon sun.

"Of course she's in town!" Blake thought as he drove the massive black and gold 1970s K10 truck down the winding roads toward downtown Nocturne. It should have dawned on him that Erika likely took advantage of his absence to spend the night out. This behavior had seemed increasingly common in recent months. Typically, if he woke up and found Erika wasn't in bed next to him, she would be wandering around the house. However, lately, she had been catching a ride or taking the couple's Subaru into town, especially on nights when he was away, engaged in his Lycan prowling.

Blake wasn't entirely comfortable with his wife's evenings out, and his insecurities nagged at him. He tried to push those feelings aside, but inevitably, intrusive thoughts crept into his mind—*Why doesn't she ever invite me to go with her? Was she meeting someone else?* Blake wasn't trying to be controlling, but his wife's unpredictable and wild behavior made him uneasy, particularly when she had been drinking, which was another one of her bad habits. The truth was that Erika was beautiful and charismatic and came across as flirtatious, even when she didn't intend to be.

He knew exactly where to find her. She would either be at that awful Goat Tavern or at the local lodge run by the three old women down the street. He pressed the gas pedal further, and the loud engine roared in response.

Chapter Eight

NO BODY

Five pints of beer were delivered to the boisterous day drinkers inside the Foolish Goat. Everyone cheerfully grasped their fresh glasses, challenging one another to maintain eye contact as they clinked them together.

"You have to maintain eye contact when you *cheers*. Otherwise, it's seven years of bad sex, and my sex life doesn't need anything else working against it," a blonde woman named Sheila rattled off in her New Jersey accent.

"Maybe you should consider coming over to *the other side*," suggested a woman named Denise, with a short fade haircut and a sly smile playing on her face.

"No, it's because of medieval times!" a muscular guy with a Bostonian accent named Daniel argued. "It's like shaking hands to avoid a sword fight," he added.

"Yeah, you would know all about *sword fighting*, ya fuckin queer," his friend Tommy snorted.

"Geez, just give up and *come out* already, would ya, Tommy! Always with the gay jokes with you. You're obsessed," his sister Denise chided.

"I'm sorry, sis. I was just jokin' around," Tommy said apologetically. "I got nothin against your people."

"How gracious of you," Erika said with a hint of sarcasm as she took a gulp of beer. Tommy glanced up, his smile fading.

"Ah, c'mon guys. Denise knows I was just kidding!" he explained defensively.

"I'm just saying you should be careful who you insult around here. You never know who the person is on the receiving end," Erika said ominously, then added, "or *what* they are."

Tommy stared wide-eyed and unblinking back at Erika while his sister Denise seized the opportunity to slap the back of his head. Tommy jumped up from his seat and yelped. Laughter erupted from everyone at the table when they realized Erika was just teasing him—everyone, that is, except Tommy, who remained standing there looking shocked.

"Haha, yeah, very funny! Look, I get that you're messing around with us, but I wouldn't be surprised if there was something like that about you. I've heard stories about your family being werewolves. I wouldn't be surprised if you all slept in coffins or some shit like that."

"Tommy, that's vampires, ya fuckin dumbass," Daniel goaded.

"Fuck you, Daniel. You know what I'm friggin' talkin' about, dude. You were the one saying that you think her family is, what do you call it? Occult! Or supernatural!"

"So, you think I'm some kind of werewolf or vampire?" Erika asked, her speech starting to become slurred as she waved her hands in a mystic manner in the air. "But if that were true, then why was I here drinking with you guys all last night and again into today?"

"So what?" Tommy retorted.

"So, genius, vampires can't be out during the daytime, and there was a Full Moon out last night, so she can't be a werewolf," Sheila correctly pointed out, prompting the other daytime drinking companions to pull out their smartphones and fact-check.

"She's right, Tommy. Look here. Worm Moon," Denise read mechanically as she showed her phone screen to the others.

"Alright, so maybe *she's* not a vampire or werewolf, but there's definitely something fishy happening in this town. You can't deny it! Just a few months ago, my neighbor Travis had a buddy visiting from Boston who disappeared. The dude just up and vanished."

"Nobody knows where he went," Sheila added in an eerie tone.

"No body?" Erika asked.

Denise retorted, "Well, I mean, I'm sure somebody's gotta know something, but if they do, they sure as shit ain't talkin'."

"No. What I meant was... did anyone find a body?" Erika clarified.

"Oh no, not that we've heard. All we know is that he went missing without a trace. Right, Tommy?" Denise asked her brother, who nodded in agreement.

"That's right, Nisi."

"You see, that's just it, though," Erika continued. "If nobody knows what happened to this guy and *no body* was found, why does it automatically have to be a werewolf that killed him? What about an accident or just ordinary foul play? Why does it have to be anything supernatural?"

"Dude vanished under mysterious circumstances; that's all I'm saying," Tommy said. "Livestock getting mutilated. People going missing. It's all just strange. And frankly, a lot of suspicion falls on your family and those other weird *Europeans* living in the area."

"Geez, Tommy!" Sheila exclaimed as she rubbed her face with her hands. "Tell me you're xenophobic without telling me you're xenophobic," she said, then glanced at Erika with apologetic eyes. "Don't mind him, Erika. He's just an asshole. He doesn't know how to be any different." But Erika remained unfazed by the conversation. She took another sip of her pint and set her glass down.

"Well, I can tell you right here and now that I absolutely... positively..." she said, making a meal out of each word she spoke. "With one hundred percent unequivocal... unquestionablah..." The group exchanged glances as she fumbled over the words. "Beyond a shadow of a doubt, I have certainly never seen any evidence that anyone in my family is a werewolf. We're just regular old folks, just like you and me," she stammered. "We are the least paranormal people you've ever met on the planet. No wolves in my family," she declared, then looked over at Sheila, who was smiling at her. "But even if I were, I promise I don't bite," Erika said, brushing a strand of blonde hair from Sheila's forehead. "At least not hard." Her comment made Sheila blush. At that moment, a shadow swept over their table.

"Hi, Erika," Blake said tensely as he approached the booth. The sudden appearance of the tall, wolfish man startled everyone, causing all of them, except Erika, to recoil.

"Hi, honey," she said sweetly, taking another sip of her drink. Blake's shaggy black hair was tousled from driving with the windows down. Feeling the weight of everyone's eyes on him, he ran his large hand through his mane, attempting to tame it. Then he smiled, revealing his large white teeth framed by his scruffy face. Everything about him radiated wolf.

"Are you ready to come home?" he inquired through his thick accent.

"What time is it?" Erika asked, and Blake looked at his watch.

"It's just after two o'clock," he confirmed calmly.

"Oh, wait, what? Really?" she asked, momentarily disoriented. "In the morning?" Her voice trailed off as she glanced through a nearby window.

"No, it's daytime," Blake confirmed. "It's alright, my love. But let's get you home."

"I know. I know. Do you know what else I know?" she added with a sly grin.

"What do you know?" he asked with a sigh. Erika was about to reply, but the thought suddenly slipped from her mind. She realized she was tired from day drinking and staying out late the night before. What she needed was a nap. Erika looked at Blake and suddenly felt confused about why her husband was staring back at her expectantly.

"Wait, what was the question again?"

"You were starting to say, 'Do you know what else I know?'" he reminded her.

"Oh right," she said, searching her mind for the point she had wanted to make. She settled on a musing that had been plaguing her for some time. "In *The Little Mermaid*, have you ever wondered what might have happened if Ariel never actually made it to shore? Like, what if she had just stayed at the bottom of the sea? She exhibited some serious hoarder-type behaviors. Maybe she would have just kept collecting sea trash. 'You want thing-a-ma-bobs?'" Erika asked in a sweet, innocent Ariel imitation before snapping into a harsher tone, "'..I have three hundred and eighty-five thousand!'"

"What are these *thing-a-ma-bobs*?" Blake asked, clearly not following his wife's train of thought.

"It's complicated," Erika said as she pulled herself away from the non-sequitur and finished her drink. Then, she grabbed her bag, took out a handful of cash, and set the bundle of money on the table.

"I want to buy your drinks. It's been lovely hanging out with all of you, even if you are suspicious of us completely, one hundred percent normal people. Then to Blake, "Alright, come on, honey. Let's go howl at the Moon and sniff some butts."

The drive home was quiet, except for the rhythmic hum of the engine nearly lulling Erika to sleep. Blake's voice pulled her back from the slumber-filled journey she was about to embark on.

"Why didn't you come home last night?" he asked, without looking at her.

She stirred and replied, "Because I wasn't in any shape to drive, and you weren't around either. You were off being woofy in the woods."

"Did you stay at The Three Sisters' Inn again?" Erika didn't answer. Blake wasn't about to let her off that easily. "Look, Erika, I'm not trying to control you. I just want to make sure you are safe. I don't want to see you get hurt," he tried to explain. At this, Erika let out a quiet, bitter laugh. Blake glanced at her as she cradled her face in her hand. "What is it?" he asked.

"The anniversary of his death is coming up," she said with deflation. "Technically, it's next week, but Ryan was killed on the night of the Full Moon in March two years ago. I just felt like going out, having a few drinks, and forgetting things for a while. That's all," her response was defensive yet filled with warning.

"I'm sorry; I forgot," Blake muttered sheepishly. After that, the conversation faded for the remainder of the drive home.

Later that evening, Blake and Erika dined together in tense silence. Guests rotated in and out of the dining hall, partaking in the large buffet before hurrying off to the night's festivities. They all seemed oblivious to the sullen couple in the corner. After dinner, Blake and Erika walked past the nightclub, which was beginning to come alive, and nodded to the security guard standing in front of the elevator doors. Erika felt exhausted and was eager to take some Tylenol to relieve the throbbing pain that had lingered between her temples for a while. The lift doors closed, and the sounds of the nightclub faded as the car ascended. By the time they reached the 3rd floor, their surroundings were completely quiet. The couple stepped out from the elevator and walked down the long hallway, illuminated by wall sconces, toward their suite. Before long, they arrived at the door to the room that Erika had once shared with her mother in her youth and now reclaimed as her own space in adulthood.

As soon as they entered their large bedroom suite, Erika stripped off her clothing, casting the garments indifferently to the floor, and then plopped down onto the couple's large white bed. Blake sighed and picked up the clothing in her wake, tossing them onto the nearby chaise lounge. He walked over to the bed and removed his shirt, revealing his muscular torso and arms. Erika closed her eyes as she felt him lift her legs and slide them over to her side of the bed. She felt the bed sink with his weight as he lay beside her, and then she heard the lights switch off.

Erika briefly considered going to sleep, but a strong urge flared up inside her. She mechanically rolled over and climbed atop her husband. In the darkness, she felt that he was still wearing his boxer briefs.

"Maybe we should wait until tomorrow," he suggested. "I want to make sure you're sober enough to genuinely want this."

Erika replied matter-of-factly, "I don't want to wait," as she pulled off his underwear.

The sex was distant and lacked passion. Once they were finished, Blake quickly drifted into a relaxed, blissful slumber. Erika lay there for a moment, listening to the soft rise and fall of his chest. After a moment, she discreetly rolled over, opened her bedside drawer, and took out a small container holding a line of pills—one for each day. She quietly popped a birth control tablet into her mouth and briefly wondered if her husband was even slightly concerned or suspicious that no offspring had yet come to them.

Chapter Nine

STERLING

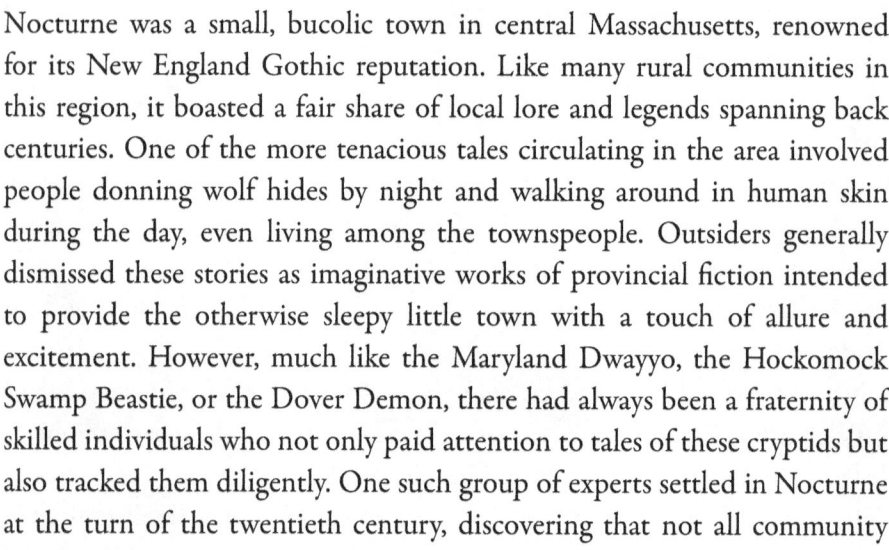

Nocturne was a small, bucolic town in central Massachusetts, renowned for its New England Gothic reputation. Like many rural communities in this region, it boasted a fair share of local lore and legends spanning back centuries. One of the more tenacious tales circulating in the area involved people donning wolf hides by night and walking around in human skin during the day, even living among the townspeople. Outsiders generally dismissed these stories as imaginative works of provincial fiction intended to provide the otherwise sleepy little town with a touch of allure and excitement. However, much like the Maryland Dwayyo, the Hockomock Swamp Beastie, or the Dover Demon, there had always been a fraternity of skilled individuals who not only paid attention to tales of these cryptids but also tracked them diligently. One such group of experts settled in Nocturne at the turn of the twentieth century, discovering that not all community rumors and legends were without merit.

Somewhere across Nocturne, a *Jeep Gladiator* pulled up beside an old *Dodge Power Wagon*. The two off-road vehicles were parked in front of a large, shadowy cabin on the outskirts of town that, by all appearances, seemed unoccupied. It was late, but since it was the day after the Full Moon, visibility outside this structure was high, with the waning gibbous Moon shining in the night sky. Three car doors slammed almost in unison as a group of hooded figures exited the vehicle and walked around to the building's side entrance. One individual tried the door handle, and as expected, it was unlocked. The door inched open, and all three figures silently slipped inside.

After quietly closing the door, the figures crept through a dark mess hall and turned the corner into a spacious room, dimly lit by a large, roaring fire in a stone hearth. Three men were already seated around a massive oak table in this room. A large, burly man with a prominent brow and a thick, strawberry-blonde beard stood up abruptly upon noticing the newcomers.

"Corbin! You startled me! I'm glad to see you all finally made it," the burly man's deep voice resonated through the quiet space. Corbin, the leader of the newcomers, reached for the nearby wall switch and flipped it on while pulling back his hoodie. A deer antler light fixture above the oak table illuminated the great room inside the log cabin-style hunting lodge. Wood, animal pelts, and various horns adorned every inch of the space. Numerous mounted taxidermy trophies lined the high walls near the exposed beams that framed the room's perimeter. However, the dim lighting didn't reach that high, leaving the posed busts frozen in time and cloaked in shadow.

Corbin stepped forward, wearing a broad smile across his face. Although he wasn't a tall man, standing at about five feet six inches, nor particularly muscular, these traits made him stealthy and agile. He sported a fade that blended into a crow-black fauxhawk. His skin was fair, and his eyes were nearly as dark as night. A large tattoo of a cross extended down the length of his throat and across his pronounced Adam's apple. He inhaled deeply, taking in the familiar scent of the place he had known since childhood. Then, he exhaled a sigh slowly through his mouth.

"Ahhh, I miss the smell of this old place. I've been away from it for too long."

This hunting lodge was called Sterling Lodge. It was situated in the woods on the outskirts of Nocturne, where Corbin Sterling, the leader of the Wolf Hunters Association, had just arrived. His great-grandfather, Elias Sterling, built the lodge and established werewolf hunting in the area around the early 1900s, when it became clear that shapeshifting monsters were prevalent in the region. Elias built similar lodges across the country in every place where the creatures lurked. Sterling's descendants carried on their ancestor's legacy, leading elite groups of werewolf hunters. Corbin had not been back to Nocturne in quite some time, spending most of his time between Elkhorn, Wisconsin; Wexford County, Michigan; and Valle Crucis, North Carolina—places where werewolf activity often got out of control.

"Good to see you, Beau!" Corbin greeted the tall man with an ocherous beard as he walked over to shake his hand enthusiastically. "Let me introduce everyone. This is my right-hand hunter, Nawn Ferris." Corbin pointed to the African American woman with platinum blonde braids and bleached eyebrows. "And this is Naiche, who is even more skilled at tracking than I am!" Naiche was a Native American from the Chiricahua Apache tribe. He had chiseled features on his smooth face and steely, stoic gray eyes.

"Tracking?" Beau exclaimed, clearly surprised. "You think we need a tracker?"

"Hey, man, at this stage, when we're getting stonewalled with the lack of cooperation, shit tends to go sideways real fast. I wanted to have a well-rounded group of skillsets at the ready. For instance, Nawn here is highly skilled at putting werewolves in the hot seat; werewolf interrogation." Corbin and Beau looked at Nawn Ferris, an impish smile spreading across her face as she brandished a mouthful of silver teeth at them.

"Wow, just what we need," Beau mused.

"And who do you have here with you, Beau?" Corbin inquired, turning to the two men who had since risen from the table.

"Corbin, I'd like to present Carter and Malik," Beau introduced. "Carter is typically based in Frederick County, Maryland, and has been with the East Coast Hunters Association for nearly five years. If I'm not mistaken, he has a neutralization number up in the fifties." The tall Caucasian man stepped forward and shook Corbin's hand. The guy was yoked.

"Honored to meet a Sterling, sir," Carter rhapsodized.

"Likewise, Carter," Corbin replied with a smile. Next, Beau turned to Malik, whose attention was directed toward the high walls and ceiling.

"And this here is Malik. Former Special Operations Forces. He's new to Lycan hunting, but eager to learn," Beau trailed off, apparently at a loss for additional introduction beyond those words. Then to Corbin, "He is the replacement sent in from HQ after Johnny Seven retired."

"Wonderful! Glad to have such a dedicated group of hunters on the case. Now, let's get down to business," Corbin said as he pulled up a seat at the large oak table. The others followed suit.

"The details of this case are as follows," Beau began. "Our brother and huntsman assigned to the Nocturne region, Curt Siodmac, went missing approximately fourteen to seventeen months ago in the October to December timeframe. In his last report, he advised that all was normal and stable in the greater Nocturne area after neutralizing a flare-up of ferals earlier that fall. After not hearing from him and many failed attempts to contact him, three of us arrived in Nocturne in January of last year and began tracing Curt's last known whereabouts. Again, Johnny Seven rolled off approximately six weeks ago, and Malik joined the detail about four weeks ago. I'll pause now for questions and a decision on the next course of action."

"Thank you for the briefing. Please remind me of the prominent Lycan families currently residing in the area."

"There are several local families—the Lupus, Vulpes, Aristides, and Landises. The most prominent family in the area is the Dragos family. I've also heard rumors of a union that has brought some new Hungarian Lycans to the area by the name of Farkas."

"I remember the Dragos family," Corbin recalled. "Their sleepy little haunted hotel business has been around for a long time. I presume that all the Lycan families have been questioned extensively to the best of your team's ability?"

"Affirmative. Almost all have been cooperative—all *except* the Dragos family. Early in our investigation, some of them cooperated and answered a few questions, but their stories kept changing depending on who we spoke with. In general, the information provided doesn't seem to line up. First, they said they had seen Curt. Then they said they hadn't seen him in months. They offered some outlandish suggestions and speculations for his last known whereabouts. It's all been very dodgy."

"Well, that's very troubling, indeed. In my experience, honest werewolves are both willing to engage and consistent."

"We have repeatedly asked for permission to search their property. First, they stalled in giving us any response at all. Then, they flat-out declined, citing an interruption to their business. This brings me to my next point—for your situational awareness, the Dragos Manor haunted hotel business has expanded into a full-blown nightclub. I mean, this thing is just ridiculous. Just like a nightclub you would see in Vegas. I've never seen anything like it. It's attracting a lot of people, not just werewolves, mind you, but actual people, into the Dragos' orbit. This has made it extremely difficult to obtain any cooperation from the family. Supposedly, they recently had a new Head of Household come into power, but honestly, it doesn't seem like anybody is steering that ship."

"A nightclub? Jeepers creepers, what are they doing? That is a far departure from what I knew of that business. They had always strived to keep it classy."

"Last but not least, since my group arrived, there have been a handful of mysterious deaths and disappearances reported throughout the past year. At least four to five cases have occurred sporadically. It feels like werewolf-related foul play. The single body that has been recovered was found in the woods, but the others have yet to be located and recovered."

"Have you tried approaching the townspeople?" Corbin asked. "See what they have to say about Curt or the other missing persons."

"We have conducted extensive questioning and surfaced some rumors that Curt may have been romantically involved with someone in the Dragos family. Her name is Erika. As you know, we have to broach the subject delicately since many people don't know exactly what their neighbors are, although some have their suspicions."

"Where did you hear this from?" Corbin asked.

"From the owner of the Foolish Goat and a couple of his patrons."

"Well, gents and lady," Corbin glanced at the wall clock. "It's almost 2200. We have time to hit the local pub before it closes and ask a few questions. I'd like to see if we can find out some more details about these rumors."

"What are those trophy heads?" Malik blurted out. The group paused and followed his gaze toward the shadows near the rafters. Corbin extracted a flashlight from his belt and shone the powerful beam up toward one of the taxidermized busts. The posed shape of a fearsome werewolf head became visible. All the mounted trophies were similar. There was only one species of creature up there. "Oh, wow!" Malik said with visible astonishment. "Are those legal to possess? What if some random person were to wander in here and see those?"

"Malik, don't go insulting—" Beau reprimanded, trying to wrangle his man, but Corbin interrupted.

"No, it's okay, Beau. You're right, Malik; it is illegal nowadays to create such trophies. Those up there are probably about a hundred years old. Back then, they would kill the beast, then quickly cut off its head and rapidly process it to retain it in its werewolf state. Werewolf hunting was more of a sport in the olden days, but now there are codes and ethics surrounding Lycan containment." Malik nodded and made a visible effort to subdue his discomfort.

"I'm glad they don't allow that anymore. It doesn't feel right," he said.

Corbin studied Malik's face for a moment. "I respect your conscience. May I ask how many kills you have?" Malik swallowed nervously and looked down before glancing at Beau, who offered no assistance.

"None, sir," he finally replied.

"I see. And I assume you're comfortable with this line of work? I mean, you're here, aren't you? It's not like someone forces you into a job like this."

"Yes, sir. No problems here," Malik stammered.

"Good. That's great to hear," Corbin said, clapping Malik on the shoulder. "Now, do you have any questions? I know that entering this career isn't something most kids dream about because, frankly, you don't even know this world exists. So, we are here as a resource for you. No question is off-limits."

"I guess I was just wondering—why don't we just kill all of them?" Malik asked earnestly. "Why are *any* werewolves allowed to exist?"

"That is somewhat complicated," Corbin began to respond.

"Politics," Nawn Ferris interjected in a polished British accent, wearing a cynical expression. This comment made Beau and Carter shift awkwardly, visibly showing their discomfort.

"Alright, let's just calm down," Corbin retorted, looking at Nawn with a warning expression on his face. "At a high level, there are two kinds of werewolves. There are the genetic werewolf families; the civilized werewolves, if you will—"

"Who happen to have deep pockets," Nawn fired back again.

"Nawn! For fuck's sake, can I please continue?" Corbin asked with a pleading look. Nawn pursed her lips and glanced away. Corbin cleared his throat. "And there are the ferals, or the bitten wolves, which are considered

71

abominations to both humankind and the genetic werewolves." Once more, Nawn scoffed. Corbin looked at her, and she said nothing further.

"Why are they abominations?" Malik asked.

"Well, for humans, it's simple—They are dangerous. Not only is it physically dangerous, but it is also dangerous from a psychological standpoint. Humans knowing about any cryptids, or aliens for that matter, is a recipe for disaster. In my experience, people just don't do well with *anything* outside the 'norm,'" Corbin stated with an ironic laugh. "For werewolf culture, they are abominations because of pedigree. A bitten wolf is a wild wolf with no roots. They are void of reason to adhere to the social constructs that the Werewolf-Hunter Pact set in place for decades. I'm assuming you at least know about the Pact?"

"Yes, somewhat. I know we only hunt and terminate the uncivilized wolves; I mean the ferals."

"A formal pact was established in the early 1900s. Before then, werewolf hunters did as you mentioned just now—they hunted *all* werewolves. Eventually, the genetic werewolf families approached the hunters while in their human forms, explained their sophistication, expressed a desire to keep Lycanthropy under control, and demonstrated an ability to contribute to human society, living peacefully among us. The Pact outlined rules and laws for a standard of cohabitation that both parties must follow. The main points are—killing humans, especially hunters, is forbidden; Lycans must take responsibility for and help contain bitten werewolves; and finally, the genetic werewolves agreed to lead simple, discreet lives. Honestly, it's nothing earth-shattering, which is why it's alarming when our colleague goes missing, townspeople turn up dead, and giant fuck-all werewolf clubs spring up in small towns. Of course, it's still manageable; short of a surge in feral activity or werewolves strolling down Main Street, we won't need to resort to nuclear options just yet."

"So, what do the townspeople know about all of this? I'm sure some of them have to know what's living next door," Malik inquired.

"Yeah, sure, some know, others deny, some suspect but are oblivious, others have had mind alterations. Some people are allies, and some are enemies; the nuances go on and on," Beau offered.

"Any more questions?" Corbin asked, to which Malik shook his head.

"Don't worry; you will get used to all of this. Okay, everyone, let's get to work."

Chapter Ten

WHY I'M HERE

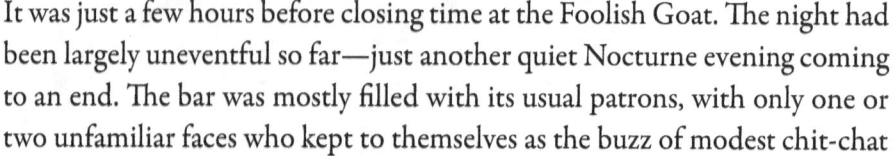

It was just a few hours before closing time at the Foolish Goat. The night had been largely uneventful so far—just another quiet Nocturne evening coming to an end. The bar was mostly filled with its usual patrons, with only one or two unfamiliar faces who kept to themselves as the buzz of modest chit-chat murmured throughout the room. A handful of regulars sat on stools, bellies up to the bar, conversing with each other and the lone barkeeper, Clarence.

He poured another shot of whiskey with a beer back, placed it before the man on the barstool, and then wiped his large hands on his bar apron. Afterward, he raised his burly arms and smoothed back his greasy salt-and-pepper hair as a booming laugh escaped his jovial, gray-stubbled face.

The front doors of his bar swung open. Clarence stood taller as he peered at the six tough-looking individuals entering the tavern. He did his best to quickly assess whether these newcomers would bring any trouble with them. The man at the front of the group was short, with a raven black fauxhawk and a cross tattooed down his throat. Clarence had lived in Nocturne long enough to recognize that this young man was Corbin Sterling, and he belonged to the family of famous hunters who had once lived in the area.

"Evening, folks! Please excuse the intrusion," Corbin flashed a friendly smile as he spoke. "My name is Corbin Sterling, and my family owns the hunting lodge on the edge of town. My associates and I would like to ask y'all a few questions if it's no trouble. But before we do, I will ask my colleagues here to hand these out." With that, Corbin reached into his coat and pulled out a leather pouch that jingled as he raised it into the air.

As the crew walked around the room, distributing the contents of the small sack, the tavern patrons exchanged confused looks. When Clarence received one of the objects, he looked down to see that it was a large silver coin.

"Alright, does everyone have a coin? Please hold them up for me if you could," Corbin requested, quickly glancing around the room and ensuring people were holding the coins in the air. "Awesome! We're seeking information about our colleague who went missing from the area approximately fourteen to seventeen months ago." Dry, defeated murmurs spread through the room in response.

"Unfortunately, I'm sorry to say that it's no surprise to hear news like this, small fella," old Hank commented from his barstool. "It's pretty common for folks to go missin', and, typically, they turn up dead somewhere out in Noctambulist Forest. That is, if they even turn up at-tall."

"I reckon if you haven't seen your friend in over a year, it's more than likely that you ain't never gonna see him again," a lady with thick, bristly red hair, called Nora, added.

"That may be, but again, as I stated, this is our colleague, so we need to make an effort to find out what happened to him so we can provide some closure to his family," Corbin pressed. The elderly man who had chimed in winced at this comment.

"I despise that word. *Closure*. What is that? Sometimes in the real world, son, you don't get fairness, and you don't get to know what happened."

"Well, I can tell you what happened to him," a male patron said belligerently. "It was those lunatics. Those cursed families that live out in the countryside!" The man speaking was a local named Travis. Clarence knew this was a sensitive topic because Travis had recently lost a friend just a few months prior. The circumstances were very mysterious—the son of a bitch had just up and vanished into thin air.

"Why do you say they are cursed?" Corbin asked.

"Because they are! The Dragos family is cursed with lunatics! They have more than their fair share of darkness that follows them around. And it bleeds out into Nocturne and curses us all as well. Our livestock keeps getting killed! It's making our farming businesses suffer. Our friends and neighbors are going missing and getting killed! And I tell ya what, we're all getting fed up with it! I know I am! We were talking the other day that someone needs to do something about it!" The agitation in Travis' voice was escalating.

"Have you reported the deaths and disappearances to the local Sheriff?" Corbin probed. At this question, the bar patrons scoffed and rolled their eyes in unison.

"That's not even worth the powder it would take to blow those beasts back to hell," old man Hank said. "The Sheriff typically classifies all deaths, both human and livestock, as wild animal attacks or wilderness accidents. They reckon all the people who have gone missing are inexperienced novices getting lost in the hundreds of acres of woodlands surrounding Nocturne. They say it's only a matter of time before those missin' turn up, but we think they're either too lazy or too scared to face what's out there."

At first, Clarence felt a little reluctant to add to the conversation. Quickly weighing the pros and cons, he finally decided to say what he knew. "Ya know, a lot of *them* like to come inta this bar for whatever reason. I think maybe my bar was named in some sorta syndicate. Also, the new Head of Household, Erika Farkas, she's been comin' in here a lot and getting very intoxicated, sometimes outta control."

At the mention of Erika's name, the stranger seated inconspicuously in the back corner booth, wearing a black hoodie pulled over her midnight blue hair, raised her face toward the people speaking. Althea's ears perked up as the conversation shifted to a topic of interest to her.

She had arrived in town about an hour ago. It took her longer than expected to secure a rental car and make the three-hour drive from Boston Airport to Nocturne. Now it was late; she felt hungry and exhausted and needed to find lodging for the night. However, for the time being, she disregarded all this as she leaned closer to listen to the discussion regarding her person of interest.

Corbin turned around and addressed his gang, "Maybe we should set up some sort of ambush for this Erika Farkas. Wait for her to come back here, then opportunistically ask a few questions," he proposed to his group. Althea abruptly stood up and approached the crowd. The quick movement startled Corbin and his crew, who quickly positioned their hands in various pockets, surely grasping some unseen weapon.

As Althea approached Corbin, she waited patiently for a premonition to wash over her. First, she felt his essence before seeing any visions. Approaching someone's aura felt like walking into a cloud of sorts. As she got closer, she felt a small amount of pressure that slowly built until it gave way to mental images. Flashes of teeth, fur, and strange canine-like creatures that Althea had never seen before appeared in her mind's eye. This was followed by an image of a crow standing atop the corpse of a dead wolf. As she emerged from the mysterious foretelling, Althea's inner voice told her that the person standing before her was the leader of wolf hunters. She also saw success in his future. Corbin would prevail in the mission his team was working toward. A chill shot down her spine as she felt uncertain about the definition of success in the context of his vocation. Corbin eyed her with suspicion.

"Excuse me, but are you all talking about Erika Navarro by chance?" Althea asked. "Because I'm actually planning to go pay her a visit tomorrow, and I was just wondering if you—"

"Whoa, whoa! Slow down! First of all, who's asking?" Corbin demanded as he continued to stare at her with a distrustful gaze. "Are you one of them?" he asked, flipping a coin toward her with the question. It flew through the air, and she caught it easily with her left hand. As she held the coin unremarkably in her palm for a moment, everyone seemed to be waiting for something more to happen. But when nothing did, Althea broke the silence.

"Sweet, thanks," she said, pocketing the coin. "My name is Althea Canere. All you need to know is that I'm looking for Erika Navarro."

"Yes, Erika Navarro is Erika Farkas, the Head of Household at Dragos Manor," the bartender confirmed. "She married last year, hence the name change."

"Excellent. Would you be able to tell me how to—"

"Look, I'm not sure what your business is, but you seem like a nice person, so I'll give you a little word of warning—you should probably reconsider your visit. We're in the middle of a serious investigation surrounding that family. I'm not sure if you heard, but people are going missing; some are even turning up dead. So, unless you have a compelling reason that you're willing to risk putting your life in jeopardy, then I suggest you go back to wherever it is that you came from," Corbin stated in a swaggering, superior tone.

"I'm here to investigate allegations of a haunted house," Althea replied flatly.

"Seriously?" Corbin snickered, exchanging amused glances with his group before returning to face Althea. "Did you hear anything I just said? I'm telling you that you *ought not* be playing around in dangerous situations that you know nothing about." Althea chuckled at his choice of words.

"Maybe I ought not, maybe I oughta. Regardless, this is a situation in which I don't need some random stranger telling me what I *ought* and *ought not* be doing. Maybe you ought not tell-eth others what to do," she said mockingly.

"Oughtn't I? You oughta know why I'm here..." Corbin said, visibly flustered by the exchange.

"Is this about a cross-eyed bear?" Althea asked, intentionally trying to throw him off.

"I'm here to remind you of the mess you could be getting yourself into by inserting yourself into a dangerous situation that you don't fully grasp and, unfortunately, one which I'm not at liberty to disclose. Now, please... do us both a favor and stay away from that place. And more importantly, stay outta our way," Corbin warned, then he turned his back to her, shutting down the conversation.

"Thank you all for your time, ladies and gentlemen. We received some good intel here tonight. We will follow up if we garner any information relating to any open cases of missing or murdered individuals. Please enjoy the rest of your evening." At this, Corbin and his group started for the door, but not before he turned to face Althea one last time and shook his head, silently forbidding her to pursue her stated intentions.

Althea stared after him, arms folded defiantly. *That was annoying.* She detested being told what to do. When she realized she was likely more irritated than necessary, she remembered this was probably due to her exhaustion. It was late; she had just traveled a long distance. Feeling tired and hungry, Althea knew she needed to find a place to rest for the night;

otherwise, she would end up sleeping in the backseat of her rental car.

She looked at the towering barkeep. He was tall and heavyset, with a burly build and greasy salt-and-pepper hair. While his height and appearance might have intimidated some, she could see that his eyes were good-natured and his soul kind. The bartender wiped his hands on his stained apron as he noticed Althea and walked over to her.

"Yes, what can I do for you, young lady?"

A wave of premonition flowed over her senses as she recognized that this man might eventually become an ally. This realization allowed her to relax slightly and extend some trust toward this stranger.

"Hi, I'm looking for lodging for the night. I know it's late, but do you have any recommendations for somewhere that would accept a new stranger in town at this hour?"

"So, you're still gonna stay in town even after the little guy's warning?"

"Yes, I have business out here. He doesn't know the details or have any other context for my life. Just because he assumes he knows better doesn't make him right."

"I admit he coulda delivered his warning with a bit more finesse, but I can vouch for his message. If you insist on going out there, you should do so with caution."

"Understood. Warning heeded. I really don't want to sleep in my car tonight, but I will." Althea's energy and ability to muster politeness were both rapidly diminishing. The bartender let out a long sigh.

"Head down the street and hang a left at the corner past the alleyway. You'll see a sign for *The Three Sisters' Inn*. Tell 'em Clarence sent ya."

Chapter Eleven

THE THREE SISTERS

With the Moon and the stars shining above, helping to light her way, Althea walked down the otherwise dimly lit sidewalk on Main Street. She watched her reflection glide across the dark windowpanes as she passed each unlit building. Hoisting her overnight bag higher onto her shoulder, a wave of gratitude for the kindness of strangers washed over her. Not only had Clarence provided a recommendation for lodging, but he also sent her off with a wrapped sandwich and allowed her to leave her car parked in his lot overnight. Arriving in a small, rural town this late had been a total gamble, and Althea felt fortunate that she would not be sleeping in her economy-sized rental car.

As she neared the alleyway, Althea stepped off the sidewalk and into the street, giving a wide berth to avoid getting too close to the unseen, shadowy depths beyond. Once on the street, however, she felt more exposed, and a strange sensation crept over her that caused her to stop dead in her tracks. She quickly spun around and looked down the street behind her. The glow from the Foolish Goat was the only sign of life on the otherwise dormant strip. Despite the seemingly humdrum appearance of the boring little town, she sensed something was out there—something unknown to her. Whether it was human or a creature, she could not discern, but she felt the gaze of something watching her. At that moment, the wind kicked up. Althea exhaled a sigh of exhaustion. She was dead tired. If something was out there, it would just have to come and get her.

Althea rounded the corner and entered a charming little cobblestone road lined with red brick buildings on either side. A lit lantern was mounted next to a black door that sat inside a large white doorframe with small windows above and beside it. Althea walked up to the short stoop and glanced up to read a wooden, hand-carved sign that read *The Three Sisters' Inn*. She quietly tapped on the door before trying the handle, which thankfully yielded to her twist.

The front door of the inn opened into a dimly lit, old-fashioned parlor. Althea poked her head inside and beheld a warm, quiet room covered in doilies. Most of the furniture—antique chairs, a sofa, and a large ottoman—was upholstered in either velvet or embroidered fabrics in varying shades of burgundy, their frames crafted with lacquered black wood. Beautiful Damask wallpaper covered every wall except for the ceiling, which was lined with red and gray Chinoiserie garden wallpaper. Impressionist oil paintings featuring countryside landscapes were mounted in gaudy gilded frames. Nearby shelves displayed small porcelain statuettes depicting men and women whom Althea did not recognize. A large Renaissance-style vase with a blue Florentine Fleur-de-lis design contained a sizable collection of peacock feathers. Heavy red velvet curtains with gold tassels covered the windows, and the few lamps in the room cast diffused light filtered through satin glass crimp shades.

At first, Althea thought the occupants must have already retired for the evening due to the low lighting in the room, but then she heard the soft murmur of women chatting. She moved through the parlor and peered into the next room. Immediately, she was amazed by the elaborate sewing room before her. Racks upon racks of spindles and spools of various sizes held many colors and styles of yarn and string. An impressive wooden spinning wheel with a massive flat iron wheel whirled and rotated as the string spun around the flyer and bobbin.

Althea noticed two elderly women wearing dark-colored glasses working diligently in the serpentine setup. Between the dim lighting and their dark spectacles, it was remarkable that the women worked so nimbly as they expertly sewed fabrics and wove complex tapestries.

"Marta, kindly bring me your scissors if you please, sweet elder sister," one of the women requested as she brandished a long piece of thick yarn attached to an intricately woven length of fabric. Her voice was velvety and sickly-sweet, with a touch of crackle like an old phonograph.

"Coming, Decima," Marta responded. She shuffled over to Decima, extended her long, sharp scissors, and snipped the string held out by her younger sister.

"Marta, would you be so good as to bring me that length of string you just cut so I may spin it back into this new batch of threading that I'm working on? I'm just now making the perfect batch of threads for *that* particular piece of string," a third woman requested. Then Althea noticed yet another sister sitting just behind the spinning wheel. Again, Marta sprang into action and shuffled over, holding the recently cut bit of string and presenting it with pride to the elderly woman working the spinning wheel.

"Here you are, sweet baby sister, Nina. Oh, that does appear to be a fine batch of threading indeed."

Althea roused, realizing she was hypnotically watching these women work and had not yet made her presence known. She felt guilty, as she did not want to startle them with her sudden appearance. Just as she was about to speak out and address the women, the middle sister, Decima, beat her to it.

"You're interested in a room for the night, my dear." The words came out more in a statement than a question, as the old woman called Decima smiled through the dark lenses of her spectacles up toward Althea.

"Oh, yes... er... apologies for the late intrusion, but yes, please. I was interested in booking a room for the night," Althea requested as she stepped further into the room. Immediately, something strange caught her attention as she approached these elderly women. Usually, when Althea got within a certain proximity to any individual, she could start to pick up some level of premonition about them. However, not one of these elderly women had any future, fortune, or fate that Althea's keen intuition could discern. *Very strange indeed*, she thought to herself. She would have to resort to old-fashioned questioning.

"Of course! We have a room available. Our last occupant, Erika Farkas, checked out earlier today; in fact," the eldest sister, Marta, confirmed as she pulled out a guest registry book and rested it on a nearby table.

"Erika Farkas? That's actually who I came to town to see," Althea said with amazement at the coincidence, still perplexed by her inability to read these people.

As she rummaged through her pockets to retrieve payment, she felt the smooth, round surface of the coin she had received earlier that night and pulled it out. She had forgotten she even had it. "Well, this is probably not enough," Althea joked. "Someone just gave this to me tonight. I'm not sure why," she commented dismissively, tucking the coin into her backpack.

"That coin is made of silver. Those people you met tonight are werewolf hunters. They wanted to know if you are a werewolf," the statement came from Nina, the sister behind the spinning wheel. While her explanation was extraordinary, she spoke the words as if they were commonplace in everyday conversation.

Althea hesitated before responding as she took in the women. All three smiled back at her from behind their dark-tinted glasses. It finally dawned on her that these women must be blind because their perception picked up more than was seemingly present in the room. Maybe they even had inner sight as she did, but this was not a subject to broach with unknown beings. You never know whom you might let in too deep.

Althea responded lightheartedly, "I can't tell if you three are messing with me."

"I assure you, dear, we are not," Marta said with a deadpan expression.

"Werewolves?" Althea's voice became uncertain as she tested the word on her own lips.

"That's right, just like the family you plan to visit. They are all werewolves, you see," Nina confirmed. Althea felt her heart sink into her feet and then fall through the floor.

"Oh, no need to worry, my dear," Decima reassured. "Most of the werewolves around here are not fierce wild beasts as the lore would state, although sometimes the younger generation gets misguided notions that they might be."

"Most of them?" Althea asked, picking up on the remark.

"Of course, it's still good to have common sense when interacting with them, as you would around any unfamiliar canine. Approach with caution and let them sniff you, but once they get to know you, they are usually quite friendly and docile. Most of the Lycan families in the area have been heavily domesticated after centuries of living among humans. This theory is testable, in fact. It's the werewolves that are created from scratch or a bite that you need to avoid. Those creatures run feral, causing mayhem and destruction during each Full Moon until they are hunted down. They might attack you if you come across them. It's rare for feral werewolves to threaten the area, but beware that it does happen."

"Okay, werewolves," Althea repeated, trying to digest the notion. "So, what else do I need to know?"

"Well, it might be good for you to learn about the local species of occupants that inhabit Noctambulist Forest," the middle sister, Decima, began to suggest, but was interrupted by her older sister, Marta.

"Oh... No, Deci. Rules, dear. She would like the rules," Marta said with delight. It was the youngest sister, Nina, who jumped in to explain this time.

"The Moon appears to be full in the sky for three consecutive nights; however, most Lycans can only transform within a twelve-hour window the evening the Moon is truly full. On the other two nights, they might experience heightened senses and mood swings and may see an uptick in afflictions such as fleas, ticks, or mange. However, about once every twelve to thirteen months, we will have a Super Moon, and during that time, they can remain in their werewolf state for a twenty-four-hour period, even into the daytime. As my sister said, beware of a werewolf's bite or scratch. A good bite will fast-track the DNA shift into your system and trigger transformation that same night. A surface bite or scratch might take you until the next Full Moon to start the transformation cycles."

"Got it," Althea said, somewhat numb with disbelief. "Do you have any suggestions for how I can get inside their home?"

"That should not be an issue," Decima answered. "Dragos Manor stands as our town's iconic haunted hotel, now turned nightclub. I hear it's *fire*, as the kids say. With the crowds going in and out of there, you should be able to slip in without problems."

Althea let out a long sigh as she tried to hype herself up despite her diminishing energy. She began to question herself and the road she had found herself on. Maybe her inner voice had gotten it wrong this time, and she wasn't where she was supposed to be. Normally, she felt assured when traveling down the right path, and the signs were clear. Here, however, she felt uncomfortable and out of her element among beings she couldn't read and creatures she was unfamiliar with. Overall, she felt a strong sense of doubt.

"Don't fret, my dear. This is nothing you can't handle. You clearly came here for a reason. Perhaps your own destiny awaits you within those walls," Marta added somewhat serendipitously. "Your guiding light will help you gain what you seek. From there, the odd Frisbee, ball, or bone should be able to assist as needed."

Althea's mental state was shattered. She was exhausted, and the riddles quickly highlighted this fact for her. She needed to get to the point, wrap up the conversation, and go to bed.

"So, I have something else to ask you because, for whatever reason, I'm unable to discern on my own, but I need to know—can I trust you three?" Althea asked.

"My dear, we're the most trustworthy spirits you could ever encounter. Heck, you don't even have to trust us; you can accept us or even love us," Nina responded, then she turned to her sister Marta, elbowing her on the shoulder. "Did you see what I did there? That's Nietzsche," Nina said with a coy smile.

Althea felt lost. "I'm asking, can we keep what we discussed here tonight between us?"

Marta answered this time. "Oh, certainly, my dear," a spindly smile stretched unnaturally high onto her cheekbones. "It'll only be between the five of us."

Again, Althea blinked with confusion and looked around the room. "Five?"

"Oh well, yes. My two sisters and I are here, you yourself, of course, and you needn't worry about the fifth person; they are outside of your dimension. They are outside the fourth wall. The one holding this book, you see. Maybe they're even listening to it. I believe in their world—to tell someone of what we have discussed here tonight would be called '*spoiler alert*,'" Marta said with a spooky inflection in her voice as she waved her fingers magically through the air.

Althea shook her head, desperately trying to emerge from the brain fog that was rapidly descending upon her after the long day and this cryptic conversation. After completing check-in, she thanked the sisters, gathered her belongings, and went upstairs.

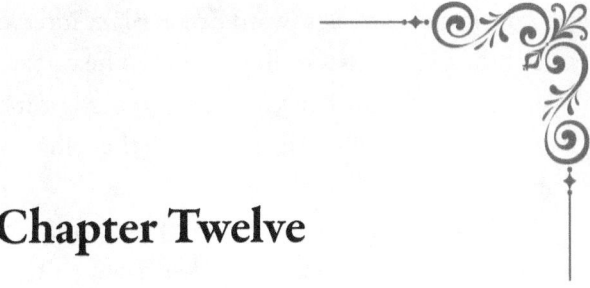

Chapter Twelve

FACE IT

Erika opened her eyes and jolted upright in bed. She was greeted by total darkness. Something had awakened her, but even as the fog of slumber lifted, she couldn't quite figure out what it was. Erika blindly swiveled her head around, desperately trying to survey her surroundings with her other senses. The shapes of familiar objects gradually started to become visible, emerging from the thick darkness of the room. To her right, she saw the bulky outline of an armoire, the curved frame of a cheval mirror, and a few chairs placed around a coffee table. To her left, a chaise lounge was positioned near the large windows facing the front lawn, hidden behind the closed curtains. An antique vanity stood in the corner, holding her mother's neglected belongings. She thought she saw a figure sitting on the vanity bench. Erika squinted, trying to determine if someone was lurking in the shadows, but once her eyes adjusted, she realized the space was empty.

Overall, everything seemed normal. The weight on the opposite end of the mattress and the soft, rhythmic breathing indicated that Blake was sleeping beside her. Erika sighed and settled back on her pillow. For a moment, she remembered the phantom she had once seen lurking in the shadows of this very room. She closed her eyes and recalled all the times she had glimpsed the feminine silhouette since arriving at Dragos Manor.

She first saw the shadowy figure the night Blake saved her from the Mischief on the evening of the Sturgeon Moon gala nearly two years ago. Erika encountered the Mischief poltergeists disguised as Curt and her friend Nicole. The imposter Curt was tormenting Nicole's apparition before directing its next attack toward Erika. Blake intervened in his werewolf form, causing the poltergeists to flee, and then he carried Erika up the cellar stairs. As she started to lose consciousness, in her last moment of awareness, Erika glanced back into the cellar and saw the silhouette of a woman watching them.

The next time Erika encountered the feminine shadow was during a visit to her late mother's abandoned bedroom suite—the one she now shared with her husband. On that occasion, she saw the spirit reflected in the mirror and was interrupted while trying to communicate with it.

She saw the phantom one last time on her wedding night. As Erika rushed toward the 4th floor to remove the first brick from the wall, she suddenly collided with the shadow woman. The encounter was shocking, but even more alarming was that while the shadow figure remained featureless as it always had, Erika could still discern a black void where its mouth hung open as she crashed through the entity. For some unexplainable reason, she hadn't seen the mysterious specter since.

Erika half-wondered where the elusive spirit had gone, always suspecting this lurking soul might even be the ghost of her late mother. However, Erika knew this was probably not true for a thousand reasons. For one, all the friendly house spirits disappeared the night of Erika's wedding and hadn't been seen since. Deep down, Erika felt guilty because she suspected that this might be related to her removing the first brick from the wall on the 4th floor that night. The second reason was that even when the house ghosts were present, everyone said her mother had never been among them. Erika vividly remembered her grandmother Daniela's ghost saying, *'Unfortunately, no, dear. Your mother never found her way back here.'* The final reason was that Erika was told spells had been cast on the 3rd floor to prevent any spirits, other than Daniela, from roaming that level. Despite all these claims that it was impossible, Erika knew she had seen someone—or something—inside this suite. There had to be another explanation for why her grandmother and Aunt Ana couldn't detect its presence.

She sighed, gently rolled over, and looked at Blake's dark silhouette sleeping peacefully beside her. He was always very tired post-transformation, so Erika suspected he was in a deep slumber. Nevertheless, she stayed quiet as she slid out from under the covers and silently opened the drawer of her nightstand. She took out the pewter hand mirror; then, tiptoeing to her dresser, she retrieved a silk nightgown.

As she slipped out of the suite and into the hallway, leaving her husband in bed, Blake opened his eyes and let out a weary sigh at his wife's departure.

The elevator chimed upon reaching the 4th floor. Light from the car spilled into the hallway, briefly illuminating the darkness before vanishing once more when the doors closed. It didn't matter. Erika had grown accustomed to spending time alone in the dark. In fact, she cherished her time in this hidden sanctuary. It was a peaceful place where she could escape the weight of expectations and constant scrutiny.

She extended her hand, resting it gently against the smooth, paper-lined wall. As she traced her fingers along its surface, Erika felt the familiar texture of the extruded doorframe, followed by the comforting roughness of brick and mortar that scratched against her fingertips—an odd sensation she had grown to love. The bricks suddenly dropped off into a void. Without hesitation, Erika plunged her hand into the opening, stirring the cool, stagnant air within.

Every time she arrived on this floor, a thrill surged inside her chest. The feeling only intensified as she neared the hole in the wall or looked upon the ghostly image of her long-deceased mother in the pewter hand mirror's reflection. Erika instinctively chose to keep these experiences to herself. She didn't want to face the endless accusations that would surely come if anyone in her family discovered what she was experiencing up on this floor. Not after the constant questioning every time Marius noticed another brick missing from the wall or the heated argument with Blake when he threatened to repair the hole. The relentless interrogations exhausted her, and she resented having to justify her choices.

An irritated scoff escaped her lips at the thought of their meddling. It wasn't like she planned to go inside the mysterious room; she simply found the space on the other side intriguing. To her, it wasn't just some forgotten room; it was the last place where her mother had lived, suffered, and ultimately died—behind this very wall.

The thought sent a sharp pang of grief slicing through her heart, catching her breath in her throat. Erika sharply withdrew her hand from the hole, suddenly consumed by a fear of the darkness that lay within. She could only imagine the profound pain her mother must have endured in that space, a torment far beyond her understanding. The longing to understand her mother's suffering weighed heavily on her soul. This went well beyond curiosity; it was a desperate search for connection, a need to confront the ghosts of her past and find closure in a story she had never truly known.

A wave of dizziness suddenly overcame her. Erika took a careful step back and sat down on the floor, using her breath to regain her composure. As she sat there, her eyes gradually adjusted to the darkness, and Ana's long-abandoned office came into focus. The door stood ajar, just as Erika had left it, the room beyond a silent witness to her countless visits to this floor. She cast a furtive glance down the hallway toward the rooftop courtyard, where so many pivotal moments had unfolded. A shiver ran through her as she remembered the first time she encountered a werewolf in that courtyard, and all her ideas of reality came crashing down around her. The courtyard was the very spot where she had been intimate with Curt, the man she ultimately discovered was her fiancé's killer. It was also where Curt met his tragic end at the hands of her cousin, Cristian. Each of these memories clung to her like a viscous shadow. Erika feared that if she didn't get a handle on her situation, she would continue to be swept up in the rapids of circumstance, drowning and grasping for a life raft.

With impetuous resolve, she stood up once more and strode purposefully into Ana's office across the hall. She retrieved the hammer, chisel, and flashlight, which she stowed away for moments when she felt bold enough to delve deeper. Erika returned with renewed determination, facing the bricks that blocked her from the unknown. She turned on the flashlight, its beam cutting through the darkness and illuminating the wall before her. Placing the light on the ground, Erika got to work, first dislodging one brick, then the next. Just as she was about to strike a third, a low, threatening growl echoed from the abyss beyond. Erika froze in place. An immediate silence followed. Although the sound had stopped, an echo of it crawled over her skin, raising every hair on her arms like scurrying ants. The growl had ended as quickly as it had started, making her question her senses. Could she have imagined it? Shaking off doubt, Erika knew she had definitely heard something. It sounded like the deep, powerful snarl of a jungle cat. For a brief moment, uncertainty took hold of her, leaving her at a crossroads about how to proceed.

Her heart thundered inside her chest. Erika craned her neck and squinted into the darkness, desperately searching for any sign of movement. The room on the other side seemed still until a shadow suddenly shifted within, followed by the unsettling sound of retreating footsteps. Adrenaline surged through her veins, and her eyes grew overbright. Erika dropped the hammer and chisel, bent down and grabbed the flashlight, and then lunged forward, thrusting the light into the jaws of the hole. Dust particles swirled in the beam like tiny fireflies. Now that she had removed two more bricks, the opening was just wide enough for her to reach through while holding the flashlight. A sudden realization hit her, sending a jolt of anxiety through her body—reaching inside would block her view unless she positioned herself right at the edge of the hole. The space looked tight, but if she pressed the flashlight right up against her cheek, she should be able to get a better view inside.

Fear gripped her. Erika took a deep breath to gather her courage. While confidence might have been elusive, she was determined that this was something she had to do. Erika stepped up to the wall in front of her. Heart pounding, she held her breath while keeping her gaze and the light focused on the ominous opening. All her senses were heightened. She listened carefully for sounds and scanned for any movement. Standing on the edge of the abyss, she gingerly raised the flashlight to her cheek. The daunting shadows cast by the flashlight beam felt like they were closing in all around her, threatening to swallow her whole. The loud rhythm of her heartbeat echoed so fiercely inside her chest that she could hear every beat through her eyes. As she moved closer into the darkness, she steadied herself against an unseen force.

The beam of light spilled into the stale room and illuminated an unsettling reality—no signs of life were present. Thick blankets of dust coated the floor, evidence of a long-abandoned time. Erika strained her eyes to their limit, her body tense as she twisted and turned, desperately searching for anything lurking just beyond her line of sight. The air hung heavy with silence that only deepened her unease, making it clear that if something had been inside this forsaken space, it intentionally did not want to be seen.

In that nerve-wracking moment, her face felt more like bait than anything else. Every second she stayed there, she taunted whatever lay in wait. Then, in a bold move or perhaps reckless disregard, Erika suddenly switched off the flashlight. The greedy shadows immediately flooded in all around her. There she was in pitch-black darkness, her face on the edge of the horrifying void. The only thing she could see were the fading afterimages of light burned into her retinas from the flashlight. Complete darkness pressed down heavily on her, disorienting her still-adjusting eyes. She listened carefully, heart pounding, using all her senses in a desperate attempt to detect any movement. The silence was oppressive, vibrating with intensity. Shadows danced mockingly around her. Every fiber of her being screamed that something was lurking in the depths. Why was it holding back? Why didn't it come for her now?

Scenarios of an impending strike spiraled through her mind, each one more vivid and horrifying than the last. She tried to push them away in vain, but they clung to her like shrink-wrap. She envisioned an unseen figure lunging at her—claws glinting, teeth bared, fingers grasping and tearing at her vulnerable face. Or worse, was the thought that the creature was sitting just inches from her in the dark, toying with her. She'd switch the light back on, and there it would be—ugly, horrible, decaying—like that *thing* she once saw in the cellar. Like a rotting, albino, earthworm-like corpse disfigured and left for dead in a damp cave. Fear pecked away at her like buzzards on a carcass. The very thought of her scream echoing through the night sent chills down her spine; each scenario she played felt more harrowing than the last.

And then something happened. Erika finally gave up. She stepped back from the frightening situation. Whatever presence lay inside that room had chosen to stay hidden that night. Erika gathered her belongings and half-heartedly headed toward the elevator, exhausted and ready to call it a night.

A moment later, the elevator doors closed with Erika inside. As the elevator descended to the lower level, a deep growl echoed from the shadows inside the opening in the brick wall on the 4th floor.

Chapter Thirteen

USUAL HAUNTS

"Ugh, I never want to leave this place, mate! I'm kinda disappointed that word has gotten out so quickly. Guaranteed we'll need to book our next holiday here at least six months in advance. And I doubt it will ever be this cheap again. We should speak with the owners before we check out. Let's make sure we establish a good relationship with them and secure some preferential treatment for future stays. Just to be safe, maybe we should go ahead and extend our checkout date one more time," Kathryn speculated. At this, Nacho almost choked on his drink. He started coughing at the suggestion. Another friend, Stanley—a skinny punk rock guy with a red mohawk—clapped him on the back to help him recover.

"You alright there, bud?"

"Yeah, I'm fine. It's just, Kathryn, *girl*, you are obsessed! We have already extended our checkout date twice! We can't just fuck-off from our lives to live in a haunted hotel," Nacho countered, then returned to sipping his bright red Happy Hour cocktail.

The three friends sat on a sofa inside the Dragos Manor lounge. Dusk had just fallen, and the lounge was already filling up as more and more people arrived to enjoy a few drinks before lining up for a chance to get into Club Dragos that night.

"Don't forget, ninety days is the longest period you can vacation in another country without a visa. Besides, you must have blown through your life savings for this trip alone. I know I sure have!" Nacho scoffed. "I need to get back to the real world soon."

"Worth it, mate. I have never experienced anything like this place before. Never in all my life. C'mon, you can't say you haven't had the best time ever; you and that busy dick of yours."

"You mean the best time walking through weird pockets of frigid air, or the constant flickering lights and floating objects, and, oh, let's not forget when the demon creature that lives under your bed tried to kill me," Nacho fired back.

"Exactly! But also, you forgot to mention—dancing our faces off, the heaps of blokes you got to bang, and all the other *tasty party favors* we've partaken in. As for that demon creature, don't be so dramatic. I saved your life, didn't I? Or did you forget?"

"Are you kidding me? I'll be paying a therapist the rest of my life to help me try and forget," he quipped.

"Whatever, you had fun. You know this is fun! This place is going to be one of our *usual haunts* from now on," Kathryn said with a coy smile playing on her lips. Nacho and Stanley both cracked a smile.

"Holy shit, that's awesome! That's totally what they should call this place! Usual Haunts!" Stanley exclaimed as the three friends cheersed their glasses.

Meanwhile, across the lounge, Cristian came rushing in from the lobby, followed by an older, gruff-looking gentleman.

"Look, sir, all I'm trying to tell you is that we're down a few guys tonight. Labor shortages are making it difficult to get shifts staffed the way we'd like them to be. So, it's up to you where we should focus resources for tonight. Do you prefer my team to work door security and collect cover charges? Or do you need guys patrolling the perimeter of the house? I won't have enough to do both."

"Whatever! I don't know what to tell you. Just get it done! Do your job. I don't care," Cristian sneered with dismissive frustration as he ducked under the hinged door on the bar countertop. "Sam?" Cristian called, getting the barkeep's attention.

"Yes, boss," Sam responded as he rose from restocking the shelves behind the bar.

"Can you please let me know when that new order of champagne arrives?"

"Yes, boss!"

"Yes, the order came in? Or yes, you'll tell me when it does?"

"Yes, boss to both, I guess! It arrived just a few minutes ago, and I am telling you now, I suppose!" Sam smiled.

"Hey, look," the head of security spoke up again. "I'm asking for assignment priorities. Please advise, and I will allocate people as I'm able to," he said, humor absent from his voice.

"The priority is working the door and collecting cover charges from non-hotel guests. Remember, the guests who paid for a room have their little wristband thingies that I showed you. Also, don't forget that hotel guests don't need to wait in line; they can enter right into the club. The second priority is having as many of your guys as possible patrol the house perimeter. Basically, make sure there's no funny business going on outside. This includes scanning the edge of the forest. Make sure no one is wandering up from the woods or, in general, that no one is spying on the hotel. Third, would it kill you to provide some valet services?"

"Sorry, we don't do valet," the head of security responded dryly. "What about the big window? Do we need us to guard that point tonight?"

"Ugh, fine. No valet, but it would sure be helpful if you did. Maybe you can at least direct the cars to park in a cohesive manner up the driveway?"

"My guys are not going to do that. You will need to hire outside services to handle tasks like parking and traffic control. We do security. Now... window or no window?"

"Forget the freakin' window," Cristian finally confirmed, exasperation overflowing from his voice as the head of security turned and left to disseminate the priorities to the rest of his team.

"You handled that well," said a familiar voice with a nonchalant tone.

"It's so hard to find good help these days," Cristian responded offhandedly as he pinched his sinuses. He then gasped and did a double-take when he finally noticed his cousin sitting across the bar. She smiled at him and sipped a clear cocktail with a lime wedge on the rim of the glass. "Erika! Holy shit! I'm sorry I didn't see you there!"

"Yeah, I can tell by that look of... What is that exactly? Shock? Horror? On your face..." she commented indifferently. Cristian quickly adjusted his tone and demeanor.

"Oh, you mean this old thing? I can't do a thing with it," he quipped, pointing at his face with efforted lightheartedness. "Yeah, sorry, I'm just running around like a chicken with my head cut off these days. This place doesn't run itself, ya know."

"I realize that," she responded pointedly. "And by the looks of it, it seems like you're doing a great job."

"I am? I mean, you think so?" Cristian asked, momentarily surprised. Erika nodded as she took another sip of her drink. "Of course, I'm totally open to feedback! If there's ever anything that I'm doing that you don't like, or if there are any changes you want to make, we can discuss them. I'm not trying to take over. I fully respect that you are the HoH around here. And look, I know this nightclub thing kinda took off *way* faster than anyone thought it would, and I know we still haven't sat down and had, like, a proper conversation about it, but you've got to realize how wildly profitable this has been for us! Like, I don't have a formal report or anything, but just the past month alone has our bank accounts overflowing! The Farkas family has been getting their kickbacks; no creditors or debts are chasing us anymore."

"Cristian," Erika interjected.

"Yes, what? What is it?" he responded somewhat erratically, worried he'd overstepped.

"It's fine," she reassured. "Everything is good. We're good."

"Oh," he responded, trying to mask his shock. "Well, good then." Cristian exhaled and silently berated himself.

He wasn't sure why he allowed his cousin to make him as nervous as she did, but he made a mental note that he needed to work on his outward confidence, even if he had any inner doubts. After all, the way things were looking, Erika didn't seem interested in her role as Head of Household. He looked at his cousin, who sipped her cocktail with her eyes cast downward at the bar. Maybe it was only a matter of time before he broached the subject of officially taking over the title from her. If that were to happen, he would have to start carrying himself like the head of the family, assured and confident, like his Bunica.

"It's great to hear that business is going well," Erika said without looking up.

"Yeah, it really is," he replied in a calmer tone than before. "Word continues to spread. The club has been steadily gaining popularity. As of right now, we have solid bookings through the end of June, but I fully expect that momentum to carry into the summer at this rate. Some of our current guests have even extended their stay a few times. They just don't seem to want to leave!" he said with a chuckle. At that moment, one of the guests came stumbling up to the bar and boisterously solicited Sam's attention.

"Oi! 'Scuse me, mate, can I please get three more of those Blood Moon cocktails?" she asked in an Australian accent. The woman pulled a compact out of her pocket and dabbed at her face. Sam quickly obliged, pouring the bright red premixed drinks into three cocktail glasses, then added a thin circular apple slice on the rim to serve as the Full Moon garnish. He handed the drinks over to the Australian guest. "Cheers, thanks. Room 216, please."

"Do you need a hand with those, miss?" Sam offered. "I can bring them over to your table if you like."

"Nah, don't trouble yourself, mate. I've carried heaps of drinks in my day," she said with a wink and an air of confidence. As the woman was about to leave, she noticed Cristian and stopped. "Oh, you're the owner, right?" she asked while balancing the glasses precariously in her hands.

"That's right," Cristian responded with pride, standing a little taller until he remembered Erika was sitting nearby. He nervously glanced in her direction. "Um, we both are actually! My cousin and I, that is. This is our little place!" he said, feigning a friendly tone, which was not his forte.

"Well, I just want to say that my friends and I absolutely *adore* your establishment. Truly a legendary setup you've got here, mate. My name's Kathryn, and those are my friends over there, Nacho and Stanley," she said, gesturing with her elbow toward her friends sitting on one of the sofas in the lounge.

"I'm familiar with your group," Cristian said to the apparent delight of the Aussie. "I was just telling my cousin Erika here that we have a few guests who have really enjoyed our little operation. Or at least, I'm assuming you do because you keep extending your checkout dates!" he remarked with gratification.

"Absolutely! We can't get enough! My friends and I were just scheming about a return visit," she admitted. "We should exchange information before we leave so we have the inside track to get in," she said with another wink. "Also, he'd probably murder me for saying so, but my friend Nacho finds you very attractive. He's too shy to say so himself," she whispered; then, she and Cristian looked over at Nacho, who smiled uncomfortably when he noticed they were looking at him.

"Well, tell him I appreciate that. Listen, if you'll excuse me. I have some pressing matters to get back to. Ya know... business-y type matters and whatnot, but I do appreciate your kind words."

"No worries at all. Just wanted to introduce myself and compliment your place. Too-ra!" Kathryn said. As she turned to leave, some of the cocktail spilled onto the floor, and with her next step, the Aussie slipped. With lightning-fast reflexes, Erika reached out and caught Kathryn before she hit the ground. Unfortunately, Erika couldn't save the drinks as all three glasses crashed to the floor and shattered, red liquid splattering everywhere.

"Mazel Tov!" someone yelled from across the room.

Kathryn appeared stunned as Erika helped her to her feet.

"How embarrassing! So sorry about the broken glassware; I'll pay for everything, of course!" Kathryn frantically apologized.

"There's no need! Please don't worry about it," Erika responded.

"And after I just assured you that I could manage it. Cheers for catching me, spunk rat," Kathryn said with what Cristian detected as flirtation toward Erika.

"We're just glad you're okay," Erika said as Sam hurried to fetch the mop and bucket from the storage closet.

"It's absolutely no problem! These things happen all the time," Cristian reassured. "Sam, before you clean up, please pour her some freshies and deliver them to her table." The Dragos bartender obliged. As Kathryn and Sam walked away with the fresh drinks, Cristian leaned toward Erika and whispered, "Good catch, Cuz. Hopefully, her flirting with you means that she's not the lawsuit-happy type."

Chapter Fourteen

THUNDERBOLTS AND SPARKS

Later that evening, outside Dragos Manor, a group dressed in post-punk fashion exited their *Sprinter* van and made their way up the long dirt and gravel driveway. It was dark outside, with the only light illuminating their path coming from the waning Moon above. The new arrivals were preoccupied with conversation as they walked along the row of parked vehicles stretching towards the gothic mansion. Excitement radiated in their voices as they speculated about the possibilities the evening might bring. This made it easy for the blue-haired stranger to sidle up from behind and blend in unnoticed.

No one would have been able to spot Althea as out of place. She looked like someone who belonged in this crowd with her midnight blue hair, black leggings, and oversized white t-shirt, which bore the phrase *Spicy Meatballz R Good*. She casually carried a small gray denim backpack over one shoulder as she stared nonchalantly forward and followed the group headed toward the daunting residence.

Her eyes traveled up the mansion's facade as she approached the massive structure. It was an awe-inspiring feat of architecture, each exterior level showcasing beautiful and unique details that had gone into the construction of this historic estate. Her gaze continued to the highest windows of what looked like the 4th floor. To her surprise, she noticed the silhouette of an elderly woman gazing out from the center window at the uppermost level. Of course, she couldn't discern from ground level, but Althea couldn't shake the feeling that this mysterious figure was looking right at her. A shiver ran down her spine as she contemplated the dismay an elderly occupant might experience as they watched their magnificent home be transformed into a glorified party house.

Once Althea finally made it through the front doors and walked into a foyer, she immediately found herself at the back of a line that seemed to lead through a large set of doors. EDM music blared from within. Not wanting to seem out of place by skipping any entry process, she patiently waited in line. To pass the time, she glanced around the lobby and noticed another room to the left of the entrance, which looked like a bar or lounge filled with a smaller, more laid-back crowd. After waiting for about twenty minutes, Althea stood before a doorman, the gatekeeper for the lively party that was occurring in what appeared to be a large ballroom behind him.

"ID, please. Cover charge is a hundred to go in," he solicited in a gravelly tone. Althea craned her neck to peer into the intensity of the fervor within. People swarmed around in every direction. It looked like sheer chaos inside. Situations like this were challenging for her; moreover, they complicated her psychic abilities. Too many people meant she would undoubtedly leave with a headache. She looked at the security guard and watched as a premonition of his life overcame her. This man did not want to be here but would do whatever it took to provide for his family. She also saw he had a steak and beer planned in the very near future.

"I'm gonna pass, but I hope you enjoy your day off tomorrow," she said, then turned and stepped out of line, leaving a perplexed-looking security guard behind.

Althea walked into the center of the lobby and slowly spun around, taking in the cavernous turn-of-the-twentieth-century manor. The place had a bewildering atmosphere, with the old Edwardian décor juxtaposed with the hordes of young people flocking to the nightclub. But it worked; she saw the appeal and charm. Yet despite the magnificence radiating from this grand home, it also possessed an undeniable foreboding quality. *Haunted house vibes, classic*, she thought to herself as she met the gaze of the woman memorialized in a stained-glass portrait above the staircase. A chill ran down Althea's spine. It seemed perfectly fine for her to roam around the lobby; only the nightclub had a requirement for entry. So, she decided to double back and inspect the lounge she had seen while waiting in line.

The mood inside the lounge was much more casual than in the ballroom. This appeared to be a more manageable place to start poking around. There were small pockets of people scattered throughout the cozy space. No one seemed to be in a rush to get into the nightclub that reverberated across the lobby. A group of people sipped cocktails near a roaring fireplace next to a retracted glass wall. Althea glanced outside and noticed a fire pit burning on the patio, bathed in decorative lighting, which gave the space a mystical ambiance. Again, she was struck by how captivating this place was and understood why it was so popular.

As she continued to survey the room, a sudden shockwave overtook her entire being. She felt thunderbolts and sparks shoot down her spine, causing a surge of goosebumps to rise across her skin and the small hairs on her nape to stand on end. Althea slowly turned, and her eyes beheld the source of the electricity coursing through her veins. Sitting at the bar was the familiar stranger from her dreams. *Erika*. Finally... after all this time, Althea was seeing her in the flesh. Erika sat alone, nursing a drink. Althea didn't hesitate; she approached her immediately.

"Is this seat taken?" she asked. Erika looked up, clearly startled by her sudden presence. "Sorry, I didn't mean to—"

"No, no. It's fine," Erika said. "Of course, take a seat." With consent obtained, Althea climbed into the chair beside Erika, even with the many empty seats around them. She slid the denim backpack off her shoulder and hung it on a purse hook underneath the bar countertop.

Althea acted as if she were patiently waiting for the bartender; however, in reality, she awaited a premonition about Erika to venture into her mind's eye. After a moment, it finally arrived. She saw that Erika was trapped in a cycle of numbness, no longer the protagonist of her own story. Her aura was dull and unreceptive. The small glimmers of light that seemed to shine through revealed her spirit in great pain. Then, something animal-like flashed into Althea's mind. For a moment, she forgot about Lycanthropy and wondered if this was what the aura of a werewolf felt like. She had never encountered one before and had no idea what to expect. Somewhat relieved, Althea speculated that the experience might not be as intimidating as she had thought.

"I apologize for the wait, Madam. What can I get for you?" the bartender asked as he stood before Althea, patiently awaiting her order.

"Oh, um," she fumbled for the words, but just then, a man with dark hair and thick eyebrows dashed frantically toward the bar. He appeared frazzled as he ducked under the countertop and started grabbing bottles off the shelves behind the bar. For a moment, Althea thought she recognized this man but couldn't recall where she had seen him before.

"I keep saying it, Sam! We really need to start upping our liquor orders. These people are bottomless pits! I have no idea how they do it. It's gotta be like a *hundred-proof* in that room. Nobody light a match in there if ya catch my drift." The man with the thick eyebrows appeared to be in a joyous mood.

"Yes, boss! Of course!" the bartender responded.

'Boss,' okay, it seems like I might have the right audience here, Althea thought.

"Yes, you can help me," she said, slightly projecting her voice. "I'm interested in speaking with someone about booking a room." Upon hearing this, the man with dark hair and thick eyebrows quickly spun around, his arms full of several liquor bottles.

"Um, yes? Hi, hello, I can help you with a booking," he said. "I'm the owner, and I manage the bookings around here. We're actually full as of now, but we can look into booking your stay in a few months." His tone conveyed an effort at hospitality.

"Oh really, what a shame," Althea said, unbothered. "You see, I'm a paranormal investigator... slash journalist. I'm interested in doing a story on Dragos Manor, which I'd like to shop around to the right network," she continued, attempting to make her story compelling enough to entice him. "Oh, how rude of me. My name's Althea Canere." She extended her hand toward him. While her story seemed effective, the dark-haired man stared incredulously at the proffered handshake. Half-rolling his eyes, he walked over and placed the bottles on the bar top.

"Cristian Dragos," he replied as he finally clasped her hand. As soon as his hand touched hers, a premonition fell heavily on Althea, like gravity on Jupiter. Cristian was the creature-man from her dream. Before arriving in Nocturne, Althea knew nothing about the existence of werewolves and wasn't able to pinpoint exactly what he was in her dream. But now, standing before her, his entire aura exuded beastliness. She saw images of yellow eyes, sharp teeth, and black fur. She now understood—*this is a werewolf.* His animalistic presence was undeniable, far more substantial than Erika's. She wondered if that meant Erika was somehow different. Althea also noticed that Cristian was deeply conflicted. Insecurity, deep-seated hurt, and distrust plagued him. At one point, his heart sought goodness and light, but his life experiences had warped him into the creature he was today, one that sometimes even he himself did not recognize.

"Um, hello?" he asked, withdrawing his hand and waving it in front of her face to capture her attention. Sarcasm was evident in his voice as he chuckled. "So, you're some kind of journalist?"

"Sorry," Althea stammered. "Yes, that's correct. I was saying, this documentary could make you and your business very famous." Her words seemed to have the desired effect of disarming him just enough.

"Hmm...*famous*..." he repeated as if savoring the word. "That does sound like something that aligns with our business model—*Become famous.* But alas, there are still no rooms available," he said, seemingly unconvinced.

"That's unfortunate. I would really need to start the research and content capture now to have a first cut ready in time for pitching season," she said, trying to balance persuasiveness without appearing overbearing. "But I guess if that doesn't work for you, I can try another New England haunted hotel."

"Hold on! I'm not saying no!" Cristian fired back. "You'll need to get a room in town for now. I promise, you won't find another haunted hotel in New England that compares to this one. Actually, the more I think about it, maybe you *should* come back in a few weeks so I can prepare! Get myself ready for prime time," he said with a self-satisfied laugh. This comment took the wind right out of her sails. Althea realized her tactic wasn't working as she had hoped, so she quickly considered the best way to redirect without souring the whole situation.

She inhaled deeply to center herself and allowed a friendly smile to spread across her face. "You're right. I know there isn't another haunted hotel that compares to Dragos Manor. Nicole Ramirez told me how incredible this place is."

"Wait, you know Nicole?" Erika asked with sudden interest.

"Yes, I apologize; I should have mentioned that. I was so distracted by the excitement of finally being here and the prospect of starting this project.

Are you, by chance, Erika Navarro?"

"The one and only," Erika sneered as she sipped her clear, fizzy cocktail.

"Don't forget, dear cousin, you're living your 'happily ever after' as Erika Farkas now," Cristian remarked.

"There's no need to make her wait a few weeks. She could stay in one of the vacant suites on the 3rd floor," Erika suggested. Cristian immediately shot her a mortified look.

"Um, sure," he said after a dumbfounded pause, his tone was tense. "I suppose we could arrange to make that happen. But we would need to charge a little extra. Ya know...VIP rates and all."

"I don't think that will be necessary," Erika overruled, then turned to Althea. "You can stay up there at no charge as our guest while working on your project."

Althea glanced nervously between Cristian and Erika. "I really appreciate the offer. Money is a little tight for this project, so I will take any generosity I can get!"

Cristian's face reddened, but he did not protest further. Instead, he ducked back under the bar countertop, grabbed the bottles, and stalked off toward the nightclub. Althea noted this intriguing dynamic. While Cristian appeared to run the show, Erika might be the ultimate decision-maker.

"Thanks again; I hope I didn't get you in trouble with your cousin."

"He'll get over it. I let Cristian have his way most of the time. He can stand to chill out a little."

"Well, I will look for ways to repay your kindness."

"Don't worry about it. The room is sitting empty. Plus, any friend of Nicole's. How is she doing anyway?"

"Oh, you know Nicole," Althea said, uncertain how to play along.

"Yeah," Erika snickered. "I do. I miss her. I've thought about reaching out, but I don't want to pull her back into..." Erika trailed off.

Althea knew what Erika was going to say. She didn't want to pull Nicole back into a haunted house full of werewolves. Althea allowed the subject to drift away, as Erika seemed to prefer.

"Again, thank you for the complimentary room. Whenever possible, I prefer to carry my fair share, so I'd be happy to trade services. Lodging in exchange for what... a paranormal investigation?"

"Yeah, I heard you mention that," Erika said, raising her hand to flag down the bartender's attention as she gestured to her empty glass. Althea eyeballed the melting ice in the tumbler as she listened to Erika speak. "Sounds interesting. I'm totally cool if you want to take a look around, but I need to lay down a couple of ground rules."

"Of course! Fire away."

"Please keep your investigation to the common areas only. The 1st through 3rd floors are fine, but we ask that you please stay out of the cellar and avoid the 4th floor." At that moment, the bartender placed another vodka soda in front of Erika. "Thanks, Sam," she said to him.

"Absolutely! Please let me know if there are any other guidelines. I want to be respectful," Althea agreed, then turned to the bartender. "Excuse me, Sam? May I please get one of those as well?"

The drink arrived in front of Althea shortly after. She picked it up and raised the glass to her new hostess.

"Here's to you... Erika."

"Why, thank you, Althea, was it?"

"My friends call me Thea."

"Well, pleasure to make your acquaintance, Thea. Whereabouts do you live in LA? I'm assuming that's where you live based on your ties to the film industry and the fact that you know Nicole."

"North Hollywood."

"I used to live out that way, but I moved here after my fiancé was brutally murdered." Erika's words sounded overly nonchalant considering the subject matter. Althea winced as she nearly choked on her drink.

"Dear God! That's awful. I'm so sorry."

"Yeah, well. What are ya gonna do? That kind of luck seems to follow me. There's a word of caution for you before you try to befriend me," Erika let out a short, cynical laugh as she took another sip of her drink.

"I'm not scared," Althea said defiantly. The words seemed to catch Erika off guard. She paused mid-sip, lowered her drink, and stared suspiciously at Althea, who smiled warmly back at her. Erika slowly nodded as if mulling over the idea.

"What the hell. Having a friend for a little while might be kinda nice. Alright, cheers, friend." Erika and Althea raised their glasses and clinked them together just as sounds of commotion floated in from the lobby. Both women turned toward the noise and saw some rough-looking people pushing their way through the line of would-be clubgoers.

Althea recognized the short man with the neck tattoo and raven-black fauxhawk. It was Corbin Sterling, along with his group of werewolf hunters. They approached the security guard at the club entrance. The guard raised his hand toward them as he urgently spoke into his walkie-talkie, undoubtedly calling for backup.

Chapter Fifteen

CONSENT

Inside Club Dragos, a security guard maneuvered urgently through the crowd, then jogged up the couple of steps onto the stage, where Cristian and the Killers laughed and sipped champagne in the owner's lounge. When the guard leaned over and whispered into Cristian's ear, the smile immediately vanished from his face. Cristian stood abruptly and marched toward the exit. As he got closer, he was shocked to hear a booming voice reverberating throughout the lobby.

"Sorry, folks! We're looking to speak with whoever runs this joint! Don't worry, this won't take long. We promise we'll get you back to your MDMA and shitty Electronica music soon enough!" the male voice called out.

Cristian emerged through the ballroom doorway and saw a group of hunters standing in his lobby and intimidating his guests. Fury pulsed in his eyes at their audacity. Just then, a few more security guards entered through the front door. The hunters were now surrounded.

"What the *hell* are you doing?" Cristian demanded. "Who the hell do you think you are?"

"Corbin Sterling," came the metallic response from the short guy who appeared to be the leader. "As you can probably surmise by my name, my family owns and operates the local werewolf hunting lodge in the area."

"Shhhhhhhh, can you please keep your fucking voice down?" Cristian said while glancing around to see if anyone nearby heard the remark. A few people in line had their phones out, recording the confrontation; others were chatting and not paying attention, while Mike—the head of security—turned and gave Cristian a funny look.

"I have to say, you've got everyone's attention with all the recent happenings in this town," Corbin said provocatively.

"Well, that's really nice, but I'm afraid you and your friends have to—"

"I think you know why we're here," Corbin interrupted, finally getting to the point. "We are hoping to have a little chat with you about a missing person case and would appreciate your *full* cooperation."

"Nope! Outside! Right now!" Cristian ordered, shutting down the conversation. Corbin and his crew turned and walked back toward the exit without protest. Christian noted that the little shit stain with the lame neck tattoo held a smug smirk on his face, most likely trying to provoke a fight. Cristian would have to work hard to keep his cool, so the situation didn't spiral out of control.

As Cristian ushered the hunters toward the front doors, a few security guards started to follow, but he fiercely rounded on them. "Oh, *no need* to trouble yourselves with this, guys," his tone was full of sarcasm. "Your team already did a *fantastic* job letting them walk right in through the *Goddamn front doors*! Just go back to your stations. I will call you if I need these trespassers ejected," he stated with authority.

Once outside, the hunters walked down the front steps and onto the driveway. Cristian trailed behind but stopped on the top step and glared down at them, his arms folded in anger. Corbin stared up at him, an instigating look playing on his face.

"No need to get so mad there, tiger," Corbin said with a short, dismissive laugh. "I was simply trying to get your attention."

"What the fuck do you think you're doing? You can't just barge in here, interrupt *my* business, and terrorize *my* customers! You probably scared half those people to death!"

"Look, we're just here on a courtesy call. Our comrade Curt Siodmac has been missing for over a year now, and for whatever reason, his trail seems to grow cold somewhere right around here, as a matter of fact."

"I see," Cristian said darkly, "Yeah, I knew Curt."

"*Knew*?" Corbin asked, shifting into a more menacing stance at the slip-up.

"Yeah! *Knew*!" Cristian reiterated. "Even when he was around, he did very little for this town. And then he just up and abandons his post. Frankly, doesn't surprise me one bit. I've already told those guys several times," Cristian said, pointing to Beau, Carter, and Malik. "We haven't seen Curt around here in a long-ass time! We don't know where he is! And I can't help you! Now, at some point, you either have to believe me, or you don't, because I can't keep saying the same thing on repeat!" Cristian said, hoping the same words he had used to gain traction with his uncle would help him now.

"It's funny you should say that," Corbin began in an even, icy tone. "Because we *don't* believe you. Not one bit. We think *you* know more than you're telling us. And we think we might just be able to find some proof of foul play right here on this property. Now, here's what's gonna come next. We're putting you on notice—we'll be doing a full search of Dragos Manor. Inside and out."

Cristian stared unblinking at Corbin's arrogance. "Well," he said, then pursed his lips and inhaled sharply through his nostrils, fighting to gain composure. "We don't consent to that." As he spoke the words, Vittoria emerged from inside the house and stood behind him, her eyes fixed balefully on the hunters. Soon, Kessler appeared, followed by Loki, Malcolm Jr., Beo, and finally River. Now, there were more werewolves in human form than there were hunters. Both groups glared at each other in this inauspicious standoff. The hunters stood alert as if bracing for an altercation to commence.

"You can't keep stonewalling this conversation," Corbin warned.

Erika made her way through the lobby, headed toward the front doorway. Althea trailed nervously behind, concerned about what her brave yet inebriated friend was planning to do. As Erika grasped the door handle, Althea finally reached out to intervene.

"Wait, Erika! Forgive me for overstepping, but do you think it's a good idea to go out there?" she asked doubtfully. Erika puffed out a slow exhale, nodding her head, then an uninhibited smile surfaced.

"Don't worry. It'll be fine. Unfortunately, I have to go. There's a good chance things will escalate if I don't," she insisted and pulled the door open.

Erika brazenly staggered outside. Althea shook her head and followed Erika outside. She watched as Erika pushed her way to the front of the crowd of her cousin and his friends. Althea had to give Erika credit; she had guts.

"Hey, hey, hey... what's this all about?" Erika demanded in a lackadaisical speech pattern as she surveyed both groups.

"Erika Farkas?" Corbin called to her from the base of the steps. "Are you the Head of Household here?" he asked in a surly voice.

"Yes, I am," she retorted coolly.

"Well, I was just telling your friend here," he said, pointing toward Cristian. "We will be conducting a search of your property. We can either do that the easy way or the hard way."

"If there are any conversations regarding the search of this property, you need to direct those requests to me." Her tone, while authoritative, was also overly nonchalant after having consumed quite a few drinks by this time. Althea pushed through the group of what she sensed were werewolves in human form and stood next to Erika on the top step. Corbin's eyes flashed as soon as he spotted her, but to her surprise, he did not vocalize any recognition of her. Instead, he kept his eyes fixated on Erika.

"Very well," Corbin said with visible exasperation. "Then we are putting *you* on notice of a search."

"I told him no already!" Cristian erupted. "We have been cooperative! They have tunnel vision!"

"I know about you and Curt," Corbin said provocatively to Erika.

"They expect us to just bend over and—" Cristian continued.

Erika raised her hand, signaling for silence. Once more, Althea was surprised by how quickly Cristian complied, even though he was still visibly seething. *How intriguing,* Althea thought.

The tension was insurmountable. It felt as though a fight would break out at any moment. Althea glanced between the werewolf hunters at the base of the steps and the pack of werewolves in their human form surrounding her. At the center of it all was Erika, attempting to run negotiations. Althea couldn't be certain how long she could keep the situation from escalating. The atmosphere felt like a powder keg in search of a spark.

"I don't know what rumors you've heard, but I echo what my cousin stated," Erika said smoothly. "Although we appreciate your circumstances, you need to acknowledge that our family has cooperated and been willing to help thus far. And we will continue to do so as long as you work with us. Don't dictate what you're going to do on our property. We will consider permitting a search, but we cannot do this at the expense of our livelihood. So, as a compromise, we will agree to freeze further bookings so you can come back at the end of June and do a search. How long do you think you will need?"

"One month," Corbin responded.

"Are you fucking kidding me?" Cristian said in protest. Erika shot him a look that told him to be quiet. Cristian said nothing further, but it was clear that anger was simmering just below the surface. Althea noted this was the second time tonight that Erika had stepped on his toes regarding a major business decision without consulting Cristian first. And she could see he was not happy about it.

"You can have one week," Erika countered.

"Very well. The last week of June, it is," Corbin agreed.

"Okay, great, thanks!" Cristian said with biting sarcasm. "Now, can you and your thugs please get the fuck off our property?"

With that, both parties started to disperse. Althea saw Erika try to place her hand on Cristian's shoulder, but he shook it off in anger. Erika followed him back inside the house, probably to run some damage control. Althea decided to hang back to give the cousins some space. She turned and watched the hunters walk down the long driveway.

Corbin turned and looked back in her direction. He was so transparent. Althea was surprised he hadn't tried to get her alone to talk. As if reading her mind, he nodded his head toward the row of parked cars, then broke away from the rest of his group, ducking behind a *Sprinter* van. Althea furrowed her brows, unsure of what he wanted. She needed to get her luggage anyway, so she might as well see what he wanted. With a sigh, she walked toward the row of cars.

"So, you didn't heed my warning, I see?" Corbin said as Althea walked past the van he was hiding behind.

"What do you want?" she asked, not attempting to mask her annoyance.

"I'm assuming you know by now that you're inside the wolf den?"

"Yes, I'm aware."

"So, what's your angle?"

"I prefer to keep my business to myself, if you don't mind."

"That response can only mean one of two things—revenge or love."

"Do you always feel the need to categorize everything? Have you ever stopped to consider that situations can have layers of nuance?"

"Look, *whatever*; since you are so insistent on inserting yourself into the equation, how would you like to make yourself useful at least?"

"You mean you would be willing to grant purpose to my pointless little life?" Althea asked sarcastically.

"I'm asking if you would be an agent for us. Ya know, gather intel. Like a secret agent," Corbin suggested as he handed her his business card. "If nothing else, you might find yourself in trouble, even if you don't want to know me... Someday, you might be glad you do."

Reluctantly, Althea accepted the card.

Meanwhile, back inside the lobby, Cristian fiercely rounded on his cousin. "I can't believe you did that! I can't believe you made that commitment without consulting with me! First, you're giving away free suites on the 3rd to some stranger, then authorizing a search of our property! Do you realize that we have the dead body of the very decaying asshole that they are looking for buried at the edge of our woods? Not to mention the incredible loss of momentum and revenue we'll be forfeiting by freezing business for a week!"

"Calm down!" Erika slurred. "First of all, Thea knows Nicole; she's not a complete stranger. Second, I was just buying us some time until we figure out our next move. Maybe we simply need to relocate... *him*."

At this suggestion, Cristian blinked approximately twenty times in quick succession, struggling to grasp the words his cousin was proposing.

"Are you out of your GD mind?" he asked in a deadpan tone. "Those hunters are probably watching this place! Plus, have you thought about the logistics of what you're saying? Interact with and transport a putrid, rotten corpse. Do you have experience moving a putrid, rotten corpse? I don't have experience moving a putrid, rotten corpse."

"Okay! Stop saying putrid, rotten corpse! You're going to attract attention. I'm not saying we need to figure it out this second, but at least we have some time."

"Oh, that's just perfect, Scarlet O'Hara! That's always your suggestion! *I'll think about it tomorrow!* Worry about it later! We'll deal with it some other time!" Cristian scoffed as he stormed off, disappearing back into the frenzy of his nightclub.

Chapter Sixteen

PHANTOMGRAMMETRY

A short time later, Althea reappeared through the front doors of Dragos Manor. She carried a padded duffle bag slung over one shoulder, her denim backpack strewn over the other, and wheeled a suitcase in tow. As she navigated through pockets of people meandering around the lobby, she searched for her hostess and soon discovered that Erika was back at the bar. An unexpected pang of sorrow struck a chord in Althea's heart, making her shoulders feel just a bit heavier under the weight of her luggage. She hung back for a moment and observed Erika as she contemplated the pain this person attempted to conceal. Erika had mentioned a murdered fiancé, yet the prognostication Althea had seen indicated that the wound ran deeper than that still. Clarence, the owner of the Foolish Goat, had noted that Erika had been married the year prior, which Althea found strange for someone still lamenting the loss of a former love. There was something to unpack in the sequence of events in Erika's life, and Althea was eager to get to know her new friend and earn her trust so that she might confide in her.

Althea glanced down at her bags and felt a surge of guilt for having initiated the friendship with dishonesty. While it was technically true that Nicole had informed her about Dragos Manor, Althea had created the ghost hunter persona and cover story to help her get closer to the situation until she could determine what she needed to know. Historically, Althea knew that revealing her ability to see aspects of past and future events often did not bode well. Her powers typically overwhelmed most people outside the context of Stellar Remnants, where individuals had the opportunity to perceive them with whatever degree of seriousness made them feel comfortable.

Erika locked eyes with Althea as she finished her cocktail. She thanked Sam, left the bar, and joined Althea in the lobby.

"I see you have your belongings. I can show you to your room now, if you'd like."

"That sounds great. Did everything turn out alright with your cousin?"

"Oh jeez, I'm so sorry. You must be wondering what the hell that whole thing was about."

"No, it's okay; you don't have to justify anything to me. I'm not here to get into your business. My business is strictly ghosts. In the spirit of friendship, I'm available to you if you feel like talking, but you don't owe me any explanations."

A sigh of relief puffed out from Erika's lips. "Thank you. You don't know how much that means to me, actually," she said with visible ease as the pair walked across the lobby toward an old elevator. "This elevator is the only way up to the higher floors beyond the 2nd floor. Usually, we only allow family members on the 3rd floor, but we have a couple of suites reserved for special guests," Erika explained as they passed a security guard, and she reached over and pressed the call button for the lift.

On the ride up, Althea noted that only three selections were available in the cart—Three, Four, and L. The button for the lobby was positioned somewhat lower than the buttons for the higher floors, almost as if a number two button had once existed and then been subsequently removed. This must mean that the 2nd floor and cellar could only be accessed via stairways. She wasn't surprised that an old place like this was not fully ADA-compliant. However, it did strike her as odd that the family would go through all the trouble to install an elevator in their home and have it bypass the 2nd floor. *Very curious*, she thought. Althea pivoted around and noticed something else. The wall behind her was also a functioning door. The dual openings suggested that one of the floors required access from the rear set of doors.

A small flame of excitement burned inside Althea's solar plexus at the thought of exploring this house and uncovering its secrets. Of course, she would respect the boundaries that Erika had established. There were more than enough curiosities to discover across three entire floors that would keep her occupied. Plus, it would provide her with the opportunity to build a friendship with Erika, who was the real key to this puzzle. Even standing beside her now, Althea sensed that she was exactly where she was meant to be.

She glanced at Erika from the corner of her eye. While Althea's inner sight allowed her to perceive aspects of the past and future for others, it typically revealed nothing about Althea's own future except for the occasional foreshadowing dream. This felt like the most natural part of her life, and frankly, she didn't want to know everything before it unfolded. The unknown felt thrilling, and she was eager to understand why her own destiny had led her down this road and to this person. What did fate have in store for her?

The elevator chimed as it reached the 3rd floor. Althea picked up her belongings and followed Erika out of the car. Several doors lined either side of the hallway before them, and another set of rooms was at the back of the house. As the pair silently traversed the large corridor, Althea briefly recalled the elderly woman she had seen in the upper window upon her arrival. Perhaps she was the reason Althea was not permitted on the 4th floor.

"Who lives upstairs?" Althea asked.

"Nobody," Erika responded matter-of-factly as they arrived in front of a doorway. She began rummaging in her pocket for the key. "This suite is vacant, so you can use it as long as you'd like. My husband and I are right next door if you need anything," Erika explained while fumbling to unlock the designated room. Once she succeeded, she handed the key to Althea just as the door next door burst open. A handsome but sleepy-looking guy with dark, shaggy bedhead peeked into the hallway. He looked surprised to see his wife standing with a blue-haired stranger.

"Erika?" he asked in a tired voice with a thick accent as he stepped out into the hallway. "I thought I heard you talking to someone out here."

"Hi, honey," she stammered. "Sorry to wake you."

"No, it's okay. How long was I asleep?"

"About a day," Erika responded. "I was showing our new guest to her room." At this, her husband looked confused. "Althea, this is my husband, Blake. Blake, this is Althea. She will be staying up here as my guest."

"Oh! Another friend from LA?" he asked, his demeanor shifting away from suspicion.

"Sorta," Erika began. "We just met downstairs earlier tonight, actually, but she's a friend of Nicole's. You remember Nicole, right? Anyway, Althea's a paranormal investigator working on a documentary about Dragos Manor," Erika added with a small hiccup. Again, a look of utter confusion returned to Blake's face. Althea could tell he was waiting for further explanation.

"What does this mean?" he asked, his eyebrows scrunched up.

"Ghosts," Althea chimed in. "I'm a ghost hunter. I asked for your wife's permission to conduct a paranormal investigation of this notoriously haunted house. My goal is to create a documentary series for television. So, you'll see me poking around with strange equipment from time to time, but I promise to do my best not to be intrusive. It's nice to meet you," she said, placing her luggage down and approaching the tall, brawny man.

As she drew nearer, Althea immediately sensed that Erika's husband was also a werewolf. Then the premonition struck—she realized that Blake possessed a quality of being devoted and loyal to a fault. She felt the jealousy stirring within him and recognized that much of it stemmed from his failure to be true to himself, especially regarding his happiness and needs. He was actively sacrificing a part of himself for this marriage. The thought made Althea feel a twinge of pity for him. She also observed an impending fork in his road that would be significant—a decision that could shape the rest of his life.

"We should let our guest get settled now," Erika suggested. "Althea, let us know if you need anything. I can have the kitchen bring you some snacks and drinks."

"No need to trouble yourself. I have everything I need, thank you."

"Your room has a large ensuite. I recommend the soaking tub; it's pretty luxurious. Anyway, have a pleasant evening, and I'll see you soon, I'm sure. Come on, Blake, let's give her some privacy," Erika instructed, reaching out for her husband's arm. Still visibly wary of the arrangement, Blake relented and allowed his wife to tow him toward the elevator. As the couple receded down the corridor, Althea heard his inquiring tone but could not make out the specific questions. He was probably confused about why Erika had invited a stranger to stay among the family on the 3rd floor, free of charge.

She shook off the speculations and refocused on the task at hand. Althea picked up her bags and opened the door to the suite. Despite the darkness inside, she could tell the space was vast. Glancing around, she noticed a lamp on a small entry table and turned it on. The dim light illuminated an enormous, hand-woven rug on the floor before her. Antique Edwardian furniture filled the room, and the walls were lined with vinyl paper showcasing a Transylvanian folk scene. This room was beautiful and eerie—an intimidating masterpiece with echoes of a disquieted soul.

Once more, Althea forcefully shook off her hesitation. There was no time to stand there feeling creeped out, she marched over to the large four-poster bed in the far corner and turned on a second lamp on the nightstand. Removing the padded duffle bag from her shoulder, she set it down on the bed, unzipped the top compartment, and pulled back the flap, revealing high-tech hardware nestled within perfectly molded polyurethane foam.

First, she extracted an iPad and a charger and then located a nearby wall outlet. After plugging in the device, she returned to the case. Next, she took out an EMF and temperature meter, a 360-degree camera rig with a couple of GoPros, a Phasm light, a handheld 8K resolution camera, and an EVP recorder with headphones. She laid the equipment on the bed, flipped the duffel bag over, and pulled out a small, lightweight tripod. Once everything was organized in front of her, Althea extracted her cell phone and scrolled through the contacts until she found the name she had been searching for—Programmer Kit. Fortunately, Kit lived on the West Coast, so Althea didn't have to worry about the late-night call due to the time difference. The number dialed, and after a moment, the line picked up. Althea heard the familiar voice of her friend on the other side.

"Did you get there okay?" Kit asked in her distinctive, husky voice.

"Yeah, I have all the gear unpacked and laid out in front of me."

"Perfect. Step one—you can forget most of that other crap for now. Those are decoy gadgets to help you look the part of a ghost hunter. Honestly, I don't think most of it really works. The cameras might help you a little, but your most valuable asset will be the app I developed, which is installed on the iPad. Is it charging?"

"Yeah, I did that first thing, just like you told me to."

"Good. Go ahead and turn it on so I can run a quick systems performance check to make sure everything is working properly," Kit instructed. Althea powered on the iPad and followed a few instructions given by her friend on the other end of the line to enable remote screen-sharing capabilities. From there, Kit took control of the device to run a systems check and confirm that it was configured to her preferred technical specs. "Okay, that's done," Kit said after a moment. "Next, go ahead and get out that custom piece of hardware I gave you and place it over the lenses on the device, then make sure the lidar setting is enabled." Once again, Althea followed the instructions, and soon Kit confirmed that everything looked operational. "Alright, everything looks good. Now launch the software on the home screen with the little Pacman ghost-looking icon called 'PhantomGrammetry.'"

Althea located the described application mainly by the long string of characters that made up the app's name. "Hm, that's a pretty long title," she commented.

"I didn't think my genius would come across in a truncated name like 'PhanGram.' Remember, this is a prototype, and while it's mostly reliable, it's not completely bulletproof yet. I haven't found a use case to test it thoroughly until now. The way it's supposed to work is through a synergy of lidar and photogrammetry—both of which are existing technologies used to generate 3D digital objects—and camera tracking techniques. It utilizes the proprietary hardware I gave you, along with the built-in camera sensor and lidar scanning capabilities, to capture suspected phantasmal activity. The backend application stitches images together to create a wireframe mesh, and the point cloud sequence keyframes, interpolates, and maps out any movement in real-time."

"That was a mouthful. In English, please," Althea asked, unimpressed by all the technical jargon.

"The primary function of my prototype is to look for anomalies in an environment. Once it picks up an anomaly, it says, 'Okay, I know this object differs from the rest of the objects in the environment based on various factors such as opacity, radiation levels, unusual locomotion—"

"Kit..."

"My software will track and make a 3D digital outline of ghosts," Kit said sheepishly.

"Neat. So how do I use it?"

"Okay, so the settings have been configured for the software to work properly. All you have to do is make sure you have the application launched and running, then lift the device up to an area in your environment where you suspect a ghost might be. Once a paranormal event is detected, you will start to see tracking markers appear on your iPad screen. If the reading is strong, you might see the tracked points connect into a form, almost like a stick-figure image. If you see the stick figure, then try physically rotating the device around the area of interest; that's where the real fun begins. If you can rotate around the spirit, we should be able to get a 3D mesh of its shape. But you will have to do this quickly. Ghosts don't typically like their pictures taken and can move very fast."

"Okay, woof! This sounds a little intimidating but cool, cool, cool. I can do it."

"Tell her we believe in her!" A familiar voice rang out in the background. Althea could not immediately place it, but then it hit her.

"Was that Nicole?" Althea asked with confusion. The other end of the line was quiet until a cat's meow broke the silence. "Is that Gingersnaps? Are you at my house?"

"Um, yeah. I'm set up over at your place," came the sheepish response from Kit. "I hope you don't mind."

"We weren't purposely trying to keep it from you!" came Nicole's voice in the background. "Kit called here the other day to see if you had left yet, and I answered the phone. Once we figured out that we both, ya know, *knew about you being at a haunted house* and that we were both helping you, we thought it might be better if we banded together so you had a solid support system back at home."

"It's fine. I'm not mad," Althea responded dismissively before changing the subject. "Say, Nicole?"

"Umm, yeah?" she asked.

"If I were to say the word—*werewolves*, does that mean anything to you?" There was a brief silence on the other end of the line.

"Oh shiiiit. That's right, that's right," Nicole muttered.

"Okay, thanks you two!" Althea said. "I appreciate the support. Kiss Gingersnaps for me. Talk soon. Bye-bye." Althea hung up the call and placed the phone on the nightstand. She sighed and stared out at the still expansiveness of the dimly lit suite. Everything was moving so quickly; she needed a moment to digest her circumstances.

"First things first. I should probably check to see if any spirits are lurking in the shadows of this room," Althea commented aloud as she grasped the iPad. Her hands trembled as she raised the screen to her face. She wasn't sure if her trembling was because she was afraid Kit's ghost tracker wouldn't work or because she was apprehensive that it would. Althea launched the application, and after about half a minute of initialization processes, some instructional text appeared on the screen that read—*Slowly Scan Your Surroundings.*

Althea began to survey the massive suite, sweeping the device in long arcs. Her gut instinct advised her to maintain a steady pace so the camera sensors could detect subtle movements. Once she finished inspecting the entire room, Althea let out a sigh of relief. It seemed she was alone.

The loud, vibrating sound of her cell phone against the wooden nightstand caused her to jump. Althea lifted the phone to see a new text from Kit—"*All clear,*" the message read. It appeared that Kit was planning to virtually ride along as a copilot for her prototype's maiden voyage. The thought brought Althea some comfort as she decided to give up on ghost hunting for the evening and unpack her suitcase.

She moved the equipment to a nearby chaise lounge, clearing space on the bed to collapse into. Althea was conscious for only a few minutes before exhaustion overtook her.

Althea awoke to see a shadowy figure standing over her. Her senses were groggy, but even so, she knew she was in danger. Instinctively, she held out her arms to protect herself. The feminine silhouette moved quickly, pinning her to the bed. Anger and fear surged within her at being restrained. It seemed that the harder she fought, the less she could move. Helplessness sank in, and she tried with all her might to push this phantom off her when suddenly—

A sudden sound jolted Althea from a deep sleep. She bolted up in bed and realized that she was alone in the dark. There was no feminine figure—only the haunting remnants of what must have been a nightmare paired with a merciless bout of sleep paralysis. But as she fought to shake off the residual terror and her senses gradually sharpened, she recognized that she had indeed heard the unmistakable sound of a door handle unlatching. Panic surged within her as her eyes darted around in the murky shadows, but she felt utterly disoriented in these unfamiliar surroundings. Althea fumbled for the nightstand, managing to switch on the small lamp. A dim glow illuminated the room, and to her immense relief, she confirmed that the door to her suite was shut. A sigh escaped her lips, slowing the rhythm of her heartbeat. She was about to lay down and try to go back to sleep when her eyes fell on a large armoire in the corner of the room. To her horror, its door was slightly ajar. A shiver ran down her spine, and the fine hairs on her arms prickled with an instinctive alarm.

At first, Althea was too frightened to move, but then she spotted the iPad charging on the wall near her bed. Summoning every ounce of courage, she slowly inched out of bed, her breath hitching as she navigated the vastness of the large room. Once she reached the wall, she bent down, unplugged the device, and tapped the screen to life. The monitor momentarily blinded her as she squinted against the brightness. Althea hurriedly tapped the cartoon ghost icon, launching Kit's app, and directed the iPad toward the armoire. Through the monitor, she could clearly see that the door was cracked open. Had it always been like that? If so, she had not noticed it before.

For a brief moment, Althea questioned herself, wondering if she was about to follow through with what she was considering. Then she realized she had to. There was no one else there to complete this task for her. Taking a deep breath, she stepped cautiously toward the antique dresser. She rotated the device around the expansive suite with each step to ensure nothing occupied any other corner. Once she arrived at the armoire, Althea took a deep breath and opened the door. She was almost too afraid to look as she peered into the tablet's screen. To her surprise and relief, the closet was empty. Althea spun around and again swept the iPad across the rest of the room, even tilting it up toward the dark, high walls and ceiling. Nothing.

A wry chuckle escaped her lips as she returned to the four-poster bed. Placing the tablet on the nightstand, Althea climbed back into the large bed just as a loud sound echoed throughout the room. Althea jumped as the high-frequency sound of her cell phone vibrated against the wooden nightstand again. She steadied her racing heart as she lifted the phone and saw another text from Kit—"*All clear.*" Althea exhaled a sigh of relief as she lay back in bed. It was late; she was not confident that the prototype Kit had built even worked. Still, she was thankful that her friend was committed to keeping watch over her.

Chapter Seventeen

SOMEONE'S WATCHING

Day of the New Moon

It was late morning outside Dragos Manor. Pillowy cumulus clouds drifted by, reflecting the sun as it ascended into the brilliant blue sky. The northern birdsong floated atop the springtime breeze and danced through the open windows into the museum-esque suite occupied by Ana Dragos. By this time of day, many of her usual morning visitors had already come and gone. Tom had brought her breakfast and opened all the curtains, and then Marius had stopped by to rattle off various news, updates, and concerns. The retired Head of Household now sat alone, propped up in bed with—what old Tom called—*her good buddy, nostalgia*, keeping her company. Despite having the constant companion of one's own memories, Ana still somehow found herself at odds with those old friends.

"It's hidden," she hissed in a low whisper. "Of course, I have it hidden. You do realize the sheer magnitude of the power within those pages," Ana paused with a furrowed brow, waiting for a response. The only problem was that usually someone needed at least two active participants for a fair and balanced dialogue. Ana was, however, ostensibly the only one in the room. The silence was broken as she began tsking at her unseen interlocutor.

"Why, of course, you do!" Ana continued. "After all, you penned the darn thing, for goodness' sake! I only brought up that old spell book because I still have yet to accomplish the pass-down ritual as you had done for me and Daniela. Handing off the duties of Head of Household did not go as I had expected, with the undesirable news of my grandson—no need to rehash that topic now. I need to teach Erika the containment spell for this house. Even though that doesn't really require the book anymore these days, I will still use it to honor the tradition." Ana again paused and listened, staring out into the room that was only quiet and still in response.

"Bring *you* the book? Well, my goodness, whatever for? What use could you possibly have of it now?" Ana challenged, then fell silent once more as she listened to what seemed to be no one in the room.

"Oh, come now, Sophia. You should hear yourself sometimes. Please understand I mean no disrespect, but *you yourself*, at one time, even warned me that this day might come, and you had said, at all costs, never to give you the book. That said, I will carry out the tradition and pass down the practices to Maricara." Again, Ana fell silent as if giving space to her phantasmal conversation partner.

"You know I meant to say, Erika! I merely misspoke! And I don't appreciate what you're insinuating, so if you don't mind, I would like to change the subject," Ana said adamantly, then rolled into another topic without skipping a beat.

"Marius stopped by earlier. He mentioned that the hunters are putting pressure on our family, which is making the local families nervous. Of course, you know how progressive and diplomatic Marius tries to be. He suggests we start granting more licenses to the younger generation since they will be in charge one day. He believes it might be time to allow some change to happen. I would agree with him if I weren't so utterly terrified that the youth have made such great strides to drive our society straight into the ground. The very idea; what a petrifying thought! Marius says this struggle between old and new thinking is a story as old as time. What would you suggest, Sophia? I'm sure you had your reservations when Daniela and I took over. Do you remember when Daniela started playing that *What's His Name Presley's* music all the time? My goodness," Ana chuckled and blushed as she listened to the silence once more. The smile slowly fell from her lips. She cleared her throat and shifted uncomfortably, sitting up more erectly on the pillows propped against the headboard.

"With that kind of thinking, soon nobody will be left in our family. God knows Cristian won't be able to give us any offspring, and Marius, well, I don't know what the hell he's waiting for. His plan seems to involve being an eligible bachelor for life. Now, if you'll excuse me, I've grown weary of this subject that you repeatedly insist on bringing up, so I think I will go for a walk," Ana said as she glanced out the window and searched for the familiar male figure she had grown accustomed to seeing.

"Maybe I'll call on that man who lives in the forest. Perhaps he has something more interesting to discuss than the demise of our family. And when I return, I must *please* insist that we talk about something else. I'm sick to death of this subject," Ana said, then defiantly pushed the covers aside and stepped out of bed, revealing a long, white nightgown.

The weather outside seemed nice and mild, so Ana quickly decided that her nightgown was sufficient. More importantly, she wanted to leave the room quickly to have a chance to cool off. Given how she was feeling, she did not want to say anything rude that she would later regret.

Outside Dragos Manor, a figure clad in woodland MARPAT camouflage sat in a portable tree stand blind, approximately one hundred twenty yards deep within the surrounding forest. His high-power binoculars were focused on the tree line near the eastern lawns of the massive Gothic Revival home. About ten minutes earlier, the man surveilling the Dragos property had seen two males exiting the front doors and walking purposefully toward the edge of the woods. Now, the two males circled a small area just beneath the tree canopies, their attention directed at the ground. The surveilling man slowly raised a short-range walkie-talkie to his camouflage facemask and pressed the push-to-talk—PTT—button.

"Come in, Base-Beau; this is Carter, over."

"Go for, Carter, over."

"What's your 20? Over."

"I'm approximately one hundred eighty yards due south of the property, over."

"Roger that. I have eyes on two males near the southeast tree line. They've been poking around for about ten minutes now. Can you see them? Over."

"Negative. All units, this is Base-Beau. Does anyone else have eyes? Say nothing, if no, over." The transmission went quiet and remained so for several seconds. "This is Base-Beau. I hear nothing. Come in, Carter, over."

"Go for, Base-Beau, over."

"Keep eyes on them. Report back if you observe anything suspicious. Reminder to use scent blocker spray, over."

"Roger that. Over and out."

The heavy front door inched open and quickly closed again as Ana slipped out onto the stoop of her magnificent home. A look of dismay weighed heavily on her face as she shuddered at the scene she had just encountered inside the lobby. To her shock and horror, the first floor was swarming with frightening-looking strangers. She exhaled a sigh of relief that, fortunately, no one had approached her nor impeded her progress as she beelined toward the front door. Now outside, Ana relaxed despite the slightly cooler weather than anticipated. Still, the change of scenery offered a nice reprieve from the monotony of her sterile bedroom suite, and the springtime breeze felt heavenly on her wrinkled skin. As she walked down the front steps and onto the dirt and gravel drive, Ana marveled that she couldn't recall the last time she had gone outside.

After a few dozen steps, she reached the edge of the driveway and stepped onto the front lawn. The cool blades of grass beneath her feet sent a small shiver of excitement up her spine. As she headed toward the eastern woods, Ana realized that she was exerting more effort than she was used to. Now, she wished she had confirmed that the man on the edge of the forest was even there before embarking on this journey.

Everything looked much different at ground level than from above. Ana squinted to see if anyone was there, but the forest's edge was still too far away to discern any details. Still, she kept trudging in the direction she thought the man would be. Finally, thankfully, his familiar silhouette came into view. His tall stature paced in circles just inside the shadows of the canopies above. At first, the man didn't notice her, but as he turned, his body language perked up when he saw her approach. He lifted his large hand and casually waved hello. As Ana got closer, she saw his shoulder-length sandy blonde hair, cool smile, and other familiar, albeit transparent, features. He had always been good-looking, that one, even for a human... even for a hunter.

"Well, I'll be damned," Ana said. "You know, there has been a lot of fuss made over you? What happened to you?"

"Funny you should ask," replied Curt's ghost. "I can't believe you can actually see me!"

"See you? Well, I've spent the better part of a year wondering who the Peeping Tom at the edge of the woods was. So, it looks like you have fallen on some hard times?" Ana asked, delicately referring to Curt's apparent demise.

"Ha! Yeah, you can say that I literally *fell* into this situation—or was pushed into it, is more like it," Curt said with a chuckle. "It's good to see you, although I must say, you are giving off quite a bit of heat."

"That's so strange that your apparition remains. All the other house ghosts disappeared the night of the wedding," Ana said. Curt nodded starkly at this remark.

"Yeah, I saw some strange flashes of lightning and electrical surges inside the house that night. I've been curious for a long time about what happened, but I'm stuck out here. My body is buried just over there, a few trees back," he said, pointing over his shoulder.

"Well, this is very interesting. I never knew the magic to retain your spirit extended out here to the grounds."

"Well, it must not be very strong. Old Tom and the werewolves have passed me a thousand times, and no one seems to be able to see me but you. But ya know what, I'll take it. Now listen, Ana. I have something extremely important to tell you that I need you to relay to Erika."

"Of course, I'm happy to help," Ana said, assuming an air of importance.

"Great. I must warn you that you might not like what you hear, as it involves your grandson."

Upon hearing that the news pertained to Cristian, Ana reacted as if she had been slapped in the face but tried to recover quickly. "Oh, very well. What is it?"

"Okay, I'm just going to come out and say it," Curt started, but before he could get another word out, he was interrupted by a shout from across the lawn.

"Ana?" It was groundskeeper Tom. "My gracious, what are you doing out here in your dressing gown? You're going to catch your death," Tom shouted as he trotted from the far side of the west lawns. Curt's ghost nervously watched the elderly man approach.

"I'm going to say this quickly," Curt's ghost hurriedly continued. "So please listen carefully. It was Cristian. Cristian killed me. He hired me to kill Erika's fiancé back in LA—Ryan. Yes, I admit that I killed the poor bastard, but the idea, the order, and the payment for his death all came from Cristian. He stole money from you and put your family's home into a financial tailspin. Cristian planned to lure Erika back here and make her available to marry Blake Farkas. Erika and I started to have feelings for each other, so he killed me too. I'm sorry to you and your family, not Cristian, and please tell Erika that I'm so sorry for what I did. I didn't know her when I took the job. I was greedy and was just following orders. Cristian's orders."

"Cristian?" Ana repeated.

"Yes, it was all Cristian. Cristian, Cristian, Cristian. He hired me to kill Ryan. Can you please tell Erika all of this for me?"

Ana was dumbfounded when Tom finally reached her. Just as Curt had mentioned, the old groundskeeper did not acknowledge his ghostly presence and was probably unable to see him.

"What are you doing out here, Ms. Ana?" Tom asked, and he took off his flannel coat, wrapping it around her shoulders. As Tom escorted her back toward the house, Ana turned toward Curt once more. Despite his translucent form, she could still discern his imploring body language.

"Please tell her for me!" Curt called after her. "I'm not sure how much longer I'll be here. I get the sense that Cristian wants to move me."

Shortly after Ana and Tom vanished into the large, haunted estate, two figures emerged from behind a tree trunk near Curt's makeshift gravesite.

"That was really fucking weird," Kessler commented with a chuckle as both he and Cristian had witnessed the entire unusual scene. Cristian's Bunica had suddenly appeared outside Dragos Manor and walked straight toward this undisclosed burial site.

"Yes, it was, wasn't it?" Cristian agreed suspiciously, glancing around to see if anyone else might be nearby. "It sounded like she was talking to someone. Also, was it odd that she came so close to his grave and said my name?" he asked, paranoia creeping into his voice. Kessler scoffed.

"C'mon, dude. You heard her! She was totally talking to herself. Isn't that what Marius said has been going on? We can take a look around if it will make you feel better, but we were both already over here when she wandered over. We would have seen if someone else was around."

"Yeah, alright," Cristian finally relented.

"So, what are we doing here, mi lobo?" Kessler asked while smoothing back his hair with both hands and then crossing his arms.

"We're just doing some recon for now. I wanted us to get reoriented with where the gravesite is. It's over there at the base of that oak tree."

"Can you remind me why we decided to put him so close to the house?" Kessler asked, furrowing his brows.

"For one, it was somewhat of a rushed decision. And two, I thought if I put it here, I could keep an eye on it. I thought if I buried it too deep in the woods, the hunters might stumble across it. Here, I can make sure the soil hasn't been disturbed and that no one's sniffing around."

"Got it. So now, what's the plan?"

"Well, my hope is that spending almost a year and a half being worm food underground has made the remains completely unrecognizable. Hopefully, there is no gross stuff left to deal with. I hate to say it, but Erika was right; we should simply move him. Tonight is the New Moon, and it will be really dark out. We come back tonight, dig him up under the cover of darkness, and relocate him."

"Not looking forward to that, but whatever, I'm in. Where are we moving him to?"

"Well, I'm still trying to figure that part out," Cristian explained as he began to scan the forest and ponder his options. He looked up just in time to catch the glint of light reflecting off some faraway lens deep in the woods. All the blood drained from his face as his pulse quickened. "Oh fuck," Cristian murmured under his breath as he spun around and quickly pretended to look at something in the other direction. Then he urgently whispered to Kessler. "Kess. Kess. Hey, listen. I need you to follow my lead, okay? Please trust me," Cristian instructed as he reached over and caressed a strand of hair from Kessler's eyes, whose face twisted into a dumbfounded expression. Then Cristian gently took his hand and walked him away from the gravesite.

"Um, what the hell's going on?" Kessler asked in bewilderment, but Cristian only shushed him. Then, without warning, Cristian planted a big kiss on his lips. Kessler's eyes went overbright as Cristian stopped kissing him, then leaned back and slapped him hard across the face.

"You bastard!" he shrieked, projecting his voice, then leaned in again close to Kessler's face. "It's the hunters; they're watching us," he hissed in a fraught whisper, then aloud once more, "How could you do this to me?" Cristian wailed and slapped Kessler again. Unfortunately, Kessler did not have the acting capacity to give any performance in return. Because of this, Cristian decided he would have to compensate. He kissed, then slapped Kessler once more before turning, arms flailing as he sobbed aloud, and ran back toward Dragos Manor. Kessler stood alone and confused as he held a hand to his scarlet cheeks.

At that moment, Kessler's cell phone chimed in his pocket. He pulled it out and saw a text from Cristian that read—"*Go home! I'll call you later!!*"

Chapter Eighteen

PROLIFIC POLTERGEIST

Two Weeks Later

Inside the Dragos library, Althea was bent over a large table, jotting down notes in a journal. The iPad sat nearby, along with the combination EMF-temperature meter, it's gauges fluctuating erratically. The room possessed a foul odor that strongly resembled sulfur or rotten eggs. As Althea continued to write notes alongside a few small sketches, she pulled her black hoodie more tightly around her shoulders with a shiver. Various books were carelessly strewn across the floor, which made her cringe as a book lover. She hoped none of the volumes were very old or sentimental, as pages lay bent and creased under the weight of their landing position.

When she heard another title begin to rattle loose from the expansive bookshelf, Althea stood up and raised the iPad. With the PhantomGrammetry app launched, she glided the device along the rows of books, searching for the source of the jostling sound. Finally, she located a simple three-point dot system displayed on the monitor. The unconnected dots floated around like a tiny swarm, apparently interacting with the book, which she could now see was wiggling. Althea braced herself and held the tablet, pointing it toward the commotion occurring with the inanimate object. Suddenly, the book was hurled violently from the shelf and hurtled toward her. She ducked agilely as the flying volume crashed on the floor near her. Althea quickly recovered and took fast-paced steps, attempting to rotate the device around the floating dots on the screen. Unfortunately, her ability to walk around the spirit was somewhat limited due to it being in the upper

133

corner of the room. Soon, the ghost shifted, the three points on the iPad monitor dispersed, and then it was lost altogether.

She lowered the device with a sigh of frustration. This had been occurring for the past several hours. The foul-smelling odor would intensify, the room would become very cold, and then the phantom would produce an audible sound somewhere on the bookshelf. Althea would locate, track, and record the event using the iPad. Finally, a book would be thrown; she would dodge it and then note the event in her notebook.

Althea was trying to determine whether there was rhyme or reason to this spirit's movements and actions. As she stood back and contemplated her notations holistically, her eyes wandered to a large drawing on the library wall. The depiction was a crude image of a cartoon ghost wearing a bedsheet, with an even more crudely drawn penis erected near the ghost's pelvis. Why was she wasting time in here? She slammed the journal shut, rapidly surmising—there was no rhyme or reason.

At that moment, her cell phone vibrated in her pocket. She pulled it out and saw the name "Programmer Kit" on the incoming call screen. Althea answered, "Hello?"

"That was a good one!" Kit exclaimed in her husky voice.

"Yeah, if nothing else, I'm thankful to know that your software works. I've been able to pick up the ghost's movement using tracking points just like you described."

"I'm honestly kinda surprised you're not getting lines connecting those dots. That tells me that this entity, whatever it is, doesn't have a body per se. It's more of a nebulous mass."

"Whatever it is, it seems to be one prolific poltergeist. Did you see that drawing on the wall I sent you?"

Kit laughed as she took a bite of something and began chewing. "Yeah. That spook draws better ghost dicks than I do. But is that drawn in blood? I can't tell."

"Okay, I'm not even gonna ask about the ghost dicks thing," Althea said, responding to the first comment before addressing the latter. "It's ash. The lighting in here is pretty dim, so I can see how the markings in the photo might read as blood."

"Is that Althea? Has she found anything? Put her on speaker phone,"

Nicole's voice called from the background at the other end of the line.

"Okay, you're on speaker now," Kit informed, then asked, "What else have you found?"

"So, I've been primarily exploring the 1st and 2nd floors. The poltergeist frequents those two stories. I have not seen any evidence of it on the 3rd floor, but I'm not convinced there's nothing supernatural up there. I get a super weird, skin-crawly kinda feeling in my room. It often feels like something is watching me sleep."

"Eww," Nicole commented. "That is really creepy."

"I also suspect something more sinister is at play in the cellar and most likely up on the 4th floor, but I promised not to enter those areas."

"Oh, please! When have *boundaries* ever stopped you before?" Kit snickered.

"What's that supposed to mean?" Althea asked, slightly offended.

"Haha, you know what I'm talking about. Just because you're all *connected to the universe* and shit doesn't mean you're not a human being full of flaws like the rest of us meat bags."

"Okay, we'll unpack that statement later," Althea said, glancing at her wristwatch. "I gotta get going. I can't believe we're in April already! Tonight is the first Full Moon since I arrived, and I think it might be safer to stay in town at The Three Sisters' Inn."

"Oh, that's right! You don't just have ghosts to worry about! I'd be curious to see what a werewolf looks like in person," Kit commented.

"Trust me, you don't want to see them. It's a frightening image you'll never forget," Nicole stated with the authority of firsthand experience.

"But you did forget them," Kit challenged.

"I meant before I forgot them!"

"Okay, thanks for the help, you two!" Althea interrupted. "And Kit..."

"Yeah, what's up?"

"Thanks for keeping an eye on me through all this. Knowing you're watching my back makes me feel a tiny bit safer."

"No sweat, friend," Kit replied.

"We got you!" Nicole called out.

Althea hung up and began to pack up the equipment just as the familiar sulfur smell returned to the air. Soon, the sound of another book started to jiggle loose from its spot on the shelf. This time, Althea ignored it. She closed the door to the library just as another volume came crashing to the floor. There was no time to follow this mischievous spirit around. As she mentioned to Kit and Nicole, tonight was the first Full Moon she would experience since arriving in Nocturne. Althea knew she needed to get moving if she intended to pack, vacate the werewolf den, and arrive at The Three Sisters' Inn before nightfall. The timing felt right to pay them another visit anyway. She wanted to discuss her findings over the past month and maybe gain some wisdom from their mysterious *all-knowingness*. Again, she recalled how she could not read their fortunes the last time she had visited. Whatever beings those wizened sisters were, Althea intended to leverage their powers to her advantage.

She checked her small silver wristwatch. It was a few minutes before 7 pm. Sundown was in about forty-five minutes, and the Full Moon would appear in the sky shortly after that. With time rapidly dwindling, the atmosphere felt daunting. Althea moved with urgency as she headed towards the elevator.

A short time later, her bag was packed, and she glanced out the window of her suite—dusk had fallen. A chill ran down her spine as she gathered her things and exited the room. Once in the hallway, Althea locked the door and turned to leave. She looked up just in time to glimpse the elevator doors closing with a dark figure inside. *That was strange,* she thought. Unfortunately, she didn't catch a good look at who was inside.

Althea approached the lift, expecting to see the needle moving toward the lobby. She was surprised to find the indicator moving in the opposite direction and halting at the number four. Her eyes slowly shifted to the call buttons on the wall beside the antique metal doors. For a moment, her curiosity battled with her better judgment. On one hand, it was getting late, and she needed to get the hell out of there. On the other hand, *who had gone up there?* The figure seemed feminine, but she was sure it wasn't Erika. As Althea tried to remember what she had seen, it was almost as if the figure lacked any distinct features.

Before she realized what she was doing, Althea slammed her palm against the up-arrow call button. The lift responded, and she could hear it descending to retrieve her. Again, she checked her wristwatch. It was getting late, so this would need to be quick.

The zipper glided up the track, snugly securing the black tactical jacket to Corbin's lean torso. He wore Flecktarn camouflage pants and combat boots, with silver blades holstered in various sheaths throughout his uniform. He turned toward Beau, who was organizing his base station to coordinate the team's course of action that night.

"Alright, Beau. Let's go over the plan for tonight," Corbin requested. Beau gave him a crisp nod and responded.

"We have five positions surrounding Dragos Manor, including two focused on the area of interest that Carter observed a couple of weeks ago. Tonight is the Full Moon, so we expect to see something noteworthy. Carter and Malik will monitor the area of interest and maneuver as needed to avoid detection while holding firm on surveilling that spot. I will handle base comms and coordinate all efforts. You, Naiche, and Ferris are positioned in a triangulated formation and will track any wolves that enter the forest tonight to see if they lead us to anything interesting. If any come my way, I will do the same. Otherwise, I will primarily manage comms."

"Excellent. With the pressure on them, I suspect they may try to make a move tonight. The main objective is to ensure that no evidence is tampered with or destroyed until we can conduct a thorough search at the end of June."

"My money is that there are some clues over where those two males were sniffing around the other day. At least, I'd like to check out that area ASAP, but it's too close to the residence for someone not to notice."

"Even at night?"

"The family regularly employs a security detail to patrol the home's exterior perimeter at night."

"Roger. Alright, let's concentrate on the present. We have thirty minutes until sundown. Radio all units and instruct them to take their final bathroom breaks. I'm going to head to my position."

The elevator dinged as it arrived at the 4th floor. It was not the doors in front of her but those behind her that opened. Althea turned and cautiously stepped out of the cart. A long, empty hallway stretched out before her. Glancing to her left, she noticed an empty office; to her right, a bricked-up doorway with a large section of demolished bricks removed. She hesitated, wondering which way the person who had ridden the elevator before her had gone. Lifting her eyes toward the far end of the hallway, Althea saw another door that was slightly ajar. A sliver of receding daylight poked through the crack.

It was getting late. As Althea contemplated whether or not to explore further, she was suddenly struck by an unnerving feeling. Her eyes darted to the brick wall. From what she could see of the space on the other side, it appeared dark and still, yet she sensed there was something malevolent dwelling within. Normally, Althea was not one to be afraid of spirits. Most were harmless souls passing through their journey and didn't pay much mind to the living outside of occasional interest or mild curiosity. However, every now and then, she would come across a hostile presence that radiated ill intentions and required her to be on guard. That settled it. Althea shook her head. Tonight wasn't the night she wanted to get mixed up in any disgruntled spirits with a score to settle. Just as she was about to turn around and go back downstairs, a voice inside her screamed, *No! There is a reason you are up here!*

A groan escaped her lips as she turned to face the massive hole in the brick wall. Despite her better judgment, she began to walk toward it, crouching low so that whatever was inside would hopefully not detect her. A shiver ran down her spine as she drew nearer to the large, gaping void. Suddenly, another wave of dread ran through her; she lost her nerve and quickly rushed past the opening. Althea hurried further down the hallway and glanced back. Whatever dark thing lurked within that space was probably the very thing fate had summoned her here to confront. *Okay, I got it. There is something I need to investigate inside that room,* she thought as she shook her head in disbelief. "Later," she whispered aloud as if trying to convince someone other than herself. "For now, I need to get outta here."

As Althea prepared to cross the ominous bricks once more and head back toward the elevator, her intuition, which she called her Obvious Voice, flooded back in—*Not later! Now! Look around now!* Althea sighed. *Divination could be such a drag sometimes.* She couldn't recall a time when she felt such inner turmoil. Every fiber of her being wanted to leave Dragos Manor and hunker down in town for the night, but the very essence of her being was forcing her to stay. She decided on a compromise. She would investigate the door at the end of the hallway and worry about the scary hole in the bricks some other time. She turned around and tiptoed to the end of the hallway. As quietly as a mouse, she inched open the door and was immediately captivated by the beautiful vista stretching out for miles before her. "Holy cow," she muttered as she pushed the door open a little wider. An elaborate spectrum of blues and teals transitioned into oranges and yellows on the western horizon. The air had cooled significantly with the setting sun. The bullfrogs croaked from somewhere in the distance, and the crickets chirped, singing their evening song. She took a moment to breathe and appreciate the magnificence of nature. As she exhaled, Althea grounded herself and returned to action. She was procrastinating. Time would not wait for her. She began to scan her surroundings methodically.

Her first thought was an observation—she seemed to be alone in this neglected outdoor courtyard. This was both a relief and a source of anxiety because it meant there was still someone roaming around on this floor. Althea's second thought was a realization—perhaps the mysterious figure she had followed up in the elevator was the same person she had seen staring down at her upon arriving at Dragos Manor. Her next thought was another burst of intuition—*Someone up here needs my help! Right now!*

There was only one thing left for her to do. Althea returned to the hallway and stared long and hard at the gaping hole in the brick wall.

Chapter Nineteen

THE DECOY PLAN

Night of the Pink Moon

The doors of Club Dragos were just about to open for the night. As was customary during a Full Moon, the large drapes were drawn shut and would later be guarded by security. While on any other night the club would feature various levels of security, Cristian paid top dollar to ensure these nights were adequately staffed. Even with plenty of security, Cristian had other concerns on his mind tonight. He sat with the Killers on stage in the VIP section of the empty ballroom, far from any listening ears.

"I can't believe it's already the end of April! The Pink Moon is tonight! Ugh, time is flying by too fast!" he hissed. "The fucking hunters will be here in two months to conduct their search! I can't fucking believe she committed us to that. It was so incredibly stupid! Plus, I know they've been spying on us," Cristian ranted. The Killers sat around, looking exasperated. Some held their faces in their hands, some sat backward in their chairs, staring despondently at the ceiling, and some fidgeted with their hands, wearing uncomfortable expressions. "And on top of everything else, I've had to put *a freeze* on any further bookings until we get this shit show sorted out! Do you know how wildly fucking annoying that is? We're literally losing money because of her stupid *fuck-ass* decisions!" Cristian seethed, then took a breath from his raging. Only Beo leaned in toward him, his body language conveyed engagement in his boyfriend's words.

"Babe, we know. We're aware of everything you're saying. It's all you've been talking about for the past month. How about we try to be less focused on what's wrong with the situation and instead try to come up with some solutions?"

"What solutions? Kessler and I already tried to..." Cristian caught himself.

"Tried to do what?" Beo asked with furrowed brows as he glanced over at Kessler.

"Tried to tell those hunters to fuck off," Kessler responded, covering for Cristian.

Beo looked at him suspiciously for a moment and then turned back to his boyfriend. "Baby, don't worry. I'm sure you'll think of a way around this mess but maybe let's give it a rest for one night," he suggested as he put a compassionate hand on Cristian's knee. Unfortunately, this did not make Cristian feel any better.

"I could fucking *strangle* Erika. You know she won't do anything to help the situation. I don't think she cares. She wants to run the show and make decisions like that without me? Then I say... have a fucking ball, pr*incess*! Maybe I *should* back off and let her deal with the fallout! But of course, she knows that I *will* step in and fix everything! Just like I always do! I'm the only one with this family's best interests at heart. I'll take care of it, just like I take care of everything else. And she'll just sit back, get wasted, and jerk Blake's emotions around. Also, why the fuck isn't she pregnant yet? Seriously! She has one fucking job!"

"Honey, I understand. Look, maybe it would be a good idea if we all went outside tonight like old times and got some fresh air. We can go to our ridge. Clear our minds a little bit. Transforming might help you to burn off some of this steam," Beo said, attempting to sell the idea with an affectionate shoulder rub.

"Yeah, maybe if we all changed into wolves, it would shake up those hunters. Stir them up out of their hiding spots," River added, visibly excited about the prospect of the group going outside to enjoy that night's Full Moon.

"Or..." it was Kessler who chimed in this time. His face was pensive. Cristian and the other Killers stared expectantly at him, waiting for him to say more.

"Ooor?" Cristian asked with exasperation.

141

"Or maybe it's not *us* who flushes the hunters out from their positions. Maybe we have a couple of ferals do the job for us. Keep the hunters busy for a while. They won't be able to keep an eye on the house and contain bitten werewolves at the same time."

"Okay, hold on," Beo interrupted with audible concern. "While I appreciate your solution-oriented thinking, we can't just defy our laws and intentionally create a bunch of ferals. Sure, it would distract the hunters, but we'll piss off our parents if we do something that reckless."

Cristian looked at Beo for a moment, considering his words, then turned to Kessler and asked, "How many are you thinking?"

"Shit. Six hunters, six ferals," Kessler brazenly fired back with a grin.

"Twelve," Vittoria corrected in a steely tone. The group turned to face her.

"*Twelve?* I was thinking of a lower number to justify it as an accident," Kessler explained.

"You need twelve," Vittoria reiterated. "Two wolves per hunter. That's two wolves pulling each hunter in two separate directions. Any fewer, and they might leave someone behind to continue spying. If you want to create a proper diversion, do it right. If you're worried about the Heads of the Households, don't be. Be bold. Tell them you are in charge and running things as you see fit. The hunters are not playing fair, so why should we? If they don't back off, then they're asking for retaliation. If pushed, we could create a whole army of werewolves so quickly that it would make their heads spin. Our kind has always upheld decency, and now they push us too far. We need to remind them that we are in charge." Her conviction seemed to inspire the group. Most notably, Kessler looked at her with stars in his eyes.

"She's right. We keep tiptoeing around and asking for permission from everyone—the hunters, our parents. Our generation is in charge now, especially with Cristian running Dragos Manor. Nocturne is our town, and we need to have the courage to run it as we deem appropriate," Kessler said as he stood up.

"Okie, I think everyone just needs to take a breath here," Beo coaxed, then turned to his brother. "Malcolm, c'mon, back me up here, bruv." But if Beo had been looking for support from Malcolm Jr., he was about to be disappointed.

"Actually, bruh. I kinda think they have a point. I don't agree with how the hunters are throwing their weight around. They have tunnel vision and have convinced themselves that the Dragos had something to do with that asshole Curt's disappearance. They simply have no proof. What if they decide our family had something to do with it? They could single out any of us at any moment. Cooperating with them feels risky."

"I get it!" Beo fired back. "I just think we all need to recognize how dangerous this plan is. Pissing off our parents or running the show how we want to is one thing. But intentionally releasing a dozen feral werewolves into the world can potentially create an explosion of subsequent propagation. The hunters might not be able to contain them for months! And who knows how many more Lycans those ferals would create during that time. It's just not a good idea."

Cristian sat back and digested everyone's positions for a moment. Then he looked at Loki, who had remained characteristically quiet throughout the conversation. Cristian knew that he was a stoic, traditional wolf with a good head on his shoulders. He would reconsider the plan if Loki were in the same camp as Beo.

"Loki, what do you think?" Cristian asked.

Loki looked alarmed at being singled out. He sighed and waited a moment before responding. Cristian appreciated this quality in him. Loki did not speak recklessly but rather contemplated his words before he spoke them.

"Create the wolves," he finally said in his quiet voice with his subtle accent. Kessler clapped his hands together loudly.

"That settles it. This happens tonight. Vittoria, would you like to accompany me?" Kessler asked, extending his arm out toward her in almost a romantic gesture. A bright red viper-like smile spread across her face as she stood up and took his proffered arm. For a moment, the two gazed into each other's eyes before River and Loki stood up as well.

"I think it's a good idea if we go too. Biting a dozen people is not going to be easy," River offered. "And remember, guys, you have to really sink your teeth in if we want them to change tonight. No scratches or surface wounds. We can't afford to wait until the next Full Moon for them to change."

"If you guys don't mind, I'm gonna hang back. I know we're taking a stand here, but my dad would still whoop my ass if he knew I was involved," Malcolm Jr. said. "Let me know how it goes, though!"

In the southeastern part of the forest, Malik sat in a portable tree blind, about sixty yards from where the tree line met the Dragos front lawn. Darkness had fallen, and his night-vision binoculars were focused on the spot Beau had assigned him to monitor. As Malik kept watch over the quiet scene before him, he heard a strange sound behind him—the distant notes of a steam organ playing what sounded like carnival music. Goosebumps rose on his skin as he realized that the only thing behind him was thousands of acres of woodland.

He lowered his binoculars and slowly turned around. Small points of light flickered deep in the forest like fireflies, although they seemed too large to be fireflies. Perhaps they were hikers, lost in the woods. The thought of the missing townspeople crossed his mind. Maybe this light was a sign of them. Malik raised a short-range walkie-talkie to his mouth and pressed the push-to-talk button.

"Come in, Base-Beau; this is Malik over."

"Go for, Malik, over."

"Does anyone else hear that? Over."

"Clarify your meaning, Malik, over."

"Circus music," Malik said in a pensive whisper as he stared transfixed on the mysterious dancing orbs in the distant woods. He had an overwhelming urge to help these poor, lost souls. After a moment, Malik's walkie-talkie came to life.

"Malik, say again, then indicate 'over'; Over." Beau's voice sounded slightly annoyed. Malik shook off the daze, moistened his lips, and raised the comms device to his mouth.

"Sorry, Base-Beau. I have ears on some carnival music. Does anyone hear it? Over."

"I hear it too, over," came the silky response of Nawn's British accent over the radio waves. If Nawn Ferris had heard the music, it must have been coming from the north or northeast of his position, where Nawn was stationed.

"Roger that, Malik and Nawn. Keep us apprised of the situation. Over," The transmission went quiet. Malik stared at the lights in the woods. For a moment, he thought he heard someone calling for help.

"Roger that, Base-Beau. I'm going to check out a possible situation. Over."

"Break, break, break," came Beau's urgent reply. "Hold your position, Malik, over."

"There are some lights in the woods. I think someone might be in trouble. Over and out," Malik said, securing his comms device in his belt holster. Beau's concerned voice crackled through the transmission, but Malik couldn't decipher the details of the message as he turned the volume dial to zero. He climbed down from the tree stand and made his way toward the lights in the distant woods.

The four werewolves in human form exited the ballroom and entered the lobby to carry out their hunt. Kessler, Vittoria, Loki, and River walked past the partygoers waiting to be admitted into the club that night. For a moment, Kessler considered pulling people from the queue, but ultimately decided against it, thinking that it might draw too much attention. He needed something more inconspicuous and glanced toward the lounge.

"We need to keep this as low-key as possible. Let's look for some people in there," he suggested, and they moved in a pack-like formation toward the Dragos lounge. The group lingered in the doorway momentarily as Kessler scanned the chill ambiance inside. At that moment, an oafish guy with thinning hair, wearing a bad suit, stumbled to the bar and obnoxiously slammed his hand down on the countertop.

"Hey, bud, can you send over another round of drinks for me and my new friends over there? See that hot blonde right there? I plan to take her to Pound Town tonight, so if you can be a pal and keep 'em coming, I promise I'll take care of you tonight. I'm known to be a big tipper!" he said pompously.

Kessler glanced over in the direction indicated by the unsavory man.

About eight people were seated together on a couch and various nearby chairs.

"Hey man, I got one for you," the goonish man offered. Then he told Sam a tasteless joke about a chickpea while a disinterested Sam prepared the guy's drink order.

"..wouldn't pay a hundred bucks to have a Kidney Bean on me!" the obnoxious guy laughed, full of self-amusement. "You can keep that one, my friend!"

"He's perfect," Vittoria whispered in Kessler's ear.

The Killers followed the man as he left the bar and staggered back toward a group of people who did not seem eager about his return. The group was still a few short of the Killers' target of twelve. Kessler would need to attract a few more nearby bystanders, without drawing too much attention.

"Alright, everyone! Drinks are on me! The bartender is workin' on them now," the obnoxious guy exclaimed with bravado.

"Is everyone having a good time over here?" Kessler asked as he, Vittoria, River, and Loki approached the crowd.

"Cheers! Yeah, not bad," a blonde woman with an Australian accent replied. Her friends concurred, seemingly grateful to divert attention from the other unpalatable acquaintance.

"Hey, amigo, we're all doing fine over here! The name's Braiden," the obnoxious man introduced, extending his hand toward Kessler, who only ignored the handshake, and carried on, focusing on his mission.

"Tonight, Club Dragos is testing out a new exclusive VIP experience," Kessler began pitching to the group. "We only have about a dozen spots available. Consider it a soft launch. So, my question for all of you is... are any of you interested in attending a secret party hosted at our new cabana in the woods? There will be a heated spa, free drinks, and a small live music performance. Again, this is a pilot launch, so please bear with management as we work through any kinks."

"Ah, sounds amazing!" a Latino guy next to the Australian woman commented. "Also, there's nothing wrong with a little *kink*," he said with a flirtatious smile toward Kessler. Others joined in with enthusiastic acceptance of the invitation.

The music blared inside the ballroom as the lights flashed hypnotically. Scores of people streamed into the room and began moving rhythmically on the dance floor. Up on the stage, Beo stared at Cristian with a look of panic.

"Cristian! You can't let them do this," Beo strongly urged.

"Well, I wouldn't have to let Kessler follow through with such a stupid plan in the first place if Erika hadn't given the hunters a formal fucking invitation onto our property!" he replied with heated justification. "Now, what I need to know from you is... are you going to tell your parents about this?"

An offended look crossed Beo's face as he exhaled angrily through his nostrils. He glanced at his brother, Malcolm Jr., who also seemed interested in the answer. Beo rolled his eyes back to Cristian and looked him dead in the face.

"I'm not a damn snitch," came his steely response. Then he abruptly stood, and Cristian watched as his partner marched down the stairs and integrated into the dance floor.

Cristian had seen this move a hundred times before. His boyfriend was beautiful, but such a drama queen. Still, he loved Beo and knew that he wanted Cristian to follow him. More than that, to chase him. Of course, Cristian eventually would, but there was no rush. Even when a tall, attractive guy wearing a black Stetson sidled up and began dancing with Beo, Cristian did not immediately jump to his rescue. Beo and the stranger gyrated to the rhythm of the music as he ran his hand across the guy's chest. This was an obvious ploy to get Cristian's attention, but he would not play his hand so quickly. Cristian sat back and sipped his whiskey. Malcolm Jr. watched the whole ordeal unfold.

"You know that my brother has always been a rule follower," Malcolm Jr. said as he leaned toward Cristian. "He would never cross the velvet ropes or write his name in wet cement," Malcolm Jr. explained. Cristian nodded but said nothing. Malcolm Jr. added, "But I must say, he has *always* been very gifted at retaliation."

While Cristian understood what Beo's brother was implying, he still felt annoyed by his boyfriend's expectations. Cristian was caught between a rock and a hard place—the hunters being the rock and the pressure of fulfilling his responsibilities as Head of Household being the hard place. Why wouldn't Beo understand and support him like all their other friends did? Why didn't he see how crucial it was for Cristian to succeed in this role so that his grandma and everyone else would start taking him more seriously and giving him the respect he deserved, regardless of his gender and sexual orientation? And who *the hell* was this asshole dancing with his boyfriend?

Suddenly, the tall, cowboy-looking asshole grabbed Beo by the hand and began leading him out of the crowd toward the exit. Cristian stood up and pursued, rushing down the steps and pushing through people dancing in the strobing lights as he hurried to catch up to Beo and his admirer.

"What the hell do you think you're doing?" Cristian demanded as he grabbed Beo's arm. Beo spun around, ready for a fight.

"It doesn't concern you," he fired back. "I'm doing whatever *the hell* I want to, just like you. Yeah, I'm leaving with someone that I don't know, but if we're being reckless, who cares, right?" Cristian could hear the pain in Beo's voice, even over the boisterous crowd and loud music.

"Hey dude, I think he wants to leave," the man in the Stetson hat drawled.

"And I think *you* should leave before I rip you in half," Cristian growled as he stepped up to the stranger, who instantly shrank away into the crowd.

"Why don't you just leave me alone!" Beo shouted.

"Because you're acting ridiculous!"

"Ridiculous, huh? What's ridiculous is my own boyfriend lying to me about a secret that he confides to Kessler and Vittoria! Don't think I haven't noticed y'all whispering and scheming. And I bet it has *nothing* to do with Curt dropping off the face of the fucking planet!" Beo yelled facetiously as he reached out and pushed Cristian hard in the chest. In a flash, Cristian caught Beo by the wrists and gently spun him around, twisting his own arms around him like a pretzel and fastening them closer together. Beo did not seem happy about this. He fought to shake him off, but Cristian only held onto Beo like he was a life raft as their bodies moved like tumultuous waves to the music. Then Cristian rested his lips on the nape of Beo's neck. By the grace of God, the gesture seemed to disarm him just enough that Beo stopped resisting. Cristian instinctively released his boyfriend. Beo turned to face him, his expression impassive. Then he lunged forward and kissed him hard on the mouth.

The lighting choreography synchronized seamlessly with the DJ's set. The two werewolf lovers in human form let the heat of their frustrations melt away as they danced together, momentarily forgetting about their troubles for a while.

Chapter Twenty

THROUGH THE HOLE AND INTO THE WOODS

Althea cautiously descended the long hallway. Each tentative step was met with a wave of apprehension as she approached the jagged hole. It yawned wide in the center of the brick-and-mortar. Pushing through the dread, she inhaled deeply, steadied herself, and peered into the void. Impenetrable blackness was inside. The air was thick and stale, yet she could still detect an unsettling vibration emanating from within, reverberating against all her senses. The darkness bore down on her, disorienting her vision. Suddenly, the faintest movement within the shadows captured her attention. A shockwave of terror coursed through her veins as she gasped and quickly ducked behind the intact part of the wall. The hairs on the back of her neck stood on end as she realized with dreadful clarity that someone—or something—was inside.

Pressed flat against the bricks, Althea fought to calm her racing heart, yet no amount of breathing seemed capable of assuaging her fears. She realized she was in over her head and shook her head in disbelief. Her eyes shone with alarm and doubt as she questioned what business she had there. Then, to her surprise, courage awoke from within a primal place inside her. Her limbs began to move. Althea stepped out from behind the wall, fully visible to whatever lay within, and stared dead-on into the void. As her sight adjusted, she was astonished to see the outline of a feminine figure standing in the middle of the room. It looked like Erika.

At first, Althea was reluctant to announce her presence in an area that was meant to be off-limits according to their agreement. However, something about the scene did not sit right. Why was Erika standing alone in the dark like that? What was she looking at? The whole situation made Althea's skin crawl. She knew she needed to intervene, even if it meant repairing some lost trust later on. So, she took a chance and called out.

"Erika?" Her voice came out barely louder than a whisper. The shadowy figure slowly pivoted and seemed to look directly at Althea, standing outside the hole. That's when Althea's blood ran cold. She noticed a second person inside this strange room—one seated on the floor while the other stood over them. In a sickening flash, the standing figure charged toward Althea. The motion was so fast and silent that Althea didn't have time to get out of the way. She winced, closing her eyes as she anticipated a blow from the incoming attack. But when no impact occurred, she opened her eyes again. This time, she saw only a lone figure sitting on the floor in the middle of the dark room.

As her eyes adjusted further, she realized that the person on the floor was indeed Erika. Althea blinked in confusion as she frantically searched for the other figure who had been there moments ago, but she couldn't see them anywhere. Either they had vanished or were hiding somewhere in the recesses of the room. Just as she was about to call out to Erika again, something inside her solar plexus told her that the other figure hadn't left. Althea's heart raced as she scanned the shadows once more but saw nothing. Stepping back to create some distance, she finally worked up the nerve to call out again.

"Erika," Althea said with more conviction this time. A deep, resonant growl reverberated from the shadowy entrance of the void in response. Chills ran down her spine. She sensed the presence lurking just beyond the edge of the darkness. Strangely, Erika remained frozen throughout all of this, like she hadn't heard a thing. Althea slowly retrieved her tablet from her backpack. The screen flickered to life, and she launched the PhantomGrammetry application. The growling persisted as Althea carefully lifted the device toward the opening in the brick wall and began sweeping the iPad with deliberate, measured movements, trying to avoid provoking the invisible malevolent entity within. After a moment, the familiar tracking points materialized on the screen, just as they had when she faced the poltergeist downstairs. But this time, the points were interconnected, forming a menacing stick figure poised defiantly in the opening of the hole. It was guarding its lair. Althea's heart pounded as she stared into the unsettling manifestation, then past it to Erika.

"Erika," Althea called out again. "This is Althea. Can you please come out of there?" This time, thankfully, Erika complied. She slowly rose to her feet and casually brushed the dust off her pants. A sudden vibration in Althea's pocket caused her to jump. It was probably Kit calling to comment on the target Althea was capturing on the device. She ignored the call, not even attempting to reach for her phone. She did not dare take her eyes off the daunting stick figure or Erika, who was now starting to climb through the hole back into the hallway. The looming stick figure remained stark still even as Erika climbed through it, it's terrible growl continuing all the while.

"Get behind me," Althea urged, her voice firm. Erika cleared the opening and got behind her. "Head toward the elevator. I'm right behind you." With steady resolve, she aimed the device at the shadowy entity lurking behind the bricks. Whatever this creature was, Althea was almost certain she had made an enemy of it at that moment.

Relief washed over her as Althea pressed the elevator call button with Erika by her side. Only when the doors closed behind them did she let out a long exhale, attempting to release the tension from her body. Her hands trembled slightly as she carefully tucked the iPad back inside her backpack. Glancing at Erika, Althea noticed that she appeared to be in a daze.

"What was that?" Althea asked with bewildered fatigue. Erika roused from her disorientation.

"Hmm? What was what?" she asked nonchalantly.

Beau pressed the push-to-talk button as the walkie-talkie squawked to life. "Come in, Malik! This is Base-Beau. I repeat, do not pursue! Do you copy? Over." He practically shouted into his handheld device. "Son of a bitch!" he fumed, this time not over the transmission. Beau knew he needed to act fast. For one thing, the mission was now compromised, leaving only Carter to surveil the area of interest. For another, who knew what Malik was chasing out there in the woods. Lastly, Malik's failure to obey Beau's orders was making him look bad in front of the big boss. He pressed the button again.

"All units, this is Base-Beau. I need backup. Malik has gone AWOL, over."

"This is Corbin. Tell us what you need, Base-Beau, over."

Beau sighed. "I need to pull Naiche to help me track down Malik. Over."

"Roger that, Base Beau. Naiche rendezvous with Base Beau at Malik's station ASAP, over."

"This is Naiche. Roger that, over."

"This is Base-Beau. Appreciate the support, team. Come in, Carter, over."

"Carter here. Go for Base-Beau. Over."

"Stay on that point. Over."

"Roger, sir. On it. Over."

"All units. We'll stay on this channel and report back as soon as we find Malik. Over and out." Beau was about to rush off toward Malik's tree stand blind when his radio came to life once more.

"Base-Beau, this is Nawn. I hear screaming. I think it's Malik. I'm going to investigate, over."

Beau exhaled another tense sigh as he closed his eyes and furrowed his eyebrows.

By this time, the night sky was still moonless, but Kessler knew this would not be the case for much longer. He excitedly glanced backward at the unsuspecting group following the Killers to the fictitious party out in the middle of the western woods.

"It looks like we may have wrangled one too many. We have thirteen people back there," Kessler whispered to Vittoria, who only coolly shrugged in response.

"How much further?" the blonde woman with the Australian accent asked.

"Oh, not far now," Kessler replied devilishly. Then he reached over his shoulders and pulled his shirt off over his head, revealing his muscular chest, shoulders, and arms. Next, he unzipped his fly as Vittoria removed her shirt, revealing a bright red satin bra that contrasted nicely with her fair skin and black hair. Similarly, Loki and River began stripping off their clothing.

"Oooh, Kathryn!" the Latino guy walking beside the Australian woman squealed. "Now, this is my kinda party," he commented enthusiastically as he eagerly began stripping off his clothes.

"Nacho, I don't know, mate," Kathryn whispered. "Something doesn't feel right. Maybe we should go back, Stanley," she suggested to her other friend with a red mohawk.

"Don't sweat it, Kathryn," Stanley confidently reassured. "If this scene is not our jam, we can just leave. Plus, Nacho and I will protect you."

Kessler heard the exchange and shot a subtle smile in Vittoria's direction. He then glanced up at the nighttime sky.

"Alright, and now the moment you've all been waiting for," he announced after a few more minutes of walking. The group stopped and looked around. For a moment, nothing happened. Everyone stared awkwardly at one another in varying degrees of nudity.

"Where's the cabana?" Nacho asked, confused.

The large, puffy cumulus clouds drifted onward in their celestial journey, and the Full Moon finally appeared in the night sky. The moonbeams spilled downward toward Earth and illuminated Kessler, Vittoria, Loki, and River, who stood completely naked. The Killers began transforming rapidly and smoothly into their werewolf forms as the humans watched in horror at the scene unfolding before them. Someone screamed while others began fleeing. Those whose fight-or-flight responses weren't kicking in stood frozen in fear.

"Aw, hell no!" Nacho exclaimed.

"Fuck this," Stanley whimpered.

"Run!" Kathryn yelled as she took off in one direction, while Nacho and Stanley went in another. Nacho was fast, but was no match for wolf Loki, who easily chased him down. Nacho screamed as the werewolf ferociously bit his arm. Wolf River paced Stanley, almost as if toying with him, then lunged and bit him hard on the thigh. Wolf Vittoria did most of the work, chasing down one human after another, catching, biting, and breaking skin before moving on to the next target. After a futile attempt to escape, nearly all of the deceived humans had been hunted down and bitten by the pack of werewolves.

Kathryn ran for her life, bobbing and weaving through the dark forest. Wolf Kessler pursued hot on her heels. He snorted and growled as he bounded after her. When he pounced, he made contact, knocking her down fiercely. Kathryn hit the ground but was nimble and somehow squirmed free from his grip. She must have found a rock or some other heavy object because Kessler felt something hard smash into his snapping jaws, followed by searing pain. He shook the stars from his eyes. The injury was merely a minor setback as he continued the pursuit.

The Aussie fought valiantly, but the werewolf was just too relentless in the end. Kathryn was about to make another run for it when wolf Kessler sprang and sank his teeth into the top of her shoulder, near the base of her neck. He bit down triumphantly as his prey drive took over. He began violently shaking her in his mouth, ragging her like a dog with a toy. When he finally released her, she fell hard to the ground. As Kathryn got up and struggled to run a few more paces deeper into the woods, Kessler had to admit, the Australian had spirit. She clutched her bloodied shoulder, but eventually, her body gave out from under her. She fell to the ground again.

The Killers stood over the wounded humans and waited for something to happen, but unfortunately, nothing did. The injured people lay scattered everywhere, clinging to their wounds, screaming and crying, some calling out for help. The commotion made wolf Kessler nervous as doubt began to creep in.

"Okay, be quiet. Just keep it down, everyone," he tried to coax. The annoying man called Braiden held a hand to his bloodied leg as he turned to wolf Kessler and staunchly rejected the order.

"Fuck you, asshole! Why the fuck did you guys do that if you can talk? No, I *won't* calm down!" Then, Braiden began yelling for help at the top of his lungs. Wolf Vittoria calmly approached the agitated man and viciously bit his jugular, tearing a wide, gaping hole in it. Braiden panicked and clutched desperately at his throat while choking and gasping for air. Wolf Vittoria watched with a maniacal grin as a fountain of blood squirted from the wound. Soon, the man ceased struggling as his lifeless body lay on the ground. She looked over at Kessler, her black fur spiked with blood.

"Okay, now we have twelve!" she said in a singsong voice. Then she turned to the rest of the struggling humans. "Keep your fucking voices down!" she shouted. The frightened humans cowered. They continued to whimper and cry, but at a much more stifled volume than before. Wolf Kessler glanced around nervously.

"How long is this supposed to take?" he asked anxiously. But none of the werewolves had the answer. After about ten minutes, something finally began to happen. Kathryn's body jerked violently forward. She began convulsing and writhing in pain. Unfortunately, to Kessler, this looked more like seizure symptoms than signs of a transition. The skinny punk rock-looking guy with a red mohawk limped over to her and tried to comfort his friend. Then he turned to wolf Kessler and pleaded.

"Please, let me take her to get some help?" Stanley begged. Kathryn struggled as she choked and gasped for air. All color drained from her face. It appeared as though her system was shutting down from blood loss. Her breathing slowed to short rattles, then faint snapping sounds, like someone walking over brittle twigs, could be heard throughout the woods. Kathryn's body began to convulse violently, and she screamed before losing consciousness as her entire body momentarily went limp. Everyone watched on and held their collective breath, unsure if she was dead or alive. Stanley reached out to touch her, wearing visible anguish on his face, but jumped when her body lurched forward with so much force that it seemed unnatural.

The bright Full Moon reflected in Kessler's steely gray werewolf eyes as the woman's body snapped and contorted into a shape that her biology had never known before. Kathryn's screams echoed throughout the night. Her face conveyed the horror of not understanding what was happening to her. Her limbs and snout elongated as flaxen fur rapidly grew on her exposed flesh. Her clothes ripped and tore, then soon fell away, revealing a sleek canine figure.

Wolf Vittoria stood beside wolf Kessler as they watched the first werewolf they had created slowly rise to her feet and adjust to her new reality. Without warning, wolf Kathryn rounded ferociously, snapping her foaming jaws at the creatures who had condemned her to this new form against her will. Soon, the bodies of the other bitten began writhing on the ground, and the sounds of agony and snapping bones grew louder.

"Come on, guys!" wolf Kessler called out to the Killers. "Let's leave them to finish changing. Our work here is done." The Killers scattered in various directions, bounding into the woods to avoid unnecessary conflict with their decoys. After all, those creatures had a job to do.

———— ⚬❀⚬ ————

Leather combat boots splashed through the mud as Malik trudged through the woods, a bright LED headlamp perched atop his head. Each time he thought he was getting closer to the people with the lanterns, they seemed to veer off in the wrong direction by some unfortunate coincidence. Malik understood how disorienting dense woodland could be. They must be exhausted and confused.

"Hey!" he shouted again for what felt like the dozenth time, waving his handheld flashlight through the air. His voice was loud, so he was surprised they couldn't hear him. The trees and vegetation must be muffling his calls. No matter. He would keep pursuing them. Malik's mind kept drifting to daydreams of finding the missing townspeople and reuniting them with their loved ones. He would be a hero. This felt better than killing civilians. Although he recognized why he signed up for the job and knew he was doing it for his late grandpa, Malik also knew deep down that he struggled with the idea of killing innocent people. Perhaps he should reconsider this commitment. Maybe there was another way for him to avenge his Pop-Pop's death.

Malik began to feel a bit fatigued and paused briefly to catch his breath. Forging through dense vegetation, away from any visible trails, was starting to take a toll on his energy. He looked up toward the lights before him as he gulped air into his lungs and noticed something. The lost hikers seemed to be heading in his direction now. They must have finally heard him or realized that he was following them.

"Boy, am I glad you guys finally spotted me," he called out excitedly. As soon as he stepped toward them, the lights began to retreat deeper into the woods again. A wave of panic surged in Malik's chest, and he stopped once more. The lights halted their retreat again and started to drift toward him. At that moment, Malik realized something was wrong.

He turned around and quickly walked in the opposite direction. The light from his flashlight and headlamp illuminated thick brush and tree trunks. Malik scrambled to retrace his steps, and panic began to set in. He chanced a glance behind him. The orbs of light were unnervingly close to him, their movements eerie and unnatural. Malik turned back and broke into an outright run. All he wanted was to return to his team. *His team!* Malik suddenly remembered his teammates and frantically reached down to his belt and pulled out his walkie-talkie.

"Help!" he shouted into the unit while pressing the button. He waited for what felt like an eternity, but no response came. Then he remembered that he had turned the volume down on his device. He cranked the dial. To his relief, Beau's voice came blaring over the other side.

"Malik! What's your 20? Over," Beau asked urgently.

"I don't know, man! I got turned around. They're chasing me!"

"Who's chasing you?"

"Balls of light!" At that moment, Malik's perspective of the world tilted upward as his leg slipped out from under him. The awkward gymnastics of his fall left his other leg as a casualty, his foot folding inward as he landed on top of it. Searing pain surged through his entire leg from two sharp points—one on the inside of his foot and the other on the outside of his ankle. He wanted to take a moment to coddle the pain, but he whirled around frantically searching for the lights. The forest around him was pitch black, except for his headlamp and his flashlight, which had landed about two yards away in the brush.

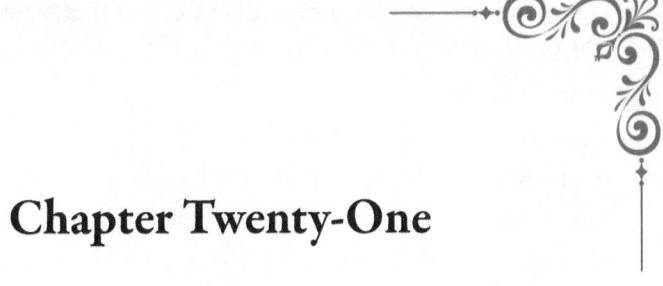

Chapter Twenty-One

LIGHTS IN THE WOODS

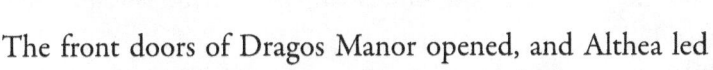

The front doors of Dragos Manor opened, and Althea led Erika out into the heavenly moonlit night. The air carried the sweet scent of springtime blossoms. A cool breeze drifted lazily through the atmosphere as the two women walked down the front steps, crossed the driveway, and then meandered onto the eastern lawn.

"What are we doing out here?" Erika asked with confusion as she attempted to shake the fog that clung to her brain like shrink wrap. She chalked it up to countless hangovers catching up with her, along with the emotional toll that spending time on the 4th floor had taken on her mental well-being.

"We're just getting you some good, old-fashioned fresh air," Althea responded with a tenderhearted smile. "Come on," she coaxed. To Erika's surprise, her beautiful, blue-haired companion broke out into a jog. Erika watched as this intriguing stranger trotted gracefully across the grassy field in the dazzling moonlight, enticing her hostess to follow.

"Ahhhhhwooooooo!" Althea released an uninhibited howl into the night. Her relaxed and carefree nature was contagious, and finally, Erika jogged onto the grass to join the fun. The two sprinted around the expansive lawn in the light of the Full Moon. They laughed and shouted as Erika let go of the heaviness she had felt on the 4th floor. Soon, her troubles subsided as the two came together and arbitrarily selected a spot to plop down on the soft grass. They sat side by side and stared up at the starry sky as Erika let out a long exhale.

"Thanks. I had no idea how badly I needed that," she marveled.

"Of course! Thanks for joining me. I enjoy your company," Althea responded warmly.

"And thanks for getting me out—" Erika stopped mid-sentence as the reality of what had occurred finally hit her. Althea seemed to notice.

"Look, I'm sorry. I know you asked me not to go up there. But I saw you get in the elevator, and I couldn't help myself. Curiosity got the better of me, and I followed you up there."

"When did you see me get in the elevator?" Erika asked incredulously. "I had been up there for a long time."

"Really? That's strange. I followed someone up there," Althea responded, then appeared to fall into contemplation.

Erika shook her head and began picking apart the situation. Part of her felt upset about the invasion of privacy, but it didn't take her long to uncover a deep sense of shame surrounding the whole ordeal. It was easy to get lost in that room, and she could only imagine how it must have appeared to an outsider who stumbled upon the scene. She felt embarrassed because she wasn't sure exactly what Althea had witnessed.

"Do you want to talk about it?" Althea asked after a moment.

"Not really," Erika scoffed. "I just like to go up there sometimes. There's a lot of family history up there."

"I understand," Althea said with a thoughtful nod. "It probably makes you feel certain emotions being up in that room. Perhaps a closeness to something you lost?"

This speculation left Erika feeling vulnerable and exposed. A burning anger swelled inside her chest. She couldn't believe that a total stranger could simply show up in her life and pretend to know anything about it.

"Okay, look—no offense, but why are you so interested? Did someone put you up to this?"

"Nobody put you up to this. I'm asking because I care," Althea responded patiently. "You don't have to talk about it if you don't feel comfortable, but just so you know, I'm a great listener. And you're right, I am interested."

"Interested in what?" Erika asked with suspicion.

"In you." The words were simple, yet they hung in the air even long after they were gone. Truthfully, it felt awful. Erika fought to reconcile her feelings as Althea watched her with tender curiosity.

"I'm going to ask you outright," Erika warned. "And if I ever find out anything you say is intentionally deceptive or misleading, that's it. You only get one chance."

"Ask me anything."

"Did someone put you up to this? My family? Or those hunters that came to our door a few weeks ago? Did anyone ask you to try to talk to me?"

"I'm acting alone," Althea said while leaning forward and brushing a piece of hair from Erika's forehead. Her touch sent a visceral sensation down Erika's spine, like lightning coursing through her veins. She stared at this fascinating blue-haired stranger with incomprehension. The moonlight created a halo around her azure hair. Althea must have fallen from the sky. She was stunning. Despite her efforts, Erika ultimately couldn't find a reason to keep her walls up, and so slowly, they began to crumble.

"My mother died," she blurted out in a small voice. "Possibly up there. I'm not sure. When it happened, I was told she died in a car accident, but then I learned recently that she had committed suicide. Nobody will explain the exact circumstances. All I know is that she would frequently go up there."

"I'm truly sorry to hear that," Althea said empathetically. "Really, I am. How long ago did that happen?"

"I was seventeen. Ugh, I hate looking back at that time." Erika felt the warmth of tears sting her eyes as she glanced back toward the memory, but she recoiled, never wanting to venture too close to it. "Honestly, my past haunts me. It's too hard for me to talk about. I carry a lot of guilt."

"You need to cut yourself a break. Guilt is a common feeling that accompanies grief."

"You don't even know that half of it. Listen to this fuckin tragic story—My fiancé was murdered a couple of years ago, and then I actually ended up sleeping with his killer! Finding that out really fucked me up. I don't trust myself anymore. I know I'm not taking care of myself right now. I know I drink too much." Erika abruptly stopped and wiped her eyes, suddenly self-conscious that she'd overshared. Althea only gazed back at her with soft kindness behind her eyes.

"That sounds very tough. Going through all of that would be a lot for anyone. I think you're really strong, considering you've made it through some extremely difficult experiences."

A wry laugh escaped Erika's lips. "I don't know about that."

"It makes sense to me that you sought the tools you needed to survive, just to get through it all," Althea commented.

"Tools?" Erika asked.

"Yeah, you said you've been drinking too much. You've been numbing to survive. That's an incredible survival strategy. But now you're starting to wake up to the fact that maybe you don't need to do that anymore. It's not a sustainable path to continue down. Also, if I may make an observation, I think you're getting something from sitting in that room up there. Even if you have trouble articulating or understanding what it is, you're trying to confront your past. I think that's a really brave thing to do. That's why I'm saying that you're incredibly strong."

"Thank you, but I think you're being overly kind," Erika laughed uncomfortably, dismissing the unfamiliar compliments. Althea held her gaze but didn't push the matter further. Instead, the two maintained eye contact and shared a comfortable silence until Erika glanced away to regain control of her heartbeat. The way this person spoke was exhilarating. She was so insightful, and maybe there was some truth to her words. Erika had felt stuck for a while now, and maybe Althea was right, perhaps it was time for her to make a change.

"Malik, come in, over!" Beau's crackling voice shattered the silence, pulling Malik's attention away from his injured ankle as fear and anxiety gnawed at him. Summoning all the strength he could muster, Malik slowly rose and stood on his good foot. He then hobbled over to the walkie-talkie, ready to press the PTT button, when suddenly he sensed someone nearby. He couldn't explain this feeling and saw no one around, yet he clearly felt someone's eyes on him.

The high-frenetic rattle of a Timber Rattlesnake sounded a short distance away. Malik froze, anxious about a potential strike. To do nothing was to lock in vulnerability, so he reached for his flashlight, which lay among the tall grass at the base of a tree. As he raised it, the beam of light flashed across the figure of a man standing just a few feet away. Malik gasped and fell backward. The man before him was short, with a powder-white face and cropped dark hair sporting a widow's peak. His bright red lips curled into a Joker's smile that somehow conveyed no life behind them, and worst of all, his black eyes were wide open, staring unblinkingly.

Malik scrambled backward, inadvertently using his injured ankle, yelping in pain and terror. The man took no steps but lowered himself toward the ground, at Malik's level, as if speaking to a child. Then he whispered, his voice emerging from his throat like the sound of a snake's tongue whipping back and forth.

"You're on the wrong side," the powder-faced man said.

"What?" Malik asked, a tear rolling down his cheek.

"This is the side you should be on. Not that terrible side you are on. Come. Come over to me."

"Nah, get away from me, man," Malik muttered, then yelled, "Go away!"

The powder-faced man's smile spread across his cheeks, yet somehow, he didn't appear happy. Malik suddenly felt two hands, one on each of his shoulders. He nearly shit himself and began swinging as he spun around and came face-to-face with Corbin Sterling.

"I got you, man!" Corbin exclaimed as he grasped Malik under his armpits and began to pull him backward roughly through the brush. Malik winced and yelped as he was manhandled backward for about thirty yards in this manner, and yet, he had never felt so much relief in his entire life. When Corbin stopped, Malik spun around and grasped frantically at his arms.

"Don't stop! Please, let's keep going!"

"It's alright, man! Let me get Beau over here. That Grizzly Bear motherfucker can carry your ass the rest of the way outta here."

"I'm serious, man! We can't stop! There's some freaky asshole out there, asking strange questions about joining him on the other side."

Corbin gave Malik a look of empathy in this comment. "I know, brother. Don't worry; I believe you. But it's best to leave it back there. Trust me. You're on the right side." Corbin's hand came down like a sledgehammer as he grasped Malik's shoulder with more discomfort than comfort. Malik quickly shoved Corbin's hand off him and looked suspiciously at the group leader. Corbin's appearance looked somewhat sinister in Malik's headlamp beam.

"Are you him? Did you just take me there?" Malik asked, his voice trembling.

"Take you where, buddy?" Corbin asked as he raised his comms device to his lips.

"To the other side?" Malik asked.

Corbin paused briefly before speaking into his walkie-talkie. Then, he shook his head and pressed the PTT button.

"Come in, Base-Beau. This is Corbin. I got your man, over."

Erika and Althea sat on the grass, gazing at the stars in peaceful silence. Erika felt a deep sense of presence, enjoying the tranquility of the moment. As she inhaled the crisp night air and surveyed their surroundings, something in the woods caught her eye. Deep in the forest, a faint movement drew her attention—a small, flickering light bobbed around unpredictably. At first, she thought it might be the hunters watching Dragos Manor, but if that were the case, they wouldn't be so obvious. She was about to point it out to Althea when suddenly, the single light split into five luminous orbs that danced like fireflies, gently spiraling in different directions. Erika watched, mesmerized by their playful dance. An inexplicable urge surged within her—she felt compelled to follow these lights. She pressed her hand into the grass, about to stand up and pursue them, when Althea's words captured her attention.

"Listen, you don't need to solve all your problems at once. Tonight, you have done the hardest part. It's not only a matter of bringing awareness to your situation but also a *willingness* to make a lasting change. Nobody can take you to this place; you must arrive there yourself. I think it's remarkable."

This observation seemed a little too astute, almost making Erika feel defiant. She searched her soul to see if she could find any falsity in Althea's speculations. However, in her search, she only discovered fears staring back at her—the fear of change, fear of failure, fear of the unknown. The sad fact was that she was comforted by her demons, comforted by her despair, but that also didn't seem right. What was her plan? To give up? Deep down, Erika knew that giving up wasn't in her DNA.

"How can you tell all of this?" Erika asked.

"I can see it," Althea replied. Erika slowly nodded. "I have only one request," Althea continued. Erika looked at her again.

"What is it?"

"May I please inspect that room on the 4th floor before you go back in there again? Would that be alright with you?" she implored.

The request instantly made Erika skeptical. The truth was that she *did* feel something when she entered that strange room behind the bricks. It felt like painful, satisfying relief—almost like scratching a spider bite until it bled. Despite worsening the wound, there were moments of indulgent, aching contentment.

"Fine," Erika finally agreed with reluctance.

"Thank you for trusting me and sharing your thoughts with me tonight. It truly means a lot," Althea said. "Would you like to—"

"Ahhhwoooooooooo!" The deep, resonating howl from the throat of a large creature bellowed throughout the night. Althea's head whipped around toward the sound; her large eyes shone brightly with fear.

"Ah shit, I forgot about those," she said, her voice sinking with fear.

"Oh, so you know about my family then?" Erika asked, somewhat unfazed, then waved a dismissive hand. "Well, don't worry about them. It's probably just my husband and our neighbors. You have nothing to be afraid of."

At that moment, a pack of large, ferocious-looking creatures emerged from the western tree line. Despite the reassurance, Althea gasped and grabbed Erika's arm, shrinking back behind her hostess. The werewolves must have noticed them, as the pack pivoted and began bounding in their direction. It was hard to gauge how many there were due to their erratic movements. Erika's surprise deepened as she realized there were more than she had expected.

"I don't know why they're acting like that," she commented as her annoyance mounted. "They must be drunk or something."

As the beasts drew nearer, the pack quickly dispersed, crouching low to the ground and strategically encircling the women. Their movements were unsettlingly aggressive as they sniffed the air and growled menacingly at Erika and Althea.

"Cristian, take it easy!" Erika chastised. "You guys don't need to act like a bunch of goddamned hellhounds! I just saw you crying the other day while watching the series finale of *Schitt's Creek*. You're not that fuckin hard."

To Erika's dismay, none of the wolves relented, nor did they seem to have registered anything she had said. If anything, their hostility appeared to escalate. Some began snapping their jaws in an unnerving manner at the women, saliva and foam flecking from their mandibles. Their hackles stood on end. Erika was at a loss; she didn't understand why her cousin and his friends were acting this way. Their threatening behavior persisted; it felt as if they didn't recognize her. And that's when it finally dawned on Erika that maybe this scenario was the other way around. Maybe it was she who didn't recognize them.

For the first time, Erika looked at the creatures surrounding her and Althea, searching for a familiar form. Most had black fur, except for two of them—a black one with a red stripe down its back and one that was a blondish color. Erika suddenly realized she didn't recognize any of these creatures at all.

The werewolves were rabid with ferocity, some starting to lunge menacingly toward them, testing their boundaries. Althea screamed and tucked her body close to Erika.

"I don't know who you guys think you are," Erika started forcefully. "But I'm the Head of Household here. The Dragos family won't take kindly to—" But before Erika could finish her sentiment, one of the unknown werewolves pounced. Erika and Althea screamed in unison. The creature landed heavily on top of the women. It was the black wolf with the red stripe down the ridge of its back. The other creatures became more vocal and swarmed triumphantly around their companion, who had pinned down the prey.

The werewolf bore down on Erika and Althea, its snarling muzzle inches from their faces. They screamed, desperately trying to wriggle free from beneath the weight of the creature. The beast's hot, gamey breath intermingled with Althea's sweet-smelling perfume. Erika's heart thundered in her chest, racing not only with horror but also with a sharp pang of guilt for having assured her friend that they were safe. Now, facing the possibility of such a terrifying mortal end, the burden of her misplaced promise loomed larger than the beast itself. How could she have let this happen?

Out of nowhere, a forceful impact struck the werewolf crouched over Erika and Althea, launching the creature backward through the air. It landed about twelve feet away with a sickening thud when its large body collided with the ground. The other werewolves pinned their ears back in a threatening manner, yet their bright yellow eyes reflected fear as they growled at the massive black werewolf that had appeared on the scene. Wolf Blake stood over Erika and Althea, guarding them while the massive figure of a silver werewolf raced past them. Wolf Marius charged at the feral werewolves, driving them away from his niece and her friend.

"Are you both okay?" Blake asked through his black jaws.

"Yes," Erika said breathlessly. "Go get 'em, honey."

With that, wolf Blake spun around to face wolf Marius and the pack of foreign werewolves. Erika could see her uncle's silver form struggling to wrangle the creatures as they scattered in multiple directions, some even doubling back to try and attack him. In a flash, wolf Blake bounded off after them, joining the effort to steer the feral wolves away from Erika, Althea, and Dragos Manor.

Erika stood up and then helped Althea to her feet.

"Are you okay?" she asked.

"Yeah, I'll be fine. Maybe a little sore tomorrow, but no permanent damage."

"I am so sorry that happened. I don't know who those wolves are, but my husband and uncle will take care of them."

"It's not your fault."

"I feel so terrible for telling you that you were safe just to have your life *immediately* put in danger."

"Again, it wasn't your fault. You were also in danger."

"This is what I was telling you about! I'm cursed! My family is cursed. You should get far away from this place and far away from me. Anyone close to me will only end up hurt or dead."

Althea put her arm around Erika's shoulder and maintained eye contact. "I already told you... *I'm not scared.* We're in this together," she said with a smile that already felt familiar. Erika shook her head. *Who is this person?* she wondered. The two had just survived a werewolf attack, leaving Erika with no strength left to fight this beautiful, blue-haired human beside her. She put her arm around Althea's waist, and the two headed inside.

Wolf Blake and wolf Marius had the feral werewolves retreating into the woods. Before werewolf Blake disappeared into the forest to continue the pursuit, he stopped and glanced back toward Erika to make sure that she and her friend were okay. He saw the silhouettes of the women walking toward the driveway. Once they emerged from the shadows into the light of the Full Moon, he noticed their arms around each other. For a moment, a twinge of discontent panged in his heart. Logically, he knew they might be injured and in need of support, but seeing his wife have close contact with someone else made his heart ache with jealousy.

As the women ascended the front steps of Dragos Manor and disappeared inside, wolf Blake turned and resumed the chase. He ran swiftly after the creatures before him, trying to outrun the green-eyed monster that followed him.

Three points of light appeared from the south. Moments later, Naiche, Nawn, and Beau arrived at the spot where Malik lay injured on the ground, with Corbin standing protectively over him.

"What happened? Beau's booming voice emerged as more of a whisper than usual. Corbin glanced from the group of new arrivals down to Malik at his feet, who looked physically and emotionally wounded.

"There were these lights. I thought someone out here needed my help. Then I saw a snake, or at least I thought I did. And there was this man with very pale skin. He..." Malik's voice cracked, and a tear rolled down his cheek. He quickly wiped it away and looked at Nawn. Her stoic expression softened slightly, but she turned her face away, almost as if to give Malik some privacy.

"The lights sound like Ignis Fatuus," Corbin stated authoritatively.

"Come again?" Beau asked.

"Will-o'-the-wisps, Jack-o'-lanterns," Corbin clarified.

"Just leave it to Corbin to know all the local cryptids in the area," Nawn said with wry amusement.

"*Foolish fire,*" Corbin said. "Nevermind. I'll explain later. For now, let's get this guy back to the lodge. I think he's had enough excitement for one night."

"What about the man?" Nawn asked.

Corbin only shrugged at the question. "I'm sorry to say, but when I found him, I heard him talking to someone. However, when I approached, I didn't see anyone there." Malik looked down, shame written across his face.

At that moment, a transmission echoed through multiple walkie-talkies at once, distorting Carter's message on the other end. Corbin signaled for everyone to turn off their units before raising his own to his mouth. With the rest of the team present to rescue Malik, only Carter was left to cover their original mission.

"This is Corbin. Say again, Carter. Over."

"Hey, Corbin. I think we've got a problem. Over," Carter responded. Even before he received the rundown, Corbin sensed it would be a long night.

Chapter Twenty-Two

JEALOUSY

The dead of night gave way to the break of day as streaks of the dawning sun appeared on the eastern horizon. Unoiled hinges whined softly as the door to the 3rd-floor suite inched open. The sound instantly woke Erika, who sat straight up in bed to see who was entering her room. She struggled to brush away residual sleepiness and was greeted with a mixture of fight, flight, and splitting hangover. Erika squeezed her eyes shut to steady the pulsating between her ears, then opened them again and saw Blake tiptoeing into their bedroom. He was barefoot, wearing dark jeans and no shirt. His body had returned to its human form with the setting of the Moon. Despite his apparent exhaustion, his stubbly face wore an expression that conveyed happiness to see her.

His demeanor remained pleasant as he drew nearer, but it slowly waned when his gaze wandered to an area just beyond the couple's bed. Erika followed his line of sight to the chaise lounge, where Althea slept peacefully—her blue hair scattered across the pillow like a sleepy ocean storm. Blake looked at his wife, his eyes full of questions.

"She was too scared to sleep alone," Erika whispered in explanation. Blake nodded solemnly, although his body language betrayed his uneasiness.

This had become a familiar dynamic between Erika and Blake over the past year, a struggle they constantly faced. She sighed inwardly at his recurring disappointment. She was letting him down, not behaving in the way he wanted his wife to, but really, what did he expect? Blake must have known that their marriage was not based on love, not true love anyway.

Any chances for that had been dashed long before they said, 'I do.' He seemed jealous whenever his wife made connections outside their marriage. It didn't matter who it was; Blake was wary of anyone she spent time with. And while Erika acknowledged that she loved him in her own way—he was a kind, good-hearted soul—still, she felt herself recoiling from their pseudo-commitment. Blake must have sensed this too.

"How did it go last night?" Erika asked, trying to steer the conversation away from the landmine. "With the ferals? I hope you and Marius weren't chasing them all night."

"Yes. They were very difficult to manage; there were so many. We tried to drive them deep into the woods but lost track of many of them."

"Where did they come from?" she asked, keeping her voice low. Blake shook his head, indicating that he had no idea, and then his eyes returned suspiciously to Althea's sleeping figure. Erika attempted to read his mind. "Blake, I know you're wondering why I would let a total stranger into our lives," she whispered, nodding toward Althea. "A lot of the time, I do things that don't make sense, even to me. But I have to say, I'm glad she's here. It's been so long since I've had something or someone to myself."

"What about me?" The wounded inflection in his voice immediately made her feel defensive.

"This isn't about you." Her hushed voice grew firm as the bricklaying for the wall inside her heart began construction. "Can't I have a friend without it being some big fucking problem? Sure, I don't really know her, but who cares? I'm glad she's here. I'm glad I met her. She offered to help me get to the bottom of what happened to my mother. Something that I've been trying to do myself, but it's affecting me too badly."

Blake let out a sigh of frustration as he turned and stared intently out the window. His arms were folded across his naked chest; he couldn't even look her in the eye.

"Erika, I'm sorry. I'm not trying to fight. Honestly, I'm just tired and would like to sleep now," he said in a defeated tone.

Guilt washed over her as she realized Blake had spent the entire evening trying to keep her and her new friend safe. Erika felt that the best thing she could do for him at that moment was to leave. She pushed the sheets aside, slid her long legs out from under the covers, and walked to the chaise lounge.

Althea's eyes fluttered open as Erika gently touched her shoulder. A warm smile spread across her face as she gazed up at Erika, but it soon faded when she noticed the other figure standing in the room. Althea gasped and shot upright.

"Blake! You startled me," she said, her voice disoriented.

"It's okay. Blake is just getting in from last night," Erika explained. "He was out chasing those creatures all night. We don't know where they came from."

Althea nodded, becoming more alert as the seriousness of the information sank in.

"Thank you, Blake. You saved our lives. It wasn't looking good there for a moment." Her gratitude was genuine, but he only nodded tersely in response.

The women vacated the room to give Blake space to rest. Now, sitting alone in his empty suite, Erika's words repeatedly played in his mind. *She offered to help me get to the bottom of what happened to my mother. Something that I've been trying to do myself, but it's affecting me too badly.* Blake sighed. He had attempted to help his wife several times, but she had only ever shut him out. And then, this stranger shows up and suddenly becomes the hero?

He lay his head on the pillow and stared at the ceiling, feeling frustrated and defeated. After a moment, he realized it was futile. Sleep would not come.

Blake raised his hand and knocked on the door before him. After a moment, Marius answered, squinting into the bright hallway; his room was dark behind him.

"Blake? What's going on? Is everything alright?" Marius asked, dazed and visibly fatigued.

"Marius, sorry to bother you. I just wanted to say thank you for helping me keep Erika safe last night."

"Of course! But you need not thank me for that. Why don't you get some sleep? You must be exhausted."

"Yes, I'm going to get some sleep," Blake replied halfheartedly.

"You didn't really come here to thank me, did you?" Marius questioned with doubt.

"No, not really."

"Well then, out with it."

"I wanted to ask you, what happened to Erika's mother?" The question seemed to catch Marius off guard. He opened his mouth to reply, but no response followed. "I'm sorry, Marius. I must know," Blake persisted. Marius sighed and opened his door wider, inviting Blake to come inside.

The suite was dimly lit and had a strong scent of jasmine tea. Marius turned on a small lamp that illuminated a modest sitting area with woven chairs. The two settled in for a chat.

"Marius, again, please accept my apologies. I know how tired you must be."

"Probably just as tired as you, I would imagine."

"Yes," Blake agreed with an exhausted smile.

"That's alright, Blake. A little sleep deprivation is good from time to time. Lest we forget what it feels like to experience any real struggle. I presume what you're looking for is far more exhausting. Trying to uncover carefully guarded secrets is not an easy task, particularly when they lie buried in the depths of someone's heart."

"I think I understand what you are saying. But I feel guilty not knowing more about my wife's past. I have tried to ask her, but she does not tell me."

"Maybe try changing your technique. Might I suggest curiosity without expectation?"

"So, you will not tell me either?"

"Oh yes, I will tell you, but to truly understand the details of the story you seek, we need to delve deeper into our familial history."

Upon hearing these words, Blake realized his endurance was waning. He had to remind himself that *he* was the one who knocked on Marius' door, and now, the sage Dragos Uncle was willing to explain. Whether it was information Blake sought remained to be seen; regardless, he dug deep into his reservoir of stamina to listen.

"To understand our family skeletons, you need to grasp certain aspects of our founder, my great-grandmother, Sophia Dragos. You see, Sophia was a powerful matriarch, unmatched in wit, confidence, and humor by anyone in our region of Romania."

"Transylvania, yes?" Blake asked.

"Naturally," Marius confirmed. "You see, Sophia was known for her boldness and often faced biting ridicule for it. But regardless of any repercussions, she lived authentically... some would say—to a fault. Despite her fearlessness and confidence, Sophia also suffered a great deal."

"From what?"

At this, Marius snickered uncomfortably. "Back then, it was known as *lunacy*. People exhibiting emotional distress were seen as vehicles for the devil. I cringe at the notion of 'mental intervention' in those days. Bloodletting, lobotomies, asylums," he said with a shudder. "Today, we'd understand that Sophia's major troubles stemmed from depression, anxiety, and possibly low self-esteem. These are all relatively common afflictions, but they weren't handled with much care or compassion back then, especially in women."

"I see," Blake responded solemnly.

"Some saw the abrupt decision to move her family abroad as reckless and mad. Rumor has it that leaving Romania also created tension in her marriage to my great-grandfather, Florin. The record of Florin living in America is mysteriously brief. Nobody knows for certain what happened to him, but stories of Sophia's legendary broken heart have been whispered throughout the generations."

"So, you are trying to tell me that Sophia's broken heart started a bad luck chain in the family?" Blake guessed.

"Very astute observation. Well done, Blake. You are correct. After that, Sophia's offspring seemed to take after our ardent matriarch, and intergenerational struggle and conflict became rampant. Take my brother, for instance—he and my mother have had a contentious relationship for some time, and now he rarely interacts with the family. The last time he came around was for your wedding, and before that, I can't remember the last time I saw him. I suspect he showed up to pay respects to the transition of power from our mother to your wife as the new Head of Household. Fun fact—the title used to be called *Leader of the Pack* back in the day. *Head of Household* was created to sound more sophisticated, I suppose. Anyway, where was I?"

"You were telling me about the chain of... problems," Blake said somewhat sheepishly, worried that the reminder might have come across as judgmental.

"Oh, yes. Thank you. Now, this brings me to Cristian. As you may have noticed, my mother and nephew have also had a strained relationship. Because of this, Cristian has made some poor choices and often struggles to process his emotions."

"Wait, you skipped Erika's mother. Remind me what her name is again?"

"Right," Marius said as a yawn escaped his mouth. "Thank you. Apologies, I have difficulty staying on track with such a tired mind."

"Please tell me what happened to her," Blake gently pressed. Marius sighed.

"It happened ten years ago this month. It's peculiar because it feels very similar to how it did back then. My cousin was cursed with the legendary Dragos melancholia. The specific crux of her pain resided in the loss of her husband. While her grief had been present ever since his passing, it seemed to amplify when she moved into this home. Erika's mother became prone to isolation and would spend her evenings wandering the dark corners of this house. At first, she appeared to be getting better. However, it soon became apparent that my cousin was almost unwilling to heal. Eventually, grief claimed her."

Blake took in Marius' words with a heavy heart. Marius observed him with kindness in his eyes.

"I understand why Erika's actions worry you. Unfortunately, your wife demonstrates signs of our family's generational afflictions. Please understand that I say this with concern, not judgment. An unattended wound doesn't heal and will decay and rot if left for too long. This is the curse that, regrettably, has befallen much of my family."

"I will save her from this curse," Blake stated boldly, perhaps with fool-hearted conviction, he realized. A similar notion must have crossed Marius' mind.

"Unfortunately, I don't think we can. It can only come from Erika. It would be best if you allowed her to own her fate. We can be there for her and show her love and compassion, but the onus to truly heal falls upon the individual. They must *arrive* at the path on their own; only then can they break through the chains fabricated in long strands of DNA."

"I just want to help my wife. I love her," Blake said helplessly.

"I understand your feelings of powerlessness. Remember—you can listen, extend compassion, and remind her of the light within. I know this must seem like the ultimate tough love, but to truly honor her, you must allow her to own her destiny. If she is to succeed, you can't do it for her. Life is hard for everyone. Of course, there are degrees of hardship, but nobody can escape *the living struggle*. It doesn't matter who you are. Whatever is happening around us is the *sign* we have prayed for. Most individuals ignore them; they choose to be numb rather than truly live. In order to experience true change, Erika must arrive at the decision herself, and then she will be open to our help. She will have to change her identity. For instance, starting with something like, 'I am capable of healing,'" Marius explained in an oversimplified manner, then tried to blink the drowsiness from his eyes.

Blake's vision was blurred. He didn't realize when his face had come to rest in his palms until his head slipped off his hand and nodded forward with its weight.

"Thank you, Marius. I appreciate the things you tell me. Maybe after I get some sleep, I will have more understanding."

"Alright, Blake. Thank you for the visit. I'm here anytime you wish to chat. Now, let's both get some rest. I need the energy to face Cristian and his friends later to inquire where the hell all those ferals came from last night."

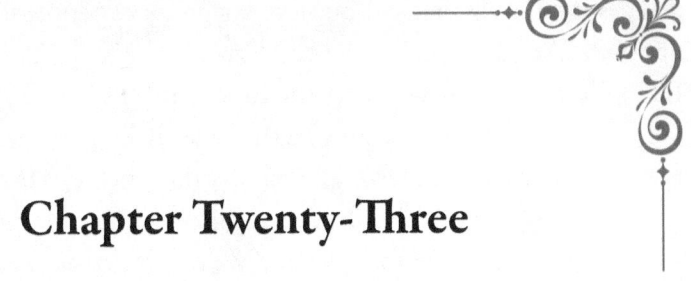

Chapter Twenty-Three

THE ULTIMATUM

It was just before 7 am. Most clubgoers, except those with rooms reserved, had left after a long night of dancing and partying. Erika and Althea enjoyed having the spacious dining hall to themselves as they chatted, sipping black tea with milk and nibbling on a light breakfast of toast and fruit.

After a short while, the first groggy guests wandered in, searching for something to soothe their obvious hangovers. Their sleepy expressions quickly gave way to wide-eyed expressions of bewilderment when they saw an intricately stacked mountain of tableware near the buffet. Plates, bowls, cutlery, salt and pepper shakers, and napkins were arranged in the gravity-defying shape of an inverted pyramid.

"How are they doing that?" one guest asked dubiously. The group hesitated, whispering among themselves, as Cristian and his entourage walked through the doorway and brushed past the uncertain onlookers.

"Exqueeze me! Coming through," he announced at an overly loud volume for a peaceful morning. He and the Killers headed straight for the stacked dishes, casually grabbing their place settings from the inverted pyramid as if the phenomenal event happening before them were trivial. Erika noticed that Cristian and his friends wore the same clothes as the night before. After filling their plates and mugs, they settled at the long dining table and started digging into their heaping servings.

"Boy, am I glad I'm not a vampire!" Cristian announced flippantly. "How much would it suck not to enjoy a hot breakfast? Just sucking blood all the time. Being a werewolf is way cooler," he said as Beo elbowed him in the ribs and gestured to the freaked-out-looking group of people still loitering in the doorway. "An emotional werewolf," Cristian clarified. "Ya know, since I'm an ESTJ Capricorn! Or whatever the fuck that bullshit is that hipsters like to talk about," he said under his breath while shaking his head and rolling his eyes, clearly annoyed at having to mollify these nervous bystanders.

"Morning, Cristian," Erika casually greeted. "Is your night just ending?"

"You know it!" Cristian jeered. "We're just grabbing a quick bite before we hit the hay. I'm so exhausted, I don't even wanna *think* about anything else for the next ten hours, at a minimum," he said, shoveling a forkful of eggs into his mouth while sporting a smug grin and chewing enthusiastically.

Everyone was engaged in conversation and enjoying their meals when Malcolm Senior silently appeared in the dining hall doorway. Erika was the first to notice him, while Cristian and the Killers seemingly did not.

"Nothing, and I repeat, *nothing* is going to get in between me and those bedsheets, ya kna wha mean," Cristian snickered as Beo tapped him on the shoulder, directing his attention to the parental figure standing in the doorway. "Aw, fuck-shit-cunt-damn!" Cristian exclaimed in a panicked voice, and his face grew tight with waning energy.

"Cristian, can you please join me in the foyer? We have something important to discuss with you." Malcolm Sr.'s demeanor was stoic.

"You're killing me! *We*?" Cristian shrieked, appearing even more distressed.

"Come with me, please," Malcolm Sr. repeated firmly. Cristian remained defiantly in his seat; bits of egg stuck in his chin stubble until Beo nudged him. Cristian scoffed and stood up, followed by his boyfriend. The two then joined Malcolm Sr., and they all headed into the lobby.

After the three had exited the room, Malcolm Jr. turned back to his breakfast and muttered under his breath, "No fuckin way am I going out there. I'm staying *right here*! Eatin' my pancakies." Then he cut off a healthy portion and stuffed the bite into his mouth. Vittoria, Kessler, River, and Loki exchanged nervous looks.

Cristian was exhausted and hoped that whatever he was about to encounter wouldn't be too painful. When he saw every major Head of Household in town standing in the lobby, he realized his chances of a stress-free morning were slim.

Typically, the day after a Full Moon transformation was regarded as a day of rest. Beo's parents and the others should have been at home, settling in for a cozy day indoors to recover lost sleep from the previous evening. Not only were they not resting, but they also took the time to shower and put on fresh clothing, while Cristian and Beo looked more haggard, still wearing the same clothes from the day before.

Malcolm Aristide Senior walked up and stood beside his wife, Shanice. That morning, she wore a satin pearl blouse with a draped neck. Her long, wavy hair was styled in goddess braids that fell gracefully over her shoulders. Beside her was Kessler's mom, Elena Vulpe, who looked more like a C-suite executive, with her dark hair pulled into a tight bun that accentuated her annoyed expression. River's mother, Serafine Landis, was dressed simply in blue jeans and a white shirt. Mihaela Lupu resembled an older female version of her son, Loki, minus the sparse, patchy beard. She was the shortest of the four Heads of Household and had a quiet presence, dressed in a modest gray floral dress. Malcolm Sr. stood next to Shanice, dressed casually but still complementing his wife.

"Good morning, Cristian and Beo," came the flowery voice of Serafine Landis. "My heavens, it looks like you two had a rough night. I trust my son is lurking around here somewhere?"

"Good morning, Mrs. Landis. Yeah, River and the Kill—I mean, everyone's eating breakfast," Cristian answered sheepishly. "I can get him for you if you—"

"No, that's quite alright. It's actually you we want to speak with first, Cristian. We're concerned about some things that have been happening around here."

"Oh, really?" Cristian asked, trying to stay calm.

"Yes, indeed. I'd say we are most alarmed to hear a rumor that a large pack of ferals was roaming around Nocturne last night. Several of our trusted neighbors reached out to inform us. Granted, those creatures could have come from anywhere, but we wanted to ask—do *you* happen to know anything about them?" Cristian swallowed hard and glanced sidelong at Beo, dreading the lie he was about to tell and what his partner might think of him afterward.

"Oh wow! No, I hadn't heard!" Cristian said, attempting to play it cool. "We've been sitting out the recent Full Moons lately, ya know, with the club and all, so we were here all night." Serafine nodded thoughtfully, wearing a quizzical expression, before resuming her line of questioning.

"Ah yes, your em... nightclub. That was the next thing we wanted to address. It's attracting some very negative attention in town, and the Town Meeting Members aren't too pleased."

"The what?" Cristian asked with confusion.

"Nocturne's City Council operates as a system of Representative Town Meetings, but we wouldn't expect you to know anything about that since it's a responsibility for a Head of Household. All you need to understand is that it's crucial for our community to stay under the radar and avoid drawing attention to ourselves. There's a lot of town gossip floating around that you have a poltergeist. Does this mean that the Mischief is running unchecked? Is your grandmother aware of what's happening around here? Surely, she would be alarmed by the escalation in paranormal activity."

"With all due respect, Mrs. Landis, Dragos Manor has always been known as a haunted house. It's *our brand*. All the prevalent ghost activity only bolsters our spooky reputation and provides a kickass experience for our guests." At this statement, Elena Vulpe expelled an exasperated groan.

"That's it, Serafine! I've had enough!" Elena exclaimed, throwing her hands wildly in the air before they landed squarely on her hips. She rounded on Cristian, her fury palpable. "I don't think we need to tiptoe around this matter while receiving nothing but uninformed *arrogance* in return. Cristian Dragos, *you* do not have the necessary power to keep this house under control," she fumed. "We are done discussing this with you. It's time we spoke with a *real* Head of Household, someone who has the power to do what's needed for this place. I need to talk to either your grandmother or your cousin at once! Dealer's choice. Bring one of them to me this minute!"

After sulking back into the dining hall, Cristian appeared in the lobby a few moments later, with Erika right behind him. As she approached the neighbors gathered near the front door, Erika noticed their angry, expectant faces. She quickly glanced at Cristian, who looked tired as he led the way with slumped shoulders. Once they were within earshot of the Heads of Households, Elena Vulpe launched into what seemed to be an ultimatum.

"One month, Erika Farkas!" the Vulpe Matriarch declared with unmistakable anger.

"Good morning, Mrs. Vulpe. What's going on?" Erika asked, trying to ease the situation.

"We're giving you *one month* to get your household in order. You have until May. By the Flower Moon," Elena commanded. "You must have the ghosts and your family members under control," she added, then shot a displeased glance at Cristian.

"What exactly is the problem?" Erika asked, though she already suspected she knew the answer because of Cristian's sullen behavior.

"With all due respect, Erika, don't be so obtuse," Elena retorted sharply. "The whole damn town is off-kilter, and it all seems to originate from the shenanigans happening *here* at Dragos Manor! The hunters have been questioning us for over a year now about the disappearance of their colleague, Curt. While his going missing is most unfortunate, it's also putting unnecessary pressure on the Werewolf-Hunter Pact, which clearly states that Lycan society will cooperate with all investigations. The rest of us are making an effort to be helpful in the matter. However, the hunters have informed us that your family hasn't been cooperative."

"What? That's not true!" Cristian fired back. "We have been *very* cooperative! The hunters are just mad because we're making a stand against them disrupting our business!"

Elena looked at him with a wry smirk. "You must realize that your so-called *business* is incredibly dangerous on several levels. For one, you're pissing off Town Hall. They think it's reckless to have all these unsuspecting humans gallivanting with poltergeists and werewolves, and I tend to agree with them. Let's start with the Mischief—exactly, when did you notice that it migrated out of the cellar?"

"I believe it happened after my wedding when the ghost of my grandma and all the other house spirits disappeared," Erika responded.

"We've always expressed concerns about the danger of keeping spirits trapped inside this house. It's too much to manage, and Ana won't be around forever. Has she even shown you the maintenance spells necessary to keep your ghosts under control? You're putting anyone who enters at risk of something terrible happening. And let me tell you, if you're relying on Cristian to maintain the magic, well then, I have some news for you... *Cristian* does not possess the power needed to control this house! Do you even have it, Erika?" Elena demanded incredulously.

At that moment, several hotel guests came out of the dining hall, carrying plates and cups as they went up the staircase.

"No way am I eating in that creepy AF room! This place seems to get more haunted every day!" one person said as they followed the rest of their friends up the staircase. Erika heard this remark and assumed everyone else did as well. She turned back to meet Elena's stern gaze.

"One month," Elena reiterated quietly, then counted her demands off on each finger. "The hunters need to be satisfied with your contribution to their investigation; you must tone down this joke of a nightclub and control your spooky occupants; and lastly, and let me be *absolutely* clear about this—there better not be *any* more unexplained feral werewolves appearing in Nocturne. We all know ferals can emerge from time to time, but it's usually tied to a compelling reason and credible source. However, it is not common for a large number of those savage beasts to appear out of nowhere without a good reason. I suspect someone in this house might know more than they're letting on. One month... or there will be consequences. You are endangering us all. We don't care how you handle it, but *handle it*. You can start by seeing Ana immediately and asking her for the incantation needed from that potent spellbook of hers to get the magic inside this house under control."

"Erika, we know you're still finding your way in your new role, but please don't make everyone pay for the mistakes of *a few*," Shanice added. "We urge you to step up and take responsibility for your family before it's too late. Let us know if you need help once you find the spell for the house. While I humbly believe that there are no Lycans in this town whose power rivals the Dragos' magic, perhaps together, we can be of service to you. Please keep that in mind, dear."

With their final words of warning echoing in the air, the Heads of

Households turned to leave. As Beo moved to follow his parents out the door, he reached back and tried to touch Cristian's hand. Cristian sharply withdrew from his boyfriend's touch. Hurt flashed in Beo's eyes, deepening the disappointment etched across his handsome face until he disappeared out the front door and was gone.

Chapter Twenty-Four

SPILL THE TEA

The cousins watched the front door close, and then Erika looked around to make sure no one was within earshot as Cristian let out a loud sigh of relief.

"Well, *that* was a close one," he hooted. "I think I'm gonna hit the sack before anything else—"

Cristian didn't have a chance to finish his thought as Erika grabbed him by the collar, pulled him over to the ballroom, shoved him inside, and closed the doors behind them.

"Jesus Christ flavored crackers and bloody wine! What the hell did ya do that for?"

"Shut up!" Erika hissed.

"You coulda tore my Todd Snyder..."

"Shut up!" she repeated. "I don't care. Listen to me. My friend and I were *attacked* by those ferals last night. One of them had us pinned down, so close to our faces we could have kissed it! I don't know what would have happened if Blake and Marius hadn't shown up when they did. Do *you* know where those things came from?"

"Ahhhh, yes, as a matter of fact, I do. We made them," he replied casually.

"You made them?"

Cristian faltered. "Kessler made them. We thought it would be a good idea to create a diversion for those hunters that you so thoughtfully invited to search our property, so *we* could buy some time to figure out that *little problem of ours* buried on the edge of the forest."

"Well, that sounds like a dumb as fuck plan! You have no way of controlling a pack of ferals running loose! How do you know they won't cause an explosion of werewolves?"

"Well, what's your idea, *Erika*?" he fired back.

"I've been thinking about that. I think it might be a good idea if we just come clean. Tell the hunters what happened."

Cristian was stunned as he blinked approximately a dozen times while staring at his cousin in disbelief. Then his hands shot up to his face, and he vigorously rubbed his eyes. "Have you lost your mind?"

"I'm serious; it was done in retaliation for my fiancé's murder, who was human and in no way tied to our world. The hunters seem to be an *eye-for-an-eye* kind of crowd. We even have a witness who can corroborate that fact if we can somehow figure out how to get our house ghosts back. Adrian can tell them everything."

"That's your best plan? We have no idea why the house ghosts even disappeared!" Cristian said incredulously. Erika knew he was right; they didn't know for sure why the resident spirits had vanished into thin air. All she knew was that it happened after she had breached the brick wall on the 4th floor. "And who are we going to say killed him?" Cristian continued.

"Huh?" Erika asked.

"Curt," Cristian hissed quietly.

Erika shook her head and shrugged at this question. "I think this might be our best course of action."

"Oh my God! I'm so tired of your wildcard *bullshit*!" Cristian groaned, then froze as he realized what he had said. Erika could tell he was worried that he had overstepped and been disrespectful.

"Look, I'm doing my best to deal with the mess *you made*, Cristian. Yes, I'm glad you killed him, but I didn't *ask* you to do that. If you're going to be mad at anyone, be mad at yourself. I'm always freakin' there for you, always defending you."

"I'm sorry... I'm just tired and cranky. I should probably get some sleep," he said, not waiting for a response as he turned and headed toward the elevator.

"Cool, *you do that*. Don't worry about anything I *just* said. You get some rest; I'll handle it. Right now, I need to visit Ana and ask her about this damn *spell* I'm supposed to learn, so I can, you know, appease the Heads of

Households and see if I can get our ghosts back. No bigs," Erika scoffed. "I honestly can't believe half the shit that comes outta my mouth these days, even though I know none of it should surprise me anymore. *Magic* wouldn't be the weirdest thing in my life at this point."

Cristian hesitated when he heard this but kept his back to Erika. "Wait. I'll join you," he muttered.

A few minutes later, Erika gently knocked on Ana's bedroom door and waited. No reply came. She reminded herself it was still quite early, and maybe her elderly grandaunt was sleeping. Erika looked to Cristian for guidance, but he just shook his head, showing visible worry on his face. She realized he was probably nervous about seeing his grandma and knew their interactions lately had often been tense and very limited.

"I'm going inside. Give me a few moments," Erika instructed. Cristian nodded in agreement, looking relieved to prolong the encounter for a little longer. She reached down, opened the door to the spacious room, then stepped inside and quietly closed it behind her.

Ana's suite was brighter than Erika had expected. The room was tidy, with minimalist Edwardian décor arranged carefully. From a distance, she saw her grandaunt lying very still, propped up in bed and surrounded by decorative pillows. Ana's eyes were half-open with an unfocused gaze. Erika waved a hand, trying to get her attention, but the elderly matriarch did not move. Exhaling nervously, Erika walked toward the bed to gently wake her grandaunt. As she crossed the room, her eyes shifted to picture frames on the shelves and walls, showcasing old-fashioned black-and-white portraits. While her curiosity was piqued, she didn't want Ana to wake up and catch her looking through her belongings. When she got closer, Ana's unfocused expression became even more disturbing, and the reality of the possible situation finally dawned on Erika.

"Ana?" she called out with concern. The Dragos Matriarch remained unresponsive. Erika quickly closed the distance, plopped down on the edge of the bed, and placed her hands on her grandaunt's shoulders. Ana yelped and sprang up from the bed, accidentally knocking over the remnants of an old cup of tea on her nightstand.

"Good heavens, Sophia, you startled me. Are you trying to kill me?" Ana asked while clutching her heart.

"Aunt Ana, it's me, Erika," she said as she picked up the teacup and grabbed a cloth napkin from a nearby table. "I'm sorry for frightening you, but you *scared* me. I thought you were—"

"Erika?" Ana blinked as she looked more closely at her grandniece. "Where did Sophia go? She was just here a moment ago."

Erika looked around the room. There weren't many places, if any, for someone to hide. She got up, moved across the room, and quickly checked the large walk-in closet and the ensuite, both of which were empty. Although Erika had heard recently that Ana's mental health was getting worse, it was unsettling to see it firsthand.

"There's no one here, Aunt Ana," she explained compassionately. Ana began muttering something unintelligible. Thinking it best to refocus on what she had come for, Erika again approached the bed and launched into her query. "I came by to ask you about the magic spells that I need to know for the house." Ana stared back at her with confusion.

"Magic? Spells? House? Oh! You must mean the magic spells for the house," her grandaunt said, finally grasping the sequence of words.

"Yes, the other Heads of Household mentioned that there is a spell that you need to teach me so we can contain the magic in the house and keep it under control. They don't like that the Mischief has left the cellar. Also, I'm hoping we can figure out a way to get our house ghosts back. I'm not sure how many spells are needed to do all of that," Erika added, shaking her head in disbelief at the words coming from her mouth.

"Oh dear, you're right. I need to teach you those spells. How dreadful of me that I haven't done so yet. You will need to retrieve Sophia's spell book. I have it hidden. It contains some very powerful spells, so before I tell you where it is, you must first promise me that you, *and only you*, will ever be in possession of this book," Ana stated with the utmost seriousness.

"Ah, sure," Erika confirmed with apprehension. "But fair warning, I don't think I know how to do magic. What I mean to say is, I'm not very magical as far as I know," she said skeptically.

"Don't worry, my dear. I thought the same thing, too, at one time. But you can rest assured that the magic is inside you. You come from a long line of powerful female Lycans. Actually, I will quite enjoy teaching you. It will be interesting to see how your power differs from my own," Ana said with delight. "Since I'm not a direct descendant of Sophia Dragos and all."

"Okay, I will have to trust your faith in my abilities. I promise that I will not let anyone touch the book. Where can I find it?" Erika asked.

"It's in the—" Ana was in the middle of responding when her demeanor shifted sharply. "*It was Cristian. Cristian killed me,*" she muttered darkly in a voice that was an octave lower than her usual one.

"Excuse me?" Erika asked with confusion.

"*Yes, I admit that I killed the poor bastard, but the idea, the order, and the payment for his death all came from Cristian.*" The words spilled out from Ana's lips as if she were reciting something from memory.

"Aunt Ana, what are you saying?" Erika asked. The Dragos matriarch did not reply but kept looking out into the room. Erika followed her grandaunt's gaze and saw Cristian standing in the doorway.

"Did she just say my name?" he asked in a loud whisper.

"Yeah, but I don't know what she's talking about. She was about to tell me where Sophia's spell book is," Erika responded uncertainly.

"Our great-great-grandmother, Sophia?" he asked with interest.

"Yes," Erika responded dismissively, then tried to refocus Ana. "Aunt Ana, where is Sophia's spell book hidden?"

"*It was all Cristian. Cristian, Cristian, Cristian,*" Ana continued, but seemed to be conversing with someone else entirely. Erika looked over at Cristian, who only shrugged.

"What is she saying?" he whispered.

"She's saying, 'It was... *you,*" Erika responded with bewilderment.

"Me?" Cristian asked, his face screwed up in a question mark. "What did I do?"

"She's saying that you killed her. And that she killed someone, but she claims you paid her to do it?"

"Okay, that's weird. I obviously didn't kill her, and I certainly have never paid someone to..." Cristian stopped abruptly.

"She seemed to get distracted when she saw you just now. When's the last time you visited her?" Erika asked.

"I mean, I don't really do it because it seems to upset her like this."

"Well, I'm sorry to say it, but maybe you should leave. Don't worry, I will tell you whatever she tells me about this house magic spell thing, but she said I am not allowed to let anyone else touch Sophia's spell book."

"Yes, it's a containment spell," Ana chimed in as she seemed to snap back into the present moment. "And yes, I will instruct you on how to do it. You must retrieve Sophia's spell book, and I can show you how to call out your Luna energy."

"Okay, great! Where's the spell book?" Erika asked, relieved to be back on track. Ana's gaze shifted to Cristian, and a dark cloud seemed to pass over her face.

"I cannot recall," she replied, scowling distrustfully at her grandson. Erika glanced at her cousin, who looked devastated. She felt sorry for him.

"Listen, Aunt Ana, I know you *think* you're doing the right thing based on your 'beliefs,' but I can tell you right now that, in the end... you'll deeply regret hurting your grandson so profoundly." Ana looked up at Erika, her mouth slightly agape as if she was about to respond, but instead she cast her eyes to the floor and said nothing. "I will come back later, and I need you to tell me where that spell book is. Remember, I am the new Head of Household, so it's *your duty* to teach me what I need to know." These words hit Ana hard, just as Erika intended. She recognized that Ana's sense of duty outweighed anything else her grandaunt felt.

Erika turned to leave but paused briefly when she approached Cristian. "Are you okay?" she asked.

"Yeah, I'm okay. Thanks for... Just... thanks," he smirked. Erika nodded and left him to have a moment with his grandmother.

As soon as the door closed, Cristian looked down at his beloved Bunica lying in bed. She started muttering to herself again and apparently didn't notice that he was still in the room. He moved a little closer, feeling a strong desire to be near her. It was hard to feel negative emotions toward someone who had raised him his whole life. Especially now, seeing her in such a weakened and vulnerable state, his heart ached with sorrow... until he heard what she was saying.

"*Yes, it was all Cristian. Cristian, Cristian, Cristian. He hired me to kill Ryan. Can you please tell Erika all of this for me?*" Ana said while staring past her grandson. A chill ran down Cristian's spine. He stared unblinking at his Bunica. A rushing sound filled his ears. For a moment, he swore his vision turned red as the blood pulsated behind his eyes.

"Who told you that?" he asked, gulping back vomit in his throat and dreading his grandma's response. Ana's icy pale blue eyes drifted up to meet his.

"Why, Curt told me," she replied as a crooked smile curled at the corners of her mouth like uneven stage curtains. Cristian closed his eyes and nodded solemnly. His stomach twisted as he thought about what might need to be done to contain the situation.

Chapter Twenty-Five

VIGILANTES AND FUGITIVES

A heavy fist pounded loudly on the front door of Sterling Lodge. The unwelcome noise interrupted the peaceful morning the werewolf hunters had been enjoying after the long night they had endured.

"Sigh," Corbin said, stretching and rolling his eyes. "Why does the *tone* of that knock sound like a pain in my ass?"

"Maybe it's someone trying to sell us a religion," Beau remarked casually, sipping his black coffee.

"Damn, I never thought I'd *actually* wish for that. I could toss a softball 'Hail Satan' at them and send them on their way," Corbin snickered, shaking his head as he reluctantly went to answer the door.

"If that's your strategy, you'd better cover up that cross tattoo on your neck, my friend," Nawn said smoothly as she blew on the surface of a steaming mug of English Breakfast.

Corbin opened the door to find a group of townspeople gathered in front of him. Their faces revealed a mixture of anger and fear. Visitors to the lodge were rare, so Corbin quickly guessed that this visit would likely be a thorn in his side. So much for a peaceful morning.

"Good morning. How may I be of service to you fine folks?" Corbin asked, casually taking a bite of toast. Instead of answering, the townspeople pushed past him into the cabin. "Won't you come in?" he added sarcastically. Corbin recognized many of the people from the Foolish Goat. Even the gruff proprietor, Clarence, was present.

"A pack of those *things* was roaming around and terrorizing our homes last night. Some of our farm animals were killed. We are sick and tired of this sorta thing happening over and over again!" an angry guy named Travis explained, his tone was tense. There were murmurs of agreement from the other townsfolk.

"What exactly did you see?" Corbin asked, taking another bite of toast.

"What do you think?" Travis shot back.

"Could you have possibly seen a Black Bear? Maybe a Moose?" Corbin asked calmly as he finished the last of the toast and noisily sucked the butter off his fingers.

"It was those beasts!" another townie chimed in.

"Alright, alright. I'm just making sure we're all on the same page. Well, we appreciate y'all coming down here to let us know," Corbin said as he sipped his coffee. "We'll look into it and see what we can do." This response didn't seem to satisfy the crowd, especially Travis, who seemed to have a chip on his shoulder from the start. Corbin looked around, waiting for someone to say more. "Was there anything else?" he asked.

"How could you let all those creatures run loose *right* under your noses? I see, one, two, three... *six* of you here! What were you doing all night? Doin' your hair up like some gay Cockatoo while the rest of us were getting—"

"Terrorized," Corbin interrupted, finishing Travis' sentence. "I heard you the first time. I can assure you we are on top of it, but we can only say so much. You understand," he said with an audacious wink.

"Looks like you're having brunch to me," Travis remarked with disdain. Corbin spun around, feigning shock, and glanced at his group of hunters, their feet casually propped up on the table.

"Oh, yes... we eat... sometimes," Corbin confirmed sarcastically as he turned back to Travis, who looked ready to throw punches. Clarence stepped in and pushed Travis back with his burly arm.

"Listen, Mr. Sterling, maybe it would help ease our minds if you could share what you can about what y'all are planning to do about this," Clarence suggested in a calmer tone. Corbin smirked, appreciating the Goat man's de-escalation of the situation.

Certainly! We are aware of the creatures you saw last night. The plan is to track them down before the next Full Moon and stage an ambush, so they don't have the chance to create more," Corbin reported militantly.

"Naiche, here, is our expert tracker and will lead that effort. Those creatures should be *normal* again by now, so if anyone sees any naked people or notices clothes going missing from your property, kindly let us know. They will most likely keep to the woods or try to slip back into town. Keep an eye out for unusual campsites, folks camping with no camping gear, etcetera. Also watch for people wearing ill-fitting clothing or anything that looks like clothing you own. They might have stolen those without you noticing."

"Another telltale sign is that they will possess healed scars of the damned," Nawn added in a silky voice, with glimmers of silver reflecting off her lush, pouty lips.

"How about we do some cutting? Let's start with cutting the crap and cut to the chase! What about the Dragos family? We all know they're responsible for this! Those creatures came from their property last night," Travis shouted as he marched over and ripped a paper map of Nocturne off the nearby wall. Then he stomped back past the gathered crowd and slammed the map down on the oak table, causing Naiche, Carter, and Beau to quickly move their legs.

"I had one on my property here around eleven last night! Those sons a bitches got another one of my flock!" Travis said while pointing to a spot on the map that was not far from Dragos Manor. "Then Darren saw one tryna get into his chicken coup over here! The Kents had one on their roof, howling at the Moon til midnight! Nearly scared their elderly grandma to death!" As Travis pointed out each position on the map, a pattern began to form, showing that the sightings all seemed to spread out from a single location, with Dragos Manor being the center.

Corbin was not impressed by what was being presented to him.

"I'll say it again—I assure you all that we are on top of this. Unfortunately, I can't share any more information about our plan. I'll just say that we potentially have an informant working on the inside."

"Potentially?" Clarence asked, seizing on the word.

"Well," Corbin faltered. "We're still working on it."

"This plan sounds pretty half-baked," Clarence scoffed.

"Maybe we should call the *real* law enforcement to get the job done!" Travis suggested, looking around and trying to garner support. However, the idea was quickly shot down.

"You idiot," Clarence fired back. "Nobody has said it, but we're talking about *werewolves* here! You know our local boys won't do anything about it. They're paid to look the other way. So you're talking about escalating it? Do you really think we want *the government* and the FBI crawling all over Nocturne? We keep it *small-town* over here." This reality was met with murmurs of agreement.

"Then, maybe we should think about some good old-fashioned vigilante justice since these peckerwoods are moving so slowly!" Travis said, again trying to rally support.

"What you need to do is get back home and keep your eyes peeled," Corbin ordered. "Keep us posted on anything suspicious, and most importantly, stay out of our way! This situation has a lot of moving parts, so we don't need your group running off half-cocked and making our jobs harder. Trust us. We know what we're doing. We'll deal with the Dragos after addressing these ferals. Those people are probably out there right now, scared shitless! We need to take advantage of their lack of resources before they catch on. Let's hope they're a bunch of pansies that don't have any survival skills. That always makes them much easier to find. Like sitting ducks."

Outside the chicken coop, two naked people crouched behind a woodpile at the edge of the farm. Stanley's red mohawk no longer stood upright but drooped from a long night of... being a werewolf. Kathryn's long blond hair cascaded over her shoulders and breasts, leaving goosebumps on her exposed skin. The two assessed their next move before taking action.

"Okay, I'm headed to that clothesline to grab those sheets and pants. You try and grab a chicken if you can. Ready?" Stanley rattled off with his eyes fixed on the suspended linen. Kathryn was dazed. She stared in disbelief at the scene before her and didn't respond. Stanley turned and looked directly at her. "Kathryn! Are you ready?" he asked more emphatically. The Aussie shook her head no, indicating that she was not ready. "Go!" he called out in a loud whisper and sprang into action.

Kathryn remained frozen behind the woodpile, watching as her male friend, with his flaccid red mohawk and stark white butt cheeks, charged toward the laundry drying in the sun. He grabbed an armful of sheets and a couple of pairs of pants, then jogged back toward the woodpile where she was still crouched. Seeing him approach awakened her senses, and she assessed the latch on the nearby coop. She jumped up and frantically unlocked the cage, startling the feathered occupants. After a minor scuffle, Kathryn grabbed one of the hens and tucked the bird under her arm like a football, subduing its flapping wings. Then she and Stanley took off running through the trees, just as the sound of a screen door swung open and slammed shut hard against its frame. A gunshot rang out into the woods. The pair kept sprinting, both unscathed, grasping onto their newly gained supplies.

The fire danced and crackled as the plucked, crudely dressed chicken cooked slowly on the makeshift spit—a stick propped up on two large rocks. It was getting late in the day, and the three people sitting around the cookout started to hear the rumble of each other's stomachs. Kathryn wore a bedsheet like a toga, while Stanley and their other male companion, who they learned was named Jerome, were both grateful for their new pairs of pants.

"Okay, I was wrong," Jerome admitted. "I'm glad you guys killed the bird. I'm hungry after all."

"I'm thankful for your Boy Scout skills, Stanley. Well done, mate. I'm pretty thirsty. Any ideas about water?" Kathryn asked.

"If you guys keep an eye on the chicken and turn it over every few minutes, I can go look for some water," Stanley offered.

"I don't understand why we don't just go back to the hotel," Jerome whimpered. "My sister Jazmine hasn't shown up yet, and I'm thinking maybe she headed back that way."

"Are you kidding!" came Stanley's incredulous response. "Don't you realize what happened to us last night? Do you understand what we are and that those things at the hotel did this to us?"

"Okay, I got it. Jeez, don't have to be such a freakin' dick about it," Jerome complained with slumped shoulders and his face resting in his palms. "All I'm saying is that we'll eventually have to figure out a way to get home. We can't stay hiding in these woods forever."

"Am I seriously the only one who watches horror movies? Do you think getting turned into a werewolf is *optional*? What about the next Full Moon? Are you going to bite all your friends and family?" Stanley challenged. Upon hearing those words out loud, neither Kathryn nor Jerome said anything. "What we need is time. We need to solve our immediate problems—food, water, shelter, clothing, information," Stanley counted off on his fingers. "We don't know anything. We don't know if we're going to change again tonight. We don't know if the town is going to roll up here with pitchforks and torches—"

"Okay, Stanley! Just give it a rest, mate. Let's just calm down for a moment. We've all been through a lot. I get that we need to figure out our next move, but can we have five minutes of peace? Nacho is still missing as well."

At that moment, they all heard rustling in the nearby brush. Stanley jumped up and braced himself for a fight, but he relaxed when three more dazed and naked people approached.

"Hey, man. You cool?" one of the guys from the other group asked Stanley. Stanley didn't respond but simply turned around and crouched back down near his chicken, almost as if guarding it. The person who spoke from the newcomers looked anxious as he glanced at his companions, a man and a woman.

"Looks like you lot had the same rough night we did," Kathryn said with a wry laugh to help break the ice. "Where are you all heading?"

"We're headed back to the hotel," the guy replied.

"And then what?" Stanley scoffed.

"And then we're going to pick up my outfitted van. I lost my keys last night, but I have an extra set hidden in the wheel well. We need clothing and supplies, which I have—just not on me right now, as you can plainly see," the naked guy laughed. Hearing this, Stanley seemed to thaw a little.

"Awesome! Let me know if I can help out in any way," Stanley offered. "What's your name, bro?"

"Kyle. This is Alice and Alex."

"Kyle, nice to meet you, man. I'm Stanley, this is Kathryn, and that's Jerome." Kathryn realized that Stanley engaging with the person who could potentially assist them.

"So, I'm counting six of us here, but there were definitely more of us who got tricked into going to that fake-ass cabana party last night," Kathryn noted. "We should look for them. Our friend Nacho is missing, and so is Jerome's sister, Jazmine."

"We're in the same boat. Alex's girl, Lena, is missing," Kyle said, casting a crestfallen look at his sullen friend. "We should get my van, and once we set up a campsite, we can organize a couple of search parties. Who knows, they might even show up."

"Kyle." It was Alice. Her look said everything. She was tired and scared. "I thought we talked about going into town and alerting the authorities," she whimpered.

"Sure, just stroll into town and tell them what, exactly?" Alex started in a snide tone, but Kyle quickly shut it down.

"Dude, I know you're upset about Lena, but give her a break! I think we can give each other a little grace right now." Kyle's compassionate words lingered in the air for a moment.

"I can tell we have a great group of people here," Kathryn said. "Let's pool our resources and support one another. If nothing else, we can watch each other's backs. We might be all we've got. May I offer you all some of our impressive bounty?" Kathryn suggested, gesturing towards the chicken that would provide everyone with a few small bites of protein.

"Thank you for the generous offer. We'll repay you once we get our van back. We have plenty of food and water, and also a couple of tents, water purification tablets, an axe, and a bunch of other survival gear. I watch a lot of *Alone* and *Naked and Afraid*, which I guess we are right now!" Kyle laughed. "See, honey! I knew my post-apocalyptic moment would come!"

Kyle's face emerged from the edge of the tree line on the perimeter of the front lawns of Dragos Manor. He spotted his outfitted *Sprinter* van parked at an angle along the long dirt driveway. With most of the other cars gone at this time of day, the van was exposed, making it difficult for Kyle to reach it without being seen. He ducked back into the vegetation to consult with Alex and Stanley.

"Okay, I think my plan is to just go for it. This shouldn't take long; I just need to grab my spare key and take off. If anyone comes out, you guys are my backup. Create a distraction or something."

"Alright, man. You got this! You want my pants?" Stanley offered.

"Nah, it's cool, bro. I'll be more aerodynamic without them," Kyle said with a sly grin. Then he turned and faced the direction of the parked van, puffed out two quick breaths, and took off running bare-assed up the long driveway. The padding of his bare feet on the ground grew faint the further he got from Stanley and Alex crouching in the tree line.

Once he reached his vehicle, he disappeared around the other side. Soon, a high-pitched car alarm echoed throughout the area. Stanley and Alex tensed as the seconds seemed to stretch on like hours, with the alarm still ringing. Finally, the large black van's headlights flickered on, and the engine roared to life. The alarm stopped chiming, and the *Sprinter* van reversed, driving down the driveway.

Stanley exhaled in relief once all three guys were inside the vehicle, heading toward the rest of the group waiting in the expansive forest. They now had the supplies that they all desperately needed.

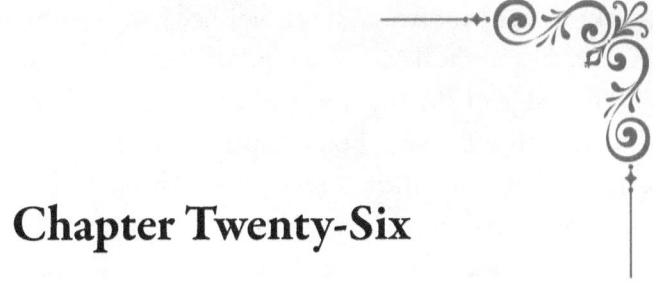

Chapter Twenty-Six

THE OTHER SIDE

The elevator cart arrived on the 4th floor, the doors opened, and Althea stepped out, carrying a small backpack over one shoulder. Her eyes immediately darted toward the daunting hole in the bricked-up doorway. She kept a close watch on the cavity, ready to retreat if the predator inside decided to strike. Despite her fear, a tiny spark of excitement grew—this was the moment she had been waiting for. With Erika's permission, Althea no longer had to tiptoe around the edges of this mystery. Yet now she faced a new challenge—solving it meant entering the unknown. There was no time to hesitate; she sensed that whatever was inside was the reason she had been called to Dragos Manor in the first place.

Althea stepped up to the opening, her senses sharp. She paused before climbing through and reached into her bag to prepare. First, she took out a headlamp and adjusted the band around her head, with the light resting on her forehead. Then, she pulled out the iPad and powered it on. The screen lit up, and she saw the battery icon in the corner—full. After tapping the Pacman ghost-looking icon to launch the PhantomGrammetry app, she raised the device and aimed it at the entrance. The monitor confirmed there was no paranormal entity inside. Althea steadied her nerves, stowed the tablet, switched on her headlight, and hoisted herself through the opening, landing firmly on the other side.

The headlamp lit up an elongated, dusty room that had been long neglected and forgotten. The air was stale, carrying an unexplainable but noticeable heaviness. Once again, she pulled the iPad from her backpack and quickly swept her surroundings. Satisfied that no otherworldly presence was nearby, she put the device away and started to scan the area visually.

The edge of the room was lined with several beds and old cots, some draped with yellowing sheets suspended from metal racks, forming flimsy barriers between them. Dusty stretchers and gurneys, along with cobweb-covered cupboards, shelves, and pantries, lined the walls. In the corner, there was a large, flat object, about the size of a person, covered with a dusty sheet. By all appearances, this room resembled a makeshift hospital that must have been used to treat people afflicted with illnesses. It was a peculiar amenity to find inside a hotel. *Unless it had been used before the hotel was established,* Althea mused.

As she looked around, trying to decide where to start her deep dive, she noticed a faint strip of light near the baseboards at the south end of the room. It seemed there might be a door there. She quickly and quietly crossed the room and tested the handle, only to find it was locked. She thought about applying a little force but ultimately decided against it. She didn't want to complicate her investigation by alerting the spirit she had encountered the night before.

Althea began working in the current room. She approached the covered object in the corner and pulled the sheet off. A cloud of dust swirled into the air as she observed the large standing floor mirror she had uncovered. Although it showed her own reflection, something about the mirror's presence made her feel uneasy. She struggled to shake off the creepy feeling. Next, she headed toward the cupboards when suddenly a flash of light reflected off a surface on the floor. She looked down and saw a hand mirror next to a disturbed dust spot on the floorboards. This must have been where Erika had been sitting when Althea found her the previous evening. Perhaps this mirror belonged to her. It didn't have the same dusty quality as everything else, though it was clearly an antique.

She reached down and grasped the handle. When she lifted the reflective side to her face, Althea was startled by what she saw. Confused, she turned the mirror over and briefly examined the backing. The pewter paisley design on the back was solid and didn't yield any clues about how this effect was occurring. Again, she turned the mirror over, and sure enough, the same unsettling image was still there. It was obvious that some kind of magic was at work, but time was precious, and she could not allow this oddity to hold her up; she needed to keep moving.

Althea tucked the mirror into her backpack and moved on toward the cupboards and shelves. The beam from her headlamp swept across several small glass bottles and vials with faded labels. *Some of the yellow labels had 'Genuine Aspirin,' 'Laudanum,' and 'Strychnine'* scrawled on them. Next to the bottles was a stack of small tin boxes labeled *'Hill's Cascara Quinine Cold Tablets.'* There were tattered cloth face masks and dusty bottles of wine that were sure to be vinegar by this point. She crouched down and opened a cupboard near the floor. After some rummaging, she pulled out a small wooden crate and set it on the ground. Inside was a thin stack of discolored monochrome photos, a box of slides, a few brass antiques, and various ephemera from another era.

Examination of a few fragile newspaper clippings revealed some telling articles—*Epidemic of Influenza Among Sailors in Boston; Spanish Influenza Epidemic Rages, Public Places Ordered Closed; Influenza Epidemic Checked In Nocturne.* Althea glanced at the dates of these articles. All fell between October and December 1918. Well, that sheds some light on what this room may have been used for, Althea thought. She recalled that Erika had mentioned the mansion was built in the late 1800s and that it once served as a boarding house. This improvised infirmary must have been part of the manor's evolution.

Next, she pulled out the stack of photos and the box of slides. Flipping through the photographs, she saw multiple images taken inside this room from different angles. There were occupied beds with various patients, with nurses wearing cloth masks tending to them. After thumbing through the photos, Althea turned her attention to the container of slides. There had to be a device to view them, so she searched and, sure enough, found a small wooden box shaped like a trapezoidal prism. Two lenses were on the narrower side, tapering out to a wider wooden stand designed to hold the slides. The word stereoscope came to mind as she recalled memories from a college photography class. She inserted the first slide into the front of the device and switched on her cell phone's flashlight to backlight the image. Althea brought her eyes up to the peepholes.

The first slide showed an image taken outside Dragos Manor. A group of people stood in front of the house—sullen and forlorn-looking individuals, some squatting or sitting in the front row. The back row was made up of plain, straight-faced people, a few dressed in nurses' uniforms. In the center stood a woman with striking features. She had dark, wavy hair parted down the middle. Her skin was porcelain white, and her lips were dark and full. Oddly enough, while Althea knew this was just a still image, she thought she saw the woman's eyes move slightly in her direction, as if to look directly at her. As she kept studying the slide, it seemed like the woman's straight mouth cracked into the faintest smirk, as if she had just heard the punchline of an untold joke.

Deep chills ran down Althea's spine, and she quickly looked around, her headlamp beam sweeping over the room that still seemed empty by all appearances. However, the temperature felt slightly colder than before. Her eyes were ill-adjusted from staring into the light. Althea sensed she should do another scan with the iPad just to be certain she was indeed alone. She placed her cellphone and the stereoscope on the floor beside her, pulled the tablet from her bag, and tapped the screen to wake it. The next careful scan of the room revealed no blips on the monitor. Doubts and worry coursed through her mind as she wondered if the device and app were working correctly. She was placing a lot of faith in this tool, hoping it was accurately telling her about the room's occupancy because her senses tingled, warning her that something was wrong.

Althea's cell phone vibrated against the hardwood floor, the loud, frenetic noise causing her to jump. She read the text from Kit—*Leave the iPad out and running.* Having someone watching her back felt reassuring. She propped up the tablet against the cupboard with the camera lenses facing into the room. This meant Althea couldn't see the monitor herself, but it made her feel better knowing Kit was watching over her. Another text came through—*That's a good spot. I can see you and see the room behind you. I know you're busy, but I can't wait to hear the report on what you've found! That place looks creepy as hell.*

Exhaling a small sigh of relief, Althea resumed her search. Next, she reached into the crate and pulled out a unique-looking oval frame mounted on a stand. The stand felt heavy like it was made of cast iron, but the light-colored metal gave it an intentionally gilded appearance. If there was an image inside the frame, it was indiscernible. She traced her fingertips over the surface and felt the intricate details embossed in the smooth porcelain. Her phone buzzed again. Kit's text read—*Lithophane, place light behind it to illuminate it.* Kit always loved the History Channel. Althea placed her cell phone flashlight behind the frame, which brought to life an etching. The molded portrait depicted a beautiful, dark-haired woman in old-fashioned clothing. The corners of her mouth were slightly turned up in a subtly coy smile. She looked remarkably similar to the woman featured in the slide.

Althea shifted her focus back to the stereoscope to compare the images. This time, when she examined the slide of the people standing out front of Dragos Manor, she noticed a gap in the crowd. The striking woman who was previously at the center of the image was absent. That's odd, Althea thought. Maybe she had accidentally selected the wrong slide.

The refrigerator door shut, and Kit's large stature emerged from the kitchen, carrying a plate of carrots, celery, and hummus. She popped a carrot stick into her mouth and headed toward the workstation she had set up in Althea's apartment above Stellar Remnants. Nicole was sprawled out with Gingersnaps across Althea's bed while the trio monitored the investigation unfolding on the other side of the US.

"Did I miss anything?" Kit asked as she offered the plate of veggies and dip. Nicole selected a carrot and took a bite.

"Nope. Not really. I mean, I can't really see exactly what she's doing with that night vision lighting."

Kit placed the healthy snacks on the desk in front of three large monitors, then took a seat and glanced at the monitor that displayed a live video feed of Althea rummaging in the mysterious room at Dragos Manor. As Kit scanned the murky environment, something caught her attention. She tilted her head to one side. In the background shadows of the room, something that appeared to be an obscured face came into view. There were distinct cheekbones, the hollows of two empty eye sockets, and a thin mouth. The face resembled a skull. Kit's eyes traced a faint outline of a feminine figure in an old-fashioned dress positioned about twenty feet behind Althea. A wave of alarm washed over her as she started to speak, but pieces of carrot lodged in her throat, causing her to choke. Nicole jumped up and clapped her firmly on the back.

"Oh my God, are you okay?" she asked. Kit continued coughing, red-faced, and pointed toward the video feed on the 8K monitor. She leaned in and turned the volume dial up. The sounds of Althea flipping through various slides and reviewing them on the stereoscope filled the room. Nicole followed where Kit pointed in the grainy depths of the dark background.

"There. In the background," Kit puffed out between gasping breaths. "Do you see that person?"

"That looks like a mannequin. I don't think that's real," Nicole speculated with a degree of confidence in her voice.

"I'm going to call Althea, just to be on the safe side." Kit picked up her cell phone, but before she could dial, something absolutely gut-wrenching happened. What they thought was an inanimate object began moving forward toward Althea. The movement seemed unnatural. The figure appeared to glide and made no sound as it moved.

As this peculiar individual became more visible, Kit realized it was an old woman with her hair pinned up in a passé bun, wearing a dark gray dress with a black lace trim. The figure drew closer to Althea, who still did not notice that anything was happening. The blood drained from Kit's face as she scrambled to dial Althea's number. The phone began to ring on the other end of the line, and a moment later, it could also be heard ringing from the video feed streaming on the monitor. Kit muted the audio to avoid feedback and watched as Althea jumped at the sudden sound. She placed a hand to her heart as she answered the phone.

"Holy shit, you—"

"Althea, listen to me. There's someone behind you. Turn around now!"

On the monitor, Althea whipped around and was now face-to-face with the old, withered woman, who appeared almost corpse-like in the night vision. The woman's face was gaunt and leathery, stretching over the contours of her skull. Kit waited on pins and needles for her friend to react to this creepy individual, but she was surprised when no reaction came. Althea craned her body around as she scanned the room, while the old woman remained still, inches away from her.

"Kit, I don't see anyone," came Althea's confused response. Kit's heart sank. A demonic smile slowly spread across the old woman's face.

"iPad! Pick up the iPad!"

On the monitor, Kit and Nicole watched Althea hurriedly turn and grab the iPad, but in her haste, accidentally knocked it off balance. The image of Althea and the creepy corpse woman tilted and fell out of sight as the device faced straight up toward the ceiling. After a moment, a shuffling sound could be heard, and the view on the monitor began pitching and rotating as Althea lifted the device and pointed it into the room. The old woman was nowhere to be seen.

Inside the abandoned medical room, Althea wielded the device, a cold sweat streaming down her face. She carefully scanned the area but grew frustrated when she couldn't see anything.

"Are you sure you saw someone?" she asked, trying to prop the cell phone on her shoulder. Then she gave up and switched the phone to speakerphone mode.

"I'm positive," Kit's deep yet feminine voice echoed throughout the room.

"We both saw her!" Nicole confirmed.

"Well, I'm not seeing—" Althea began, but her words trailed off when a cluster of dots slowly flickered to life on the iPad screen. Lines quickly connected them, revealing a rudimentary stick figure standing menacingly in the far corner of the room, near the locked door. "Is that what you saw?" Althea asked, frightened by the unexpected apparition.

"No. It was a full-blown old woman. What we saw wasn't just dots and lines. She didn't look like a ghost, except maybe in the way she moved," Kit's voice was tense. "Althea, I think you should leave *right now*. I have a bad feeling about this."

"Let me try to rotate around this thing and see if the sensor can pick up more details of its form," Althea said, taking slow steps and moving the device around the entity. The shape of a beautiful woman with dark, wavy hair parted down the middle, porcelain white skin, and full lips began to emerge on the device screen. She wore an old-fashioned, turn-of-the-twentieth-century gray dress with black lace trim at the bottom. It was amazing how much more detail Althea could capture compared to the poltergeist she had been monitoring downstairs. "Holy crap, do you guys see her?"

"Yeah, except she looked like a withered corpse before. She's younger now but looks like a cobra ready to strike. Get outta there," Kit urged.

As if on cue, the shape of the ghostly woman suddenly grew larger on the iPad monitor. It was too late when Althea realized that the entity was charging. She looked up just as an unseen force violently collided with her, knocking her to the floor. A white-hot, searing pain began radiating through Althea's torso like something was cutting her flesh. Althea fought and struggled to regain the upper hand; the only problem was that she couldn't see her attacker and didn't know which direction would offer an escape. Still, she battled until she finally managed to scramble to her feet. She quickly grabbed her gear, ran straight for the hole in the bricks, and clawed her way back to the other side.

Althea fell onto the hallway floor on the other side of the wall, then quickly raised the iPad to the opening, her heart pounding with anticipation. To her surprise, the entity was there before her, but it had transformed back into a simple stick figure instead of the captivating image of the beautiful woman she had seen moments earlier. The stick figure seemed to briefly fix its gaze on her, giving a silent warning, before it slipped back into the shadows beyond.

"Thea! Thea! Are you okay?" Kit and Nicole's voices were overflowing with concern. Althea lifted her phone, still held tightly in her hand.

"Hey," she answered breathlessly. "Yeah, I'm fine—a few scratches, but nothing serious. I can't believe that thing can push me over like that."

"Thank God! That looked freakin' terrifying," Kit commented. "Please tell me you're done and won't go back in there."

Althea was quiet for a moment as she considered Kit's request. But in the end, she knew it was one she wouldn't be able to fulfill.

"I'll call it quits for now, but I *have to* go back in there. All this bitch did today was demonstrate that she has secrets to hide. And I intend to find out what those secrets are."

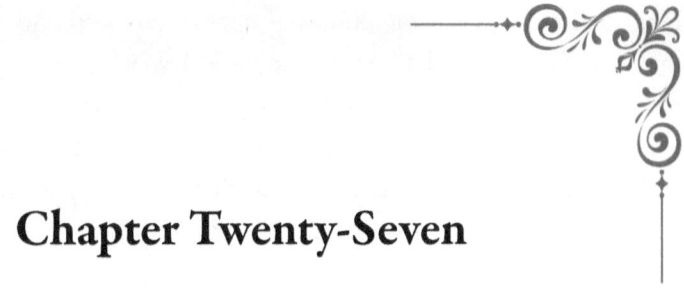

Chapter Twenty-Seven

THE POWER

Erika sat on the chaise lounge near the large windows in her bedroom suite. She was attempting to do something she hadn't done in a long time—relax and read a book. At least, that was what she was trying to do. Unfortunately, she found it hard to concentrate on the story in her hands. Erika read the same sentence a third time but finally gave up, rested the novel in her lap, and looked out the windows. The fading sunlight cast long shadows across the front lawns.

If she was being honest with herself, Erika recognized that she had been hiding in her room to avoid her Uncle Marius. Ever since the other Heads of Household issued their ultimatum earlier that morning, she had been preparing herself for the inevitable lecture. She was surprised that Marius hadn't come looking for her to discuss the incident. Surely, he had heard what happened by now.

She glanced at a nearby clock. It was nearly 5 pm. Erika briefly considered heading downstairs for a cocktail to ease the dull headache she'd been carrying with her most of the day, but that would mean leaving her room. Ultimately, the idea of delaying a potentially tedious conversation was more appealing than *the hair of the dog*. So, in an effort to distract herself, Erika allowed her thoughts to drift off to more pleasant contemplation.

Erika daydreamed about Althea. Her heart ignited at the thought of their undeniable connection. At first, Erika had reservations about agreeing to stay away from that room behind the brick wall on the 4th floor, but something about Althea's intriguing nature ultimately convinced her. Erika now realized that the spellbinding quality was authenticity. It had been a long time since Erika had trusted anyone. A wry laugh escaped her lips as she reflected on the reason why—*The last time I let myself trust someone, I ended up fucking my fiancé's killer.* Perhaps she was foolish to be putting her faith in another stranger so soon, and yet, a small flame had sparked inside her. Erika's heart had been left out in the cold for so long now that she reveled in this tiny bit of warmth.

At that moment, a knock sounded at her bedroom door. Erika rolled her eyes as she suspected who that might be.

"Yes, what is it?" she called out, irritation bubbling up in her voice. The door opened, and Marius stepped inside. He glanced around the room as he approached.

"Evening, Erika. Is, ah... Blake around?"

"No, he woke up a little bit ago and went downstairs to get something to eat."

"I see. I was just about to do the same thing myself, but then I received a phone call from Malcolm Sr."

Oh boy, here it comes, Erika thought. She shifted awkwardly in her seat.

"He told me about the visit this morning and mentioned the families' concerns," he said, attempting to muster diplomacy. Now, Erika kicked herself for not going downstairs to get that drink after all. If she got cornered at the bar, and then at least she'd have a cocktail in front of her to make this conversation more bearable. Marius must have noticed her restlessness and immediately assured her. "Let me be clear—I am not here to lecture you. Rather, I am here to strategize solutions to these problems with you."

"What do you mean?" she asked with a soft sigh.

"Right now, our biggest concern is finding out where those ferals came from. I'm not necessarily asking you this question, but it's something very serious that we need to get to the bottom of. By the way, are you alright after that close call with them last night? Was your friend bitten or scratched at all?"

"No, fortunately, she wasn't injured. Thanks for showing up when you did. It might have been a different story if you hadn't."

"I can imagine those creatures must have given you two quite a fright. I'm glad you're both okay. As I mentioned, it's crucial that we determine where they came from. Granted, ferals happen. It's unfortunate when they do, but usually, we have some idea of their origins. It's our responsibility to assist the hunters with mitigating any potential spread."

"I know. It's truly awful. The bitten, or whatever you call them, didn't ask for their fate and now face death because of our kind's recklessness," Erika responded with disdain. "I think the 'solution' is not only cold-blooded, but frankly, I think it's lazy."

"I agree with you. However, our circumstances are such that we live alongside our human neighbors, which brings certain responsibilities. Here in Nocturne, we have something called *Representative Town Meetings*, led by Town Meeting Members. A small group of these members is aware of our presence and discreetly advocates for Lycan interests in exchange for semi-annual dues to Nocturne."

"Bribery?"

"Not exactly," Marius said with a slight wince. "Think of it more like a de-escalation tax; revenue that helps keep our families out of the crosshairs of suspicion from the larger population. The *informed* Town Meeting Members alleviate any anxieties that arise about us. For our part, the werewolves of Nocturne strive to maintain a low profile. Suffice it to say that the emergence of a large pack of ferals that nobody seems to have any knowledge about doesn't support our effort to remain low-key. Neither does operating a large nightclub in our conservative, small town. Cristian's nightclub attracts many outsiders, both human and werewolf. Now, I will be the first to admit that Dragos Manor, as a business, must be allowed to adapt to the changing times. This idea applies to our community as a whole. I believe we all, including our neighbors, could benefit from being more flexible to allow room for change. After all, according to the philosopher Heraclitus, the only constant thing in life is change. The future will inevitably belong to the younger generations, so it's only fitting that you all leave your mark on it."

Erika nodded, feeling hopeful that this conversation might not be as painful as she had initially feared. She realized that she had underestimated her uncle's ability to see multiple perspectives.

"Thank you, Marius. For a moment, I was worried that you might side with Elena and the other Heads of Household." Marius smirked at this remark.

"On the other hand," he continued. "If the changes push our community too far, too quickly, they could create the unintended consequence of causing friction and division. The expansion of our business must not come at the expense of such a significant liability. There's always a balance to strike between the old ways and the new." Erika groaned as she stood and began pacing the room.

"I'm *trying* to navigate balance, but it's tough because I can't make everyone happy," she said, her voice tense despite her efforts to keep it steady. "Plus, I have my own shit to deal with too, you know."

Marius exhaled slowly. "I'm not concerned with pleasing everyone. My only concern is you and your cousin. I want to help guide you both towards happiness and stability."

"Me?" she scoffed. "You don't need to worry about me. I get why you'd worry about Cristian. That guy's rapid-firing bad decisions left and right! Get this—he's mad at *me* because the hunters want to search our property, even though I never told him to kill the *very person* they're looking for, and I didn't tell him to hide the body at the edge of our lawn! And now, we all have to deal with the fallout! Did any of that, *by chance*, come up in your conversation with Malcolm Sr.?" At this, Marius stared out the window, frowning. Erika rolled her eyes, immediately feeling guilty for taking her frustrations out on her uncle. "Ugh, look, I'm sorry, Marius."

"No need to apologize. I understand the precariousness of our situation and your frustrations with it. As I mentioned, I came here this evening to strategize solutions with you," he reiterated, his words making more sense to her now. Erika's eyes roamed around the room as she recalled each point of Elena's ultimatum.

"I'm open to being solution-focused when it comes to growth within our community. I think we can stand to tone things down around here," she remarked after a moment. "But for the record, I don't think Cristian's success is a bad thing. I think he simply wants acceptance, which has not come easily for him in this family. And now he's finally finding it through his business and the patrons who appreciate it."

"Your perception runs deep, and I agree with your assessment. However, I must make one correction—my mother is the only member of this family who has not yet found acceptance for him. The rest of us have always accepted him for who he is," Marius pointed out.

"About their other concern—that I get the Mischief under control—Elena Vulpe mentioned that there's some magic I need to learn. I talked with Ana earlier today, and she agreed to teach me, but I'm worried I might not have the power everyone thinks I do. At least, I've never seen any evidence that I can perform any *magic spells*," Erika said sarcastically. "Do you, by chance, have any advice?" she asked.

Marius raised his eyebrows at the question. He began pacing around the room, eventually stopping in front of the window and staring intently at the front lawns, now wrapped in a gentle cloak of dusk.

"The power is a very mysterious thing," he mused aloud. "Even I cannot claim to understand it fully. You were born with inherent magical abilities, which is why females of our species are revered as superior and more sacred than males. This is also why you all lead the packs and the households," he said with a smile as he turned to face her. "The strength of the power varies from individual to individual. Your great-great-grandmother, Sophia, the founder of Dragos Manor, possessed powerful magical abilities that have been passed down to all her female descendants. So, to answer your question—yes, I am quite certain you should have it, and my mother will need to show you how to use it."

"Did my mother possess the power?"

Marius seemed thoughtful before he responded. "She did," he finally confirmed, somewhat cautiously. "I mentioned that it was quite strong in her, and yet, this is the same reason I'm so concerned about you," he stated soberly.

"You keep saying that," Erika said with exasperation. "Why are you so worried about me?"

"I'm worried because of what you said a moment ago—that *'you've got your own shit you're dealing with*,'" he echoed her words back.

"I appreciate your concern, but as I mentioned, you don't need to worry about me," Erika insisted.

"With all due respect," he persisted. "The reason I am so worried is that, quite honestly, I have seen this all before." His words blindsided her. She opened her mouth to retort but stopped short as she turned away, realizing where her uncle was heading with this remark. "It feels all too familiar," he said gently. "I don't want history to repeat itself with what happened to your mother." Once more, the sentiment struck her hard as she tried to conceal the pain creeping onto her face. "You have a connection that runs deep inside you, one that you do not fully understand. You must be careful to maintain a healthy mind and heart to keep it under control. Depression, despair, resentment, overindulgence—all of these can lead you to dark places. It has sadly happened to many individuals in our family. These troubles, unfortunately, run deep in our DNA."

"I'm fine," she reiterated defensively.

"Erika, I'll be direct—I know you've been spending time on the 4th floor; you're going into that room that was sealed off. Your mother did the same thing. She tried to bury her pain by digging into the shadows of the past, but you need to be careful. You'll end up chasing reflections in a house of mirrors. You can't let darkness overtake your life."

"You have nothing to worry about," she said, suppressing the bitter lump that swelled in her throat at the thought of the tragedy that had befallen her late mother.

Marius nodded solemnly. He must have sensed that Erika was overwhelmed, so he walked over and hugged her.

"I'm sorry to be so straightforward about this, but you mean a lot to me, and I can't afford to lose you too. We don't have to delve into it any further right now, but please know I will always be here for you. You're not alone. Together, we can weather any storm, and when we emerge, you'll come out stronger on the other side," he said, kissing her forehead. After that, thankfully, he turned and walked toward the door. Erika watched him leave, relieved that the conversation had wrapped up for the time being and grateful to Marius for knowing when she needed space. As a token of appreciation, she decided to extend a small gesture to him.

"I'm not going up there anymore," Erika blurted out. Marius paused at the door and turned to face her. "To that room on the 4th floor. I promised Althea that I wouldn't. She offered to investigate it before I go back in there again. It's so strange; we only met recently, but she's already proving to be one of the best friends I've ever had."

"Well, I'm relieved to hear that, but please tell your friend to be careful, for her sake. At least she should be better prepared to handle what's up there with her experience and those fancy gadgets. Again, please express my apologies for what happened with those ferals last night."

"You know, as funny as it sounds, we actually had a pretty good time last night," Erika said as the warm feelings returned and washed away her lingering heartache. "Right before the ferals showed up, we were jogging through the grass under the stars and moonlight. We were having a nice conversation, and... and I just remembered, I saw something strange in the woods last night."

"What kind of something strange?" he asked with mild curiosity.

"Lights," Erika said pensively, remembering the feeling inside when she saw them. "At first, I thought it was the hunters, but the way they moved... almost like fireflies, but they were too large to be fireflies."

"It doesn't surprise me. There are many strange and unsavory occupants in those woods. The Full Moon tends to bring them out," he replied.

"I felt an irresistible urge to follow them," she confessed, as her thoughts returned to the captivating allure of those mesmerizing dancing orbs again. "But Althea distracted me, and then the ferals appeared. I forgot all about those lights until now."

"Well, I'm glad your night wasn't entirely traumatizing after what happened to you two. We can discuss this more later. Right now, I need to find that cousin of yours and see what he has to say about those ferals." Marius shot her an exhausted glance before continuing out the door.

Cristian was wildly frustrated. He frantically paced inside the ballroom as doubt swarmed around and gnawed at his mind. The pressure was beginning to feel overwhelming. The constant complaints from the local families surrounding his nightclub, the hunter's relentless probing, and Erika's unpredictable behavior weighed heavily on him.

"I can't believe she actually suggested that we tell the hunters that I killed Curt. Like that won't automatically be a death sentence for me!" he exclaimed ferociously.

"Darling, do not fret, my love," Vittoria drawled as she watched Cristian walking back and forth.

"And what am I supposed to do about your mom, Kessler?"

"Ya know, there is always the option to just blow off all of their demands," Kessler suggested. "We're adults. Our parents want to order us around like we're little kids, but the reality is that you're running the show at the biggest Lycan household in Nocturne!"

"Oh really? I didn't see you running out and telling your mom to back off when she was telling me I have one month to get my shit together!" Cristian fired back.

"Don't worry about it! I, like, disagree with her. This is just the typical parent-child struggle. Personally, I think our parents see your power and influence and are intimidated by it. You should really let that sink in. Be proud of your success and accomplishments. I don't think you should give in to them at all. What we should be talking about is how to keep you as Head of Household permanently. Otherwise, we're just surrendering all this power," Kessler remarked.

"Speaking of power, what is this *great power* that Erika is supposed to possess?" Cristian wondered aloud. "We need to find out the magic spell to maintain the house magic. Ana clammed right up as soon as she saw me when she was talking to Erika about it earlier. Why are females so secretive about that shit?" he scoffed.

"Yeah, Vittoria. What do you know about this magic business? I know it's, like, a *feminine thing*, but I wonder if it's something males can learn, too. Do you have it? What can you do?" Kessler asked as he and Cristian both eagerly turned toward Vittoria.

"I mean, sure, I know a few family charms and spells—memory charms, love spells, protection spells," she said, listing them on her fingers. "But it's not like I can shoot lightning bolts from my hands or anything," she said, then melodramatically gesticulated into the air. Nothing happened. Cristian and Kessler exchanged amused looks. "But I also have never seen anywhere near the level of magic that exists within these walls," she admitted dryly. "Bringing spirits back from the dead seems like advanced work."

"Maybe you can learn the Dragos spell," Cristian suggested. "Maybe you can even teach me, or something. Then we wouldn't necessarily need Erika to fulfill any HoH duties at all."

"That's a great idea. Then, when Erika *'goes missing,'*" Kessler chimed in with air quotations. "We will be completely self-sustainable without her."

"What are you talking about?" Cristian asked incredulously.

"I just mean in terms of the *Erika problem*—What if there was an accident? What if there simply *was* no female HoH to take the role? Then it would have to be you. No questions asked. That would solve all your problems."

"What the hell are you talking about?" Beo demanded as he approached the group. Everyone spun toward him in shock. He must have slipped through the doors without them noticing. "Cristian, are you seriously entertaining this?"

"Beo! I didn't hear you come in. We are just shootin' the shit. Of course, we weren't serious," Cristian said with an offhanded wave.

"Uh-huh, just like when you were kicking around the idea of creating all those ferals last night, and then guess what happened? You guys are taking this all way too far," Beo chided.

"Oh my God, Beo! Would you do me a favor and crawl outta my ass for five fucking minutes? I was just asking Kess a question, for fuck's sake! You're always so ready to assume the worst of me and jump down my throat!" Cristian fired back. Maybe it was a bit of an overreaction, but his fuse was short. There was too much on his plate right now, and he didn't need anyone to pile on more bullshit.

"I'm sorry that my *valid concerns and reasoning* are such a burden to you while you're in the throes of making your poor choices. My... fucking... bad. No problem, Cristian. I'll back off. You can have all the space you need. I'm done!" he said, his voice full of steel that sliced through the atmosphere. Cristian watched the mistake unfold in real time, but his pride kept him from undoing what was happening. When he said nothing, Beo gravely nodded, turned, and marched out of the room. Cristian was too angry to pursue him, and he rolled his eyes bitterly as Beo disappeared through the ballroom doors.

"Well, maybe it's better that I'm single right now. I need to bury myself in problem-solving anyway," Cristian sneered as he brushed off the encounter. The door opened once more, and Cristian's head shot up hopefully, but then his shoulders slumped when he saw Marius approaching, wearing that same old look of concern that Cristian realized he was so tired of seeing.

"What happened to Beo? I just saw him leaving. He seemed upset," Marius commented. Vittoria and Kessler exchanged glances, but no one offered any explanation. "Very well," Marius said after a moment of silence, then turned to his nephew. The gravity that accompanied his demeanor was instantly irritating. "Cristian, I was wondering if I might have a word with you?"

"What is it?" Cristian groaned in response. Marius ignored the tantrum and continued.

"There was a large pack of ferals roaming around last night, and I was wondering—"

"We made them," Cristian blurted out before he could think it through. Everyone was stunned. The room fell silent as the words still hung in the air. *Oh well, fuck it!* Cristian thought to himself. *Looks like we're doing this.* "We were trying to create a diversion to keep the hunters busy."

"My God. What were you thinking? You cannot create those creatures so recklessly!" Marius scolded. "You know our duty to this town! To society, to ourselves! You are way out of line!"

"Honestly, I just need *you*, Beo, and everyone else to get off my back! I've had it!" Cristian fumed as he started to march away from his uncle.

"Cristian!" Marius yelled after him. Cristian froze, groaned, and turned around. Marius visibly fought to maintain his composure, surely angry at his nephew. "I will not force you to accept my help, but know that I will always be there if you find yourself in over your head," he said earnestly, though with subdued tension in his voice. But Cristian didn't care.

"Well, I don't need your help," he replied indignantly. "I'll handle it myself."

Marius stared at his nephew with pain in his eyes, but to Cristian's surprise, he didn't protest or pursue the matter further. Instead, he turned and walked out of the room.

Cristian returned to where Vittoria and Kessler sat, plopped down into a nearby chair, and buried his face in his hands.

"Ugh, I have the *worst* headache," he whimpered. "How am I gonna get Marius and everyone else off my back?" Cristian, Kessler, and Vittoria were silent for a moment. It was Vittoria who finally broke the silence.

"Maybe we should consider removing your uncle from the picture, darling. I know he has been stressing you out for some time now," she suggested. Kessler and Cristian snapped their heads in her direction.

"What do you mean?" Cristian asked nervously. "What do you want to do to him?" Vittoria merely smiled at his anxious line of questioning.

"Oh, darling, don't worry. I would never harm him," she clarified. "But we could distract him. I'll try to dig up some dirt on him to use as leverage to help manage his movements for a while."

"Ha! Good luck, my uncle is a saint," Cristian said almost deliriously. Vittoria grinned mischievously.

"Give me some time. I will do a little digging. I will find something." Her words came out like silky poison. "Trust me, darling. Everyone can't be a good guy all the time. I'll find something."

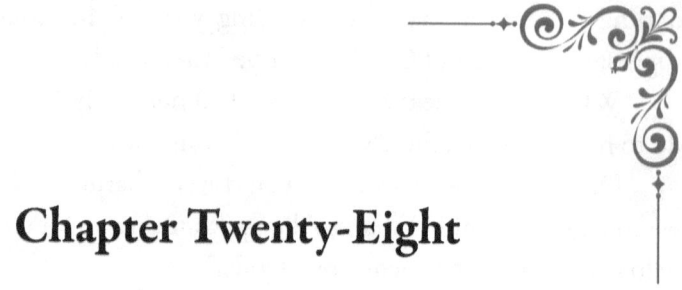

Chapter Twenty-Eight

SOMETHING SMELLS ROTTEN

One Week Later

The door to the *Sprinter* van swung open, and Kyle stepped out into the morning sunshine. Alice soon appeared behind him, followed by Alex, who looked like he hadn't slept in days. Kathryn, Stanley, and Jerome were already seated around a small fire that Stanley had built. Two tents stood about thirty feet away, which Kyle had lent to them. They all exchanged sullen morning greetings as the group from the van joined those around the fire.

So far, they had been unable to find Alex's girlfriend Lena, Kathryn and Stanley's friend Nacho, or Jerome's sister Jazmine, nor any of the other people who had been ambushed on their way to the ill-fated party in the woods just a week prior. After acquiring Kyle's van and establishing a hidden campsite, Kathryn, Stanley, and the rest of the group conducted daily searches for their missing friends. Yet, with each passing day yielding no results, despair began to weigh heavily on Kathryn. She pictured those poor, frightened souls wandering lost in the woods. It was her hope that they had found each other and worked together to seek out resources and shelter in their time of need. Kyle must have sensed the turmoil in Kathryn's heart.

"Don't worry; we'll find them," he said, trying to reassure her. His remark was met with glum expressions. While the group attempted to remain positive, a sense of hopelessness had escalated. "We were just saying that maybe a few of us should venture into town to grab some extra supplies. I'm still fairly well-stocked in the van, but there's no reason we shouldn't aim to keep it that way. We can take turns so everyone can enjoy a little change of scenery. Who knows, maybe we'll find our lost friends or discover some news about them."

"But what if someone is looking for us?" Jerome asked.

"Like who?"

"I don't know. Anyone. Like those *things* from that house."

"I'm pretty confident that we can slip into town without being noticed. When we first arrived in Nocturne to check out that club, there seemed to be a lot of tourist-type people on Main Street. I'm sure we could blend right in."

"I must say, mate, that I agree with Jerome. I'm somewhat hesitant to go into town, but on the other hand, you're right; our friends might be there. We could be sitting out here for nothing," Kathryn added.

"Why don't Alice and I just go, then?" Kyle suggested. "We can pretend to be on our honeymoon, and I'm sure people will leave us alone."

The group reluctantly agreed to the plan, and Kyle and Alice began preparing for their trip to town.

Corbin Sterling ascended the concrete steps of a red brick building with white trim in downtown Nocturne. A large, forest-green sign that matched the shutters and door displayed the words *Town Hall* in bronze lettering. Upon entering, Corbin proceeded down a narrow hallway with creaking floorboards that groaned with each step until he reached the end of the corridor and a staircase leading to the 2nd floor. He trotted up the steps and found himself in front of a closed door with a brass nameplate reading, *Vincent Smith*. Corbin knocked on the door and waited for a response.

"Come in," called a friendly male voice from inside.

This office belonged to the current de facto leader of the Town Meeting Members, who had requested Corbin's presence that day.

"Good day, Mr. Smith. You wanted to see me, sir?" Corbin asked as he walked through the door.

"Yes, Corbin. Come on in," Mr. Smith invited, gesturing to an empty chair beside one occupied by a woman who appeared to be a corporate executive. "Do you know Mrs. Vulpe?"

"Oh, Vincent. You know you can call me Elena," she said with a warm smile.

"My mother raised me to be polite and to respect women, which is why I typically lead with formalities. Now, where were we? Oh yes, Elena was just mentioning that *the families* are committed to doing whatever it takes to assist with our little pest control problem."

"Thank you kindly, Mrs. Vulpe. As you know, we have extensive experience in that area. The most helpful thing *the families* can do for me is inform us of the whereabouts of our missing hunter, Curt Siodmac," Corbin said matter-of-factly.

Mr. Smith laughed nervously. "Now, Corbin, let's not throw around accusations. The reason I called you in here today is to secure your ironclad assurance that *none* of Nocturne's residents will be disturbed over what is quite possibly a misunderstanding."

"A misunderstanding? Our man is missing! My team has spent over a year trying to track him down. Then, when I arrive with reinforcements and confront the Dragos family, a dozen ferals are miraculously released in the area. Some might see that as intentional enemy action."

"Corbin! You are out of line! You don't have any proof of those allegations. People are innocent until proven guilty, not the other way around. I did not invite you here today to insult Mrs. Vulpe or me," Mr. Smith barked.

"Mr. Smith, Mr. Sterling. Please, gentlemen. Let's sit down and talk this through in a calm manner. Now, Mr. Sterling, is it alright to call you Corbin?"

"Knock your socks off, Mrs. Vulpe."

"Thank you. Now, Corbin. You probably don't remember me, but I've known you since you were a small boy when your dad worked in this area. Our families and hunters have always maintained a good working relationship. I asked Vincent to invite you here today so that you know you have the backing of the Vulpes, Aristides, and Lupus. As a gesture of good faith, we wanted to extend some funding toward your effort to help us with that *pack of problems* we both share." With that, Elena unclasped her purse, reached in, and pulled out a large envelope that bulged with the shape of three neat rolls inside. "Remember what I'm saying—the Vulpes, Aristides, and Lupus. I'm sure you know our sons."

Corbin stared momentarily at the envelope offered to him. He knew that everyone in the room had experience with moments and transactions like this. What was implied was that all Corbin needed to do was take the money, which bought a certain level of grace for the families Mrs. Vulpe mentioned. However, this time, there was more at stake than usual. Corbin looked at Vincent and Elena as he stood up.

"What about our missing man?" he asked of the room.

"Mr. Sterling, I don't get paid to solve crimes. I suspect Mrs. Vulpe doesn't either."

Corbin pursed his lips and nodded, reached out, and took the proffered envelope. "Thank you kindly, Mrs. Vulpe. We need all the support we can get to handle our little pest control problem. Just to clarify, no price could compensate for our missing man. The Pact states this very clearly, so I'm sorry to say, but if the Vulpes, Aristides, or Lupus are involved, this," he waved the envelope, "doesn't cover it." Then he turned and stalked out of the room, leaving the door wide open behind him.

Once Corbin reached the bottom of the steps and the creaking of the wooden floorboards receded, signaling his departure from the building, Elena turned back toward Vincent Smith. She glanced at his desk and picked up a photo of Vincent with his two young sons on a fishing trip.

"Vincent, you know what it's like to be a parent. You would do anything for them, right?"

"Why, yes, certainly, Elena."

"I need *your* assurances that no matter what, you won't let the town, or those hunters, retaliate against our boys," she said, pulling a larger envelope from her purse and sliding it across to the Town Meeting Member.

"Elena, like my predecessor before me, I sympathize with Nocturne's *unique* residents and am eternally grateful for what *the families* do for our community. You all ensure that Nocturne doesn't have to rely heavily on tourist dollars, which helps keep our town the way we like it—quiet and peaceful. Of course I understand, Elena," Vincent said, taking the envelope. "You have my full support, which also comes with the backing from

Nocturne's Sheriff."

The large *Sprinter* van was parked in the woods, about one hundred fifty yards from the outskirts of downtown Nocturne. Kyle and Alice wove their way through the brush, quietly emerging at the edge of town. After another fifteen minutes of walking, they reached Main Street and entered the first general store they encountered. A small bell sounded as they stepped through the door. The store owner was chatting with a local man, who immediately cast a judgmental glance in their direction.

"Damn hipsters," the townie muttered, not-so-quietly under his breath. Kyle and Alice ignored the remark, picked up a basket, and began perusing items in the small store. They were giddy as they filled their basket with excitement. When Kyle and Alice entered the canned goods section, they started grabbing cans until a comment caught their attention.

"So, has anyone seen any sign of those *cursed* people?"

"Naw, that little queer-boy hunter thinks they're keeping to the forest."

"So? Go out to the forest and get them, then! Shesh, are they even really hunters? I can name a dozen good Nocturne men who would have already shot those beasts. Has that short-girly-fella even confronted the Dragoses about this yet?"

"I hear they've been too busy chasing fairy lights in the forest to do anything about the Dragos or those beasts lurking in the woods."

"That Corbin guy is just a bunch of gibber jabber. '*Watch out for people stealing clothes, or stockpiling food, or setting up camps with no equipment,*'" the shopkeeper laughed, then his voice caught in his throat. "Uh oh... here the little fancy-man, come now."

At that moment, the bell above the shop door jingled as several footsteps entered the store.

"Well, look what the cat drug in. We were just talking about you boys... *and lady*. Any luck finding those creatures y'all are lookin' for?"

"Not yet, friend!" a short guy with a black fauxhawk replied. "We're wondering if anyone has come in here to purchase a large amount of food recently?"

Alice's eyes went overbright as she made eye contact with Kyle, who signaled for her to remain calm. He slowly started returning canned goods to a nearby shelf. As he reached to place another can back on the shelf, he dropped it, and it rolled down the aisle, colliding with a combat boot flecked with dried mud. He quickly stashed the full basket behind a nearby shelf.

An African American woman with platinum blonde braids and bleached eyebrows leaned down and picked up the can.

"You dropped this," she said with a silky British accent as she extended the can to Kyle.

"Whoops," Kyle said as casually as he could and accepted the can. Then, in a move so quick that it surprised even him, Kyle turned to Alice and began flirting with her, grabbing her thighs and tickling her stomach. With his back to the crowd, he quickly shot her a glance that signaled her to play along. "You dropped this, you little butterfingers," he teased. It took her just a moment to catch on, but fortunately, she did so quickly.

"Kyle!" she squealed, immediately going on the defensive, laughing and squirming at being tickled.

"Do you think you can hold onto it this time, or do I need to carry this big, heavy can for you?"

"You're a jerk," she giggled, playfully swatting at him. He leaned in and kissed her, resulting in an endearing display of affection, though intentionally nauseating.

"Gross," said the African American woman as she turned away in disinterest.

"Damn hipsters," the shopkeeper muttered, shaking his head.

Kyle finally emerged from a long kiss with Alice and walked to the counter with his solitary can of beans.

"That all?" the grocer asked.

"Yup! Going to make my famous chili tonight and just needed some beans to round it out," he stammered. After paying, Kyle grabbed Alice's hand as casually as he could and tried to ride the wave of performative affection out the door.

As the couple walked by, Corbin's Spidey senses began to tingle as he detected the faintest scent of raw onions. He continued to watch them as the pair pushed open the door and stepped out onto the sidewalk.

"Man, smells like that guy only eats chili. Those two really need a shower," remarked the townie to the shopkeeper. Corbin's eyes widened as the realization struck him. He rushed out the door and was soon joined by the other hunters. Corbin and his team scanned the streets outside the general store.

"Spread out. Search inside the shops and check for any hiding spots large enough for a person to conceal themselves. They can't have gone far. Find and follow them; they will lead us to the others. Move!" Corbin instructed. The hunters dispersed, ducking in and out of storefronts and peering into parked vehicles along Main Street.

Nawn Ferris rushed into an antique store filled with large furniture. She scanned beneath the desks and tables, peering into massive trunks and inspecting every potential hiding spot. A sudden movement caught her attention, prompting her to spin around and look at two heavy drapes near a beveled stained-glass window featuring a floral and geometric design. She noticed that one of the curtains shifted slightly as if it had recently been disturbed. She crept closer and drew back the fluttering curtain, immediately feeling a rush of cool air on her skin from above. Glancing up, she noticed a vent releasing air into the room.

She turned around and noticed a ladder leading up to an A-frame loft. A smile crept across her face as she approached it and grasped the first rung. The outlines of several figures came into view as she completed her ascent, but she soon realized that none of the shapes belonged to living beings. Mannequins were staged in a retro sitting area, giving the appearance of a gathering frozen in time.

"Can I help you?" asked the store owner, an older woman with half-moon glasses, looking up with an inquisitive expression on her face. Nawn glanced from the mannequins to the shop owner below.

"Barmy shop, ya got here, innit?" Nawn commented.

Corbin hurried up the steps of a nearby church and swung open the door. A surprised pastor at the altar looked up in shock at his sudden entrance.

"Forgive me, Father. I was wondering if two people, a man and a woman, have passed through here?"

"Around here, forgiveness is ubiquitous, Son."

"Thank you, Father."

"You are the only person who has come in here this morning," the Pastor stated, holding Corbin's gaze.

"I see," Corbin said, glancing around the pews. "I hate how this will sound, but would you mind if I took a look around?"

"Not at all," the Pastor smiled. "Take as much time as you like." Corbin nodded and briskly walked up and down the aisles, looking between the pews. "I have an office in the back, and there are also a few storage rooms if you would like to look in there too, my son."

These words surprised Corbin, and a wave of shame washed over him for questioning the Pastor.

"No, thank you, Father. We are both men of God, you and me. I trust your word," Corbin said. He paused to cross himself, taking in the crucifix behind the Pastor before turning and rushing out the door again.

Alice and Kyle slowly rose from behind the altar at the Pastor's feet.

"We can't thank you enough, Father," Kyle said in a trembling voice.

"Stay as long as you like. When you do decide to venture out, remember to conceal yourself either above or below the eye line. Try to make yourself as small as possible or use objects to help you blend in. That should help you reach your destination and avoid detection."

Chapter Twenty-Nine

LE FEU FOLLET

Day of the New Moon

    The last year of marriage has not been what I expected, Blake reflected quietly while folding a pile of laundry on his marital bed. *Things have not been ideal ever since our wedding night. That night, Erika moved into this room that she once shared with her mother. We were married, yet we both spent the night alone. I celebrated our nuptials under the light of the Full Moon, while she went to bed. When I returned the next morning, I heard her weeping softly. Of course, she stopped when she noticed me. I realized then that she felt disappointed in her decision. I have never forced her to be with me. It was several months before we finally consummated our marriage, and when we did, she was intoxicated. When I tried to tell her that we should wait until another time when she was sober, she became angry with me, and in the end, I gave in to avoid a fight. The experience was cold and distant, and while part of me felt grateful to finally be close to my new wife, another part was saddened by the absence of any real love from her. The next morning, Erika was plagued with guilt. She was apologetic and embarrassed by her behavior. This only made everything feel worse.*

    Blake reached out and ran his fingers across Erika's black dress with the small white flowers. He reflected on how much he loved the way she looked in that garment. He sighed and picked up a pile of folded shirts and carried them to the couple's walk-in closet.

    There are moments when I glimpse the connection we once shared before we were married; now most of the time, she feels like a stranger. He glanced at a photo that rested on a built-in shelf. It was a picture of Blake and Erika standing at the altar on their wedding day. He was still in his human form, and both wore stone-faced expressions.

Right after our wedding, her visits to that room on the 4th floor became increasingly regular. I've tried talking with her about it for a long time, only to have her get angry with me or avoid the topic altogether. Now, she tells me she has stopped going up there because of a promise she made to her new friend. How is this stranger better at communicating with my wife than I am? Blake wondered in frustration. He felt confused as he placed his folded shirts inside a drawer, then his eyes wandered up to his suitcases on the top shelf. He stared at them for a while, and an idea began to formulate in his mind.

Maybe we could take a trip. The thought quickly began to lift his spirits. *Yes, a trip might do us both some good.* Excitement swelled inside his chest. *I should take her on a holiday to spend some time together. We could visit Hungary and even Romania for a little bit. Erika told me that she had never been there. Getting her away from this place for a while would be good.*

Blake started scheming about the places they could go. They would visit Budapest and Eger; Erika would also enjoy Pécs. Then, they would head east to Romania and visit Bucharest and, of course, a few towns in Transylvania. This was a fantastic idea. He would book everything immediately and surprise her.

He trotted off eagerly to retrieve his laptop and get to work. Laundry could wait.

Marius pulled his motorcycle up the driveway of La Maison d'Aristide, a beautiful French-inspired château manor. Although it was a sizable estate, it measured only about one-third the size of Dragos Manor. The massive front door opened, and Malcolm Sr. stepped outside, closing it behind him. Marius killed the bike's motor, propped up the kickstand, and removed his helmet.

"Bonjour, ti-Marius, how are you? Thanks for coming by, bruh," Malcolm Sr. greeted.

"Of course! I always enjoy the ride over here," Marius replied. As he stowed his helmet, he noticed Shanice Aristide looking suspiciously from a window on the 2nd floor. Marius smiled and waved hello to her.

"Jeepers creepers, bruh," Malcolm Sr. said and tried to duck out of his wife's eyeline. The Aristide Matriarch opened the window and called down to her husband.

"Don't bother Malcolm. Why are you acting so suspiciously, anyway?"

"I'm sorry, Cheri. I thought you had gone out for the day. You just surprised me, is all," he said sheepishly.

"Elena had to cancel," she confirmed, wearing a dubious expression. "You're a big boy! You're allowed to play with your friends. Let me know if you want me to make you two some sandwiches or something."

Malcolm Sr. smiled at his wife. "Thank you, Cheri. Maybe some steak sandwiches would be nice."

"Oh, Shanice, please don't go to any trouble!" Marius called up.

"It's no trouble, Marius! Now you two play nice. I'll call you when lunch is ready," she called out, then disappeared inside the Aristide home. Marius looked over at Malcolm Sr., who blushed.

"What was all that about?" Marius asked with a snicker.

"I'm sorry, bruh. I don't want to give the impression that I have something to hide from my wife. I only wish to speak with you privately. About the kids."

"I see."

"Shanice and the other Heads of the Household have warned those kids of ours, but I feel like they are still not taking those warnings seriously. Maybe we should do something to help push them in the right direction. No disrespect to you, bruh, but if Beo and Malcolm Jr. spoke to me the way Cristian does, they'd be getting the poop spanked outta them. There would be poops flying all over this yard, bruh!"

"You know, I felt that way at first. I was trying to guide Cristian toward making the right decision, especially regarding his nightclub. But honestly, as I watch him continue to resist input and advice, I'm starting to think maybe he needs the space to figure things out on his own. Sometimes, small struggles and failures can be healthy for growth to occur."

"It's not just the nightclub, bruh!" The two friends stared at each other long and hard at this statement. Marius now understood why Malcolm had asked him over. "There is something fishy going on with that missing hunter. Now, I'm not accusing anybody of anything, but there is talk. A lot of talk. You've got to understand that I'm worried for my sons' sake, especially Beo. I'm worried they're gonna get dragged down into something they got nothing to do with," Malcolm Sr.'s face was tight with concern. "Now, I'm approaching you as my friend. We found out that information from that busboy in the Gather at the Goat circuit a while back. You had said you were going to talk to Cristian about it. Then suddenly, that Adrian fellow turns up dead, and Curt is missing! As someone who knows the particulars of what we were investigating, I'd say the pieces could fit the puzzle. Now I just gotta ask, what's going on?"

Marius averted his gaze from Malcolm Sr. and looked toward the vibrant green landscape. The late morning mist lingered on the horizon, resting at the base of the tree line near the edge of the forest. He glanced up at the cloudy gray sky and noticed dark rain clouds approaching from the east. It pained him not to be honest with his dearest friend. A strong feeling of conflict burned inside his chest, and beneath it, Marius recognized that the dark murk of resentment was beginning to fester around his heart.

The fact was, Marius couldn't share everything he knew with Malcolm Sr., not about Curt and Adrian murdering Erika's boyfriend. Admitting so would put them too close to Curt's disappearance. Marius, Cristian, and Erika had agreed that nobody was to know the truth about Curt killing Ryan. Adrian's ghost had not lingered around long enough to be questioned, and then he disappeared with the rest of the house ghosts the night of Erika and Blake's wedding. Marius knew his attendance at that event was reckless, and now he kicked himself for not pushing back harder against the idea.

While he hated keeping all these ugly secrets locked away, Marius had decided he would take them to his grave. This was the most he could do to protect his nephew, despite Cristian's insistence that he didn't need him. If Cristian continued down the path he was on, then no amount of intervention would save him. However, maybe there was a middle ground to be found between these polarizing feelings.

"I have asked Cristian repeatedly, and he has assured me that he truly knows nothing about what happened to Erika's fiancé or Curt. Unfortunately, it appears that Adrian wandered onto a farmer's property and was killed. While his death is regrettable, according to our agreement with the Town Meeting Members, there is no recourse. There are clear restrictions regarding trespassing on properties that grant the farmer certain rights."

"That's another subject I wanted to discuss with you, Marius. Our families have been covering town dues for your family, and now we are having to pay even more to offset the damages caused by the recent chaos involving those unexplained ferals, Cristian's nightclub, and the disgruntled hunters. This situation is not sustainable."

"I'm uncertain what else to say except that I understand the strong desire to intervene; however, I believe we should do the opposite. Let's pull back." It pained Marius to utter these words. "At least, this is my plan for Cristian. And I'm sorry to say, but I don't think he's acting alone in this. These kids believe they can do whatever they want, knowing we will always be there to bail them out. While I love my nephew, I believe he needs a hard lesson in accountability."

"What are you saying, bruh?"

"We will pay back all the money that the Dragos owe you for our previous dues. The club is generating plenty of revenue. After that, please don't cover any more dues for the Dragos family. You can inform the other families of my plan and advise them to do what they think is right. We can't force our kids to make the right decisions, and we can't protect them from their poor choices, so I plan to step back and let them face their fate," Marius explained resolutely.

"I understand what you mean, Marius. Sometimes, there is only one way to learn the hard lessons in life. My only fear is that this thing gets a lot worse before it gets better," Malcolm Sr. said grimly.

"That may very well be true. I suspect the situation will get worse before it gets better. But maybe even just giving the appearance we're pulling their safety nets is enough to scare them in the right direction. Please know that I will not let the situation get too out of control for my mother's sake. She has not been well lately."

"I'm sorry to hear that, bruh. Truly."

"She's been talking about seeing a man in the woods," Marius said. "I assumed he was fictional, but then Tom told me she even wandered out to visit this mystery man a few weeks back."

"A man?" Malcolm Senior asked with alarm.

"Yeah, it's strange. I know that many unusual things inhabit these woods, but we seem to be attracting more than usual lately."

"What do you mean? What else?"

"Erika told me she saw some lights in the woods during the night of the last Full Moon. She said she felt a strong urge to follow them."

"Hmm, well, maybe that is something I can help explain. It sounds like Le Feu Follet," Malcolm Sr. mused.

"What's that?"

"Le Feu Follet are the Creole bayou fairies. The word translates to fire fairy. They are the small beings made of light that inhabit the marsh. They appear in the darkness of the bayou as flickering flames. Many people who see them believe they are something else and follow them. But it's a trap. You will attempt to follow these fire sprites but can never reach them. Their sole purpose is to lure you into the swamps to your death."

"Is that real?" Marius asked with skepticism.

"Some will tell you that the story of Le Feu Follet is folklore disguised as a lesson not to wander too far from home. But yes, they are real. They are evil entities, and you should warn Erika that if she sees something like that, she should never follow them."

"Good thing we are a long way from the bayou," Marius commented.

"No, bruh. It doesn't just have to be the bayou. I saw them in the mausoleums once when I was a kid. My mother told me that the devil himself gave brimstone to these lost souls to light their way through purgatory."

"I see. I was about to say if you only saw them in the bayou, it could be swamp gas or naturally occurring bioluminescence," Marius commented thoughtfully.

"What? Biolumin... No! Those pretty lights are intended to be distracting, so they can lead you further into the swamp, making sure you lose your way. When you finally realize how far you have wandered, it's too late. You're either lost or worse. A good thing to know is that they cannot cross anything iron. Drive an iron needle into the ground between you and them, and they cannot cross it."

"Thank you for telling me about these creatures. I will pass along the info to Erika."

"Bioluminescence," Malcolm Senior scoffed. At that moment, beads of rain began to fall. Malcolm Sr. squinted up toward the storm clouds looming overhead. "Now is the perfect time to see about those sandwiches, bruh. And please, do not bring up these things we discussed in front of Shanice. She is very worried about what is to come."

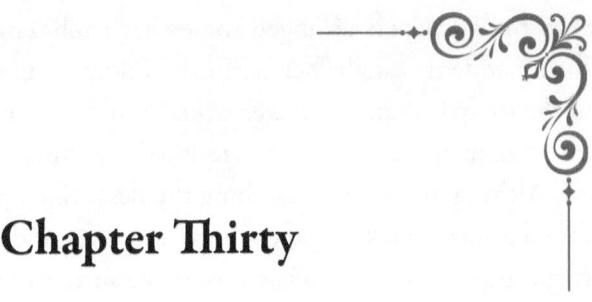

Chapter Thirty

THE WARD

The storm clouds gathered round and made themselves at home in the New England sky. Heavy rain had been descending all afternoon. Despite the early hostile encounters, Althea had returned to the unusual medical room on the 4th floor every day for the past couple of weeks to continue her investigation. Oddly enough, Althea had not seen any sign of the malignant entity ever since the altercation where she was attacked and knocked down by an unseen force. It was like the spirit had vacated the premises. And yet, somehow its absence seemed almost more unsettling. Regardless, Althea had a job to do, so she pressed on while cautiously keeping her guard up.

After an exhaustive search of the primary room, Althea was finally ready to try her hand at lock picking to gain access to the next. The beam of light from her headlamp rolled across the closed door as she approached it. Althea reached down and grasped the handle, and to her surprise, the door unlatched and drifted open. Daylight spilled into the main room. The breath caught inside Althea's throat. She braced herself for another encounter with the malevolent spirit, but after several minutes without incident, she carefully inched the door open. Raising the iPad with the PhantomGrammetry app running, Althea entered the well-lit space and swept the monitor around the room. No sign of any ghosts. She exhaled a sigh of relief and began to take in her surroundings.

Overcast daylight flooded in through a small, rain-flecked window, revealing a simple, seemingly unoccupied office space. There was a modest desk and chair, a few wooden crates stacked nearby, and a large trunk filled with bound papers arranged somewhat haphazardly. A dark, human-sized shape suddenly caught her attention. Looming in the shadows in the corner of the room was an old duster jacket suspended on a coat rack. Even though it was an inanimate object, the residual fright made her skin crawl.

Althea got to work searching the desk. She opened the top drawer and found a small stack of papers impaled on a spindle. Thumbing through the fragile pages, she found what looked like an announcement written in looped cursive. It read:

It is with good conscience and a strong commitment to our neighborly duty that Dragos Boarding Home will provide dedicated quarantine space until such time that this tragic influenza no longer plagues our community of Nocturne. We will offer nursing aid, various elixirs, catholicons, and other antidotes within this quarantine space, which will henceforth be known as The Ward. For terminal patients, we will provide an exclusive experimental treatment that we can state, with a high degree of confidence, is not available anywhere else in the world. The Dragos family is pleased to offer all stated services free of charge as a contribution to our esteemed community and beloved neighbors. However, all treatments require strict confidentiality and absolute nondisclosure to any persons outside our care.

This was a curious letter. Althea mulled over the words again—*The Ward*. On one hand, the offer seemed like a selfless contribution to Nocturne. On the other hand, something about the arrangement felt underhandedly suspicious. There had to be more to the story than what was on the surface. The whole situation gave her the creeps.

Althea carefully closed the desk drawer and turned her attention to the large trunk full of documents. It was an impressive chest made of solid oak and brimming with numerous bound records. She crouched down, lifted up a couple of stacks of yellowing papers, and examined the date ranges scrawled across the cover pages. As Althea thumbed through the documentation, she noticed several names listed within. These appeared to be the medical journals that the family kept from their days of serving patients in their makeshift medical ward during the 1918 flu. Althea was instantly curious to see if she could find any information about the '*very exclusive experimental treatment*' mentioned in the announcement. After reading a few entries, nothing particularly unusual caught her eye. She tried flipping to the back of one document, then looked through another, but to no avail. *If only I knew what I was searching for,* she thought in frustration. She moved another stack of papers and spotted a volume that looked different from the rest. It was a small leather-bound diary with gold lettering embossed on the cover that read SD.

A loud bang suddenly broke the silence, followed by the sound of breaking glass that echoed sharply from the main room. Althea hurriedly got to her feet and rushed to the doorway. Light spilled from the office into the dark room, revealing an unsettling stillness inside the ward. She quickly pulled out the iPad and raised it toward the room, desperately scanning for any signs of the spirit. A flicker of reflective light on the screen suddenly caught her eye. She saw where a bottle had fallen to the floor and shattered. Althea looked over at the nearest shelf and saw an empty space where the bottle had been. The problem was that this shelf was approximately twelve feet from where the bottle now lay. Either it was carried to this new position, or it had been thrown there. Her phone vibrated in her pocket. She pulled it out and saw Kit's urgent message, *"You know she threw that bottle! Where did she go?"*

Where, indeed, she thought. Althea continued to scan the room with the iPad as she took tentative steps toward the shards of glass on the floor. The ward was unnervingly quiet. When she reached the broken glass, Althea looked down and nudged a large piece with the toe of her shoe. The shard had a label on it—*Strychnine. That was daunting.* Althea realized that whether or not she could detect the ghost, she was being threatened. It was probably a good idea to wrap up for the day... after she read that journal.

A deafening clap of thunder rumbled outside the 4th floor office windows. Althea eagerly leafed through the pages of the intriguing leather-bound journal. She learned that it once belonged to an individual named Sophia. Based on the initials "SD" boldly embossed on the cover, this could only lead her to conclude one thing—this was the diary of Sophia Dragos.

Althea found herself captivated by the exquisite handwritten script in her hands. As she delved deeper, intriguing details of the early history of Dragos Manor began to unfold. She read that the Dragos Patriarch, Florin, abandoned his wife and family shortly after the grand estate's construction—a monumental endeavor that took over twenty years to complete. Although the text offered no clarity on his fate or the reasons for his departure, Sophia poignantly described a day when he was simply gone, leaving a profound void in her soul. It was undeniable that in the wake of his absence, the Dragos Matriarch was left utterly heartbroken. Sophia's entries from this tumultuous time resonated with palpable distress and debilitating anxiety, drawing Althea deep into a vortex of emotions.

Sophia tirelessly fought to keep her head above water over the next several years after Florin's departure. Despite earning a meager income, she was determined to maintain the expansive house for her family. But she felt immense pressure closing in around her. Her journal entries reflected this struggle, which soon spiraled into profound mental and emotional anguish. Then a turning point emerged during the nineteen-teens. Sophia devised a plan to tackle her converging issues head-on.

First, she realized that she needed to secure a more reliable source of income for her family. In 1914, she converted Dragos Manor into a boarding house primarily for travelers and war workers leading up to the beginning of 'The Great War,' as she referred to it in her writing. She acknowledged that running a boarding home for humans was a challenging undertaking, considering that the home was owned and operated by werewolves, but it soon became the new way of life for the Dragos family. Then, in 1916, Romania declared war against Austria-Hungary and officially entered World War I. This led to an influx of overseas travelers fleeing Eastern Europe as their hometowns became battlegrounds. Finally, when the war ended, a second problem arrived in Nocturne soon after. The pandemic struck in the fall of 1918, intensifying the third problem that the Dragos Matriarch had been experiencing for some time—isolation. Sophia had never fully recovered from her husband's departure, and despite having family and community, her deep-seated loneliness was evident. This sequence of events motivated her to devise a plan to solve all her problems with a single solution—*magic*.

Sophia wrote that she began practicing and refining a few defunct family magic spells. Her objective was to use a protection spell as the foundation but enhance it to create a new product capable of containing spirits. Althea realized this made perfect sense, and Sophia must have succeeded in her efforts since Althea herself had witnessed some of the most haunting experiences she had ever encountered in her life within the walls of Dragos Manor.

The journal entries revealed two fascinating types of spirits—the house ghosts, which comprised deceased Dragos' relatives, friends, and neighbors. Althea wondered if this spell might have been the very 'experimental treatment' that Sophia alluded to in her letter to the community during the 1918 flu. The second category of spirit mentioned seemed to have emerged unintentionally, as a shadowy byproduct of the primary spell. These apparitions, unlike any tethered to a living being, appeared to intensify with each death on the property. Their reckless and mischievous actions made them both a nuisance and a liability, prompting the decision to confine these malevolent spirits to the cellar. Sophia dubbed these entities—*the Mischief*.

Althea leaned back and digested these entries. The descriptions of each type of spirit didn't line up with what Althea had encountered so far. While she was certain that it was the Mischief poltergeist she had been tracking downstairs, it was noteworthy that it had left its confines of the cellar. Furthermore, Althea had not seen any signs of the benign and amiable house spirits described in Sophia's writing. Lastly, there was no mention of the dark entity living in the ward, although Althea had a pretty good idea of who that might be.

The next section of the journal described the containment spells required to gain control over all types of spirits residing within Dragos Manor. Sophia explained that she recorded a collection of her most powerful spells in a separate volume, which she referred to as her *grimoire*. She used this grimoire—also referred to in her text as her book of spells—to teach her female heirs the necessary magic so they could pass the knowledge down to future generations. Without these incantations, the house would, quite literally, fall. No future dwelling could exist on the land without extreme paranormal events or misfortune befalling anyone who attempted to live there.

A small sigh puffed out from Althea's lips. Had she inadvertently stumbled upon a method to combat or possibly control the hostile entity behind the brick wall? Ironically, Sophia herself had authored her undoing, assuming that Althea's assumptions were accurate. She felt that the original

Dragos Matriarch may have dabbled in a bit too much dark magic and, whether intentionally or unintentionally, ended up with her soul trapped inside Dragos Manor for all eternity. With a better understanding of what they might be up against and sights on a possible way to combat it, Althea was determined to help Erika gain the upper hand and put this particular demon to rest. Althea's plan was to locate Sophia's grimoire and bring it to the three sisters. Perhaps they could assist her in figuring out how to leverage it.

In her final entry, as Sophia was getting on in years, she wrote about the last pass-down ritual she would ever perform. Sophia taught her magic to two new family members who had married her grandsons in the 1940s. Their names were Daniela and Anastacia. More than just her magic spells, Sophia knew that her time on Earth was limited, and she wanted to make sure her legacy lasted beyond her physical presence. With a strong sense of duty, she chose to share her deepest secrets and wisdom with her beloved granddaughter-in-law, Anastacia.

Althea looked up from the journal and gazed out the rain-streaked window into the stormy night.

"Ana," she whispered softly.

Another flash of lightning was soon accompanied by a crack of thunder reverberating throughout the dark New England sky. The elevator door opened on the 3rd floor, and Althea exited the cart. She glanced around to ensure the coast was clear, then pretended to head toward her suite. However, she quickly pivoted and ducked across the hallway. Althea inched the door to Ana's room open, stealthily slipped inside, and closed the door behind her.

The room was dimly lit. Only a single oil lamp flickered on Ana's nightstand, casting light on the old woman sitting upright in bed and muttering to herself. Her eyes slowly drifted toward Althea, her gaze clouded and unfocused. Ana seemed devoid of any recognition or emotion.

"I'm sorry to disturb you, Mrs. Dragos. I hope I didn't startle you. I was wondering if I might have a quick word with you regarding some of

238

your late relatives," Althea asked politely. At first, the elderly matriarch did not acknowledge her. It wasn't until Althea drew nearer that Ana seemed to register her presence. The elderly woman looked up and quizzically inspected her face.

Like clockwork, Althea's inner sight manifested, conjuring a vivid image of Ana Dragos before her. Instantly, Althea was struck by heart-wrenching sorrow; although she couldn't pinpoint the exact cause, the palpable sense of isolation and profound loneliness was evident. Then she saw the figure of a man. At least, she thought he was a man. He appeared elfin in nature as he stood among thick trees. Suddenly, the man vanished, and a silver lynx stood in his place. Finally, an image of an elegant woman with striking features, dressed in a tailored black satin dress and wearing large pearls around her neck, emerged in the premonition. She had dark, wavy hair parted down the middle, porcelain white skin, and bright red lips. The hairs on the back of Althea's neck stood on end as she realized she was looking at an image of Sophia Dragos.

"Ah, there you are, child," Ana said, interrupting Althea's focus. "You see, I told you she would come," Ana said with a chuckle. "She was here the other day asking about your spells, so I was quite certain that she would return soon," Ana explained, but Althea had the distinct impression that the words were not directed toward her. Althea looked around the room but saw no signs of anyone else.

"I'm sorry, Mrs. Dragos, are you speaking to me?" she asked uncertainly.

"Good heavens, child. Whatever have you done to your hair?" Ana asked with visible disdain. At that moment, Althea finally realized that, despite her blue hair, Ana was mistaking her for Erika. While she was not exactly keen on taking advantage of the old woman in this way, she hoped her reasoning was admirable enough that the karmic fallout would not be excessively punitive. Althea decided it was best to press for the information she needed and get out of there as quickly as possible.

"You mentioned some spells, Mrs. Dragos?" Althea paused and searched her mind for how Erika might address this family member. "I mean, dear Aunt Ana. Are you talking about the grimoire?"

"Indeed, child. You will need to fetch the family spell book from within my safe. It's upstairs in my office. Bring that to me; make sure you are alone.

There is some... *very* sensitive information in there that I need to explain to you. Do not bring that grandson of mine back here with you this time. This sort of thing is not for—" Ana abruptly fell silent. She craned her neck like she was carefully listening to something. When she began speaking again, as before, it was not to Althea but to some unseen individual. "Of course I must show her your spellbook! Come now, Sophia! You know I will not be around forever. These were your orders! You even told me that one day you may try to convince me to do something that deviates from your original instructions and that I should unequivocally disregard such advice." At the mention of *Sophia*, Althea nervously glanced around the shadows in the room.

"Ana, are you speaking with Sophia?" she asked anxiously. The elderly woman looked up but did not respond. "Is she here now?" Althea persisted. A blissful smile crept over Ana's face, but again, she provided no answer to the question. Maybe she didn't understand. Or perhaps she was being elusive. Regardless, Althea unholstered her backpack and reached inside. Her hand brushed past the hand mirror and found the iPad. She pulled out the device and switched it on.

A cursory scan of the suit revealed no apparent spirits present. Even so, a chill ran down Althea's spine. She hoped to God that Kit's gear was still functioning properly. Whether or not they were actually alone, Althea couldn't be certain. She put the iPad away and looked back at the retired Dragos Matriarch lying in bed.

"Ooh, Sophia," Ana whispered softly. "I think she's onto you."

A thought suddenly crossed Althea's mind. Perhaps Ana Dragos was suffering from a cognitive impairment and might not be able to discern what was real and what wasn't. Althea had heard as much from various family members around the house. Still, she would try another tactic to get the old woman's attention. Althea reached into her bag and pulled out the pewter hand mirror.

"Ana, do you know what this mirror does?" she asked. The elderly matriarch focused her gaze on the shiny metal object.

"Why yes, my child. That mirror belonged to your great-great-grandmother, Sophia. That is a magic mirror that shows individuals their fate."

This was exactly what Althea was afraid of. Slowly, she turned the mirror toward her face to check if the image she had initially seen on its reflective surface was still present. Sure enough, the dark, featureless woman stared ominously back at her. The figure resembled a living shadow. Althea suddenly heard a low growl near her ear. She quickly tucked the mirror back inside her backpack and grabbed the iPad, wielding it around the room. To her dismay, there was still nothing. She stowed the device in her bag, maneuvering it around Sophia's journal.

"Ana, what did Sophia tell you before her death? She shared her most personal secrets with you, isn't that right? Do you remember what she told you?" Althea asked in rapid succession. Ana appeared stunned by this barrage of questions. She opened her mouth to respond.

"I recorded those secrets... inside the spellbook," she said quietly. Out of nowhere, Ana's demeanor suddenly shifted. "He told me, '*I'm going to say this quickly, so please listen carefully,*'" Ana said with notable urgency.

"He? He who? Don't you mean—she? Sophia?"

"He said that it was Cristian who killed him," Ana explained, but Althea was confused by this remark.

"Killed him? Killed who, Mrs. Dragos?" she coaxed.

"Curt," Ana replied emphatically. "Curt told me, '*Yes, I killed the poor bastard, but the idea, the order, and the payment for his death all came from Cristian,*'" Ana continued as if reciting something she had heard.

"Okay. And who did Curt kill?" Althea asked.

"Curt said, '*Yes, it was all Cristian. Cristian, Cristian, Cristian. He hired me to kill Ryan.*'" Ana spoke more erratically, but then suddenly seemed to calm down. Althea didn't know who Curt and Ryan were and was about to ask, but the sound of footsteps approaching behind her caught her attention.

"What are you doing in here?" came the icy voice of Cristian Dragos. Althea's blood ran cold. How long had he been there? "You shouldn't be in here! You need to leave right now!" he ordered, visibly angry.

"I—I'm sorry," Althea stammered while hoisting her backpack onto her shoulder. "I was just—"

"Leave! Now!" he repeated. Not wanting to escalate the situation, she did as he asked and swiftly exited the room.

Cristian turned back and stared in disbelief at his beloved Bunica lying in bed. She looked at him but did not seem to recognize him. She was muttering again, just as she had been during his last visit.

"What did you tell her?" Cristian demanded in a quivering voice. His head was spinning. He didn't need his grandma to tell him what she had said. *I heard what she told that little blue-haired snoop,* he thought. He didn't know what to do. His mouth felt exceedingly dry. *How the hell does Bunica know about Ryan?* Cristian realized how big of a problem this could become. What if his Bunica told these things to Marius? What if she told Erika?

Cristian felt utterly unhinged. His eyes snapped toward his grandma, urgency racing in his pulse. He approached her bedside and gently lifted one of her pillows, grasping it firmly in both hands. Ana's gaze remained fixed on the window, her expression hauntingly vacant. The flickering oil lamp cast a glow on her face. Cristian felt his breath hitch with a mix of fear and determination. His heart thundered with the weight of his decision.

"Don't be ridiculous, Sophia. He would never harm me," Ana said, but not to him.

Cristian's blood ran cold. His clenched hands gripped each side of the pillow so tightly that he could see his knuckles turning white. He took a deep breath, summoning the courage to follow through. She would not fight very hard. All he had to do was apply even pressure and maintain a firm grip. It would be over quickly.

"Sophia, you don't know everything. No matter what, I will always forgive him. I already have," Ana said. The words caught him off guard. The false nerve he had mustered floated away. Cristian sighed, shame burned inside his chest, and he placed the pillow behind his grandma's head. Cristian turned and left the room.

Chapter Thirty-One

CONFLICTING PLANS

Feminine leather boots splashed frantically through mud puddles. A soaked hoodie was pulled down over this individual's eyes, while a few wet strands of blue hair clung to her cheeks. Althea ran as fast as she could toward the garages behind Dragos Manor. The door to her rental car flung open and seconds later she was inside, slamming it shut to shield herself from the torrential downpour. A flash of lightning snaked across the night sky, soon followed by a bellow of thunder. The car was relentlessly pelted by heavy raindrops as the engine turned over, and Althea punched the gas. The vehicle fishtailed down the driveway, hung a left onto the road, and sped off in the direction of town. Althea was in desperate need of guidance. In this madhouse of circumstances, there was only one person she could think of turning to… Make that three people.

The economy-sized rental car screeched to a halt in front of the entrance to the alleyway that led to The Three Sisters' Inn. Althea hopped out and scurried up the familiar stoop, reaching the key fob back toward the street to lock the car. There was so much swirling around in her mind; all she could think of was that she needed help sorting through it. She opened the door and tried to make her presence known to avoid startling the sisters. Once again, she found the elderly women in their sewing room, working vigorously.

"Aw, here she is now, Marta. Right on time," Decima stated triumphantly and turned an elongated smile toward Althea. "Hello, dear."

"Hi, sorry to interrupt your evening, but I was wondering if I might ask you some more questions about the Dragos family? Your candor was very helpful the last time I visited," Althea commented with trepidation. As before, she was still unable to sense any clairvoyant information about these beings. It gave her chills to work blind like this, but what she said was true. These women had provided very useful information during her last visit.

"Of course, my dear. It is *the Mother* you have questions about this time," Decima asserted.

"The Mother?" Althea asked with confusion. "Is that the thing that lives on the 4th floor of Dragos Manor?"

"Yes, indeed. Inside the ward," the eldest sister, Marta, chimed in. Upon hearing this, Althea briefly thought that perhaps she should have come here sooner; however, she understood that timing was everything. Had she visited earlier, she might not have been armed with the right information or questions. She knew she was on the right path, and the events happening around her were the signs she sought. She would not rush.

"Is *the Mother* Sophia Dragos? The founder of Dragos Manor. The one who created all those spells?" she asked.

"Hmm, yes and no," Decima responded coyly. "Right now, the Mother could even be Erika Farkas herself."

Althea's blood ran cold. "What?"

"This is an extremely powerful family you are dealing with. The magic you are dealing with is embedded in their DNA and inside the foundation of that grand home. *The Mother* ebbs and flows with familial pain. She is the one who keeps the wound healthy and thriving. Or should I say, festering and rotting? Right now, the Mother may be too large to control until Erika and other family members confront their demons."

"Wait, how can that *thing* be Erika?" Althea asked incredulously.

"My dear, instead of dwelling on the problem, perhaps turn your energy toward the solution," Marta suggested.

"And the solution?" Althea inquired anxiously.

"A riddle. Answer me these questions three—" Marta began, until her younger sister elbowed her in the arm.

"No, dear. A quest. A quest," Nina quickly corrected.

"A quest!" Marta agreed in a singsong voice. "Oh, yes. That's right," Althea blinked and shook her head, indicating her confusion.

"A quest? What kind of quest?" she asked.

"Through the Noctambulist forest to the summit of Mt. Saudade. There, Erika will find a means to break the Dragos family curse. Throughout the journey, help her explore the root causes of her pain. In doing so, she will have an opportunity to fortify herself against that which threatens to consume her," Nina instructed.

Althea was perplexed. This sounded like a quest comprised of riddles. Although she understood that it was fate that had summoned her here, the true purpose and reason she was there eluded her. Doubt and uncertainty swirled in her mind. The entire situation felt surreal, as if it had been taken from the pages of a book.

"There will be moments when you feel tempted to stray from this path," Decima mused. "Whether driven by fear, self-preservation, or even situations of life and death, you may want to give up, but believe in your purpose and remain steadfast in your journey. The *easy road* will not yield the answers you seek."

"I'm not sure what I'm seeking," Althea confessed, realizing the depth of vulnerability and fear hiding behind her uncertainties.

"The true answers lie in wait at the cross-section of providence," Nina said with a smile. "Here, take my sewing needle with you. This is a sturdy needle made of iron. Use it to help keep you on track."

"Okay, thank you," Althea said, taking the needle. She pierced it through the side of her backpack for safekeeping.

"Now, a warning," Marta advised ominously.

Althea sighed, the wind deflating from her sails. Of course, nothing about this would be simple. "Now, a warning? Okay. I'm listening," she said while rubbing her face. "What is it?"

"Use the mirrors, but do not linger in reflections for too long. That mirror in your backpack is a tool. It shows you your future. To do that, it must access the future. The only way to access the future is via a portal. Meaning that *it is a key*. Be careful with it. Do not look upon it again until *you have no way out*." Marta's words rang in Althea's head. She almost felt that this effect was intentional, as if the message was imprinting itself on her memory. Althea finally sensed something for the first time in the company of these women.

"You aren't able to tell me anything more, are you?" she voiced her realization aloud. Three spindly smiles crept up the elderly, wrinkled faces.

"We *would* wish you luck, but we never touch the stuff. Go create your own luck," Decima whispered with a wink behind her half-moon spectacles.

"Erika!" Althea called out as she hurried up to the bar inside the Dragos Manor lounge.

"Hey, Thea," Erika greeted with a smile as she sipped a cocktail. "Jeez, you're soaking wet. Were you jogging in the rain?"

"Something like that. Listen! Let's go on a backpacking trip together," Althea proposed. "Get out in nature for a while. It will be healing for us! The weather is going to be great after this storm passes. We can take our time; stay out there for a couple of weeks."

"Yeah, ya know, that sounds great! I haven't had an adventure like that in a while," Erika eagerly replied. "Where should we go? There are so many state parks and forests to choose from."

"How about Mt. Saudade? That's nearby, right?"

"Oh, I didn't even think of that. Yeah, I think it's about twenty-five miles through the Noctambulist woods. I think we can get there if we use the Questhaven trailhead."

"Did you say Questhaven?" Althea appeared surprised.

"Yeah, I'm pretty sure that trail goes straight to the base of Mt. Saudade, but I'll double-check just to be sure. We'll need to put together a solid pack—lightweight with a good mix of supplies. This trek will take us a little while."

"Okay, great! Maybe we can leave after the next Full Moon, so we don't have any unexpected run-ins again," Althea suggested.

"Probably a smart idea. The Flower Moon is just two weeks away. That should give us plenty of time to get supplies together," Erika agreed with rapidly growing excitement.

"Awesome!" Althea clapped triumphantly, then leaned in and hugged her friend. Erika was surprised but welcomed the affection as she nuzzled her face into Althea's damp blue hair. Althea's now-familiar essence put Erika at ease, and the closeness sent goosebumps down her spine. At that moment, Blake rounded the corner and entered the lounge, triggering Erika's enthrallment to shift into guilt as she released her friend.

"I'm going to start packing!" Althea eagerly announced, trotting off toward the lobby and waving to Blake as she passed him.

"Hello, my darling!" Blake greeted his wife with a light kiss on the cheek. "I have a surprise for you. But first, did I just hear your friend will be leaving us?" he asked, wearing a somewhat pleased expression.

"Huh? Oh, no. She was talking about packing for our camping trip. We're going on a backpacking trip for a few weeks out in the woods. I'm so excited! I think it will be good for me to get out of here for a little while, don't you agree?" For some reason, Blake's face looked as though someone had died. "What is it? What's wrong?" she asked, feeling her guard rise as she recalled their last argument regarding Blake's jealousy over Althea.

"It is nothing," he said, appearing defeated.

"Stop it. You're acting like a child. Tell me what you were going to say," Erika's tone emerged icier than intended.

"I wanted to inform you that I will be taking an extended trip home to Hungary," he finally said.

"Oh, why didn't you just say that? That's fine with me," she said nonchalantly, taking the last sip of her drink. Blake nodded solemnly and stared into the distance. The next time he spoke, it was to Sam behind the bar.

"Excuse me, Sam. Double whiskey, neat," he ordered. Erika could tell he was upset, but she didn't feel like playing games. If he wanted to share what was on his mind, he would.

"So, when are you leaving?" she asked as his drink was delivered.

"As soon as possible," he said, tossing back the sweet, oaky liquor.

Later that night, inside the ballroom, Club Dragos buzzed with energy. The place was packed, and everyone was already in full party mode despite the storm raging outside. Cristian and the Killers, minus Beo, sat near the large windows in the owner's lounge area on the stage. Tonight was the New

Moon, so the curtains were drawn open, revealing the cloudy, moonless night. Occasionally, a bolt of lightning flashed like shattered glass against the dark, stormy sky.

"Listen, I know my brother really cares about you. He's just mad right now. It'll blow over!" Malcolm Jr. attempted to console Cristian, who was not in the mood to be comforted.

"He always thinks the worst of me! I know my methods can sometimes be a bit *brute force*, but I'm a *results guy*. I make shit happen! I know I'm not perfect. He just needs to accept me for who I am, but he won't, so there's nothing I can do about it." Cristian was flustered. "Look, I appreciate you trying to make me feel better, but I honestly just wanna forget about it right now. It's been two weeks! I don't think he's coming back!" Cristian said, retreating into his glass of red wine. Malcolm Jr. reached out and placed a sympathetic hand on Cristian's shoulder and didn't press further.

As Cristian sat back, brooding with his Barolo, he noticed Vittoria approaching through the crowd. Even in the strobing lights, he could see the pleased expression on her face. As she ascended the steps of the stage, her long legs peeked out from the slit in her black form-fitting dress. Cristian loved her style and wished he could pull off her look.

"My love, I have some exciting news to cheer you up. I need to speak with you privately," she told him, the smile never leaving her face.

"Yeah, no problem," Cristian replied, then said to the rest of the group, "Hey guys, you heard her; give us some space." With that, Malcolm Jr., River, and Loki walked off stage and mingled with the crowd on the dancefloor. Only Kessler remained on stage with Cristian and Vittoria.

"Can I stay?" he asked hopefully.

"Very well, but don't say anything. I need to tell Cristian something very important, and I don't need a peanut gallery making quips," Vittoria said with an eye roll.

"Dear God. What is it? My heart can't take any more heart-spooks. Please take it easy on me," Cristian exclaimed dramatically.

Vittoria started, "I found out some news about our dear Marius that I believe will get him out of your hair for a while."

"Holy shit! No way! What is it?" Cristian asked. Vittoria leaned in, a playful smile on her lips as if she would burst into laughter at any moment.

"He has an illegitimate child with a human woman in Romania," she whispered with one raised eyebrow. Cristian was stunned as his jaw dropped.

"Shut up! Oh...my...Gawd! Are you... kiiiiiiiddding me?"

"No, darling. I'm not. Get this—the woman didn't know he was a werewolf when she fell pregnant. They broke it off when he moved back to America. She hasn't even told him that his daughter exists." Cristian rolled backward onto the sofa cushions beside him, his feet in the air like a dead bug.

"Oh my God, oh my God! This is so crazy! *Jerry! Jerry! Jerry!*" Cristian was beside himself with giddiness. Then, he composed himself starkly once more as he rolled back into a seated position.

"Can I say something?" Kessler ventured to chime in.

"No!" Cristian and Vittoria responded in unison.

"Oh my God, Vittoria! I am so gay for you sometimes! I would dyke out with you so hard if I were a lesbian! How do you do it?" Cristian shook his head, marveling at her cunning ingenuity.

"I have my ways, darling," she sneered, plucking a cigarette from a pack and placing it between her bright red lips.

"Oh, yes please, give me one of those," Cristian said, taking a cigarette. Vittoria lit the tip for him, and the two friends sat back and giggled together, enjoying their smokes.

"This news is huge! It couldn't have come at a better time. After what I told you about what I've been going through with my Bunica," Cristian explained, then squealed with delight. "We should tell Marius immediately! He needs to get his ass to Romania! See that baby girl of his!" Then, something dawned on Cristian. "Wait, so is the baby a werewolf?" At this question, Vittoria took a long drag of her cigarette. "*Is she?*" Cristian demanded.

"I don't think so," Vittoria confirmed through a long exhale of smoke.

"Errr, are you sure it's his?"

"Oh, what difference does it make!" Vittoria said with an eye roll as she snuffed out her cigarette. "You said we needed to get Marius out of the way for a while. This was the best reason I could find. He'll go out there and spend time trying to figure out if the kid is his or not."

"You're absolutely right; this is a fantastic distraction. Knowing him, he won't come right out and ask this woman, '*Hey, does our baby, by chance, change into any unusual creatures once a month?*' Let's figure out how best to get the word to him and ship his ass outta here pronto," Cristian said.

"Can I say something?" Kessler tried to interject again.

"No!" Cristian and Vittoria responded in unison.

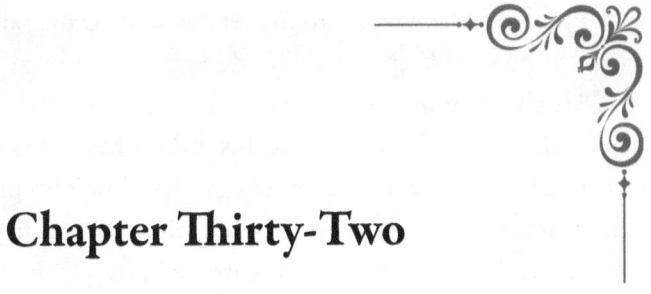

Chapter Thirty-Two

HAPPY CAMPERS

The New Moon hung dark and obscured in the night sky as the storm clouds finally started to clear. The rainfall had eased, but the air remained damp. The sharp hissing of a zipper opening gave way to the rustling of nylon as the tent flap unfastened. Two figures ducked through the entrance, then Stanley and Kathryn stood and stretched after waiting out the storm inside the recreational shelter.

"Christ, am I glad that storm finally let up. I couldn't stand being locked in there with your bloke farts any longer," she said as another nearby tent unzipped.

"I wasn't even farting. I'm just in desperate need of a shower," he replied. "My nether regions are a little swampy if you catch my drift."

"One, fuckin rank, mate. And two, your *drift* is what stings my eyes," she quipped.

"I hate to break it to you, Kat, but you don't smell like a rose either. The first body of water we find that isn't our little freshwater stream, I don't care who's looking. My white ass is jumping in," Stanley stated matter-of-factly.

"Missed opportunities; y'all should have bathed in the rainfall like we did," came the cheerful voice of Kyle as he, Alice, and Alex hurried up to the campsite. Their hair was wet, and they all had towels wrapped around themselves. Alice shivered as she kept walking toward the camper van. Alex and Kyle, seemingly unbothered by the chilly night air, hung back to chat with Kathryn and Stanley. A second tent unzipped, and Jerome emerged with an armful of dry firewood.

"I pulled some wood into my tent as soon as the rain started. I figured it would be good to keep it dry. Should I get a fire going?"

"Alright, Jerome! Way to go, man!" Stanley said as he walked over to help with the fire. By this point, his red mohawk was surrounded by fuzzy brown hairs on his scalp. Jerome began handing him pieces of wood, which Stanley stacked into a pyramid inside their makeshift firepit. Once the flames crackled and danced, the group gathered around the fire and absorbed its warmth into their souls. At least small comforts still existed.

"Are you all in the mood for black beans again tonight, or should we treat ourselves to a can of turkey chili?" Kyle asked pleasantly.

"It depends, man. How are we doing on provisions?" Stanley asked with concern.

"We're still good for a while, Stan, my man. I set up this van to be prepared for the zombie apocalypse," Kyle said with wry laughter.

"Whoa. Easy, mate. We're already juggling enough paranormal realities right now," Kathryn cautioned. "The last thing we need is to summon zombies."

"Sorry. Sorry. You're right," Kyle admitted, then looked up toward the sky. "Cancel the zombies. We don't want them. Hey, speaking of spooky shit, I almost forgot to tell you that when we were out taking our rain shower, we saw a bunch of weird lights zig-zagging around deep in the woods. Something about them didn't seem human."

"Fantastic news," Stanley said sarcastically. "That's creepier than that freaky circus music we heard a few nights ago. Maybe we should think about pulling up stakes and relocating. We could look for some good fishing spots and set up camp near there. Fresh protein in our bellies would do us all some good."

"I'm open to that," Kyle said. "But we should also think about getting some more gas first. I have a little less than half a tank left."

"We still have a couple of weeks," Kathryn chimed in. "Ya know, until the next Full Moon. Maybe we should consider sneaking into town again."

"I don't know, Kat. After the last time—"

"Hey, did you guys hear that?" Jerome interrupted. The group looked at him in surprise and then started nervously glancing around. Jerome was quiet, his nose tilted up into the night air.

"What did it sound like?" Alex whispered.

"Shhh," Jerome fired back, his eyes fixed on the shadows in the woods beyond. "There's someone out there," he said, gesturing into the darkness.

Stanley, Kyle, and Alex puffed up their stance and gazed in the direction Jerome indicated. Everyone waited for several minutes. Soon, Alice returned from the camper van.

"Hey guys, I was just thinking—"

"Shhhhh!" Jerome reprimanded. Alice looked startled as she clammed up and quietly joined the others by the fire.

"What's going on?" she whispered, fear evident on her face.

"Jerome thinks he heard something in the woods," Kyle replied in a low voice.

"I *did* hear something. Someone's out there, but you all need to be quiet. It's moving." Jerome was tense. He closed his eyes and tilted his nose toward the breeze. His head turned more east now as he opened his eyes again. "There they are," he said. The campers collectively snapped their heads toward the indicated direction and saw a handful of shadowy figures approaching from a distance.

"Okay, everyone, be cool," Kyle whispered, though his body language suggested readiness. "Let's see who they are and what they want. It could be Lena, Jazmine, and Nacho."

"I see six," Alice muttered. *Six!* The number made Kathryn's heart leap, hoping it might not only be their missing friends but also some of the other ambushed people.

"Evening, friends!" Stanley shouted, startling everyone around him. "Awfully late for a hike, isn't it?"

The mysterious group didn't respond right away but kept approaching the campsite. As they got closer, Kathryn realized they weren't the people they'd been looking for. The group was mostly men and one woman, and they certainly looked like a rough crowd.

"Sorry, I hope we didn't frighten you," a shorter guy with a black fauxhawk said as soon as the crew was close enough not to shout.

"No, man, you're good," Kyle said, trying to mask the tension in his voice. As soon as all six were close enough, Kathryn saw their faces illuminated by the flickering flames of the campfire. The short guy with the fauxhawk had a tattoo running down the front of his neck. Kathryn could make out that it was a cross in the flickering firelight. *Cool, bro,* she thought. Right behind him was an African American woman with platinum blonde braids who looked strong, like an MMA fighter. There was another man who seemed to be either Latino or Native American, a big, burly white guy with a beard, another muscular white man, and an African American man with a slight limp, trailing behind the group at a slower pace.

"Y'all out on a little camping trip?" the short guy with the fauxhawk asked.

"Obviously, dude. What's it look—" Alex began to say, but Kyle placed a hand on his friend. Kathryn guessed that Kyle and Alex might now feel a little vulnerable with only towels wrapped around their waists.

"Don't mind my friend," Kyle said, sounding lighthearted. "His mother never hugged him. Yeah, we're just out here enjoying nature. Again, please forgive our apprehension. You have to understand that being approached by six strangers in the middle of the woods at night is a bit unnerving."

"Oh, no doubt, friend," said the guy with the fauxhawk. "We didn't mean to frighten you. We're looking for a group of people who might have gotten lost out here. They could be dangerous. Have you seen anyone or anything in this area that seems suspicious?"

"No, we haven't seen anyone else," Kyle replied in a calm, steady tone.

"So, just you folks then?" the short guy asked with a smile that said more than his words.

"Yeah, man, like I said. It's just us out here. We've got the whole spread! Sorry we can't be more helpful, but we appreciate the warning," Kyle said to the strangers before turning to Alex. "Maybe it's a good idea we hostler up," he added loudly enough for everyone to hear, and Kathryn suspected it was mainly for the benefit of the short guy with the fauxhawk. This was the first she heard about any firearms at their campsite.

"Might be a wise idea," the short stranger agreed as he looked around their campsite suspiciously. "Say, have we met before?"

A look crossed Kyle's face that he struggled to suppress, yet Kathryn could almost sense his anxiety lingering in the air.

"I just have one of those faces, I guess," Kyle responded coolly.

"I guess so. Welp, I suppose we'll be on our way, then. Hope you folks enjoy your evening. How long did you say you'd be out here again?"

"We didn't say. Haven't decided yet. Just playing it by ear," Kyle said, his 'cool guy' persona fading. The short guy with the fauxhawk and neck tattoo grinned, nodded, then turned and walked back into the shadows of the forest. His crew followed, each one eyeing the campers with suspicion. The night air felt even chillier after they disappeared. Everyone at the campsite remained alert, their collective nerves palpable.

"Those are the same people who chased us in town. What do you think they're going to do to us?" Alice's voice trembled.

"Stan, my man. I think you were right. Maybe it's a good idea to pick up stakes tomorrow after all," Kyle said as Alice's question went unanswered.

Corbin Sterling crouched down and raised the scope with night optics to his eye. He observed the group of so-called campers scurrying around their campsite. Their body language conveyed distress. Corbin felt sympathy for their situation. He, too, would be distressed if he had recently turned into a Lycan and, as a result, had to become a fugitive on the run. Self-preservation—he understood that completely. Unfortunately, that sympathy didn't change his duty as a werewolf hunter. Humanity came first. Period.

"What's the plan?" Beau asked in a low whisper, his baritone voice persisting.

"The plan," Corbin said while lowering and stowing his night vision scope, "is to keep tabs on this group. Beau, you and your team will monitor them. They will most certainly change locations after tonight. Nawn, Naiche, and I will continue our due diligence and search for more. I only counted six of them, but my gut tells me there might be more out there. We have two weeks."

"And then what?" came the concerned whisper from Malik. Corbin's gaze shot over to him before darting to Beau.

"And then, hopefully, your foot will be healthy and you can do your job!" Naiche retorted.

"Guys!" Beau hissed. "Don't worry. When it's 'go time,' Malik will perform. This is just first-time jitters."

"I'm sorry, I'm just struggling with the idea of terminating human beings," Malik said quietly with conviction.

"You see, that's where you're mistaken," Corbin replied calmly. "These are not people. There's no turning them back once they've transformed. And look, there is no shame if you don't have it in you; no one is forcing you to be here." Malik lowered his head and looked at the ground.

"Malik, this is just like training, and the reason we seek out people with your skillset," Beau chimed in, trying to hype up his man. "We only terminate the creatures in their werewolf state to prevent mistaken identity. The first course of action is to utilize silver blades in hand-to-hand combat to put them down as humanely as possible. Firearms are used only in extreme cases, if necessary, but it's worth noting that regular bullets are ineffective against them, even when they're human. Close combat allows you to look into their eyes, pray, apologize, or do whatever soothes your soul and theirs as you transition their humanity to the other side and send their beast to hell. Try not to slice. Go for one decisive blow to the temple or the throat. Clean. Your knife is sharp. The metal is meant for this task."

"We also assist in getting the bitten ID'd," Naiche added. "If possible, we set it up so their bodies can be found and returned to their families. We work with law enforcement and medical examiners to reclassify the cause of death as something more benign. That is the best we can do for these people."

"Okay," Malik finally relented. "I understand. You know, I signed up for this job because a werewolf killed my grandfather. He never transformed, thank God. That thing just straight-up killed him."

"I'm sorry for your loss, Malik," Corbin said. "Embrace that. Lean into it. You're doing something good that will help ensure that doesn't happen to another family. I'm sorry when it happens to anyone." Malik nodded stoically. "Alright, are we good here?" Corbin asked.

"I'm sorry, boss. It won't happen again," he said sheepishly.

"Good. Now, let's get to work. We will be in communication over the next couple of weeks and will come back to assist with the first round of terminations, provided we don't find any more suspicious characters squatting in the woods. If these folks here are just a normal bunch of *happy campers*, we'll move on. However, the fact is that we saw that guy and his girl in town the other day and pursued them. It's no coincidence they are out here now. They all match the profile of the creatures we are looking for—a sizable group of people lingering in the woods for an extended period. Granted, they have more camping gear and even a vehicle that I didn't expect, but that makes them even more dangerous if they are who we think they are. Imagine if they decide to drive into a big city before the next Full Moon. Can you picture the Lycan flare-up? People talk about a zombie apocalypse, but they've never considered a werewolf apocalypse. And werewolves are almost harder to kill than frickin' zombies."

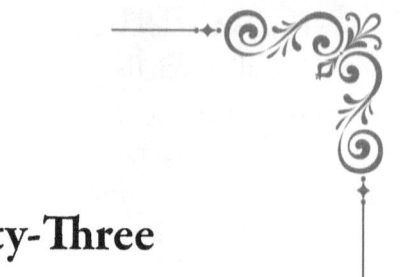

Chapter Thirty-Three

SAFE

Day of the Flower Moon

A sudden tapping sound caught Althea's attention. She looked through the open door of Ana's abandoned office toward the hole in the bricks. The tapping came from inside, an ominously taunting invitation from the spirit dwelling within. Althea had been avoiding the 4th floor ever since speaking with the three mystic sisters a few weeks earlier, when she learned that not only did she not have a clear understanding of the entity inside the ward, but she also wasn't sure how to combat it. Instead, she and Erika had spent the past two weeks preparing for their upcoming journey. They were leaving in the next day or two, after the Full Moon that was due in the sky that evening. Erika was in town purchasing last-minute supplies needed from their list, giving Althea the perfect opportunity to finally search for the Dragos spellbook. She ignored the tapping coming through the brick opening and continued inspecting the antique cast-iron safe located behind the desk in the retired matriarch's office.

Testing the handle confirmed Althea's suspicions; it was locked tight. Mistaking her for Erika, Ana had unknowingly revealed the location of Sophia Dragos' grimoire to the fortune teller. Unfortunately, Althea couldn't stay long enough to ask how to access the safe, as Cristian had discovered her inside his grandma's room and immediately ordered her out. Running her fingers over the antiquated locking mechanism, Althea knew she needed to find the key. So she started with the most obvious place in sight—the dusty office desk.

After rifling through each drawer, she came up empty-handed. Continuing her search through the rest of the room, she looked around the door frame, under the rug, and behind the black-and-white pictures on the walls. No key was found in any of these places. She stood and stretched, reassessing the situation. As much as she tried to remain optimistic, a feeling of hopelessness came creeping in. This was an impossible task. Dragos Manor was massive; the key could be anywhere, and time was not on her side. If she wanted to get her hands on the spell book before she and Erika left, Althea would have to risk another visit to Ana, regardless of the potential consequences. With everything happening, there was too much at stake to allow something so important to be left behind. And now she kicked herself for allowing fear and doubt to fuel her procrastination.

Her eyes returned to the safe. She examined it carefully, contemplating it. Then Althea noticed something she hadn't seen before: the door was ever so slightly misaligned with the edges of its container. *That's odd,* she thought. Althea moved closer, grasped the handle again, and although it still wouldn't turn, she pulled the door back. To her surprise, with a little force, the door gave way and swung open. She laughed in astonishment as she realized the mechanism must have been rusted or broken.

A handful of items were stacked inside, but one immediately stood out—a small, leather-bound book with frayed pages sat atop a small pile of books. The rustic-looking book could have been mistaken for an old Bible if it weren't for the absence of gilded edges on the pages. Before Althea could reach in and grasp it, the chime signaling the arrival of the elevator cart rang out through the hallway. Panic surged throughout her body. She had no idea who would be coming up here, as it wasn't often that she encountered others on the 4th floor. Althea immediately shut the safe door with urgency, making sure not to accidentally latch it, then pivoted and scrambled underneath the antique desk.

"I swear to God, she better be up here," came Cristian Dragos' seething voice. Althea felt his presence appear in the doorway of the office. Her heartbeat quickened, pounding so hard that she was almost scared he could hear it. She silently berated herself for hiding in such a visible place. If he caught her, the optics would not look good—Althea sneaking around, hiding in the office beneath a desk. She remained as still as possible and fought to control her breathing. Fortunately, he did not linger in the doorway for long. She heard him walk over to the brick wall and stick his head through the hole. "Erika!" he shouted in a sharp tone that made Althea jump.

"Maybe she's outside," another male voice suggested, and then Althea heard footsteps receding down the hallway toward the rooftop courtyard.

"I'm so pissed, I could just scream! I just found out that she's planning to leave on some camping trip!" Cristian fumed. "And what, she's just going to leave me here to deal with everything?" His voice faded away when the door at the end of the hallway closed behind them.

While Althea could still hear their muffled conversation, she couldn't make out the details. Her intuition told her that she needed to know what they were discussing. The only problem was that in order to get closer to the courtyard, she'd have to move away from the safety of potential hiding spots. She decided to take the risk. Althea jumped up and slung her backpack over her shoulder as she headed toward the door at the far end of the hallway. Cristian's muffled voice became clearer as soon as Althea reached the door.

"She invites the hunters to come back here in a month to search our property, and *this* is what she decides to do to help us prepare for that? I've been turning down requests for reservations for weeks now. Am I just supposed to handle everything?" Cristian ranted to the other unknown individual.

Curiosity got the better of her. Althea inched open the door and peeked through. She saw Cristian with his friend Kessler and Blake's sister, Vittoria. None of them seemed to notice her as Cristian continued his tirade.

"Blake freakin left! I can imagine he's getting tired of her bullshit! Erika is not doing her part! She hasn't produced any offspring for him; she hasn't lifted a finger to help with our situation with the hunters, and still hasn't done shit about the house magic problem. Where's that magic spell book? She was supposed to get it! She spends all her time drunk or with that ghost hunter. By the way, I think something is going on between them. Have you noticed? Erika doesn't bring anything good to the table. I'm the one earning a living for our family; I'm the one doing everything! And she just decides to *fuck off* into the woods to *lez-out* with that blue-haired ghostbuster!" Cristian groaned when he finished.

"Just let her leave then, my love!" Vittoria countered. "We don't need her. Let her leave! Kessler and I are here for you, darling. We are not going anywhere. Maybe this will be your moment to really claim your power! Become the true Head of Household. Everyone will learn to accept it. And please do not fret about the hunters, my darling. We will figure something out. They will have their hands full with those ferals for a while. In the meantime, we just need to get rid of the body. This whole ordeal does not need to escalate. The hunters' trail will grow cold. It's already cold if you ask me. And whatever this magic is, it can't be that hard to learn. As for my brother, maybe you are right. Maybe it's better that he left. If you think your cousin is going to be a lesbian with the ghost hunter, perhaps it's good he is not here to see such things."

"You know, that's another thing. I think that ghost hunter is full of it! I haven't seen any footage or been asked to do interviews. She's probably just another con artist looking for a free ride," Cristian continued, though less emphatically than before.

"Are you starting to feel better, darling?" Vittoria asked in a soothing voice.

"Yeah, kinda," he admitted. "All I can say is, *thank God* we got Marius out of here with that kid in Romania story! I'm so glad your anonymous letter idea worked, Vittoria! I've never seen someone get on a plane so fast."

"I even had someone I knew in Romania send it," Vittoria said with a Cheshire cat grin.

"Let's just hope he stays out there for a good long while. The last thing I need right now, on top of everything else, is one of his insufferable lectures. I've had it with everyone's judgment and criticism. I have proven time and again that I am willing to do what it takes to be a good Head of Household. I was the first Dragos to reach across the divide and seek a resolution with you and your family, Vittoria. I'm the one who paved the way for Erika to come back to this place. I'm the one who has single-handedly saved our family home with my nightclub. And I'm the one who is realizing now that I made a big fucking mistake with one thing. I should have just let Erika marry that human! You're right; I don't need her here. Frankly, it would make my life way fucking easier if she never came back."

"Everyone might have to accept you as Head of Household," Kessler chimed in. "It's a dangerous forest out there, filled with vicious creatures and

261

treacherous obstacles. She could get lost, have an accident. You know, I've heard that there are many ferals running around."

Cristian listened but remained silent. Althea couldn't believe what she was hearing. Perhaps she was misinterpreting the message.

"And you know, there is always the option that we could help *increase* those odds," Kessler suggested.

There was no mistaking that comment. Althea let out a small gasp from the hallway. Her hand shot up to her mouth. She froze, hoping they had not heard her. Fear washed over her, sending a cold chill throughout her body.

Outside on the rooftop courtyard, Vittoria caught a whiff of a familiar scent in the vicinity. It was a fragrance she recognized well, as she had often been the catalyst for this particular emotion throughout her life. Still, she tilted her head back and sniffed lightly at the air to pinpoint its direction. The smell was fear, and it was coming from inside the hallway.

Back inside the hallway, Althea suddenly felt very exposed as she sensed the group approaching. Realizing she didn't have enough time to retreat to any hiding spot, she quickly reached into her backpack and grabbed a pair of headphones and a device she had never used before called an EVP, or Electronic Voice Phenomena recorder. She placed the headphones over her ears and started sweeping the device across the walls while pretending to walk casually down the hallway. Less than a moment later, the door at the end of the hall swung open with a bang, and the long shadows of three ominous figures stretched across the floor.

Althea continued sweeping the device across the wall, pretending to follow a compelling lead. White noise echoed through the headphones until she approached the hole in the bricks, then she heard a faint, scratchy voice. The wavelength bars suddenly bounced on the EVP.

"*Murder*," the disembodied voice whispered. Althea shook her head in disbelief before turning around and catching sight of the individuals at the far end of the hallway. Despite anticipating their appearance, she was still startled when she saw the daunting trio. Althea decided to leverage the surprise in her performance.

"Oh, hi! I didn't know anyone else was up here!" she shouted, trying to hear herself through the headphones. Cristian's mouth moved, but Althea couldn't make out his words. This inability to hear was the precise act that she wanted to emphasize and demonstrate to the group to show them that she hadn't just been eavesdropping on their conversation. "I'm sorry, what? I can't hear you," she shouted again, before adjusting to a more normal volume as she removed the headphones. "Here, let me take these things off." Cristian looked her up and down suspiciously.

"So, ya doing a little ghost hunting?" he asked in an exaggerated tone of insincere friendliness.

"Yeah, just collecting materials. I'm excited to get this content into the editing bay. Once I've crafted a rough cut, I'll need your help with voice-over audio and interviews," she stated, fighting to maintain composure.

She fought hard to keep her nerves steady. Erika had told her that Cristian and his friends were the ones who made the werewolves that attacked them during the last Full Moon. This, combined with Kessler's unsettling threats in the courtyard moments ago, made Althea understand the gravity of the situation. She had to stay calm, even with the heavy realization that both she and Erika were truly in danger.

"Vittoria, Kessler, can you give us a moment?" Cristian requested.

His friends obliged, leaving Cristian's side and heading toward the elevator while casting distrustful gazes at Althea. As Vittoria passed by, Althea felt a distinct absence in her aura, almost as if something present in most sentient beings was missing. It wasn't so much nefarious as it was purely animalistic. When Kessler passed by, a full-blown premonition overcame her. He was desperate to prove himself and was on a path to take bolder actions to do so. She sensed that it wouldn't be long before Kessler had the blood he so desperately desired on his hands. Althea needed to get Erika as far away from this place as possible. Again, she worked hard to steady her nerves. The two continued glaring at her as the elevator doors closed, and soon, the cart began descending to a lower floor. Althea was now alone with Cristian Dragos. She directed her inner scope toward him.

"I want to know what you were doing inside my grandma's room the other night?"

"I'm sorry. I didn't mean to overstep. I've been going through a lot of old documentation and was trying to ask her for some insight."

"It didn't sound like you were talking about documentation when I got there. It sounded like you might have been asking about a murder. Are you working for the hunters?" While his voice was calm, his tone was menacing.

"No, of course not," she responded emphatically. "My loyalty is to Erika. I will be honest—the hunters asked me to send them information, but I haven't. Not once! I've had no contact with them."

"Do you know what they are looking for?" he pressed.

"No, I don't. And frankly, I don't care," she fired back with overstated ambiguity. It almost seemed as if she had convinced him, but his eyes still swam with distrust.

Cristian took several steps toward her. Althea braced herself, unsure of his intentions. He walked right past her and toward Ana's office. She was stunned when he reached for the door handle. Althea had just discovered Sophia's spell book inside the broken safe. She couldn't allow it to slip through her fingertips. Althea sprang into action, reached into her backpack, and this time extracted a blue racquetball.

"Um, hey," she said casually. Cristian stopped just before the door and impatiently looked at her until he noticed the blue bouncy ball in her hand. They both stood very still until Althea bent down and rolled the ball down the hallway. As soon as the toy left her grasp, Cristian seemed impassively intrigued. He cleared his throat and nonchalantly followed it. Her plan worked. Cristian walked away from the office and down the hallway to retrieve the ball.

"I would like you to give me a report on the progress you have made with your little paranormal investigation," he said in a haughty tone as he approached with the retrieved ball in his hand, offering it back to her. However, as soon as Althea reached for it, to her surprise, Cristian pulled the ball away from her, keeping it at arm's length, just out of her reach.

"Well," she said, doing her best not to react to the strange encounter. "I have captured a lot of footage and kept careful records of the different types of paranormal activities I have encountered," she replied, then gave up on reaching for the ball still in his hand. As soon as she stopped trying, Cristian lowered his arm and offered her the ball again. This time, Althea didn't make another attempt to grab it. To her surprise, he started pressing the ball into her body. First, he pressed it into her arm, then her stomach; he kept pushing it into her until she finally took it from him. Once she did, he became fixated on the ball in her hand while continuing to talk.

"You can't just expect to stay here for free with nothing to show for this project of yours. *Throw it*. We're gonna need you to leave soon. *Throw it*. Once I see this *rough cut* of yours, maybe I'll consider letting you come back. *Throw it*," his voice grew more and more anxious with each *'throw it'* command in between his eviction sentences. Althea tossed the ball down the hallway, and Cristian jogged after it this time.

"I fully understand. You and your family have been very gracious in allowing me to stay here and work on my project. I'm new to filmmaking and appreciate the gesture of goodwill you all have extended to this indie artist." She watched him retrieve the ball, walking with as much composure as he could muster. Her response seemed to appease him for the time being as he looked down thoughtfully at the ball.

"Well, I appreciate you seeing things my way," he said genuinely. "Ya, know... this was fun," he said, holding the ball with subtle triumphant body language. "Maybe we can do it again sometime. Before, ya know... ya get the fuck outta here," he said with droll laughter. Althea thought it best to mirror his temperament, so she laughed, too. Cristian sighed out the remainder of his chuckle and said, "Well, I gotta find that bitch cousin of mine. I hear you two are planning some little camping adventure. How..." Cristian shook his head while seemingly searching for a fitting descriptor.

"Fun?" Althea offered.

"Sure," he scoffed, then brushed past her as he headed toward the elevator. He must have forgotten what he intended to do with Ana's office, as he walked by it without a second look.

A pleasant grin rested on Althea's lips when she realized she might have a chance to grab the Dragos family spell book after all. At that moment, a new premonition finally floated into her consciousness. She sensed that Cristian was experiencing tremendous pressure and also noted that he was feeling introspective over a major life decision. Since she was aware of the danger some of those decisions posed, and that Marius and Blake were not there to ensure their safety, Althea shifted her thoughts to grabbing the spellbook and Erika away from Dragos Manor as soon as possible.

Cristian was about to get on the elevator but suddenly switched directions as if he remembered something. He pulled a set of keys from his pocket, walked down the hallway, and then closed and locked Ana's office door. Althea's heart sank through the floor; she had come so close, but now she could not get her hands on the Dragos spell book. Cristian headed back to the elevator and pressed the call button. As he stepped into the cart and pressed the button to head downstairs, Althea realized that she didn't have any other reason to remain on the 4th floor.

"Wait," she called out. "Hold the door; I'm headed down too."

Cristian's mind raced as the elevator cart descended toward the 3rd floor. *That was way too close for comfort! What if the ghost hunter had heard Kessler's dumb remarks and told Erika? Imagine the shitstorm it would create! Killing someone has already caused me enough problems. I'm not going to entertain killing my own family member. I mean, maybe I daydream about it, but I sure as shit would never act on it! That's it! This has all gone too far! First, I need to speak with Erika and tell her that I need her here. Then I'll find Kessler and Vittoria and tell them that I'm not on board with harming my family. Not Erika, not Bunica, or anyone else! We need to deal with the hunters, tone down the nightclub, and empower Erika to figure out the house's magic maintenance. It's time to fucking grow up. It's time to listen to the other Heads of Household.*

When the elevator dinged upon arriving on the 3rd floor, Althea quickly thought of a way to distract Cristian long enough to grab Erika and make their escape. It was too dangerous to let him get anywhere near Erika; much less be alone with her. Althea realized she had to create a distraction so she could finish preparing for the trip and convince Erika that they should leave immediately. She needed something convincing to divert his attention. When the elevator doors opened, she and Cristian stepped out of the car, both heading toward Erika's room.

"What are you doing?" he asked incredulously.

"I just want to apologize once more for overstepping by going to visit your grandma," Althea blurted out. "Ya know... it was very strange," Althea continued.

'What was?" he asked, eyeing her suspiciously.

"Ana mistook me for Erika," Althea said. "She mentioned something to me that I feel I should share with you." It worked. Her words captured Cristian's attention. He stopped and stared at her with something resembling dread.

"Did she?" he asked, taking the bait.

"Yeah, she said something about a family spell book hidden behind a secret panel in the ballroom. I'm not sure if that means anything to you," she said, feigning ignorance. Cristian's curiosity seemed piqued. Althea needed to push the idea just a little further. "It's funny, I look nothing like Erika. I'm worried your grandmother might mistake any woman for Erika. She seemed quite eager to talk about several subjects. Again, I just wanted to let you know in case Vittoria or anyone else went to visit her." Althea hoped her plan was not too obvious, but it didn't seem so.

"Thank you for letting me know. I will make sure we monitor my Buncia's visitors more closely," he said as he changed directions and headed toward his bedroom suite adjacent to Vittoria's. Cristian seemed so intrigued that it appeared that he had forgotten all about wanting to talk with his cousin.

Althea exhaled the breath she had been holding for a long time. She didn't have much time. She would quickly gather her things, do a quick dye job to avoid being easily spotted, and then get Erika.

Chapter Thirty-Four

CUT OUT

A wide range of backpacking supplies was spread out on Erika's bed. All the essential items were included—two full water canteens with built-in UV purifiers, a ferro rod with a steel striker, a small multitool with knife blades and pliers, lightweight sleeping bags, a two-person tent, a map and compass, a mini first aid kit, two small pots, and, of course, pack food. Additional items included a flashlight, survival blankets, utensils, mugs, extra water purification drops for backup, and a ground tarp. They planned for a modest amount of clothing and toiletries.

Erika meticulously reviewed every item, carefully considering whether anything essential was overlooked. With their departure scheduled in the next one to two days, they still had the opportunity to acquire any last-minute necessities. She reached down and lifted a small, lightweight pack onto the bed, eagerly experimenting with the optimal order for loading it.

A sudden knock at the door startled her. Erika called for the individual to enter, and when she saw Althea step inside, she was taken aback—not by her friend's presence, but by the striking transformation. The vibrant blue hair that had once flowed like a river was gone and was now replaced by long, luxurious black strands that cascaded gracefully over her shoulders.

"Wow, you look great! I mean, your hair... Your hair looks great," Erika stammered, feeling slightly mystified. "I was just about to text you. I think we have everything," she began, but Althea hurriedly walked toward her and interrupted.

"Erika, please, you have to listen to me," she urged in a low yet urgent tone. "We need to leave immediately. I can't explain everything right now, but trust me—something is very wrong. We must put as much distance between us and this place before nightfall."

"What's going on?" Erika asked with mild alarm.

"I promise that once we're a safe distance away, I will share everything with you. All I ask for now is your trust. We need to leave immediately."

Erika nodded resolutely. That was all she needed to hear because she trusted her friend. They quickly began packing their gear.

A quiet knock sounded at the door, followed by the latch unfastening and a squeak from the unoiled hinges. In the next moment, Vittoria's face appeared in the doorframe. She stepped into Ana's bedroom suite, while Cristian slipped in behind her but quickly retreated into the recesses of the room to avoid being seen. Ana sat in a chair, gazing dreamily out the window that overlooked the front lawn and the eastern woods. In the distance, the peak of Mount Saudade loomed over the land, as the remnants of spring lingered for one more month in its kingdom.

The retired Dragos Matriarch looked peaceful. Cristian watched as Vittoria approached his Bunica, her hips swaying gracefully with each step, making her movements resemble a slithering snake closing in on a mouse. Vittoria sidled up close to Ana and crouched down to her eye level.

"Hello, Ana," Vittoria said, a bright red smile spreading across her face. "My, you're looking well. It's so good to see you." Ana roused; her wrinkled face scrunched as she seemingly tried to place Vittoria's face.

"Oh, it's wonderful to see you, my dear," Ana said with a tone of surprise that obscured whether she recognized Vittoria's identity.

"I swear you look younger every time I see you." The compliment made Ana's cheeks flush as she fidgeted.

"Thank you, my dear. Thank you. You know, it's like I've always said, it's good to live a clean life of temperance, free of sin and indulgences."

"Ana, I hope you can help me with something important," Vittoria said with an earnest tone. Cristian quietly positioned himself just behind his grandma, ensuring he remained out of her sight. Vittoria's eyes shifted upward to meet his. "I remember you mentioned the other night that the Dragos family spell book is safely tucked away behind a secret panel in the ballroom. Could you please remind me exactly where it is? It's crucial that I locate it."

Ana seemed flummoxed by this question. "Secret what? Panel? No, my child. No panel. It's upstairs in my office, inside the safe."

Bingo, Cristian thought, as a wave of relief flooded through him. Now, they could finally get to work. He was grateful that Vittoria was willing to try her hand at the magic before deciding whether or not they needed Erika in the mix.

"Oh, silly me. That's right. You did say inside the safe. Tell me, is there a combination or a key that I need?" Vittoria continued.

"No, my dear. The mechanism is long broken. You should be able to pull on the handle. I suppose there really is no sense keeping it in there any longer," Ana laughed. "I'm glad you brought up this subject, you know; we really should practice soon. I won't be around forever, you know."

Hearing those words struck Cristian's heart, causing his breath to catch in his throat. Even amidst the chaos that surrounded their relationship, his love for his Bunica was unwavering.

"Of course, Ana. I will fetch it and bring it to you immediately," Vittoria said triumphantly.

"Good, I'm glad you are taking such an interest. As I said, I won't be around forever, and furthermore, I will be leaving my entire estate exclusively to you. You can manage the family affairs at your discretion."

This time, Vittoria looked up at Cristian in astonishment. Confused by his grandma's words, he gestured with his hand, signaling for Vittoria to continue and find out more.

"Ah, ah, what do you mean, Ana?"

"Cristian and Marius are cut out. Marius has his own money, and Cristian does not need mine. I'm trying to ensure the Head of this Household remains where it should, namely with the next living female Dragos heir," she stated matter-of-factly.

The sting of those words resonated so profoundly within Cristian that he felt utterly numb. He was devastated. How could his Bunica dismiss him so carelessly? A wave of anger began to infiltrate through the cracks of his shattered heart.

"The good news is..." Ana continued. Vittoria returned to look at Ana. "..that I forgive him."

"Forgive who?" Vittoria asked.

"Cristian," Ana replied simply.

Vittoria followed Cristian out of Ana's suite and closed the door behind them.

"That's not the first time she's said that. That she *forgives* me. What do you think she meant by that?" Cristian asked with his back to Vittoria. "*She forgives me.* Forgives me for what? I didn't even know I was sorry," he questioned in disbelief as he turned to face Vittoria.

"It doesn't matter right now, darling. Put it out of your mind. We know where the spell book is, and Erika is still leaving, correct?" Cristian nodded, but he still couldn't shake the bad feelings surrounding his grandma's words.

"Yeah," he said. "You're right. It doesn't matter. It's better that she's leaving." Cristian said, feeling completely deflated. Vittoria watched him for a moment before casting her eyes to the floor. Anguish nestled in Cristian's heart at the realization that his Bunica—the only one in his family who raised and cared for him—was cutting him out. He felt dead inside.

"Are you alright?" Vittoria asked, her face conveying a knowing expression that what had just happened in that room most likely destroyed her best friend.

"You know what, Vittoria? No. No, I'm not alright. Everything I've ever done has been to earn the love and respect of my Bunica. What she values most are tradition and the honor of the Dragos name. In her eyes, I will never embody either of those values simply because I'm gay. All my life, I've felt inferior to my cousin, and those feelings haven't diminished in adulthood. I've always wished my life were as easy as hers. The only reason Erika is Head of Household is because it's tradition. It was handed to her on a golden platter, and I'm sorry I ever brought her here."

"What are you saying, my love?"

"I'm saying that I don't care anymore. I don't care what happens to her out in those woods," he murmured as his eyes met Vittoria's.

Althea's mind raced as she sifted through the items in her backpack. Many of the gadgets and tools that Kit had provided would be useless to her in the wilderness. She had to consider keeping her pack light to avoid carrying around unnecessary weight. She wrapped the pewter hand mirror in a scarf and shoved it into her pack, along with the iron needle the three sisters had given her and the mini travel kit she always carried to mix elixirs and tinctures. Finally, she grabbed two books. One was a small encyclopedia of plant species, which might be useful if they needed to forage or mix any rudimentary medicines during their journey; the second was Sophia Dragos' journal. She tucked everything in her bag and zipped it up.

Glancing out the window, Althea saw the afternoon light beginning to fade into dusk. They needed to hurry. It seemed that her plan to distract Cristian had worked; he never came to knock on Erika's door. Althea's mind began to swirl with doubt as she fought to maintain her nerve. Perhaps instead of going on this hike, they should hop into their car and leave Nocturne. Maybe they should drive into town to surround themselves with people, or call Marius or Blake and tell them the situation, and ask them to return immediately. But something inside her insisted they needed to follow this road that stretched out before them.

The sisters' words suddenly echoed in her mind, as if playing on an obscured stereo—*There will be moments when you feel tempted to stray from this path. Whether driven by fear, self-preservation, or even situations of life and death, you may want to give up, but believe in your purpose and remain steadfast in your journey. The easy road will not yield the answers you seek.*

The time was nigh. Althea watched as Erika loaded her pack onto her shoulders, pulling her long, ash-brown hair from underneath the straps and gathering it into her hands before tying it into a flowing ponytail. Then, Erika turned and met Althea's gaze. A light shone from within Erika's spirit that ignited a flame inside Althea's soul. She was meant to be here, with this person, at this time. Althea understood that she, Erika, and this moment were merely a blip in the vast scheme of all that had transpired throughout time and all that was yet to occur. All fear melted away. Althea walked over and stood beside her friend.

"Should we cut out?" Erika proposed.

Chapter Thirty-Five

TENSIONS RISING

Dusk enveloped the Noctambulist woodlands. Beau felt a rising anxiety as he glanced at his tactical watch—7 pm on the dot. Nightfall was expected just before 8 pm, with the Moon set to appear soon after. Where was Corbin and his crew? He looked over at Carter and Malik, who were speaking in hushed tones as they surveilled the group of campers they had been tailing for the past two weeks. Their campsite was located approximately ninety feet away. Although Beau was confident that his team could take down at least some of the beasts, three against six could be a daunting task, especially with a rookie crew member. If any of those creatures survived another Full Moon, they would become increasingly difficult to capture and would have the potential to reproduce more like them. Beau realized it was time to assume a three-man operation as he walked over to strategize a game plan for moonfall.

"My question is, why aren't there more consequences for the werewolf families? Why not enforce some accountability?" Malik asked.

"Normally this isn't a huge problem that stems from civilized families. If a feral happens, it's usually an accident—one, maybe two, can be considered an accident. This amount was done intentionally. Don't worry; there will be accountability and consequences," Carter assured.

"Listen up, men. I have decided that we need to proceed with the assumption that it will just be the three of us tonight."

"Someone's coming!" Carter said in a low, urgent whisper.

Beau's fears were soon quelled when he spun around and saw a lone figure approaching from a distance behind them. He exhaled a sigh of relief upon registering a short male frame with a fauxhawk. Thank God. For a moment, Beau was worried that they had moved so much while tracking the group of campers that Corbin and his crew would be unable to locate them. He silently laughed as he chastised himself for having any doubt. Corbin could find anything.

"Am I glad to see you," Beau greeted as soon as Corbin was close enough that he didn't need to shout. "I was worried for a minute there. Where is the rest of your crew? Did you guys find any more targets?"

"Hey man, I'm sorry to have worried you," Corbin said as he stepped over a fallen tree and joined Beau's team. "Yes, we found three white males with little clothing in a makeshift campsite about six miles east of here. They don't have as many supplies as this group and certainly didn't have a vehicle, but they're managing. Naiche and Nawn stayed behind to track that group. I realized I needed to get back here and help you with this large group," he said, gesturing toward the direction Carter pointed his binoculars.

"Let's hope that's all of them, and we can close this thing out tonight," Beau said. "If not, we're out here for at least another month."

"Not to worry, brother. We will get them," Corbin reassured. "These woods have so many other occupants that we'll close in on any outsiders sooner or later. Speaking of which, remind your guys to be careful with those forest lights. We accidentally wasted some time chasing them for a short while, thinking they were more of those bitten people. It's just those damn Will-o'-the-wisps. We have enough going on without wasting time on demonic red herrings."

"Copy all," Beau said, glancing at his watch again. "We're about forty minutes from sunset. Do you think we should move into position soon?"

"Just let me know how I can assist," Corbin said. "This is your party."

"I think we keep it simple. Now that there are four of us, we can surround their camp from the north, south, east, and west positions."

"Great. Also, because these campers have a vehicle, I parked my *Jeep* a few hundred feet back in the woods," Corbin said. "Just in case there's a vehicle pursuit."

The door to the Sterling Lodge banged shut on its hinges. Travis sauntered out to meet the townspeople who stood waiting anxiously outside.

"Just as I suspected, not a one of them is anywhere in sight. Matter of fact, I don't think I have seen those supposed hunters in weeks," Travis said. Angry murmurs of unrest rose in pockets from the crowd of about two dozen townies. "They said '*trust us*!' They said they would handle it! Instead, it's only gotten worse! Tonight is yet another Full Moon, and where the fuck is that little fancy-haired asshole with his dumb-fuck neck tattoo?" Again, the crowd's audible nods of agreement, coupled with angry furrowed brows, encouraged Travis to continue his discourse. "Okay, boys, we're heading over to Dragos Manor tonight! Let's confront these animals. See what's really going on over there!" The proposal was met with a resounding roar of consensus.

Two sturdy pairs of hiking boots stepped gingerly outside Dragos Manor. Althea and Erika were as ready as they'd ever be to embark on the adventure that lay ahead. Their packs were light yet brimming with preparedness. Althea's gut told her to manage her sense of urgency; they needed to press forward into the woods at a steady pace. Just as one would move cautiously around any wild animal, she understood that any hurried or erratic movements could potentially attract unwanted attention. She stole a glance back at Erika, whose eyes met hers. There was a spark of determination in them as a small, reassuring smile played at the corners of her mouth, an unspoken promise that whatever lay ahead, they would face it together.

A quiet knock sounded on Erika's bedroom door, soon followed by it opening and Cristian's head peeking inside.

"Hellooo. Is anybody home?" he called out in a low voice as he glanced around the room. Everything was silent and still. The bed was made, and nothing looked out of place. Cristian opened the door fully and stepped inside. "Erika?" he called out louder this time. There was no response. As he stepped further into the room, his eyes began to scan the area. He was unsure of exactly what he was searching for but hoped to find some clue about Erika's life.

He felt the weight of his own misguided notions bearing down on him like an impending storm. Luring Erika back to Dragos Manor had been his idea. Now, as Cristian reflected on the magnitude of his mistake, he grappled with regret. He had once convinced himself that he needed his cousin and that his intentions were noble for the sake of the family. But now, his grandmother's haunting words echoed in his mind—*I'm trying to ensure the Head of this Household remains where it should, namely with the next living female Dragos heir.* Cristian found these thoughts tightening around his throat like a noose. He could no longer deny the truth—this was likely how it was always meant to be. Ana's unwavering commitment to tradition made it clear—the estate would never be passed down to him or Marius. It was always Erika's destiny. He had to face the facts and acknowledge the inevitable. The future of Dragos Manor was sealed long before he ever contemplated his own place in it. He couldn't deceive himself any longer.

Cristian wandered over to the window and glanced down at the front lawn. Headlights from vehicles were beginning to arrive for that evening's events, bringing a crowd of visitors eager for an evening of merriment and delight. Cristian had done that. He was the proprietor of the feelings those strangers sought. He smiled, proud of his accomplishment, but that feeling quickly gave way to a quiet sob that surprised even him. He surrendered to the emotion and wept into his hands as the blue light of the evening spilled upon him.

"I'm just so conflicted," he sobbed aloud to no one as his heart squeezed and ached. The sorrow could not keep him for long, however. Cristian had a job to do, and he knew that he needed to move away from the window to avoid an undesired transformation should the Moon suddenly decide to poke its face out in the night sky. He straightened up and wiped the tears from his cheeks. As he was about to turn away, he noticed two women wearing packs nearing the woodland tree line. "The fuck?" he said aloud as he grabbed his phone from his pocket and dialed Erika's number. The line went straight to voicemail. He quickly tried again, but it was too late. He watched as the two reached the edge of the forest and disappeared among the trees.

The darkness of the night felt impenetrable in the woods, surrounded by trees and thick vegetation. A new instinct told Kathryn that something within her was changing. It was happening to all of them. She acutely sensed her companions' fear and agitation; more than simply sensing it, she could almost taste it.

Ever since that dreadful night when she and the others were bitten, her senses had heightened beyond the normal human range. But tonight was different. The group had discussed the impending transformation at length, but no amount of reasoning or rationale could prepare them for what was about to unfold. The thought of her body twisting and breaking into another species frightened her. More than the pain, the fear of not knowing exactly when it would happen loomed. It felt similar to stepping into a haunted house attraction; you knew something was coming, but had no idea where or when. On top of it all, they all knew that people were hiding in the woods, stalking them. They could now smell them.

"We don't have much time. I can feel the tension in my bones like they're gonna snap," Stanley said, his face contorted in discomfort.

"They're just out there waiting for us," Alice whimpered. "Why can't they leave us alone?"

"Well, we're sure as shit not going to make this easy for them," Kyle said. "I think we should split up now. Remember the plan—no matter what happens, we'll reconvene at the spot we discussed closer to the base of the mountain."

"I'm scared," Alice said.

"I know, love. We're all scared," Kathryn said, trying to comfort her new friend.

"After tonight, I think we should seriously consider moving on from this area altogether," Kyle suggested.

"No!" Jerome protested through gritted teeth, his fangs starting to grow inside his mouth. "I'm not leaving Jazmine behind."

"Yeah, unfortunately, that's not really on the table for us either," Stanley said, looking at Kathryn. "We need to find Nacho."

Everyone's eyes turned to Alex, anticipating a similar protest, but he merely looked at the ground. The group stood in somber realization that perhaps their friends were already dead.

"Don't worry; we'll figure something out, but for now, I think we should move," Kyle said.

"I agree with you, brother," Stanley said. "Okay, we're going to stash the supplies you loaned us so we have that stuff at our disposal until we can reconvene." The six people whose lives were changed forever stared at each other a moment longer.

"Be safe out there," Kyle said.

"You too, my friend," Stanley replied. Then everyone got moving. Kyle, Alice, and Alex climbed into the *Sprinter*. When the engine turned over, Kathryn, Stanley, and Jerome started packing up their gear—tents, a fire starter, water purification tablets, and first aid. In the distance, Kathryn heard the faint sound of a second vehicle engine starting up. Kathryn, Stanley, and Jerome locked eyes, then they whirled around to look at their friends through the van's windshield.

"Go now!" Kathryn shouted.

As the van sped away, Kathryn heard the distant sound of the other car's engine. Out of the corner of her eye, she noticed a *Jeep* appearing from behind its cover in the distance.

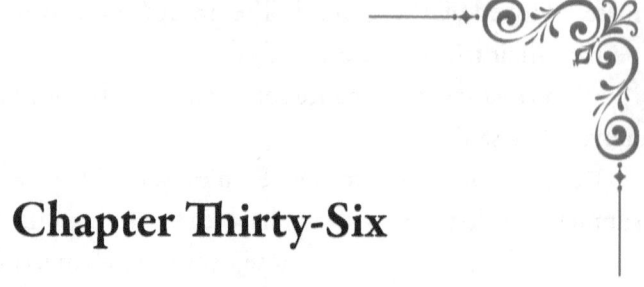

Chapter Thirty-Six

INDECENT EXPOSURE

Night of the Flower Moon

The drinks flowed, the DJ set was in full swing, and everyone inside Club Dragos was having a great time—except for Cristian Dragos. A tear rolled down his cheek, landing in his shot of whiskey. Vittoria and most of the Killers, minus Beo, sat with him in the owner's lounge on the ballroom stage. The curtains were drawn shut, blocking the massive east-facing windows from the Full Moon, which was about to make its grand appearance in the vast sky at any moment.

"Is there anything I can do to cheer you up, my darling?" Vittoria cooed.

Cristian shrugged and tossed back the whiskey. Responding would only lead to more tears. He was trying to mute his sorrows, not give them a platform or a megaphone. After all, what good would it do to examine his current situation? His boyfriend was gone, his grandmother had rejected him and denied him the only home he had ever known, and his cousin had left him to face all the problems they were dealing with alone. Sure, Cristian thought he wanted Erika to leave, but to actually see her disappear into the forest with that woman had enraged him. The bright side was that with her gone came the clarity Cristian needed about taking charge. He would stand his ground against the hunters, the other Heads of Household, and anything else that crossed his path. And he was going to do it his way. Cristian looked out hollowly at the sea of people before him.

"You know what? Fuck it. I've just decided I don't need anyone's permission anymore. My Bunica isn't going to accept me no matter what, so

I'm done spending even a second longer playing nice. I don't need any of them," Cristian proclaimed as a tear rolled down his cheek.

"Good for you, darling. That's the spirit," Vittoria beamed as the other Killers voiced their support for the idea as well.

"Does this mean... you're not stepping down?" Kessler asked. "Even to our parents' demands?"

"That's right, Kess. The buck stops here with me. This is my home, my nightclub, my success. I'm the Dragos Head of Household. Erika might not even make it out of those woods alive," Cristian said nonchalantly. Kessler and Vittoria exchanged quick glances. "Even if she does, I don't see her sticking around. Not after what she's done to me. She left me holding the bag for everything. Fuck her."

His intrusive thoughts crept in once more. *What would life be like if Erika were no longer around?* he wondered as he poured himself another shot. For a moment, Cristian thought of his childhood with his cousin. He recalled the games they used to play and the laughter that flowed from their hearts and lungs. No matter how much he understood what most likely needed to be done, following through felt impossible. Cristian looked over at Kessler and Vittoria. The pair chatted and sipped champagne, resembling the wolf-in-sheep's-clothing version of Bonnie and Clyde, except if Faye Dunaway had black hair and fire engine red lips and Warren Beatty had been bypassed for a young Marlon Brando instead.

For a moment, Cristian considered leaning over and clearly stating that no one was to bring any harm to his cousin, and that he himself would eventually face her and sort it out. That's not to say he intended to kill her; even if his life depended on it, he did not believe he could harm his own flesh and blood. Cristian stared at his friends, but for some reason, the words would not come out of his mouth.

The two security guards standing in front of the large, sealed windows began shifting around nervously while listening to their earpieces, then responded on their walkie-talkies. One left his post, walked up the stairs, and onto the stage. Cristian was surprised to see the man hold out his walkie-talkie. "The boss says we've got a situation out front. He's asking to speak with you for further instruction," he explained.

"What's happening?" Cristian asked. The guard captured the attention of the other Killers as they all watched him offer Cristian the short-range communication device.

"The Boss says there's a disturbance in front of the home and is asking if me and the other guard can join him," the guard responded with a thick Bostonian accent.

"Absolutely not! Return to your post. I'll deal with this," Cristian said, raising the walkie-talkie to his mouth. "Hello, this is Cristian. What's happening out there?"

"Sir, you have to hold down the button," the guard instructed. Cristian rolled his eyes and tried again.

"Hi, hello, this is Cristian. What's happening out there?"

"Say 'Over,' sir."

"Over," Cristian said in a mocking tone into the walkie-talkie. Shortly afterward, a crackle of audio preceded the transmission response from the head of security.

"Sir, we have a situation out here. Requesting to pull all guards from their stations to help keep things under control out here, over." Then, the static sound fell silent.

"Ummm, request, like, denied," Cristian replied. "Tell me what's happening! Who's out there?" He let go of the button and rolled his eyes as he remembered. "Over."

"Just a moment, let me ask them to identify themselves." The walkie-talkie fell silent for a moment. Cristian looked at the Killers and laughed, shaking his head at the situation. Again, a crackle brought the communication device back to life as the head of security's gruff voice returned once more. "Mob; Angry mob—is all I can get outta them."

Cristian's face fell into sharp dismay. He took a moment before responding. It was a month early. That better not be those freakin' hunters out there. If it was war they wanted, they would get it.

"Nobody leaves their posts. Stay right there. We're coming out," Cristian said, anger fuming from the core of his being.

People chatted and conversed outside the ballroom, seemingly unaware of the events unfolding on the front steps of Dragos Manor. Cristian and the Killers weaved through the crowd and approached the front doors. River lurched forward and grabbed Cristian's arm.

"What are you doing? We can't go outside unless you're ready to transition for the night," he said with alarm.

"Dude, no duh! I was just going to see if we can find out more about this so-called *angry mob*," Cristian fired back. "If those hunters rolled up here before our agreed-upon timeframe, I think we need to be ready to chase them off this property," he said, bristling with anger.

"We're with you, Cristian," Kessler stated with conviction.

"I agree. I don't think we should allow the hunters to push us around," Loki quietly agreed.

"My daddy's gonna kick my butt, but I'm in too. I think this is important," Malcolm Jr. added. Vittoria, River, and the rest of the group nodded in agreement. Looking around at his friends, Cristian felt touched. A pang of gratitude reverberated in his heart and caused his eyes to fill with moisture.

"You guys are my real family, my chosen family. Thank you for your unconditional support; I mean it," Cristian said as he wiped his eyes. Vittoria placed her hand on his shoulder and leaned in.

"Let's raise hell," she whispered.

Cristian nodded and lifted the walkie-talkie to his mouth. He licked his lips, then pressed the button.

"This is Cristian Dragos. I need your team to pull back. Come inside and clear the lobby. Everyone needs to either be inside the club or inside the lounge. We need space in case this thing gets outta hand. Over."

A crackle, and then, "Sir, I would advise against my team pulling back. We have an agitated crowd out here. Torches, pitchforks, the whole nine yards. Over."

Cristian cocked his head to the side. *Pitchforks?* That didn't sound like the hunters' MO.

"Wait, can you find out any more info from them? Ask them where they are from. Over." Cristian inquired. After a moment, the guard responded.

"They said they are from right here in Nocturne, Massachusetts. They wanted me to tell my boss to come outside and face them. They said something about sending you back to hell, I don't know. In my opinion, you should not come out here. They're a little all over the place, sir. Over."

From Nocturne. These people were not werewolf hunters, which could only mean one thing—Cristian had a good old-fashioned neighborly dispute on his hands.

"Thank you for your advice. We'll be fine. Tell them we will grant them an audience. Your team needs to pull back, but stand by in case we need you. And Mike, remember, I am paying you very good money. I hope that buys a certain level of loyalty. Over."

Shortly after, the security team returned inside the lobby and escorted the crowd of partygoers into the ballroom or lobby. Now, there was only one thing left to do. Cristian and the Killers removed their clothing and kicked their underwear aside.

"The good news is, it sounds like we only have angry townies outside, and not the hunters. They're probably just upset after all the ferals were set loose during the last Full Moon. I bet they're trying to pin us down and think if they prove we're werewolves, they'll have the right to murder us or something," he said dismissively. "I think we'll be okay. I doubt there will be a silver bullet among them," Cristian said. The group laughed momentarily, and then Cristian became serious once more. "*Only scare them.* No killing. Do you guys understand?" Oddly enough, Cristian had meant to utter these words earlier that night but couldn't get them out when it came to Erika. Now, he knew that he did not want that to happen. He looked at Kessler and Vittoria and repeated his message. "No killing *anyone* tonight. Got it?"

The moment was upon them. There would be no turning back from what they were about to do. Cristian knew there would be consequences for his actions, but he didn't care. It was high time the whole town recognized the benefits he brought to the town. If they would not willingly give their respect to the name Dragos, he would force them to respect him. He turned and swung both large front doors wide open.

Kathryn fought for every breath, her heart thundering in her chest as she sprinted through the darkness. The cool air stung her lungs, yet she pressed on, desperate to escape. Behind her, the sound of heavy footfalls loomed closer, echoing in the night. Though she couldn't see her pursuer, the scent of danger was unmistakable. Her legs felt as if they might crumble, each step a battle against exhaustion. She knew that if she fell, it would give her relentless stalker those crucial seconds to catch her. The thought sent a wave of terror coursing through her veins, urging her to push harder, to flee faster. Her life depended on it.

The ground suddenly dropped beneath her feet. She stumbled head over heels, rolling down a hill. Kathryn's body landed with a thud in a clearing where the Moon sat center stage in the sky like the main event. She cried in anguish as her body contorted and broke, seeking a form unfamiliar to it. Her clothing became extremely tight all over before tearing. Thick swatches of golden yellow fur replaced the surface area of her body. Her tears gave way to a sense of predation. All emotion surrendered to instinct.

Soon, the form of the hunter who had been chasing her emerged from the brush. The man raised his weapons while yelling something indiscernible. Kathryn lay there in her new werewolf state. He began to charge forward but hesitated. She could smell his fear and rounded on him, jaws snapping ferociously. She pounced, knocking him to the ground.

Under the glow of the Flower Moon, Cristian and the Killers boldly marched outside the house, stark naked. The unexpected sight stunned the townspeople, many of whom recoiled in disbelief. Suddenly, the naked figures transformed as the townspeople watched on in horror. Fur sprouted across their bodies, their jaws elongated into formidable maxillae and mandibles, while tails erupted from behind. When the transformation was complete, all that remained were powerful, canine figures standing bipedally before the terrified crowd. For a tense moment, both groups locked eyes in a silent standoff. Then, with a calm yet commanding presence, wolf Cristian stepped forward to address the crowd.

"You are all trespassing," he declared through his wolf lips. The townspeople were frozen as they stared in utter shock at the talking canine figure before them. Wolf Cristian suddenly raised his right hand as if conducting an orchestra and unleashed a powerful, thunderous howl that resonated deeply across the grounds. In an instant, the Killers mirrored his intensity, joining in on Cristian's foreboding howl.

Apparently, that was enough for the townspeople. Sheer panic erupted as the crowd let out terrified screams. They began scrambling in all directions while the werewolves descended the steps and chased after them. Although the wolves could have easily hunted down and caught the fleeing mob, they snarled and bared their teeth from a safe distance. The townsfolk zig-zagged frantically across the lawn, desperate to get away.

One man in overalls stopped and turned toward his werewolf attacker, throwing his pitchfork like a javelin. Wolf River rose from all fours and easily caught the pitchfork. The man in overalls looked petrified as he stared at the werewolf holding the pitchfork.

"Really, bro? Come on," wolf River said incredulously. The man in overalls pivoted and continued running.

Malcolm Jr., the werewolf, chased down another man wearing jeans and a red flannel shirt. Unfortunately, the man tripped and fell hard, hitting the ground face-first. Wolf Malcolm Jr. raced to his side and helped him back onto his feet.

"Whoopsie, that looked really bad!" wolf Malcolm said, carefully dusting clumps of dirt from the man's face and clothing with his paws. The man stood wide-eyed, staring at the werewolf who was acting so compassionately toward him. The two found themselves at an impasse. "Um, I guess you should start running again," wolf Malcolm Jr. suggested. The man slowly nodded, and the two took off more slowly this time.

Wolf Cristian pursued a man who unexpectedly turned and aimed a shotgun directly at Cristian's face. Wolf Cristian let out a high-pitched shriek and swiftly batted the shotgun's muzzle away just as the farmer pulled the trigger. The blast illuminated the night as the gun fired into the air. Wolf Cristian seized the firearm from the man's hands and rapidly racked five more shells, unloading the ammunition onto the ground.

"What's wrong with you?" he demanded, then threw the gun over his shoulder into the grass. "Ugh, that was such a dick move. You could have hit me! Start running again, now!" wolf Cristian ordered. The farmer looked terrified as he followed the command. He resumed running while wolf Cristian shook his head and resumed chasing him once more.

Wolf Kessler aggressively pursued the ringleader of the mob, who was screaming and flailing his arms as he attempted to escape the werewolf hot on his heels. It's true; Cristian had said no killing would occur that night, yet the manner in which wolf Kessler chased the man made it seem as if he had not heard the message. The werewolf was gaining on the man, who screamed in terror. Wolf Kessler lunged. The man bellowed in horror just as the werewolf pinned him to the ground. Wolf Kessler pressed his large face close to the man's face.

"You're lucky I have more important things to do tonight," wolf Kessler whispered through gritted fangs. "If you're still here by the time I get back, you're dead." Then, taking advantage of the chaos as his cover, wolf Kessler pivoted and darted off into the forest.

Distant howls pierced the stillness, echoing ominously through the night as Erika and Althea sprinted through the shadowy woods. They instinctively sensed danger behind them, which fueled their urgency to put as much distance as possible between themselves and whatever was happening back at Dragos Manor. There was no turning back.

As the pair sprinted through the underbrush, Erika suddenly became aware of an ominous sound—the rhythmic pounding of galloping paws through the twigs and leaves behind them. The creature was gaining on them at a terrifying speed. Sharp stitches ripped through Erika's side, yet she pushed herself to run even harder, driven by a primal urge to survive. Suddenly, a massive, dark werewolf appeared on the trail ahead. Erika and Althea abruptly stopped in their tracks. The beast's chest heaved with exertion, but it recovered quickly and with alarming speed. The creature closed in on the terrified women, a fearsome growl rumbling in its throat.

Inside the sewing room at the small inn just off Main Street, Marta lifted her face toward her two sisters. Decima noticed her eldest sister watching her through tinted spectacles.

"I was wondering if you needed to borrow my scissors tonight, dear sister?" Marta asked, offering her sharp shears toward her sister, Decima.

As the dark werewolf slowly advanced toward the women, an unexpected rustle from the nearby bushes drew everyone's attention. A flaxen werewolf suddenly emerged, growling menacingly at Erika and Althea. Erika felt her heart race with hope as she briefly mistook the creature for her uncle. Yet, when she noticed the werewolf's golden fur, distinct from her uncle's silver coat, she was quickly reminded that her uncle had abruptly departed overseas. It became painfully clear that this creature was not Marius. Fear and despair set in once more.

The women were now surrounded. The dark wolf was on one side of their path, and the blond werewolf on the other side. It seemed that Erika and Althea had made the wrong choice by marching off into the night like they did. They should have stayed home and faced whatever Althea was worried about. But then, something strange happened. The flaxen werewolf locked its intense gaze on the black werewolf, pinned back its ears, and let out a bone-chilling growl that reverberated with an unmistakable disdain for the dark wolf's very existence.

"Take it easy, newbie," the dark werewolf warned. Erika recognized his voice. It was Kessler! *Thank goodness,* she thought with relief.

"Oh, Kessler, thank God," she exclaimed.

"Kessler?" Althea repeated with alarm, grabbing Erika's arm and quickly leading her away from both wolves.

Erika felt a rising fear as she struggled to keep up, scared of the looming threat of werewolves right behind them. Just then, a frightening cacophony of snarls erupted behind them, halting her and Althea in their tracks. They turned to witness a shocking scene—the flaxen werewolf was viciously overpowering wolf Kessler, who desperately tried to fight back. To their disbelief, the blonde wolf was gaining the upper hand. Kessler, in stark contrast, resembled a frightened house dog, powerless against the wild and untamed ferocity of a true predator.

"Should we help him?" Erika wondered aloud.

"No. He is no friend of ours," Althea said firmly. "Let nature sort itself out."

Back inside the sewing room, Decima contemplated the scissors that Marta offered her before responding.

"No, I don't think I will need to borrow those after all, dear sister. At least, not tonight."

Chapter Thirty-Seven

DAWN

First light was on the verge of breaking, and Erika eagerly awaited its arrival, desperately trying to shake off the overwhelming despair that had gripped her, wondering if daybreak would ever truly come. She and Althea had spent the past few hours wandering deeper into the woods. Once the thick fog bank rolled in, they decided to take a break and seek refuge from the unknown dangers lurking in the nighttime mist. Now, Althea leaned against Erika with her eyes closed as they rested at the base of a large oak tree. Erika would sleep once the sun broke the horizon, and then she would finally feel certain enough that the wolves wouldn't suddenly pounce through the haze of fog.

Her eyelids were half open as she scanned the surroundings. Because of the thick mist, she had to depend on her other senses to detect what was out there. She heard a babbling brook nearby and birds beginning to sing, their melodies echoing through the dense haze hanging in the air. For a moment, Erika let the calming sounds soothe her as she took a short break from surveillance. She glanced down at her friend's black hair resting against her shoulder. A surge of guilt washed over Erika. This stranger had come into her life, willing to offer so much support, protection, and comfort, and all Erika did in return was to let the monsters that haunted her life repeatedly attack her.

The birds fell silent. Erika hadn't realized how much she had come to rely on their song until it disappeared. Her eyes scanned the area around her. With the heavy fog, there was only about fifteen feet of visibility. Everything was dead silent except for the misleadingly peaceful sounds of the nearby stream. Yet, she was certain that something lurked out there. *Oh, why wouldn't the sun rise more quickly?* Erika thought. She could only hope that the fog was hiding their presence just as much as it concealed whatever else was out there. Then, the faint outline of the blond werewolf emerged from the mist. The creature wandered past with waning energy, seemingly oblivious to the two women huddled at the base of the oak tree.

Deep in another part of the forest, Corbin, Beau, and Carter were relentlessly searching for Malik. The weight of worry, combined with the exhaustion from the job they had to perform the night before, etched itself into Beau's brow.

"Try not to worry, Beau," Corbin attempted to reassure his associate. "We will find him. I can see you tearing yourself apart, but we did a good thing last night. We put down that entire van of Lycans. And now we have them, their van, and everything we need to work with our coroners to return those poor souls to their families. I know losing a man is stressful, but we will find Malik."

Beau did not immediately respond, and Corbin suspected he was searching for something to say other than casting self-blame. Corbin knew this feeling well. It wasn't an easy job to lead a group of brave people willing to risk their lives to terminate dangerous creatures in a clean, dignified, and respectful manner so they could return those poor souls to their loved ones. He understood the entire situation wasn't fair. He recognized the cursed individuals didn't choose to become what they were, and it was unfair when any misfortune befell one of their teammates.

"I keep fighting the urge to say I should have stayed with him. I know in my heart that he was ready to be out here with us. And I know that I did the right thing by getting the job done on those three in the van."

"The good news is that I spoke with Nawn Ferris this morning, and she confirmed that she and Naiche were able to get the three Caucasian males they were keeping tabs on. That means we put six down in total last night."

At this, Carter lowered his head in defeat. "I'm sorry I couldn't get mine last night, guys. That one with the red streak down its back was a real shitbag. I got caught up trying to chase him and that black one, and I saw Malik run off after that yellow werewolf."

"I'm proud of this team. We put down *six* wolves last night. All things considered, it sounds like we got most of them. So long as the remaining ones don't bite or scratch anyone else, hopefully, we're down to those last three. And who knows, when we find Malik, he might have gotten that yellow wolf!"

A knock at the front door of La Maison d'Aristide roused Malcolm Sr. and Shanice Aristide from their morning coffee. The two had hoped for a quiet morning after transformation, but this seemed unlikely as they opened the door to find Elena Vulpe, Mihaela Lupu, and John and Serafine Landis.

"I would wish you a good morning," Shanice began, "but I can see by the expressions on your faces that this may not be as good a morning as we'd hoped."

"Are your sons home by chance?" Elena asked.

Malcolm Sr. and Shanice exchanged a glance. "I'm not sure," Malcolm Sr. responded. "What has happened?"

"It wouldn't surprise me if they were over at Dragos Manor. It seems our kids..." Elena cleared her throat. "..exposed themselves to a large group of townspeople last night," she said with evident anger despite her measure.

"My God," Shanice whispered.

"Indeed. We have a problem on our hands. We tasked our children to get their act together, but they have failed," Elena said. "More than failed, they have blatantly defied us. Now, that leaves us with the burden of deciding the consequences. Additionally, we will need to run damage control to mend any issues that may have arisen with the townspeople. The Town Meeting Members will be furious, and I'm afraid Vincent will only be able to do so much to calm their nerves on the matter. We can offer increased dues and memory charms for those who have been greatly traumatized. I don't know about you all, but I was not planning on moving or being driven out of town like Mary Shelley's monster."

"I think it's safe to say we've all had enough," Shanice replied. "The question is, should we even try to engage the Dragos family any further in this matter? I regret to say that Cristian is at the core of all these issues. Erika does not seem capable of handling the responsibilities of her role. At the same time, I realize that Ana is no longer suited for the job, and no one can reach Marius, leaving us with no one else to turn to. So yes, it appears we need to bypass the family unless someone thinks they can get in touch with Marius." At this suggestion, the entire group turned to Malcolm Sr.

"I have already spoken with Marius about this," he said. "He thinks we should pull back and let these kids learn the hard way."

"So, do nothing?" Serafine asked incredulously.

"We cut them off. No more paying for their mistakes. They need to get themselves out of their mess," Malcolm Sr. replied.

"Don't you think that might be a little too dangerous?" Shanice asked with concern. "We're talking potential retaliation from the town. Someone could get killed. It might even be one of our kids."

"It might be dangerous," Malcolm Sr. agreed. "But we must trust what is written. What's meant to be will be. If we continue to try to save our children from themselves, they might never learn that the world has real consequences. They need to understand that *it is possible to lose everything*. If this is meant to be the fall of the house of Dragos, maybe it was meant to stand no longer."

A rustling in the nearby brush made Corbin, Beau, and Carter spin around on their heels. Malik stepped out, and although he should have been happy to see his comrades, he momentarily hesitated. The horrors of the night before had him on edge. Beau's face lit up with relief as he let out a booming laugh and walked over, throwing his massive arms around Malik and lifting him off his feet.

"You had us worried there, friend!" Beau beamed as he set Malik back down on his feet.

"Yeah, sorry to worry you," Malik replied quietly.

"So, how did it go?" Corbin asked with a smile.

"What? Oh, I didn't get it," Malik confirmed.

"That's alright," Carter added. "I didn't get mine either. That was a tough bunch last night. We're just glad you're okay, brother."

"Yeah, I'm okay," Malik responded.

"Well, now that we've found you, let's head back to the lodge. Nawn and Naiche are probably there already. Between all of us, we got six of those creatures last night. Let's eat some breakfast, then we'll get that bunch to the coroner for processing."

As the team set off toward Corbin's *Jeep*, Malik trailed behind. While he usually did not mind Beau's hearty bear hugs, unfortunately, this time, his titan leader might have inadvertently reopened the wound Malik had spent the evening tending to. It was just a scratch; hopefully, it was small enough to heal on its own without any issues. Even so, Malik made sure the other guys weren't looking as he glanced at it. He pulled back his jacket and looked down at the claw marks that had torn through his t-shirt. Sure enough, a small red smear began to soak through the fabric.

The sun was now rising higher in the sky. As soon as the birdsong resumed, Erika knew that whatever creature she had seen was no longer there. Finally, she allowed her body to power down and rest. Normally, Erika could not sleep if it was light outside, but now she found comfort in the brightness that shone through the redness of her closed eyelids. It felt good to keep them closed.

Just before sleep overtook her, she sensed someone or something was watching her. With her last ounce of strength, Erika opened her heavy eyelids and looked out into the dissipating fog again. At first, she didn't see anything. Her surroundings were peaceful and still. But then, a slight movement caught her attention, and she saw the figure of a naked woman standing among the trees and looking in her direction. Erika wondered if this person was real or if she was dreaming with her eyes open. The woman was pale with long blonde hair. She was a lovely creature, with long and graceful features like a forest nymph.

Whether or not she was real, nothing about this mysterious woman made Erika feel threatened. A sense of calm enveloped her, and sleep slowly took hold. Hopefully, the enigmatic figure would still be there when she woke up, as curiosity ignited within her to find out who she was.

Epilogue

A SIZE TWENTY SANDAL supporting a massive foot approached the chicken coop as a large shadow cast across the structure. The hens did not stir or fuss when a hand the size of a dinner plate reached in and gently plucked a few eggs from the nesting boxes. Standing straight, his figure loomed taller than anyone he had ever met. At eight feet four inches tall, his stature solidified him in the gigantic category. It was this physical trait that Homer used for his livelihood.

Homer the Humongous had worked in carnivals for as long as he could remember. He never knew who his parents were, only that they were in the same line of work. Homer spent his life searching for them, moving from one carnival to another. From what he could tell, he could never find them in any mainstream circuit, which is why he expanded his search to circus attractions that operated more *off the beaten path*. This led him to work at Barker's Fun Fair, a carnival of oddities hidden deep within the Noctambulist Forest in Nocturne, Massachusetts. Over the decade since Homer joined this outfit, something unexpected happened—the owner, Mr. Carnie Val Barker—C. Val for short—made it impossible for Homer to leave. This wasn't so much due to any physical chains per se, rather, C. Val was a man who had done a lot for Homer in the absence of having any real family of his own. And even though Homer was not fond of C. Val's disturbing hobbies and peculiar interests, Homer felt so deeply indebted to his employer that the thought of leaving never seemed like a viable option.

Homer plopped a few eggs into a pot of water that bubbled and boiled over a small outdoor fire pit. Once the eggs cooled, he fetched a couple of apples and a banana from Gilda the Ape's bunch and loaded the food into three small bowls. As he strode across the grounds toward the cart containing the fair's newest attractions, he whistled a quiet tune from *The Greatest Show on Earth.*

Having a fair located deep in the forest meant visitors were very rare, although it was always a big event when outside guests stumbled upon their humble carnival outfit. The boss insisted on putting on a massive show with all the bells and whistles. The only problem was, for some terrible reason, bad luck always seemed to befall their guests, and almost always, those unfortunate souls wouldn't make it out of the fair alive. It was always such a shame when that happened. Fortunately, their most recent guests to enter the fair's *"admission trap"* about two months ago turned out to be anything but ordinary. In fact, they were suspected of being werewolves, although they refused to confirm or speak at all, really. The suspicions were finally confirmed just the night before, after the trio transformed inside their cage, much to C. Val's delight, earning them the prestigious title of Barker's Fun Fair's latest attraction. *Those lucky ducks,* Homer thought.

As Homer pulled back the curtain, the three occupants wearing tattered clothing inside the barred train cart scrambled backward, away from the flood of light. The male and two females looked wide-eyed at the giant holding the food bowls.

"You all hungry?" came Homer's baritone voice. No one inside the cart responded. "Well, here, you should eat anyway. That was quite a trick you all did last night. Can't say I've ever met a werewolf before, let alone three of them." Homer tilted the food bowls to fit them through the bars, accidentally dropping one of the boiled eggs. "Whoops," he said, picking it up and dusting it off on his shirt before placing it through the bars and back inside the bowl.

The werewolves, now in their human form, snatched their food bowls. Homer stood and kept company with the trio while they ate. Once they finished, they pushed the bowls back toward him.

Homer collected the dishes and said, "Well, I have some chores to do, but I'll be back to take care of you three later." He was accustomed to them not speaking to him, so he turned and began to leave when he heard the male utter his first words.

"Thank you, Homer," the Latino guy said in a small, hoarse voice. The giant stopped and eagerly looked back at the captives.

"You're welcome," he replied. "Do you have names I can call you?" he asked, hoping not to push the conversation too far.

"Jazmine," the small African American girl replied.

"My name is Ignacio, but my friends call me Nacho," the Latino man said.

The third woman sat quietly for a moment before she muttered her name, "Lena."

The End

THE OTHER SIDE - DISEMBODIED LIVING

A Note to the Reader

Thank you, kind reader, for sticking with *The Other Side* series for two books so far. This series has four books planned unless inspiration drops from the heavens. The last two books may take a little while to complete; I want to ensure they are the stories I intend to tell, so I will take my time in getting them out. Please be patient and buckle up for the marathon. I plan to live life, not race it.

These stories are crafted for entertainment. I put a lot of effort into writing them; they are my labor of love. I hope you relax and envision the story unfolding with pleasure and amusement. If you enjoyed them, please leave reviews for these books in any format and on any platform you use. Reviews greatly assist indie authors, like me, in sharing these stories with readers who will appreciate them.

Not into reviews? Here are some other ways you can support—recommend these books to friends and family, give me a shoutout or share on social media, and follow, like, and engage with posts on my author pages. Any and all of this is appreciated.

All my love and appreciation,

Sea

More info at www.seaellewolf.com[1]

---

1. http://www.seaellewolf.com

Acknowledgments

A huge, mushy, affectionate thank you to my friends and family for always helping me share my stories with the world. Through your support and collaboration, I learn so much and continue to grow and evolve as a writer. Words can't express my sincere gratitude for you all. While there are so many of you out there, I especially want to give shoutouts to:

My darling wife, Raquel, thank you for your unwavering love and support, thoughtful feedback, and strong editorial skills. I love you, honey bunny. My daughter, Frankie, thank you for being the light of our lives and my reason for smiling. My sister, Ashley, thank you for your thoughtful insight and for believing in my writing. My dad, Evan, thank you for always being in my corner and being one of my biggest fans.

I'd also like to thank Samantha Shear for her insightful feedback; you are a true mentor and a powerful conduit that helps my creativity flow. Thank you, Anny Beck, for your beautifully crafted book descriptions. Thank you, Alejandro Colucci, for your masterful cover designs. Thank you, Cara Oberfoell, for your expert design skills and all the hard work you put into my author website. And last but not least, thank you to Jack, Amber, and Sylvia for your unwavering support and friendship. As always, many other people have contributed to Team Wolf, so please know that I am grateful to all of you from the bottom of my heart. I couldn't have done this without all of you.